# WILDFIRE

## STREET RATS OF ARAMOOR
### BOOK 5

written by

M I C H A E L
# WISEHART

# Copyright

*WILDFIRE* is a work of fiction. Names, characters, places, and incidents are products of the author's imagination or are used fictitiously. Any resemblance to actual locales or persons, living or dead, business establishments, or events, is entirely coincidental.

# WILDFIRE

Street Rats Of Aramoor: Book 5

# Books

### STREET RATS OF ARAMOOR

*(First book takes place 20 years prior to The Aldoran Chronicles)*

Book 1 | Banished

Book 2 | Hurricane

Book 3 | Rockslide

Book 4 | Sandstorm

Book 5 | Wildfire


### THE ALDORAN CHRONICLES

Prequel | Shackled

Book 1 | The White Tower

Book 2 | Plague of Shadows

Book 3 | The Four-Part Key

# Map of Aldor - West

Hi-Resolution maps in the Shop:

« www.michaelwisehart.com/aramoormarket »

# Map of Aldor - East

Hi-Resolution maps in the Shop:

« www.michaelwisehart.com/aramoormarket »

# Map of Aramoor

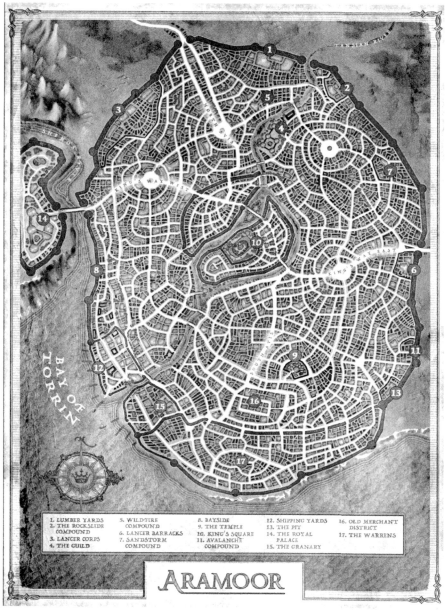

**Legend:**

1. LUMBER YARDS
2. THE ROCKSLIDE COMPOUND
3. LANCER CORPS
4. THE GUILD
5. WILDFIRE COMPOUND
6. LANCER BARRACKS
7. SANDSTORM COMPOUND
8. BAYSIDE
9. THE TEMPLE
10. KING'S SQUARE
11. AVALANCHE COMPOUND
12. SHIPPING YARDS
13. THE PIT
14. THE ROYAL PALACE
15. THE GRANARY
16. OLD MERCHANT DISTRICT
17. THE WARRENS

## ARAMOOR

Hi-Resolution maps in the Shop:

« *www.michaelwisehart.com/aramoormarket* »

# Foreword

**W**ILDFIRE is the fifth book in the Street Rats of Aramoor series, a prequel to the Aldoran Chronicles saga. If you haven't yet read the first four books, *Banished, Hurricane, Rockslide,* and *Sandstorm,* I recommend doing so.

This series ties directly into the Aldoran Chronicles saga, twenty years prior to the first book: *The White Tower.*

As with my other books, there is a Character Glossary at the back if you need it.

## Street Tribes of Aramoor Logos

Hurricane    Avalanche    Rockslide    Wildfire    Sandstorm

# WILDFIRE

## Chapter 1

"QUIET," I WHISPERED AS I PEEKED out from the tall reeds along the bank of the Pyruvian River. This was one of the few narrow spots that could be forded without drowning during the late summer months before the fall rains set in.

"You don't actually plan on us getting in that, do you?" an irritating voice whispered from the darkness behind me. "It's filthy."

I grabbed a handful of reeds and squeezed, imagining that it was Dakaran's neck that I was strangling. Taking a moment to regain my composure, I slowly backed out of the thick undergrowth and made my way over to where the members of Room Eleven were waiting with the horses.

"It looks clear enough," I said, keeping my voice low in case there were patrols on the other side. "The water's not too swift. If we are to cross, looks like we found the right place."

"How can you tell?" Gellar asked. "I can't see the hand in front of my face."

Barthol raised his hand and acted like he was going to slap Gellar, and Gellar flinched. "Fine," Gellar said. "Point is, if we can barely see each other, how are you able to tell if this is a safe place to cross?"

"My eyes," I said, pointing at my face, not thinking about the fact that they probably couldn't see me. "Living underground for so long has given us Upakans the ability to see where others cannot."

"That's a rather helpful gift," Fipple said, moving his hand away from his face, trying to determine how far he could see.

"I hate agreeing with the recruit here," Waylen said, nodding toward Dakaran, "but I don't relish the thought of paddling myself across the river in the middle of the night, horseback or not. If it escaped your attention," he said, grabbing his hefty midriff, "I'm not exactly built to go floundering across a river like a water vole."

"Nonsense," Gellar said with a sharp smile as he tightened the end of the braid on his red beard. "As big as you are, you should float no problem. In fact, we could probably use you as a buoy to tie the horses off."

Dakaran started to laugh, and Fipple grabbed his mouth. "Shhh. Don't forget where we are," he whispered.

"Yes," Barthol agreed, turning in Fipple's general direction, "we don't want to alert your countrymen that we're coming."

Fipple released Dakaran and turned, his eyes hot. "Cylmar hasn't been my country for a very long time."

Barthol raised his hands. "My mistake."

Mjovic, or Stumpy, as we affectionately called him, was the only one who hadn't given an opinion about the water, or the darkness, or whether or not to use Waylen as a buoy. He stood quietly next to Dakaran, his dark skin helping him blend in with his surroundings, that and the simple woodsmen outfits we were wearing. We had traded in

our crimson-and-gold Elondrian uniforms for dark-brown leathers and hooded cloaks.

I was certainly missing my black leather jacket, but unfortunately over the last two years, I had outgrown it. Even though I kept telling myself I'd get a new one, I never seemed to get around to it, what with all the time I now spent with the Lancers.

"Don't forget why we're here," I said.

"We're here because we were ordered to be here," Fipple groused, adjusting his topknot.

"We're here to rescue the ambassador and his wife."

Dakaran snorted. "Hang both of them. Anyone stupid enough to try meeting with the overlord of Cylmar deserves what they get. Besides, I'm not getting in that water, and that's that. I'm the crown prince—"

"Out here, you ain't nothing but another recruit," Barthol huffed. "Your father done tossed you to the wolves, boy. The sooner you get to realizing that, the better off you'll be."

Dakaran looked at me as if expecting me to take his side and tell them that he didn't have to go.

"Sorry," I said with a slight shrug. "Barthol's right. In the Lancers, titles mean nothing for those of us commissioned as common foot soldiers. The king told Overcaptain Tolin to treat you as any other recruit."

Dakaran ground his teeth. "I don't think this is what my father had in mind, us sneaking around in the middle of the night, swimming through muck-infested waters, risking our lives for an idiot and his idiot wife."

"Then I guess you shouldn't have forced Overcaptain Tolin's hand and demanded to go."

"Did you think I was going to let you leave me behind to do all your duties while you're out gallivanting around the kingdom? Over my dead body."

"Afraid it's not your choice," Gellar said. "Nor ours, unfortunately. We got our orders."

"We do tend to get the short end of the straw when it comes to assignments," Waylen pointed out.

"Or maybe," I added, "we should look at it as: of all the people the overcaptain could have chosen for such an important mission, he chose us because he knows we're the best."

The others looked at each other, then at me. "Nah."

"More like we were picked because we're the most expendable," Gellar said.

No matter the reason, we didn't have time to sit around and debate. We had a mission to complete, and I wasn't about to let Room Eleven's reputation down by failing to finish it, not after Overcaptain Tolin had given me the charge of leading this mission.

We had passed through Belbridge the previous day and stocked up on supplies before crossing. There was no telling when we'd next come across another town large enough to purchase from, so we thought it prudent to stop. Besides, the bridge at Belbridge was the main crossing point between the two kingdoms, and it gave us an opportunity to scout out the other side before moving upstream to find a safe place to cross on our own.

With a mission this important, the king had spared no expense. They sent us by ship south through the Bay of Torrin and then west between the mainland and the Copper Islands, where we continued on around past the Isle of Delga to the coastal town of Laneer. From there, we purchased horses and started north along the Pyruvian River.

The river would eventually split farther north at the bottom of the Black Hills, one branch leading into Cylmar, the other into Elondria. From what I'd heard, there had been a lot of debate over who owned the rights to the Black Hills. More importantly, the rights to the ore in them.

Several battles had been fought between the two kingdoms over that very subject.

In fact, it was the sole reason the Elondrian ambassador and his wife had been sent to Cylmar in the first place—to work out negotiations between Overlord Saryn and King Rhydan. Apparently, those negotiations consisted of the Cylmaran overlord kidnapping the ambassador and holding him for ransom, stupidly believing that would earn him the upper hand in the negotiations.

"Let's get going," I said, untying my cloak. "We need to get across while the clouds are thick enough to hide the moon. I want to be on the other side and several miles inland before the sun rises. As close as we are to the Belbridge crossing, I don't want to take the chance of running into patrols." I rolled my cloak up and stuffed it into a weather-sealed satchel before turning to look at the others. "What are you waiting for? Strip!"

"Are you crazy?" Dakaran shot back. "I'm not taking my clothes off."

"You will if you don't want to chafe all day by riding in wet ones."

It was a good thing it was dark, because the sight of seven naked men climbing down the embankment would have drawn the entire Cylmaran army. This was one time I was not very thankful for my Upakan sight, and I did my best to not look at the others as we carefully walked our horses down the embankment and slowly waded into the water.

As warm as the evening was, the water felt refreshing. Dakaran was the next to last in, and only after Barthol threatened to toss him in if he didn't get a move on. Barthol's looming presence behind him was no doubt the only thing keeping the prince from trying to bolt. That, and the fact that his father had made his appointment to the crown conditional on his service to the Lancers. If he didn't finish his commission, he wouldn't inherit the throne.

From the bank to the reeds was extremely rocky, so we decided to walk our horses down into the water before mounting. I waited at the edge for the others to find their way down the embankment, Dakaran purposefully taking his time. I shook my head.

It had been a little over two years since the king had first requested that I join the Lancers on a temporary basis; two years since Noph had turned over Sandstorm to Sapphire, Reevie, and me; two years of weekly visits to the palace in hopes of getting His Royal Pain in My Backside ready for his upcoming commission in the Lancer Corps.

I watched as Dakaran fumbled his way down into the river, a scowl on his face the entire way. I didn't think anything could be worse than trying to run a tribe of street kids, but nothing could have prepared me for working alongside a prince who had lived his entire life in the lap of luxury, only to find himself demoted all the way down to a simple lancer recruit. I wondered if his whining would ever end.

I hated dropping this burden on my roommates, but as Tolin said, there was no one else in the entire garrison capable of handling such a charge but Room Eleven. I wasn't sure if he was trying to pay us a back-handed compliment or simply butter us up. My guess was the latter. The only upside to having Dakaran there was that Captain Henzlow had re-frained from sending us on Warrens patrol out of fear of something happening to the young princeling and him getting blamed for it.

Once everyone had finally made it in the water, we mounted and let the horses do the brunt of the work as we focused on keeping our clothes out of the water. There were several bridges spanning the border river, but each was manned by guards on either side—Elondrians on the east side, Cylmarans on the west—which made traveling across impossible if you wished to remain unseen. Even though we weren't wearing our lancer uniforms, it would have seemed strange to have a full company of men crossing from Elondria into Cylmar, especially when tensions be-tween the two kingdoms were so high.

I was the first out of the river, quickly sliding out of my saddle to dry off as best I could with a spare shirt before dressing and climbing up the embankment on the other side to see if there were any signs of a river patrol nearby. Crawling along on my hands and knees, I reached the top and took a moment to stare out across the flat plains ahead.

There was no one for miles in either direction.

Quietly, I crawled back down the embankment where the others were now dressed and waiting.

"What did you see?" Barthol asked.

"Not much." I took a quick swallow from my waterskin, then hung it back on the side of my saddle. "I don't see any patrols." I looked up. The clouds were still covering the moon. "Best we get a move on while we still can."

Using a long stretch of rope that had been tied to the back of Stumpy's saddlebags, we mounted and turned our horses northwest. With the rope, I was able to guide them safely forward, keeping a slower pace as I did, making sure the horses didn't step in a hole. Over the last two years I'd spent in the Lancers, my horsemanship had grown. I remembered how nervous I used to be around them. Now, I found I rather enjoyed riding, not that I got the chance to spend much time in the saddle. Most of my lancer duties were within the confines of the garrison, which made me long for patrol days.

There was nothing quite so relaxing as spending a morning or afternoon slowly trotting through the streets of Aramoor.

I spared a quick glance back over my shoulder. The others looked ready to fall out of their saddles. Deep yawns and drooping eyelids let me know there was no way they were going to make it through the night without stopping. But I wanted to make sure we were far enough away from the river and the Cylmaran patrols that traveled the road alongside it before we stopped and set up camp.

A mile or two farther in, we reached a small outcropping of rock, which looked like it might help shelter us for the night, so I pulled to a stop. "We'll catch a few winks before heading on. I'd say we're far enough from the river that no one should spot a campfire." The fire would keep the wolves away—wolves and any other sort of animal hunting these lands at night.

Prairie grasslands stretched for miles around us, though a forest lay to the north along the lower foothills. There was the occasional copse of hardwood scattered between us and the forest, providing enough deadwood for our fire. It didn't take long to gather up what we needed, and soon enough we had a small pit dug and a fire stoked.

With the light from the blaze, we set up our blanket rolls, keeping our backs to the rock. No one seemed much in the mood for food. Even Waylen forwent his usual evening snack in exchange for crawling into bed and shutting his eyes. I took first watch to give the others a chance to sleep.

I crawled up on the rocky embankment behind our camp and stared out across the open landscape, not seeing much more than the grass. If I squinted hard enough, I could just make out the shadow of mountains off to my right. Or it might have just been a passing cloud formation. It was growing hard to tell.

The air out here smelled different. It was clean. The city had its own smell. I wouldn't say it was sour—some quarters were. It was mostly just different. Still, I had to admit, living inside Sandstorm Manor seemed to cut back quite a bit of the less pleasant aromas, as the people living there had the wherewithal to afford proper sanitation.

I suddenly found myself missing home. I wondered what Sapphire and Reevie were up to. No doubt snoring away in their feather beds and soft linen sheets. They had no idea where I was, and I had been forbidden to leave any word. The mission was supposed to be a secret, which,

according to Overcaptain Tolin, meant absolutely no one could know. I hated to think what Sapphire and Reevie were going to do when I didn't show up on Seventhday as I usually did. Even without any unforeseen complications, this mission was going to take weeks. I felt bad, but there was simply nothing I could do about it.

My duties as a co-chief of Sandstorm had begun to slip over the last year. Now that Dakaran was being pushed into service, the king had insisted that my time spent in the Lancers go from part-time to something more permanent.

It wasn't a choice I wanted to make, but one I had a feeling was coming. My co-chiefs also suspected as much and had begun to plan ahead, starting by limiting my duties at Sandstorm. I was still expected to try to make Sapphire's dinner parties when I could, since they were the main source of income for our tribe, but with me being required to stay in the garrison, it was difficult. She was doing a remarkable job following Noph's example and building a network of contacts who used our tribe to facilitate anything from secret meetings to undisclosed shipments of goods, and a wide variety of other arrangements, just so long as they weren't of a more personal nature.

After Kore's initial attempt to take over our tribe, and the consequence of that choice left him bedridden for nearly a month, Rockslide had kept mostly to its own borders, at least where Sandstorm was concerned.

Wildfire was a different story. It seemed neither Red nor Kore could make it through a single Guild meeting without nearly coming to blows.

If it were up to me, I would have liked to have found a way to get rid of the tribes altogether. Integrate them through the orphanage into proper homes, or possibly use Queen Ellise's funding to help get them apprenticeships. The queen had been very good about keeping her word to Master Fentin and Mistress Orilla. The orphanage was running at capacity, and our work with the local merchants was proving rather profitable as well, not only for the kids, but also for the merchants. There was even talk of opening a second orphanage.

The queen had gone above and beyond her initial offer of a monthly stipend and arranged for members of the aristocracy to sponsor kids themselves, encouraging them to put their charitable coin to good use. I was surprised by how many of the upper class were willing to participate, having always looked on them as nothing but conceited, selfish stuckups. Many turned out to be very generous.

A groaning noise below brought me out of my musings, and I barely got a chance to smile before whoever did it was snoring once again, blending his voice with the others. Even Dakaran looked at peace, probably one of the only times he ever did.

I yawned, finding it rather hard to keep awake myself. After a while, my eyes drooped, and I shook my head, even going so far as to pat my cheek to keep awake. I'd gotten little sleep on the journey so far. I never did well away from my own bed, my own routines. It was hard to sleep when your surroundings were constantly changing. In fact, the only thing that seemed to stay the same was my roommates' snoring.

The clouds passed overhead. Whatever storm had been brewing had evidently gone around us. The moon was only half-full, but more than bright enough to light the open land we were traveling through. I could see movement off to the west, possibly wolves or coyotes. Whatever they were, they didn't seem to know we were here, or care.

I yawned again, then shook my head. Sleep was doing its best to take over, and I was doing my best to fight it. I thought it was winning. I raised my hand and stared at the black onyx ring on my first finger and the white rune crest at its center. A smile broke across my face.

Four years I'd been waiting to wear it. Four years it had taken before my fingers had thickened enough. My father had said the day I could

wear this ring was the day I would be considered an Upakan warrior. It was still a little loose on a couple of my fingers, but I found that I could wear it quite comfortably on my first finger without fear of it slipping off.

I wondered what my family was doing. I wondered if my father would be proud of the man I'd become. There were times when I found it difficult to remember their faces, which scared me. I didn't want to lose those memories.

"You ready to get some sleep?"

I startled from my perch, nearly falling off the side as I turned to find Barthol climbing up over the rocks to join me.

I took a deep breath to steady my nerves. "You're getting quieter by the day. If I didn't know any better, I'd think you were Upakan trained. Oh, wait, I guess you were."

Barthol chuckled and took a seat beside me, letting his long legs hang over the side. Even with my growth spurt, Barthol still stood a good head and a half taller, and twice as wide in the chest. We sat in silence a while before I finally noticed him staring.

"What?"

He pointed at my chin, then rubbed his own thick black beard. "I like it."

"You do?" I asked, rubbing at the growth on my face. "You don't think it looks strange?"

"Makes you look older."

I smiled. I had always wanted a jawline beard, ever since seeing Captain Talbot's the day we had sparred in front of the garrison. It had taken me nearly six months to grow it long enough to be noticeable, but I had finally managed it, and to be honest I was quite proud of the way it had turned out. I looked at least nineteen or twenty, even though I was only halfway through my seventeenth year.

"The other lancers look at me different now that I have it. Like I actually belong. I don't get mistaken for a simple runner anymore."

"Who are you kidding?" Barthol said with a grin. "You'll never belong."

"Speak for yourself."

He smiled. "I was."

I yawned and looked back down at the dwindling fire. "Guess I'll turn in."

Barthol nodded. "Get some sleep while you can. No telling when you'll get another chance."

I bid him good night and climbed down from my perch and back to where the others lay around the fire. I threw a couple more logs on top, then crawled into my bedding between Stumpy and Dakaran. Dakaran was the only one not snoring. It didn't take long before my own drowsiness won out, and I drifted off.

I woke to a hand on my shoulder.

"You awake?"

I groaned as I peeked through my lids to see the sky lightening in the distance. The stars were all but gone. "I am now, I suppose."

Dakaran grunted. "Good. What's for breakfast? I'm starving."

I wanted to roll over and pull my blanket over my head, but we needed to get a move on. The sooner we reached the capital city of Ecrin, the sooner we could rescue the ambassador and his wife. We hadn't been gone a few weeks, and I was already missing Aramoor.

# WILDFIRE

*Chapter 2*

FTER A QUICK MEAL of hard meat and dried berries, we covered our fire and were on our way, doing our best to stay as far from any roads as possible as we traveled northeast.

According to our map, the Ryne River ran directly west of us from Lake Nari in the north of the kingdom all the way south to the Rhunarin Ocean, splitting the kingdom in two. We had to be careful, though, because most of the bottom half of that river was marshland. If there was one thing I knew from my experience traveling near the Slags in Keldor, you didn't want to get too close to a marsh.

"How far are we going today?" Dakaran asked. He wiped the sweat from his face with his sleeve, which was soaked completely through thanks to the blazing sun overhead. It was barely midday.

"We go as far as we can," I said, doing my best not to sound abrasive. "The less time we have to spend in this kingdom the better. It's not exactly known for its friendly, welcoming people." Out of the corner of my eye, I could see Dakaran casting about as he twisted in his saddle, no doubt looking for highwaymen.

The land around us had yellowed, as the summer sun had dried up all the grass, but occasionally we would cross a small patch of green, which typically meant there was a water source nearby for us to fill up at. It wasn't too long before we found such a spot and stopped for lunch.

The Black Hills were sitting off in the distance over my right shoulder, and as long as I kept them there, I knew we were heading in the right direction. From the map, it appeared we would be riding through more open plains over the next couple of days, keeping the forest and its foothills on our right and the swamp surrounding the Ryne to our left. As long as the ground remained firm, we should be safe.

"What's that?" Fipple asked, pointing ahead to a wisp of a dark cloud rising from the ground.

We pulled the horses to a stop, and Gellar leaned forward in his saddle, his brows lowering slightly, of which there were three, since one of them had been split with a nasty scar. "Too big to be a campfire."

"Prairie fire, then?" Waylen asked, his thin braided beard swinging from the bottom of his chin as he looked around for any other signs of burning.

I studied the plume as it rose all the way into the sky. "It's not big enough for a prairie fire. Too confined. I accidentally burned down part of the grassland around the Slags when fighting off a couple of razorbacks with my father. The smoke from those fires was lighter and spread nearly across the horizon."

The others looked at me funny but didn't say anything.

"Perhaps we should check it out," Stumpy finally suggested. "Could be someone needs help." Mjovic was the most softhearted of the group, always looking for ways to be of service.

"Could be highwaymen," Dakaran said. "If we stick around, it could

be us they try burning next."

I wanted to roll my eyes. "We'll check it out," I said, as it seemed the others were waiting on me to make a decision.

"Of course we will," Dakaran grumbled.

I reached over and slid my lancer sword partway from its sheath and let it drop, then did the same to Noph's former sword on my back. I liked the feel of having one sword on my back. It didn't escape my notice that it also looked impressive. I had found sheathing it difficult at first, but with time and practice, it became easier, almost second nature. It also didn't hurt that the opening had been made much larger than your common carrier, and since the hilt of the sword was aiming upward, I never had to worry about it falling out.

I sent Fipple on ahead to scout for possible troops in the area, then kicked my horse into a trot, and we slowly picked up speed as we headed for the source of the smoke. I kept the horses at a steady pace, not wanting to push them to exhaustion as we rode from one hilltop to the next, watching the smoke grow in size the closer we got.

We slowed as we made our way toward the final rise, where Fipple was waiting.

"No soldiers," he said, "but looks like trouble."

There were faint shouts coming from the other side, and we dismounted. I left the horses with Dakaran, Stumpy, and Waylen, while the rest of us climbed to the top on foot. As we approached, I waved the others down, and we crawled the rest of the way.

Below us, in the cleft of a small valley between rises, was a circle of colorful wagons. Three of the wagons were on fire as men and women and even children in colorful baggy clothing scrambled to put them out.

I pointed at the front of the wagons where a group of colorfully clothed men were trying to fend off a dozen or so armsmen. The attackers were dressed in common everyday garb, not a uniform in sight.

Probably highway bandits. Even from where we were, it was pretty obvious that the three wagons were done for, and if we didn't intervene,
the people would be as well.

"Tinkers," Gellar said, disdain in his voice.

"Rhivanni," Fipple corrected.

"What're Rhivanni?" I asked.

"Nomads," Barthol said. "Tend to keep to themselves mostly. Travel
from town to town selling wares."

"Trouble is what they are," Gellar added.

Fipple shook his head. "Misunderstood is what I would call them.
We had tinkers who came through my village every year when I was a
child. Nice enough folk."

"Speak for yourself," Gellar said. "I've heard they steal the children
of towns that don't let them in."

"Rubbish," Fipple shot back. "Superstitious nonsense."

Gellar rolled his shoulders. "I'm just saying."

"Superstition or not," I said. "There're women and children down
there, and if we don't do something now, they're going to be slaugh-
tered."

"Fine," Gellar said, and we quickly scooted back far enough to stand
without being seen. "But don't say I didn't warn ya."

We rushed back down to our horses and mounted.

"What's going on?" Dakaran asked. "What did you see?"

"Draw swords," I ordered as I pulled mine from the sheath on my
back.

Dakaran reached for his sword. "Why are we drawing weapons?"

"You were right. There's highwaymen." Before Dakaran could voice
his certain complaint about charging headlong into a fight, I kicked my
horse into a full gallop, as did the others, forcing Dakaran to do the same
or get run over. I could hear him calling objections as we rode up the

hill.

We crested the top and continued down the other side, picking up speed as we did. The sight of the armed thugs setting fires and killing those below had my mind racing back to Gustory the bard, who had lost his wife and child to a bunch of mercenaries. I could have used his gifts right about now to put the fear of the Creator into these men.

I shook my head to focus on the task ahead and urged my horse faster.

Several of the tinkers were down already, and the highwaymen had them flanked, moving in for the kill. We were nearly to the bottom of the rise before the first of the armsmen spotted us and shouted a warning. The majority of the highwaymen pulled back to meet us, but instead of grouping together, they spread out, making it easier to pick them off individually, which was a clear sign these men weren't trained in any kind of combat warfare. Their first instinct was every man for himself.

We swept through with a single gallop. Fipple trampled one of the men who wasn't smart enough to get out of the way of a galloping horse. I cut another down on the first pass. Preferring not to leave my legs open for them to cut on, I leaped off my horse and rushed the armsmen head on, pulling my second blade from the sheath at my waist.

The rest of Room Eleven was right behind me, eager to join in the fight. We might not have been wearing uniforms, but that didn't mean we had forgotten any of our training. The rest of the highwaymen pulled away from the wagons to engage us, leaving the tinkers free to attempt to put out the fires before they spread to the other wagons.

All around me, my roommates fought just as I'd trained them. They were swift and deadly, keeping their movements small and clean, not wasting energy on frivolous showmanship.

Barthol was the only exception. He cut one man's sword from his hand, then grabbed the man and lifted him over his head and threw him on top of two others, sending all three to the ground, where he quickly disarmed them with a strong kick to the face and a slash across their forearm.

Gellar kicked one man in the knee so hard it snapped, then finished him off with a quick thrust to the chest.

Fipple fought two at once, his sword arm moving in perfect form as he blocked and parried and beat back both men's attacks. He stabbed one in the leg and opened the wrist of the other, leaving both incapacitated.

Stumpy, who was on my direct right, was just as proficient with his left hand as he would have been with his right, if he still had it. His sword was fast, beating back every swing with little effort, playing with his opponent. He had the man fumbling around, swinging wildly and hitting nothing. Finally, Stumpy finished him with a solid kick to his gut that had the man doubling over far enough for Stumpy to hit him with the pommel of his sword. One strike and he was on the ground, begging for mercy.

Waylen kept back with the horses and Dakaran.

Even though Dakaran was a lancer recruit, and trained by me, he was still the crown prince, and we weren't going to thrust him into immediate danger if we didn't have to. Dakaran had his sword drawn, but at the same time he seemed all too happy to remain behind and help Waylen protect the horses.

I took down one of the four remaining with a feint and cut, before the others threw down their weapons and fled, bravely leaving their comrades behind. I was tempted to chase after them, but we had more pressing issues to deal with. Namely, the wagon fires.

Behind us, the tinkers had formed a line and were trying to pass buckets of water as they desperately fought to save their gear.

"Come on," I shouted to those of the highwaymen who could still

stand.

Barthol grabbed the closest and shoved him toward the circle of wagons. "Get a bucket and start dipping!" The rest quickly rushed to help, especially when Barthol raised his sword, which still had some of their blood on it.

As soon as the flames were down to a manageable level, we gathered up the bandits and took them to the edge of camp and as far away from the tinkers as possible, tying them to a wagon wheel. The tinkers were too busy putting out the rest of the fires to notice.

"Please, don't kill us," the highwaymen begged.

"That's up to the tinkers," I said. "They're the ones you've harmed. It falls on them to seek their own justice."

About that time, an older man in a very colorful cape and a large staff walked out to greet us. "May the Great Father bless you for your kindness to us, and we hope that you will share our fire this evening."

"Seems a fire is about the last thing you folks need right now," Gellar stated.

I could only shake my head and hope the old man didn't take offense to Gellar's rather uncouth and untimely jest.

The old man smiled. "Yes, I see what you mean." He seemed in a daze. I guess fighting for your life and watching family and friends die around you for no logical reason would have that effect.

Several of the tinkers lifted the bodies of those of their group who'd not been lucky enough to make it through the battle and laid them respectfully in a row near one of the wagons. The injured were carried to a different wagon on the left and lifted inside, most likely to have their wounds seen to by their healer.

Several of those who'd carried the wounded drew their swords and started for the highway bandits.

"No!" the old man said, seeing what his people were about to do.

"That is not the way of the Rhivanni!" The old man's words were direct, but I could see the way he was squeezing the life out of his staff. If I had just witnessed the senseless slaughter of my own people, I can't say I would have been as forgiving.

The old man turned to us. "My name is Brishad. I am the leader of this clan. We are of the Sil'Rhivanni. It is rare to find those willing to help their neighbors in this part of the world. Cylmarans aren't exactly known for lending aid unless it benefits them, especially to those of the Rhivanni. Where are you gentlemen from?"

"We're from—"

"Not from around here," I interrupted Dakaran. I wouldn't have put it past him to mention that he was the crown prince. "We are passing through on our way to Ecrin."

"Then you are in luck," Brishad said, "for that is where we are headed. You can travel with us, share our meals. In return, perhaps your presence will deter other such men as those." He pointed his staff at the armsmen on the other side of the encampment.

"We can't wait that long," Gellar said briskly. "We have business that needs tending to." Whatever his dispute with the tinkers was, he didn't seem to be backing off it.

I smiled, trying to assure the man we didn't mean to offend. "I'm afraid he's right. Our journey will be a swift one, though we wouldn't say no to sharing your fire this evening." It looked as though they could use a hand with the charred rubble anyway. I wondered how they were going to be able to carry on, having lost that many of their wagons.

"I see," the old man said, looking disheartened by our refusal to travel with them. "Well, we certainly wouldn't want to keep you from your business, that is for sure." His smile returned. "And though we can't offer much, we can promise a night of song and dance and some of the finest mead you'll taste this side of the Khezrian Wall."

"Now that does sound right neighborly," Waylen said with a firm tug on his belt. "I've always heard that Rhivanni mead was as sweet as a woman's kiss and as strong as her father's right arm."

Brishad chuckled. "You've heard correctly, my friend."

"Doesn't seem quite appropriate," Gellar said, "drinking and merriment with your dead lying there."

Brishad smiled. "Yes, I believe it's your custom to mourn your loss, but there will be plenty of time for that later. We of the Rhivanni prefer instead to celebrate a life, to send them on their way with joy in our hearts for having known them."

I liked that idea. It was certainly more pleasant than some of the ritual send-offs that I'd seen, especially military ones, though with the Lancers, there seemed to be a sense of great pride in their traditions as they honored those in passing.

"What do we do with them?" Fipple asked, looking over at the prisoners.

Brishad turned, and his face tightened for a moment when he looked at the bound men, but then he sighed. "We will see to their wounds, feed them, and then send them on their way."

"Are you crazy?" Dakaran asked. "They just tried to kill you. You can't just let them go."

"What would you have us do?" Brishad asked. "Murder them in return? How would that make us any better than them?"

"If not, you risk them coming back to finish the job."

"You killed more than half their number. The rest are either wounded or have fled. I don't foresee them trying anything again, at least not anytime soon."

"Don't you have some form of law out here?" I asked.

Brishad turned and pointed northward with his staff. "The closest town is Khartag, and to be perfectly honest, I wouldn't doubt if half these men were from there. The law out here is what you make it."

Seemed a dangerous way to run things. No law, or those to uphold it, bred anarchy, which led to things like this happening in the first place. Not a place I would ever want to live. Even those of us on the streets had rules we followed.

With nothing left to be said, we tied off our horses and went to help the tinkers sift through the damage. They'd managed to get the fires out, but now they needed to strip away the damaged wood to see if anything was left to salvage. The charred wood was still hot in places, smoke filling our lungs as we worked to clear away the rubble. Everything we touched left our hands and clothing black with soot and ash.

After removing the burnt, unusable areas, the tinkers stretched a large piece of treated canvas over what was left of the frames, creating a makeshift shelter that could at least keep out the rain. By the time we'd finished, the sun was nearly down and the cookfires lit.

We washed the soot off in a nearby stream, even going so far as to strip off our shirts to clean the sweat, before joining the Rhivanni for their evening meal. Brishad was correct; the food was excellent and the mead even more so. Fine enough that even Gellar's frown vanished as he sat back and sipped on the very sweet drink.

The Rhivanni were a friendly people, and they loved to sing and dance. More than once, I found myself caught up in a song whose tune was familiar, but the words were not, as though having been rewritten to fit their personal experiences. "The Butcher's Wife" became "The Tinker's Daughter." "The Rusty Ol' Plow" became "The Rusty Ol' Wagon." And there were several others as well whose titles I had forgotten, but the rhythms were all too familiar.

Waylen hadn't been exaggerating when he said the Rhivanni mead was as strong as a father's right arm, and I limited myself as to how much I drank. Unfortunately, most of my roommates, including Dakaran, did

not. In fact, before the night was done, Stumpy was regaling the clan with songs from his childhood, while Gellar was on his feet demonstrating the dance of the fae, which he'd learned back home when he was a boy. The man was surprisingly nimble, and quite inebriated.

By the time the fires had died down, I was helping tote my compatriots over to their bedding. I left them in their clothes to sleep it off, hoping a full night's rest would sober them up. Either way, the ride tomorrow was going to be an unpleasant one for them. For me too, since I would have to be the one to listen to their complaints for having let them drink so much.

The Rhivanni were true to their word and fed the highwaymen before releasing them. They kept the men's horses and let them go on foot, making sure it took them some time to reach wherever they hailed from.

It didn't take me long to fall asleep, and with the Rhivanni keeping watch, I was able to sleep the whole night through. It had been several weeks since that had happened, and I clearly needed it.

By the time morning arrived, the tinkers had breakfast already cooked and waiting on us. As expected, my roommates were the worse for wear, already squinting even though the sun had yet to rise, and complaining of everything being too loud. Gellar emptied his stomach at least twice before filling it with some fresh-cooked meat and a bowl of honeyed oats and sliced figs. The meal was a wonderful break from our supplies, which had been selected more for storage than flavor.

Saddling our horses, we said our goodbyes and wished the Rhivanni well. They gave us some of the leftover meat to eat along the way and thanked us for our timely rescue, once again wishing us blessings from the Great Father. By the time the sun was peeking up over the horizon on our right, we were back underway.

We'd barely been in Cylmar two days and had already found ourselves in a small battle. Didn't bode well for the rest of our trip. I hoped our luck turned before we reached Ecrin.

# WILDFIRE

## *Chapter 3*

I KEPT THE PACE SLOW, making sure to keep the woodlands in front of the Black Hills within eyeshot, ensuring we didn't stray too far west and end up running headfirst into the marshlands and whatever creatures hunted there.

It wasn't until lunch that my roommates' heads finally began to clear and the ache of the constant up and down in their saddles, jostling what little brains they had, began to lighten. They even attempted a few light-hearted conversations while they ate, something none of them had any desire to do earlier. In fact, the majority of the morning had been re-freshingly quiet, with the exception of the periodic moan from a bout of dizziness or complaint that the sun was too bright.

As promised, the Rhivanni's mead had been sweet and packed quite the wallop.

The next two days, we traveled as far as possible while we had light, then looked for a place to shelter at night. Other than the occasional

traveler—who did their best to pass by as far from us as possible—we didn't see many people on the rather indirect route I'd chosen for us to take. If we had stuck to the roads, perhaps we would have seen more.

I was surprised we hadn't come across more farmland. There were a few scattered fields here and there where we found ourselves forced to travel around fenced-off areas, but for the most part, it was nothing but wide-open, unsettled land.

The fourth and fifth days were spent on a more westerly approach as we made our way toward the Ryne River. I figured we were far enough north that we would miss the marshlands, but there was no telling how accurate our map was, so it was a bit of a guessing game. Had we taken the main roads through Cylmar, it would have no doubt cut down on our time, but it was safer to take the longer route than risk running into a contingent of Cylmaran lancers, which the Rhivanni said patrolled the main trading routes across the kingdom.

Most Cylmarans, like Fipple, had olive-colored skin, which would have made our paler skin stand out had we been stopped. Fipple didn't talk much about his heritage, other than to say he didn't consider himself one of them. I was sure there was a sordid history there, but none of us had the nerve to ask.

Thankfully, about halfway through the fifth day, we reached the edge of the Ryne. The river was wider than I had anticipated, not something we would want to attempt swimming across, which meant we were going to need to find a crossing, and unfortunately that most likely meant finding a town large enough to have a ferry.

"Dorwall looks to be our best bet," Stumpy said, staring at the map, which he had spread out on the back of his horse, while the rest of us gathered around.

"I agree," I said. "Now we just have to determine where we are. Are we south of Dorwall, or north?"

"I doubt we've traveled far enough north to pass it," Fipple said.

Most of the others agreed. Dakaran didn't seem to care one way or the other. He was too busy trying to rub the stiffness out of his backside as he walked bow-legged over to the edge of the riverbank to pick up some rocks and toss them in the water.

"North it is, then," I said.

Stumpy rolled the map and tucked it back in his saddle. The rest of us took a moment to join Dakaran by the bank as we, too, worked out some of the soreness of sitting in the saddle all day. The dark water moved along at a steady pace. It was muddy, probably from rains farther north stirring up the sediment.

We spotted a ship in the distance making its way slowly in our direction, its lone white sail blending in with the thick billowing clouds overhead. We watched as it passed before mounting and getting back underway.

My mind drifted to Dorwall as we rode along the river's winding course, picturing what it would be like. I'd always heard tales of how dangerous Cylmaran cities were, but I couldn't imagine Aramoor being any less dangerous. One of the worst places I'd ever been to was Norshag, a small mountain village that my father and I had come across after making our way out a pass in the Northern Heights. We had barely made it out of that woodland community with our lives; surely Dorwall couldn't be any worse.

We passed through a couple of small fishing villages along the way. The villagers lived in shanties, their clothing no better than mine had been while living on the streets. In fact, those living in the Maze, where Hurricane used to be, would have been considered very well off compared to the condition of these wretches.

It wasn't until late afternoon that we caught our first glimpse of Dorwall from atop a small rise a quarter mile southeast.

"Not much to look at, is it?" Gellar said. "Reminds me of some of the riverside communities in Briston. They don't have much going for them except the river."

"Probably doesn't have more than one good inn," Fipple said, "and calling it good might be an overstatement."

"Only way we're going to find out is by going down there," I said. "I'm hoping we won't have to stay the night. Better to get passage over and be on our way."

Barthol took a swig from his waterskin and wiped his mouth with his sleeve. "I second that." He hung the skin back on his saddle. "Well, no sense sitting here in the sun." With that, he spurred his horse down the stretch of winding road along the riverbank toward town.

The rest of us hurried to catch up, especially since the horizon in front of us was beginning to darken as an approaching storm drew near.

Sure enough, the clouds rolled in about the time we reached the city's outskirts, which wasn't much more than a shanty town that had attached itself to the main city along the roadway. We'd barely made it into the city proper, and I already wanted to turn around. The rain coming down in sheets on our heads didn't help.

The buildings were a wash of old river stone, chipped plaster, and rotting wood. Upkeep looked minimal. Our horses' hooves sank in ankle-deep muck. Each step produced a squishing, popping sound. Either side of the main road leading through the center of town was littered with debris: anything from broken pieces of table to shattered window frames with shards of glass scattered about for some unsuspecting passerby to step on. The menagerie of junk included old chamber pots, pieces of clay jars, even broken broom handles.

I pulled my horse to an abrupt stop and pointed at something hanging out of one of the narrow alleyways between buildings. "Is that what I think it is?"

The others turned to look.

"If you think it's a rotting corpse," Barthol said just behind me, "then yes, that's exactly what you think it is."

"I don't like this place," Dakaran whimpered on my right. "I want to leave."

"You and me both," Fipple said, keeping his hand on the hilt of his sword.

I nudged my horse, and we kept going. I had only seen a few of Dorwall's citizens so far, and only from a distance, as it seemed they were quick to disappear when they saw us coming.

The only indication that we were reaching the center of town was that the buildings were clumped a little closer together. A few of them actually had signs over the doors indicating a place of business, though most of the signs were so faded they were all but unreadable. A single branching street crossed at the center, with a covered well that sat in the center of the town's square.

We reached the crossroads, and I twisted in my saddle to see if I could spot the closest tavern or inn in order to ask whether the town had a ferry. I spotted a man to my right making his way in our direction.

"Excuse me, sir, can you tell us where—"

The man disappeared into one of the shops before I could even finish my sentence.

"Friendly town, this," Stumpy said.

"I get the feeling we aren't wanted here." I turned to look down the left side of the connecting roadway but was stopped when Dakaran grabbed my arm.

His face was white as a sheet. He pointed up at something on the other side of the connecting street, and my stomach clenched. There was a man hanging from a sign off the side of one of the two-story buildings farther down. His arms had been lashed to the sides of the sign like two

featherless wings trying to flap away. The body had clearly been left up there for some time.

I'd barely gotten turned back around when Dakaran leaned over the side of his horse and emptied his gut, nearly causing a sympathy reaction from the rest of us. Curtains parted in the surrounding windows, and doors cracked just far enough to let us know we were being watched.

"Best we keep moving," Fipple said.

"I second that," Waylen agreed from the back.

Even if we had found a tavern, I didn't think it would be in our best interest to go inside—we might not come back out. Not wanting to linger, I turned my horse down the left branch of the connecting street, partly hoping that it would lead us toward the river, but mostly just to get away from the sight of the swinging corpse.

We rounded a bend and caught our first sight of water ahead. I prayed they had a ferry. The closer we got to the water, the worse the living conditions became, to the point that the buildings weren't much better off than the shanties on the outskirts of town.

"I see boats," Dakaran all but shouted, just to be heard above the downpour, which was now coming down at a pretty hard pace.

Sure enough, the road we were on ended at a small wharf, which was made up of a few piers with some boats tied alongside, but nothing that resembled a ferry.

"Over there." Gellar pointed off to the right. There was another building farther down, just off a small roadway that ran along the river-front. It had its own small dock and what looked like a large flatboat attached.

My heart leaped, and I waved our little group forward. I didn't care if we had to shelter in the rain or even ride straight through it, I wanted to put this place behind us and never look back. The line of smoke rising

from the chimney of the ferry station was the only indication that someone was home.

We tied the horses to the rail in front and quickly sheltered up under
the covered porch, shaking as much of the water from our cloaks as we
could. I felt like a half-drowned rat that had just swam through sewage
and was in need of a good cleaning. I knocked on the door and waited
for a reply.

I couldn't hear anything from inside, what with the downpour, so I
waited. When no one came, I knocked again, louder this time, hard
enough that my knuckles twinged under the force.

"What do ya want?" someone shouted from the other side of the
door. "We're closed!"

"We seek passage across," I shouted back.

I thought I heard what sounded like chains rattling from the other
side just before the door cracked and whoever was inside peered out. All
I could see was a single eye and part of a beard. "I told you, we're closed."

"We need to cross."

"Not in this rain, you don't. I ain't takin' no one across in weather
like this. One slip on a wet board and over you go."

I looked at the others. They appeared about as frustrated and desperate to leave as I was. "Where's the closest ferry or bridge from here?"
I asked, turning back to the ferryman.

"Closest crossing is Pirn, about a three-day ride north to Lake Nari."

I figured it would almost be worth it just to be gone from here, but
that didn't mean that Pirn would prove any better.

"We really need to cross. Is there anything you can do?"

"Yeah, I can go back to my supper." He started to close the door
when Dakaran desperately shoved his boot in the crack.

"We can pay," Dakaran said. "Coin is no object."

"I don't care if you was carrying the queen's jewels, no one gets across

tonight, and that's that. Now get your foot out of my door or I'll stick a bolt in it." The ferryman yanked open his door a little further, revealing he had a loaded crossbow which he aimed at Dakaran.

"No need for that," I said, slowly moving Dakaran back behind me and out of the way of the man's anxious-looking trigger finger. "This is our first time to Dorwall. Where do you suggest we go?"

"Back to wherever it is you came!" And with that, the ferryman slammed the door, and I heard chains once again from the other side.

I huddled with the others on the front of the porch. "That man is scared of more than just the weather," I said.

Barthol nodded. "Did you notice all his windows were not only shuttered but boarded?"

"These people are scared of something," Fipple said. He grabbed his topknot and squeezed the water from it. "Don't think I want to hang around and find out what."

I nodded. "Well, it appears we aren't going anywhere tonight. Any suggestions?"

"Leave, just like the man said," Dakaran stated.

Waylen wrapped his thin wisp of a beard around his fingers, attempting to wring the water from it. "Can't say as I disagree. This place doesn't seem safe enough to travel through during the day, let alone at night."

"We could head north toward Pirn," Stumpy suggested. "Perhaps we'll have better luck there."

I shook my head. "There's no way of knowing whether it would be any safer than this place, and it would take us three days out of the way." I leaned in and lowered my voice. "The longer it takes us to get to Ecrin, the greater the chance that the ambassador and his wife will be dead when we get there."

"What do you suggest, then?" Gellar asked, leaning against the porch rail, his hand resting on his sword.

I turned and looked out across the grasslands just north of town and the storm clouds that had all but darkened the sky, growing darker by the moment, as the last remaining vestiges of the day were quickly slipping away. Pretty soon it would be too dark to see. "We could try holing up somewhere outside of town, but clearly a fire is out of the question, and I don't like the thought of being out in the open with that coming." I pointed toward the flashes of light off in the distance that seemed to be getting closer.

The others turned as the first roll of thunder echoed across the grasslands.

"Where does that leave us, then?" Barthol asked. "I didn't see much in the way of an inn when we first rode through, let alone somewhere to stable the horses."

I thought a moment, then turned and banged on the ferryman's door once more, waited a moment, then banged again.

"I told you to get off my property!"

"At least tell us where we can find shelter for the evening!"

There was a moment of silence before he spoke again. "Head back into town, then take a left at the square, and you'll see a sign on the right for the Spotted Pike Inn. I suggest you get indoors before it gets any darker. Now be off with you, and don't let me catch you banging on my door again!"

"Let's go," Dakaran said, heading down the porch steps for his horse. "It's already getting dark."

I looked at the others and shrugged. "You heard him. Let's go."

We mounted and rode back to the docks, where we took the main street back toward the town's square. As much as I tried, I couldn't pull my eyes away from the rotting corpse on the other side, a clear warning. I just wished I knew what the warning was. We took a left at the center

of town and skirted the covered well in the middle as we made our way up the next street.

We didn't have to go far before Dakaran was all but hopping out of his saddle to point us toward a building on the right. As the ferryman had said, there was a sign out front that read THE SPOTTED PIKE INN. There was also the image of a long, spotted fish painted underneath, though several of the spots seemed to be missing, since the paint was chipped and fading. We pulled our horses in front and climbed down, tying off at the rails.

Beside the inn was a rundown-looking shamble of a barn that I assumed was for stabling the guests' horses, not that I imagined they got guests all that often, or ever. However, we waited to stable the horses until we knew for sure we would be staying, though at this point, I'd have been fine bunking with the horses, just to be out of the weather.

Dakaran was the first one to the door, but I grabbed him and pulled him behind me. "Might be another crossbow waiting on the other side."

Dakaran quickly scooted to the back, more than happy to let the rest of us go in first and find out.

With my hand resting on the hilt of my blade, I opened the door and stepped inside. The common room wasn't all that big, certainly nothing like the Rose and Crown, or even the Fishnet, for that matter. It was dark and smoke-filled, nearly every table and stool around the bar taken. Like every other building in town, the windows were shuttered and boarded from the inside. The only time I had seen behavior like this was in Aramoor, during times of heavy storms off the ocean, and only in those areas closest to the water.

I turned and nodded to those behind me, and they stepped in as well, Dakaran in the lead. Every eye in the place turned in our direction. Those seated closest stood, shifting their seats completely around, not wanting their backs exposed to the band of rough-looking riders who'd just entered. Several of the men and even the women had long knives in their hands, looking like they could explode out of their seats at any moment and be on top of us. Though, it seemed that most of the eyes were looking past us to the—

"Shut that door!" someone near the back shouted, others coming out of their seats.

Stumpy, who was the last in, turned and shut the door. The patrons glanced nervously at the entrance again, not quite looking at us but rather staring at the floor and open spaces between the door and the tables. Their curious looks became so unnerving that I, along with the rest of my roommates, turned to look as well.

"What is everyone staring at?" Fipple asked.

Barthol leaned in. "Don't reckon I like the look of this place."

"Or the smell," Waylen added.

I scanned the room, looking for anyone who might resemble an innkeeper, and spotted a frightened-looking man in an apron on the left, holding a tray of drinks. It was a wonder they hadn't spilled the way his hands were shaking. When he saw me catch his eye, he laid the tray down on one of the occupied tables and hesitantly started our way, rubbing his hands nervously down his apron.

The innkeeper was average height, though skinny, his apron hanging off him like a bedsheet, seemingly having been made for someone with a little more girth. He had brown hair, brown eyes, and three-day stubble, with no other distinguishable features.

"Can . . . can I help you gentlemen with anything?" He looked each of us over, spending a little more time on Fipple.

As he got closer to the door, he raised his hand out toward the empty space between the tables and the wall and continued to hold it there until he reached us, as if attempting to sweep up any unseen cobwebs from the side wall with his hand. As soon as he reached us, he lowered his arm

back to his side, and those in the room slowly began retaking their seats, though their blades stayed close at hand.

"What in the flaming stones is going on around here?" Gellar mumbled under his breath. "These people are right mad. Might be safer outside with the storm."

I wanted to agree but held it in as I turned to address the innkeeper. "We are looking for rooms tonight."

"Here?" the innkeeper asked. "In Dorwall?"

"Yes, here," Gellar huffed. "Do you see any other towns nearby?"

The skinny man wrung his hands. "You must not be from around these parts." Once again, he glanced at Fipple. "No one comes to Dorwall. Not even the boats stop anymore."

The hairs on the back of my neck were beginning to rise. "And why is this? Besides the fact that your town looks like it's about to fall apart and you have dead bodies quite literally hanging in the streets."

"Clean the place up a bit," Waylen suggested, "and maybe you'd get more people passing through."

The innkeeper shook his head. "We don't want more people."

"Dead if they do come," one of the patrons called out on the right. Another man with a bent back, sitting about two tables from the front, nodded. "Those that ride in don't ever ride back out."

# WILDFIRE

## Chapter 4

I TRIED TO SWALLOW, but my mouth had gone completely dry.

"I'm beginning to see why you wished to recant your heritage," Waylen whispered to Fipple.

"What do you mean those that ride in don't ride back out?" Dakaran asked, his face looking even more pale than before, if that was possible.

"He means, best you leave while you can," the squirrely innkeeper said.

"Have you looked outside?" Gellar asked, pointing toward one of the boarded windows. "Where do you suggest we go?"

Barthol leaned in. "Sleeping in the field is beginning to sound really good to me."

"We aren't leaving," I said. "This is the closest ferry crossing for days, and that storm outside isn't something we want to challenge." The cracks around the door and windows flashed with white light, and the

building shook with the sound of thunder. I turned to the others. "We need to get those horses stabled."

"Me and Fipple will see to the horses," Stumpy said, "while you find us some lodging."

The two men turned and opened the door, and half of those seated nearby stood and drew their weapons as the rain flew in.

"Whoa!" I shouted, raising my hands. "They're just going to see to our horses. No need to get carried away."

Fipple shut the door behind them, and one of the men at a table on the left walked over and swung his sword blindly through the air between us and the door. Hitting nothing but the stone wall, he returned to his seat, as did most of the other patrons.

These people were nuts.

"What in the Dark One's name is going on around here?" Gellar asked, looking ready to draw his own weapon if the innkeeper didn't give us a straight answer.

The skinny man with the apron gulped, then glanced around the room, but not at the patrons. Instead, he looked nervously toward the empty spots where no one was seated or standing, especially along the wall. "Something evil haunts this town," he said, his hands clenched tight in front of him.

"You mean *hunts* this town, don't you?" a woman in the back called out.

I couldn't see who it was that had spoken, as the room was tightly packed and the smoke fairly dense, but it was easy enough to tell that whoever she was, she was scared.

"Are you trying to tell us you believe there are spirits haunting your town?" Waylen asked, nervously wrapping his finger around the bottom of his thin beard.

"No other way to explain it," the innkeeper said. "People murdered in their own beds with no one around. Others dying in the streets while walking home alone."

"What about the corpse we saw hanging in the middle of town square?" Barthol asked. "You can't tell me spirits hoisted him all the way up there."

"That was Dreese," an older man by the bar said, tankard in one hand, knife in the other. "Town carpenter. We woke three days ago to find him hanging from his own store's sign."

I shivered at the thought.

"Whatever it is," the innkeeper said. "It can't be seen."

In a strange and perverse sort of way, it made the crazy things these people had been doing make a little more sense. They weren't scared of us. They were scared of the shadows, afraid of what they couldn't see, afraid of opening a door and letting in something hidden. I found myself suddenly glancing over my shoulder toward the empty space between the door and the first tables on the left. Then again, if it was a spirit, shutting the doors and boarding the windows wouldn't make any difference.

"You're saying the people around here have been dying and no one has seen anything?" Barthol asked. "You've got to have some idea of what this is. People don't just up and die for no reason."

No one answered, though pensive looks were traded amongst the patrons.

Barthol shook his head. "Why am I getting so worked up? It's not like I have to live here." He looked at me. "The sooner we get to sleep, the sooner morning comes, and we leave this mad town."

The innkeeper shrugged. "On your heads what happens. Don't say we didn't warn you." He walked over to the bar—beside an open door with a set of stairs that no doubt led up to the inn's guest quarters—grabbed a few keys off a rung on the wall, along with a single candle and holder, and motioned us over.

Before following the skinny man up to see the rooms, I turned to Waylen. "Wait here for the others. When they finish with the horses, tell them we've headed upstairs to see to our rooms."

"Were you dropped on your head as a boy?" Waylen said. "I'm not waiting down here by myself." He leaned in. "These people look crazy enough to try roasting me over a spit. Who's to say they ain't the ones doing the killing?"

"Fine. Who wants to stay with Waylen?"

"Don't look at me," Dakaran spouted when I glanced his way.

"Oh, for pity's sake," Gellar grumbled. "I'll stay." He turned and grinned at Dakaran. "Besides, who's to say that the killer isn't waiting up in one of those rooms for you?"

I left them to their squabbling and headed across the room. Dakaran was quick to catch up, Barthol just behind. I passed one last glance over my shoulder before following the innkeeper through the door and up the narrow staircase. Both Waylen and Gellar had taken up positions behind the door and as far from the tables as possible, though they kept a close eye on those seated at them.

This was really turning into a nightmare. I was starting to rethink my decision of not taking the Rhivanni up on their offer to travel with them.

We reached the top of the stairs and found a small dark corridor running the full length of the building. On the left side was a wall with windows that overlooked the alley below, and on the right were the rooms. It was clear from the amount of dust collected on the floor that this inn hadn't seen occupancy in some time.

The innkeeper didn't bother showing us our rooms. He simply handed us the keys and the candle and waited for payment. "One silver and three."

"That will include our meals, I hope," I said as I dug around in my pocket and pulled out my coin pouch.

"Meals included," the innkeeper acknowledged as I handed him the fare. It was a more than reasonable price for four rooms in Aramoor, but out in the middle of nowhere, in a town where people were dying for no known cause, it seemed steep.

The innkeeper nodded his appreciation and stuffed the coins in his apron pocket. "I suggest you get in and lock the doors as soon as possible, and keep them locked." With another sad shake of his head, he turned and started back down the stairs. He stopped about three steps down and turned. "Oh, I almost forgot, my name's Tobar. Welcome to the Spotted Pike Inn." With that, he continued down to the common room.

"Welcoming bunch," Barthol said.

"Welcoming enough to get you killed in your sleep," Dakaran grumbled.

I looked down at the keys, using the light from the candle, which Barthol now held, to read them. Each key had a number attached, matching a number on a tarnished silver plate that had been nailed to the front of each door. "Looks like some of us are going to have to double up," I said, looking down at the four keys Tobar had given us.

"I'm staying with you," Dakaran was quick to announce.

"Fine." I took one of the keys—Number 3—and handed the rest to Barthol. "Pick your room. I'll let the rest of you decide who sleeps with who. Honestly, it might be best if we all double up."

"That might prove difficult," Barthol said, looking at Dakaran. "There's seven of us now."

I ran my hand back through my hair. He was right. Either one person slept alone, or three shared a room. At this point, I doubted anyone was willing to sleep on their own. "We'll figure it out when the rest get here." I walked down the dark hallway to my door and stuck the key in

the lock. Dakaran had his sword drawn and at the ready as I turned the handle and pushed it open.

The door whined the entire way before coming to a stop with a bump against the wall. I was actually quite thankful for the squeaky hinge. It would be hard for anyone, or anything, to sneak in with a door that loud. Barthol stood just behind us, holding out the candle as we all peered into the cramped quarters.

The room was small, with a single bed on the right, though it looked wide enough to sleep two, but not comfortably. There was a small table beside the bed with a candle on top, a stone fireplace in the left corner, a stand beside the door with an empty washbasin and a towel, and a window on the far side between the end of the bed and the unlit hearth. It looked down on the alley on the other side of the inn.

"At least there's no dead body lying in the bed," I said, trying to lighten the mood. I drew my own sword and started in, waving it around the empty spaces of the room, feeling somewhat ridiculous. Satisfied that there wasn't anything in there with us, I nodded for the others to come in.

Barthol walked over and lit the candle on the nightstand, then started for the fireplace, but the sound of footsteps coming up the steps out in the hall had us all moving back to the door instead.

"They're up here," Gellar called back down the stairs as he reached the top landing and headed our way. He was toting a couple of our saddlebags in his hands. Fipple and Stumpy, who were carrying the rest of our meager belongings, tracked water all the way down the hall, the two looking like they'd just taken a swim in the river with their clothes on.

"How are the horses?" I asked.

Fipple, who was still trying to wring the water from his topknot, glanced around the dust-covered hall and sneezed. "Better off than us, it appears."

"What's it look like?" Gellar asked, pushing his way past Barthol to get inside. "Kind of small, isn't it?" He wiped a finger across the wash table on the left, and it left a line where the dust had been. "Not much for cleaning around here, are they? Hope you didn't pay much." He glanced around the room. "Which one is mine?"

"Tobar only gave us four keys," I said, holding them up. "So we'll have to double up tonight."

"In beds that small?" Gellar asked.

"You rather bunk by yourself?" Stumpy asked. "And hope no shade wanders into your room while you're snoring?" Apparently, Gellar and Waylen had filled Stumpy and Fipple in on what the innkeeper had said about the strange killings taking place.

Gellar grumbled something under his breath, but he didn't say anything more.

Apart from Gellar's initial complaint, no one seemed too disturbed by the sleeping arrangements. I doubted any of us were going to sleep all that much as it was. Another flash lit the window on the far side of the room, and the building shook with the aftershock of the thunder.

"And which lucky room gets to sleep three?" Stumpy asked, quick to notice the discrepancy in the number of rooms to the number of people needing to go in them.

"We'll sleep three," Dakaran volunteered without asking me. He clearly wanted as many people in his room as possible.

I nodded. "Fine, yes, we'll sleep three. We're the smallest of the lot anyway. In fact, here, I'll make it simple. Stumpy, you're with me and Dakaran. Fipple, you're with Waylen. And Gellar, you're with Barthol."

They all nodded, and I handed out the keys. Before they made it out the door, Waylen stopped. "What did they say about our meals? Afraid all we have left at this point is some stale biscuits. We weren't expecting to go this long without passing a town with provisions."

"The price includes meals," I said. "But we better make it fast. It's getting kind of late. We'll be lucky if the kitchen is still open."

Waylen's face darkened, and he abruptly handed his key to Fipple. "You go check the room. I'm going to go make sure the cook hasn't cleaned up for the night." With that, Waylen shuffled himself out the door and down the hall. I could hear the wooden boards creaking under him as he went.

The others dispersed to their own rooms, leaving me, Stumpy, and Dakaran to ours. While Dakaran did his best to shake out the bedding, Stumpy and I saw to the fire. It was a little warm for a blaze, but at this point, we were more eager to have the extra light.

We placed our packs under our beds and met the rest of our party in the hall. Barthol and Gellar were the last to join us, but as soon as they shut their door and locked it behind them, we all headed down to see if Waylen had been able to scrounge us up something to eat. With all the excitement taking place, I hadn't realized how hungry I was until we reached the bottom step and made our way back out into the common room. Even with the strong smell of pipe smoke, there was a lingering smell of something coming from the kitchen that had my stomach grumbling.

Surprisingly, the room was still packed, though we did manage to find a couple tables close to the door that apparently no one wanted to sit in. We pushed them together and sat down. Conversations that had ceased as we first entered slowly began to pick back up. Waylen walked over from where he'd been conversing with Tobar and sat down with a smile on his face.

"I take it you caught the cook before they shut down the kitchen," Barthol said.

Waylen tucked his gut up under the lip of the table as he tried scooting his chair a little closer. "Aye. It seems the patrons weren't all that hungry tonight, so he had quite a bit of wasted stew he was going to dispose of. They'll have it out to us shortly."

Waylen had barely gotten the words out when Tobar walked over carrying several empty tankards, which he plopped in front of each of us at the table. Another man, who'd been serving drinks behind the bar, carried over a couple of pitchers, which he filled our tankards with, then left on the table and walked back to the bar.

Tobar waited around long enough for us to take our first swallows, evidently making sure we were satisfied before moving on to other things. The ale was warm but welcoming, and it soothed my throat going down. From what I could tell, it didn't have quite the bite that the Rhivanni's mead had, which I was thankful for.

"Don't fill up on drink," I cautioned. "We need clear heads tonight."

Several of those with tankards to their mouths lowered them, the first being Dakaran. In fact, I didn't see him lift his tankard again the rest of the evening.

By the time we'd managed to relax in our seats, a man and woman wearing matching aprons stepped out of the open doorway on the opposite side of the bar and started in our direction. They carried two large trays between them as they carefully wove their way across the room and over to where we were anxiously awaiting our food. They placed the trays down and began passing out the wooden bowls.

The smell was better than the taste, but we hardly had room to be choosy. It was that or stale biscuits. The overly peppered sauce seemed to be meant to cover the somewhat sour flavor of whatever it was they were using for meat. I didn't remember seeing any farm animals on the way into town, and after some of the gruesome sights we'd witnessed so far, I tried not to let my imagination get carried away on what that might be.

Waylen, on the other hand, clearly had no such preconceived notions, as he had finished his second bowl before most of us made it halfway through our first.

"So, what do you think is really going on around here?" Barthol asked no one in particular, though he looked at me as he finished the question.

I stuffed another bite in my mouth and quickly swallowed, washing it down with a small sip from my tankard. "I'm hoping we don't have to find out."

Gellar noticed some of the men from the table next to ours staring and turned to address them. "What do you think is going on around here?"

A few of the other tables, those that were close enough to hear us, turned as well.

"Surely, some of you have some kind of notion as to what is really going on."

The men shook their heads and went back to their own conversations, pretending we weren't even there.

"What's wrong with you lot?" Gellar asked, looking out across the room, which had now quieted once more. "You can't tell me no one here has a better guess as to what's happening in this town than flaming shades."

The patrons sneered and tightened their grips on their weapons as they turned their backs to us, some going so far as to tell us to mind our own business, others waving their mugs at us angrily and grunting.

"How long have the killings been going on for?" I asked, turning to face the room. "When did they first start? Something had to have changed."

"It was when the new magistrate took over," a woman in the back said. It sounded like the same woman who'd spoken out earlier about their town being *hunted* and not *haunted*.

Some people at a table on the back right stood and moved, leaving the woman to herself.

"You yellow-livered cowards, the lot of ya! Whatcha runnin' for? I'm just sayin' what we's all thinkin'! These killings didn't start till he showed up." The woman was stout at the waist, with disheveled hair and eyes of such a bright green I could see them from the other side of the room. She was older, with grey streaks in her brown hair, and was full-on sloshed by how slurred her words were.

"Who's this magistrate?" Dakaran asked.

The woman stood and stumbled across the room with a tankard in her hand, grabbing the backs of chairs she passed to steady herself. She then proceeded to plop down in one of the seats at our table, not paying the least mind that Fipple was already in it.

Fipple quickly shot up before she landed in his lap, then fetched a vacant chair from a table next to ours, whose patrons had decided it best they call it a night and leave. In fact, several other tables cleared out as well, as though not wanting to be around as this woman gave her opinions on who was possibly behind the terrorizing of their town.

By the time she'd drained the last of her mug and reached for the pitcher on our table, half the tavern's patrons had left.

"I'm tellin' ya, it's that Magistrate Nezrit. The one sent in from Ecrin. When he first stepped off the boat was when the killings began." She half-hiccuped, half-burped, then drained her glass and wiped the froth with her sleeve.

"Best you were on your way, Matty," Tobar said nervously as he scurried over from the bar. He ran his hands down his apron as he cast about the emptying room. "I think you've had enough for one night. Best go sleep it off."

She glared at the skinny innkeeper and sneered, but eventually she stood, her legs wobbling enough that I thought she was going to land on top of Waylen. "You'll leave this town if ya know what's good for ya." She stared at us a moment as though trying to decide who we were or where she was, then stumbled her way to the door with Tobar's help.

Tobar quickly shut the door behind her, to keep the wind and rain—and anything else—out, then turned. "Don't pay Matty much mind. Gets a bit carried away when she's had a few." He left us to our drinks and walked back to the kitchen, disappearing inside.

Stumpy set his drink down on the table. "I think I'm going to call it a night."

We all nodded in agreement and made our way over to the stairs and up to our rooms.

As before, I had to sweep our room with my sword before Dakaran would step foot inside. This time, though, I had Stumpy to help. Dakaran stood in the hall, swinging his sword in a full circle around him as he waited for us to finish.

"All right," I said, tossing my sword on the bed. "There's nothing here, unless it crawled up the chimney."

Dakaran stopped halfway into the room, his eyes shooting straight for the hearth. "And do we know there isn't something up there? Did you sweep it?"

I released a frustrated sigh. "No. But you're more than welcome to try climbing inside to find out. Though I wouldn't recommend it—with the fire still going." I shook my head and walked over to the bed. "Which side do you want?"

Dakaran looked at me like I was mad. "You're not sleeping on there with me."

"I most certainly am, and if you don't like it, you can sleep on the floor."

"Where do I sleep?" Stumpy asked.

"In the bed," I said.

Now both of them were looking at me like I'd lost my mind.

I smiled. "We will sleep in shifts, two at a time, while one of us stands watch."

"Oh." Dakaran rolled his shoulders. "Right. That's a good idea. You can go first." With that, he shot over to the bed and hopped on top, sliding over to take side nearest the wall.

"You sure?" Stumpy said, sitting down on the edge of the bed.

I nodded. "I'm not all that tired anyway."

"Suit yourself." He lay down beside Dakaran and closed his eyes.

Dakaran turned over on his side with his back to Stumpy, neither using the covers, deciding instead to sleep on top with their swords in their hands. I took a seat on a chair in the corner and listened to the sound of the rain beating down on the roof and the wind blowing against the window, producing a rather haunting moan as it seeped through the cracks.

Between the storm outside, the crackling fire in the hearth, and my roommates' snores, I found myself periodically dozing off. I was clearly more tired than I thought. It was during one of those times of half-consciousness that I found myself suddenly jerking awake, my ears catching a noise that didn't quite fit.

I looked around the room. Everything seemed to be just as I'd left it—the candle burning low on the table, the fire hissing and popping in the corner, my roommates snoring—but there was this nagging feeling of something being wrong. Had I heard something or just imagined it? As jumpy as I was, I'd probably dreamed I'd heard something, and it had startled me awake. Not seeing anything out of the ordinary, I slowly leaned back in my seat. Just as soon as I'd resigned myself to the fact that I'd made the whole thing up, there was a slight squeak by the door.

I turned my head slowly, and with the dim light from the hearth, I could see the handle on our door slowly begin to turn. I reached for my sword and quietly pulled it from its sheath as I leaned forward in my seat. The boards under my chair creaked when I shifted my weight, and the handle stopped.

I waited, keeping my eyes and ears glued to the door, but there was no movement, no sounds at all over the storm outside. Slowly, I pushed up to my feet and slid my way across the floor, trying not to press down too hard or too fast and give away my position. Grabbing the handle, I took a deep breath and yanked it open and leaped into the hall.

There was nothing there.

# WILDFIRE

## Chapter 5

**W**HAT'S GOING ON?"

I turned to find both Stumpy and Dakaran out of bed with their swords up, casting about tensely as they tried to determine why I'd leapt into the hallway.

A door opened two down from ours, and Barthol stuck his head out. "Ayrion, is that you? What are you doing?" He held up his candle to get a better look around.

"You weren't just down here at our door, were you?" I asked.

Barthol stepped halfway out of his room and shook his head. "No. Why?"

The door between ours suddenly opened, and Fipple's and Waylen's heads appeared. "What's going on out here?"

"Neither of you were just at our door, were you?"

Fipple shook his head. Waylen simply yawned, looking like he'd just woken from a deep sleep.

Barthol stepped out of the room completely, Gellar following him as they walked down the hall in our direction, both with their swords in hand. "Did you hear something?" Barthol asked.

"Yes. There was someone at our door."

"How do you know—"

"Because the handle turned," I said, interrupting Dakaran before he could finish. "But by the time I made it to the door and opened it, the hall was empty."

Several of the others turned and looked around the hall.

Waylen rubbed his arms. "I think I just got chill bumps."

"Wasn't your door locked?" Barthol asked.

"Yes. And here's the key," I said, holding it up for the others to see. I walked over to the stairs and looked down to the bottom, but I couldn't see anything but a dark stairwell, so I headed back. "If you weren't already, I suggest you take turns watching in your rooms tonight. Whoever, or whatever, this is, they can apparently get into locked rooms."

Fipple looked at Waylen, then at Barthol. "I think we'll bunk with you two tonight. Four to a room is safer than two, and easier to keep watch on. Get more sleep that way."

Barthol nodded. "Don't know how much sleep any of us will be getting after this."

"Bring your own mattress," Gellar said sharply. "'Cause you ain't sharing with us."

Waylen and Fipple grabbed their belongings and their bedding—all but the frame—and headed down to Barthol and Gellar's room. Once they were in and the door shut, I headed back into ours, shutting and locking it behind us, for all the good it would do.

Dakaran walked over to his bed and swung his sword all around it, even slapping the sheets on top before sitting down on the edge. Stumpy joined him on the side while I walked over and tossed another couple of logs on the fire. The storm outside didn't seem to be waning any, the thunder rolling and lightning striking at random intervals, just enough to keep us unnerved.

"Who wants to stand watch now?" I asked with a sheepish grin.

Both Dakaran and Stumpy raised their hands. In the end, we all stayed up and kept watch, none of us wanting to risk falling asleep and waking up to find ourselves hanging from the sign out front. By the time morning arrived, the storm had mostly passed, or at least the lightning had. It was still raining a good bit, and the wind was still beating against the shutters outside.

Dakaran yawned. "I can't believe we paid good coin to sit here all night and stare at the walls."

"Better than sitting outside, I guess," Stumpy said.

Creaks on the boards in the hall had all three of us up with swords in hand. The creaking stopped just outside our door.

"It's come back for us," Dakaran whispered.

There was a knock, followed closely by Waylen's voice. "You up in there? The rest of us are heading down for breakfast."

Dakaran was the first to the door. "We're ready," he said as he opened it and shot into the hallway.

Barthol peeked in. "Get any sleep?"

"About as much as you lot, probably." I couldn't help but notice the dark circles around Barthol's eyes.

"So that's a no," he said with a forced smile.

After locking our door, I followed the rest of the group down to the common room. Apparently, not even Tobar had been through yet, since none of the candles had been lit, and with the storm still looming outside and all the windows boarded, the room was dark.

"Stinks worse down here now than it did last night," Gellar said,

pinching his nose. "They must not have cleaned up afterward."

Fipple used a striker from his pocket to light one of the candles near the bar, then turned to light some of the candles on the tables. He stopped halfway to the first one, his eyes going wide as he stared at the front door.

"Holy flaming Pits. What in the name of the Dark One is that?"

We all turned to find something nailed to the door. With horror, I realized it was a body—and that I could still recognize the face, despite how mutilated the rest of the corpse was. Its green eyes seemed to be screaming as they stared at nothing.

"It's Matty," I said.

Dakaran looked like he was about to retch and quickly turned away.

"How did we not hear any hammering?" Fipple asked.

Gellar hmphed. "As loud as you snore, it's a wonder any of us heard anything. Not to mention the building shaking from the thunder."

The lock on the front door snapped to, and the door opened.

Tobar screamed when he came face-to-face with Matty's remains, and he rushed inside before the door could shut on him. He stumbled over to where the rest of us were standing and took a moment to catch his breath before turning to look. "I told that fool woman to keep her mouth shut." He shook his head and clicked his tongue. "Poor thing didn't deserve this."

"You didn't happen to be in our hall last night checking the doors, did you?" I asked to my left, none of us able to pull our eyes away from the gruesome sight.

Tobar shook his head, at least from what I could see from the corner of my eye.

"As soon as the last patron left, I told Cook to take off, then I headed around to my chambers at the back and locked myself in." He finally turned away from the door, prompting the rest of us to do the same.

"Why? Did something happen?" He scanned our faces as if to see if any of us were missing.

"Someone tried coming into our room last night, and apparently had their own key."

Tobar shuffled over to the left wall beside the bar and looked at the rack of keys displayed there. "I keep a single spare key for each door, but they all seem to be here."

I nodded. I didn't know how I felt about there being another key to our room lying about for anyone to take, but at this point I didn't see any sense in debating the issue. We were hopefully going to be miles from this place by evening.

The door opened once more, and we all reached for our weapons.

The cook screamed when he saw the body and ran inside, just like Tobar.

"Don't reckon anyone is up for breakfast?" Tobar asked, almost as an afterthought.

We all looked at the door and shook our heads.

"Didn't think so." He put his arm around the cook, and they left us at the front and made their way across the common room and into the back.

"I say we get our stuff and go see if the ferryman will be willing to take us or not," Barthol said.

"Doubtful," Fipple said. "Not with it still raining like it is."

"Can't hurt to try," Stumpy said.

I nodded. "Sounds like a good idea. I think I've seen enough of this place for one night."

"For the rest of my life," Waylen mumbled to himself, joining me and Barthol as we headed for the stairs.

It didn't take us long to pack, and by the time we did, there was light pouring in from the cracks in the shutters. It wasn't the warm amber light of a new sun, but the overcast grey of a sun hidden by thick clouds. The rain was still coming down, but not quite as strongly as it had been the previous night.

The horses seemed to have weathered the storm well enough but looked just as anxious to be gone from this cursed town as we were. We saddled and rode down to the waterfront. The roads were even worse today, making it a slow trudge through town. No one appeared to be up, no lights in the windows, no sounds of movement inside. Dorwall looked completely deserted.

"The water is up," Fipple pointed out, his topknot hanging down in front over his right shoulder.

He was right. The river was cresting close to the tops of the piers, sending the tops of the boats rising above the walkway.

"It's also moving rather swiftly," Stumpy added.

Both of which were clear signs that the trip across would be a rough one.

We reached the ferry station and reined in out front. This time, the others stayed on their horses while I went to talk with the ferryman, hoping that having only one man on his porch would make him more agreeable. I shook the water from my cloak as I made it up under the overhang. My boots were coated in mud all the way to my ankles. I tried shaking the thicker clumps off, but it didn't help.

Three raps on the door, and I waited.

Not hearing anything, I knocked again, this time louder.

The familiar sound of chains rattled from the other side just before the door opened. I found myself facing off against the ferryman's crossbow once more as he stared me down with a frown that said he wasn't in any better mood this morning than last night. He looked beyond me to the rest of Room Eleven.

"I see you survived. Can't say I'm not surprised. The storm must have dampened the creature's appetite."

"Not hardly," I said. "We woke to find a woman nailed to the front door of the inn. Not much left to look at."

The ferryman's frown deepened. "Who was it?"

"Innkeeper said her name was Matty."

The man sighed, his crossbow lowering slightly as he shook his head. "Whatever, or whoever, it is, it's getting bolder."

"Which is why we're here. We seek passage across."

The crossbow shot back up. "Are you deaf as well as stupid? I told you, I ain't taking no one across in this weather."

"The storm has passed, and—"

"The rain ain't. Look out there, boy," he said, pointing behind me with the crossbow. "And I don't even have to look to tell you the river's running high and fast. I can hear it from here. Dangerous at the best of times, but you add in slick boards and a fast current, and what you'll end up with is an upturned ferry and a bunch of drowned men and horses."

"Then what do you suggest we do?"

"Wait and see if the sun returns. Give it another day and we'll discuss it further." With that, he shut the door, and the chains rattled once more.

I walked over to the edge of the porch and shrugged. The men looked about as distraught as I felt. None of us wanted to stay a moment longer, especially after last night.

"What now?" Dakaran said. "We can't stay here."

I walked out through the mud and untied my horse and mounted. "We can either try to push on to Pirn, which in this weather would put four or five days more onto our journey, or we can try waiting it out one more day and see if we can get across tomorrow."

"If we weren't in such a rush," Barthol said, "I'd vote to take the trek north. As it is, I say we try sticking it out one more day. Besides, right now, we don't have enough provisions to make it two days, let alone four or five. We'll need to see if there's a shop to buy from and whether or not they have people willing to sell to us."

"Don't get your hopes up on the latter," Gellar grumbled, pointing at the ferryman's front door. "If he's any indication as to the type of welcome we'll receive, we might be better off fishing the river than finding someone willing to open their doors to us."

Stumpy tucked the end of his arm further up into his sleeve to keep the rain off his stump. "Perhaps with so few visitors, they'd be overjoyed to have someone willing to purchase their goods?" He held his legs out from his saddle to rinse the loose dirt from his boots in the rain.

Waylen grunted. "If they have any goods left to sell. If these killings have been going on for any length of time, I doubt anyone has come this way to help restock the shelves. Remember what the innkeeper said. 'Boats don't stop here anymore.'"

Waylen made a good point, though I hoped he was wrong. "I say we head back to the inn to talk with Tobar. Perhaps he can point us in the right direction for provisions. Then we hunker down in the inn like we did last night and wait it out. Hopefully, the sun returns, and the ferryman will be more inclined to take us across."

Gellar sneered as he shook the water droplets from the thick red braid hanging from his face. "If not, I'm going to lash him to the boat and take it across myself."

A couple of the others nodded in agreement, and we started back through town.

We stabled the horses once more, taking off the saddles, since we figured in a town this size, we could get around just as easy on foot. After making sure the horses had enough feed and water, we headed for the inn.

"You're back?" Tobar asked. He and two other men were busy trying to remove Matty's body from the door, one piece at a time. "Thought you'd be long gone by now."

"Not for a lack of trying," Gellar grumbled.

"It appears we might be needing our rooms for another night," I said. "This time, better make it just two instead of four."

"And meals," Waylen added. "We don't want to forget those." He looked at the corpse, and for a moment I thought he'd change his mind, but he didn't. Like the rest of us, his face pinched at the sight of the dead woman.

The men managed to get the final nail pulled, and Matty's body dropped onto the walkway. I tried not to look.

"Is there a good place in town for us to restock supplies?" I asked, hoping to be away from the poor woman as quickly as possible.

Tobar stopped what he was doing long enough to point us back the way we'd come. "The butcher is just around the corner. Take a left at the square, and his shop will be the second on the left. That is, if he has anything left. Meat has been kind of sparse lately, what with the boats no longer stopping and the farmers no longer wanting to come into town."

We thanked him and headed back out into the rain, which had lessened since we left the ferry. It was down to a heavy sprinkle. By the time we rounded the corner, we spotted a few more of Dorwall's citizens moving through the streets, keeping close to the edges, no doubt so they could hop inside a doorway if they felt they needed to. Seeing a group of seven hooded men coming down the road was enough to send most scrambling back inside.

We found the butcher, whose shop was unfortunately directly across the street from Dreese, the dead carpenter hanging from his sign. And as our poor luck seemed to be holding out, Tobar was correct: The butcher and his son had little enough to sell us but scrap meat, cuts usually reserved for dog food or the very poorest to use for soup—nothing smoked, nothing salted or dried. We purchased a few small strips of something, figuring we could at least get Tobar to cook it for us to take on our way. And apart from the butcher and a single farm wagon that rolled through town long enough for us to purchase some fresh vegetables off the back, there wasn't much in the way of provisions for our travels, which meant we would have to spend more time hunting and cleaning and less time actually traveling.

We took our goods, what little there were, and headed back to the Spotted Pike. By the time we arrived, the rain had stopped and the sun was just beginning to peek out from behind the clouds, letting us know it hadn't deserted us after all. Tobar had managed to dispense of Matty's body, though the wood was still stained with her blood.

"Not sure if I'm all that hungry after all," Fipple said as he clapped his boots on the stoop before stepping inside.

Even with a courtesy shake and a stomp, we still tracked quite a bit of mud into the common room as we looked around for a table away from the door. So far, there hadn't been any sign of whatever had killed Matty the previous night, which left me wondering whether this thing killed during the daytime as well. Perhaps it wasn't unseen after all; maybe it was a skilled assassin who had been trained to keep hidden, like the Upakans.

Could it possibly be one of my people?

I shook the notion off before it festered any further. We weren't paid to terrorize people in this way. This was sloppy, messy work. This was done by something that enjoyed killing. Whatever it was, it was a rabid creature that needed to be put down.

"What can I get you gentlemen?" Tobar asked, back in his usual white apron.

"What do you have?" Waylen was first to ask.

"Same as we had last night," the innkeeper said dryly.

Waylen's cheerful expression slipped. "I guess I'll have that. And some of your finest ale," he added afterward with a bright smile.

Tobar frowned. "Only got the one."

"Oh. Guess we'll be having that as well."

Tobar nodded and headed back to the kitchen to put in our order. He didn't seem in much of a hurry. He didn't seem all that much awake, either. Like the rest of the town, he seemed to be walking around in a daze.

The food was out shortly and tasted like it was last night's batch of stew, heated up just enough to soften the gravy. The ale wasn't much better, strong and a bit on the sour side. We ate in silence, no one wanting to do much more than lift their spoons to their mouths.

With little to do to occupy our time as we waited for night to fall, most of us spent it in the common room, watching people come and go, listening in on their conversations. Tobar was quick to spread the word about what he'd found waiting for him on his door this morning. Those listening responded about the same as he had. No one seemed all that shocked or horrified. Most wagged their heads sadly; some blamed Matty for her loose tongue.

I was surprised there weren't more people trying to leave the town, and I asked Tobar about it the next time he came by the table.

"There were some that tried a while back, but they barely made it a day out of the city when something tracked them down and murdered them all. A farmer found their campsite, and what was left of them, and reported it the next time he came into town." He took a deep breath and wiped his hands nervously down his apron. "Their bodies are still sitting out there."

When the innkeeper left to refill our pitchers, Barthol turned to the

rest of us. "Guess it was a good thing we decided against sleeping out on the plains."

"I feel sorry for these people," I said. "Imagine having to live here, under constant terror, and not being able to leave."

"It's a sad situation they've found themselves in, that's for sure," Stumpy said.

"I . . ." I couldn't believe I was about to say this. "I almost wish there was something we could do for them."

"Don't even think about it," Dakaran shot back. "I can see that look in your eyes, and you can forget it. We have to get to Ecrin, remember?"

"I know, but that doesn't mean we can't try to do something while we're here."

"We *are* doing something. We're trying not to end up like that drunk fool woman last night."

"Yes, but it couldn't hurt to—"

"I command you to quit thinking about it. I'm the crown prince. Your job is to protect me, not this flaming town."

A tray crashed onto the floor behind us, and we all turned to find Tobar staring wide-eyed at Dakaran. And he wasn't the only one. The idiot had said it loud enough for most of the tables around us to hear. Tobar quickly dropped to the floor and began cleaning up the spilled stew, casting furtive glances our way as he did. Those at the other tables turned away when they saw us watching, hushed whispers spreading around the room.

I laughed loudly and leaned forward and slapped Dakaran on the back of the head. "I've told you for the last time, you oaf. You are not the crown prince. Your father's a bricklayer and your mother works for my aunt. Be thankful we agreed to give you this position. If I hear another word from you, I'll throw you in the river myself."

My roommates looked stunned at first, but one by one seemed to catch on, as they too badgered Dakaran before going back to their drinks. I reached over and pulled Dakaran to me. "Are you trying to get yourself killed? You say something stupid like that in front of a full tavern, and it won't be some unseen creature you'll need to worry about. It'll be every fortune hunter this side of the Black Hills, looking to make a quick profit by kidnapping the high prince. I promised your parents I'd look out for you, and that's what I intend to do."

I released my grip on his cloak, and Dakaran scooted back in his seat, a scowl on his face. I hated calling him out like that, but it was safer than the alternative.

The rest of the afternoon and evening passed much the same. We took a stroll around the city, not finding much more than we'd already seen. We did come across a small bakery that had some hard tack to sell us, which we paid handsomely for. The dried bread wasn't much to look at, but we were grateful to find it.

We sat quietly in the inn that evening, finishing off another bowl of leftover stew as we sipped slowly on our sour, watered-down ale. The storm had passed completely, and the sun had begun to slowly harden up the streets, though it would be several days before they hardened enough not to sink our boots in.

The inn wasn't quite as full tonight, undoubtedly due to what had happened to Matty the night before, and those loyal patrons that did show up didn't stay as long.

"'Bout time we turned in, isn't it?" Waylen said with a deep yawn.

Fipple drained the rest of his tankard. "I couldn't agree more. The sooner we get to sleep, the sooner morning will arrive, and we can leave this cursed place once and for all."

"You said that last night," Waylen pointed out. "See how well that turned out for us?"

The others finished off their drinks, and we all headed upstairs for

our rooms. After taking several minutes to clear the space, Dakaran, Stumpy, and I locked our door and threw a couple of logs on the fire.

"Who goes first?" Dakaran asked, looking at the chair in the corner.

"I'll go," Stumpy said with a yawn that had me yawning as well. After not getting any sleep the previous night, it didn't seem as though they wanted to try making it two.

As soon as my head hit the pillow, my eyes shut on their own. "Wake me next," I said just before falling off to sleep. I wasn't even sure if I'd heard Stumpy's reply.

A loud noise yanked me out of my sleep, and I fell out of the bed, trying to get to my feet. Stumpy was already heading for the door.

"What was that?" I asked, sword in my hand. I glanced back at the bed, where Dakaran was just getting out. He stumbled a bit himself, clearly not quite awake.

"It came from next door," Stumpy said, reaching for the handle. About that time, the room next door exploded into chaos: men shouting, furniture being thrown around the room, swords clanging.

Stumpy got our door open, and I beat him through it. "Stay here with Dakaran and keep that door shut!"

I tore down the hall and tried opening the next door, but it was locked. It sounded like a battle going on inside. I leaned back and kicked the door as hard as I could. The handle gave way as the trim around the jamb splintered.

I rushed into the room. All four roommates were swinging their swords wildly at nothing, shouting and cursing at the darkness. Gellar was bleeding from one arm, and Fipple had a gouge on his forehead and a trail of blood down the left side of his face.

"It's come for us!" Fipple bellowed from on top of the bed, chopping at the side wall.

"What's going on?" I shouted, holding my sword in front of me, not seeing anything.

"It's here!" Barthol said, swinging in all directions, barely missing Waylen, who was doing the same. "The creature's come for us! It's in the room!"

"There's nothing—"

About the time I said it, a vision struck, and I dove into the room and spun. There was a man in the corner holding a long dagger with blood on the tip. He looked . . . wrong, and it wasn't just his white hair and amber-colored eyes. It was the fact that I could see through him. Holy flaming faeries, the townspeople were right! It was a shade!

# WILDFIRE

## Chapter 6

HE SEE-THROUGH MAN looked right at me and froze. "Impossible." He looked about as shocked as I did. "How is it you see me?"

I was about to tell him I had no idea when he pulled a second dagger and dove for me.

I deflected his blades and kicked him back against the wall. As soon as our weapons touched, everything in the room lost its color for a brief moment. I shook my head. What had just happened? The shouts of my men behind me dulled, then, as soon as our blades lost contact, the sensation vanished and everything went back to normal—whatever normal was in a situation like this.

"Where'd you go?" Barthol shouted.

"He was there and then he wasn't," Fipple said.

"He's over here!" I yelled, beating back several more attempts at my neck and chest. The man, or whatever he was, fought like a cornered beast. My blade once again struck his, and I felt as though someone had put a shroud around me to cloud my senses. Was this truly a shade? Was I fighting death itself?

The daggers once again struck my blade, and I parried and countered with a quick upward cut, fighting to keep from getting hit by one of them. I had no idea what they would do to me if they did. Anticipating an attempt on my right side, I switched positions and caught him in his instead. The see-through man howled like a wild animal as my blade struck flesh, and he rushed out the door before I could stop him.

There was blood on my sword. This was no shade.

I ran after him, all the way down the hall and then down the stairs into the common room. He was fast. A few of the candles were still burning, as Tobar and the cook were busy cleaning up for the night. Tobar turned at the sound of me charging into the room.

"Watch out!" I shouted, and the see-through man hit the innkeeper with his shoulder on the way to the door.

Tobar squealed as he flew backward into one of his tables. The cook shrieked and ran for the back, leaving the innkeeper to his own fate as he dove inside the kitchen. I chased after my assailant, but he managed to slip outside before I could catch him, and by the time I reached the door, he was gone.

Out of breath, I turned and helped Tobar back to his feet. He was shaking all over. Thankfully, the white-haired man hadn't stabbed him on the way by, evidently too worried about getting away from me.

"What . . . what just happened? Was that . . . was that the creature?"

I nodded. "He's gone for now."

"He?"

"It's not a creature, and it's not a shade. It's a man."

Tobar shook his head. "But there was no one there."

"He was there, I assure you."

The door in the back squeaked, and the cook stuck his head out. "Is it gone?"

"Get out here, you coward!" Tobar commanded. "If you weren't my cousin, I'd fire you on the spot, just leaving me out here to die like that."

The man grinned sheepishly. "Sorry, I thought you were right behind me."

"How could I be right behind you, you fool, when you plainly saw I'd been thrown across the room? It's a wonder I'm still alive. If it hadn't been for this young man, I might have been the one hanging from the door next."

"Ayrion!"

I spun, raising my sword as the sound of heavy footfalls thundered down the stairs behind me. My roommates flew into the common room, ready for war, sending Tobar shrieking back under one of his tables.

"What is it?" I asked, my eyes darting around the room, expecting to see another one of those see-through people chasing after them. But nothing was there.

"It's Dakaran," Stumpy said, his face pale.

"What about him?" I scanned the faces, realizing for the first time that Dakaran wasn't with them. "Is he hurt?" I started for the stairs. "Did you just leave him up there?"

"No!" Barthol grabbed me on my way by. "He's not up there."

Every hair on my body stood at once. "What do you mean he's not up there? Where is he?" Before I got the words out of my mouth, I knew what was coming next.

"The creature took him," Stumpy said.

My worst nightmare had just come true. I'd lost the king's son. Worse, I'd lost a friend.

"It came in through the window. I was knocked unconscious before I even knew what happened. But there was nothing there. These people are right. It's a shade. By the time I came to and managed to get back to my feet, Dakaran was gone." Stumpy rubbed the back of his head, and there was blood on his hand afterward.

"It's not a shade!" I all but yelled, too upset to control myself. I held up my sword for them to see the blood, then turned and looked at the table Tobar was hiding under, doing my best to take a breath to calm the sea of emotions swelling inside me. "Matty mentioned something about a new magistrate. Who is he?"

Tobar's eyes widened. "Are you crazy? Look what happened to her. I don't want that happening to me."

"Who is this man?" Barthol growled, walking over and flipping the table backward off the trembling innkeeper.

Tobar hesitantly climbed back to his feet with Barthol's help. His cousin, the cook, made another quick exit into the kitchen. "He's . . ." Tobar gulped. "He's the magistrate."

"We've already established that," Gellar said, his eyes narrowing.

"He . . . he came from Ecrin to replace Magistrate Ferka."

"And what happened to him?" Fipple asked, studying the darker corners of the room.

"He died."

Fipple turned back to the innkeeper. "Died like the rest of the people in town?"

Tobar shook his head. "No. He was just old."

"And where does this new magistrate live?" I asked. "I reckon it's time we paid him a visit."

Tobar looked at my roommates, then back at me, clearly wondering if we'd lost our minds. "He lives where all the magistrates do, in an estate about a mile east of town. There's a small grove, and the house is just inside. But you can't go there. No one goes there."

Clearly Matty hadn't been the only one to think that whatever was going on had something to do with this new magistrate.

"If it is him, then he's got one of ours," I said. "We're going."

"Right now? It's the middle of the night."

"Perfect," Waylen said. "Then I guess he won't see us coming."

Tobar stared at us a moment, then shook his head and threw his arms in the air. "You're all mad. I want no part of this." As soon as Barthol released him, he rushed to the back and disappeared into the kitchen.

Barthol turned. "What happened up there? Were my eyes playing tricks on me or did you vanish right in front of us, several times? One minute you were there swinging at nothing, and the next you were gone, then suddenly you were back again."

"I did?"

Those who had been in the room at the time nodded adamantly.

"It wasn't a shade. It was a man, but I could see through him." I didn't know how else to describe him. "He was about my height, with white hair and golden eyes. I couldn't tell much else because even though I could see him, I couldn't."

"What does that mean?" Gellar asked, casting about the common room, his sword still up and moving.

The others looked about as skeptical as Tobar at my sad attempt to describe what I'd seen.

"I don't know how else to explain it. It was like looking through a wineglass. I can see the glass, but I can also see through it. And clearly, he can't walk through walls like a shade, since he was forced to use the door to escape. And my sword drew blood." I raised the blade for them to see once again. "Shades don't bleed."

"No," Stumpy said, examining my sword closer. "They don't. And if it bleeds, it can be killed."

Gellar hmphed. "My question is, why is it you can see him and no one else can?"

"I've been wondering the same thing. I can only guess it has something to do with my Upakan eyes."

Barthol, like the rest of my roommates, stared at my eyes a moment, then shook his head. "Whatever the reason, we've got to go now. Our duty is to . . ." He caught himself and then added, ". . . our friend."

I turned and headed for the stairs to grab the rest of my gear. "Our duty is to Room Eleven. He's one of us, and we don't leave our own."

It didn't take us long to gear up for what might be coming, and before Tobar or his cousin had stuck their heads out the kitchen door to see what was happening, we were dressed, armed, and heading out the front door. We saddled the horses and rode out into the night.

The streets were dark. The sky above was clear after the storm, but the moon was just a sliver of its size, giving little in the way of light, though it was still enough for me. I guided the men through the city, keeping my eyes open for any sign of movement. Not being able to trust my own eyes, what with that man running around, I had to be extra cautious. I couldn't imagine what my roommates were going through, not being able to see anything of this assailant and having to rely solely on me. It demonstrated not only their courage but how far they were willing to go to protect one of their own.

The wind picked up outside of town as we crossed the open grasslands for the crop of trees ahead, which covered a rise overlooking the small river community. I stopped the men as we reached the tree line and dismounted.

"We leave the horses here and go the rest of the way on foot," I whispered.

The others dismounted, tethering their horses to some of the nearby trees. With swords in hand, we started through the woods. Tobar had said the magistrate's house was just inside, so I doubted it would be that

far of a walk.

Sure enough, the trees eventually opened into a small clearing with a brick home built squarely in the middle. It wasn't exactly what I would call grand, certainly nothing like Sandstorm Manor back in Aramoor, but when compared to the rest of the rundown wood-and-stone structures in town, it was luxurious.

The home had two stories with several chimneys running throughout, though none were in use. There were windows across the front of the house, including the entryway. The side of the house facing us had several as well, all dark, all without shutters, making it easy for anyone inside to be watching the surrounding grounds.

I wished I knew why the magistrate had taken Dakaran. Was he just the most convenient, or was there another reason? And what was it with this kingdom and their incessant need to kidnap people?

I studied the windows as best I could, but as far as I could tell, they were empty. Somehow, I doubted whether the magistrate would have believed a rescue attempt possible, having struck the fear of the Dark One into these people. Still, it was best to be cautious. If this magistrate knew who it was he had taken, which was likely, given Dakaran's propensity for blabbing his title, then he might be less eager to kill him. He might try holding on to him in an attempt to extract a ransom, much like the overlord of Cylmar was doing with the Elondrian ambassador.

I could only hope that was the case.

Worst-case scenario, the magistrate decided to do the same to Dakaran that he had done to Matty. If that were the case, I hoped he took his time with it. Not because I wanted to see Dakaran tortured—though at times the thought had crossed my mind—but because the longer the man took, the more time we had to try rescuing the prince. Clearly, this magistrate was a very sick person. The gruesome way he was killing said he was a man who found great pleasure in pain. I only wished I had thought to ask Tobar what the magistrate looked like. I could have kicked myself for not doing so.

I waved the others forward, and we slowly crept our way through the underbrush to the edge of the trees. There was a waist-high brick wall surrounding most of the estate, only open in the front where the drive entered from the road and circled around to the entrance.

"No lights," Waylen whispered. "Perhaps he took our young prince-ling somewhere else."

"Let's hope not," I whispered back. "We'd have no way of tracking him if he did." It was odd that there would be no lights on inside. I doubted the magistrate had gone to all that trouble to capture Dakaran just to crawl in bed and go to sleep. Not to mention the wound he'd sustained at my hand. He would need to clean and dress it. "We can't wait to find out. We need to get inside and take a look."

Keeping a firm grip on my sword and a close eye on the open-facing windows, I slipped over the wall and knelt in the shadows, waiting for the others. One by one, they climbed over as well. With a nod, we rushed across the yard for the back corner of the house. So far, I'd seen no move-ment inside.

We crouched at the corner, and I peeked around the back. A small courtyard sat off the central entrance, with a garden just behind. It was empty. As with the front and side of the home, there didn't appear to be any lights on. I motioned my men forward, and we made our way quietly toward the back door. The sword on my back bounced lightly as I kept to the balls of my feet.

I peered in the windows we passed, but other than what I would expect to find—a few chairs, a sofa, some basic furnishings, walls lined with portraits, mirrors, and sconces—I didn't see anything out of the ordinary. From the horrors I'd seen in town, I was half-expecting to find dead corpses lying about. Had the townsfolk gotten this wrong? Was it

not the magistrate? It seemed a mighty big coincidence to have this man show up exactly when the killings began.

After stopping at the door to listen, I reached up and felt the handle. It turned, and I released a small sigh of relief. Apparently, the man didn't even believe he needed to lock his doors. Then again, from the way Tobar had been acting, I couldn't see anyone coming up here to pay the magistrate a visit.

I took one last look around the grounds before sliding open the door and slipping inside. The others moved in behind me.

The house was quiet, other than the typical creaking of the rafters as the foundation settled. I ran my finger across a nearby table and was surprised to see it come back covered in dust. Apparently, the magistrate didn't keep any staff on hand to help him clean.

We were crouched in what appeared to be a large room for the family to sit in during the evenings, as the room held a westward view, but it looked to have been a while since anyone had used it. The hairs on the back of my neck were beginning to rise. I nodded at the others and started forward, but an arm pulled me back.

"Where are you going?" Barthol leaned into whisper. "We can't see a thing."

Sometimes I forgot that they couldn't see in the dark. I grabbed a candelabra off the dusty table on my right and handed it back to Fipple. He generally carried his striker with him. Waylen steadied it as Fipple lit the three candles on top.

The room brightened, color seeping back in as my eyes adjusted.

Barthol took the candle holder and held it up for the rest to see as we started forward, me in the lead. We'd barely made it across the room when a muffled voice, barely distinguishable, brought us to a stop.

"Did you hear that?" Gellar asked.

I held my finger to my lips for everyone to keep quiet, and we listened. It happened again. It was definitely a human voice, possibly gagged, but I couldn't tell where it was coming from.

I kept my sword in front of me as my eyes darted about the darker corners of the room, half-expecting the see-through man to jump out and attack. "Let's keep going," I whispered.

Quietly I edged my way toward the door on the opposite side of the room, and we headed into a narrow hall that ran toward the front of the house. The floor under our feet groaned as the weight of six men passed over. Still, other than the faint whimpers we'd heard, the place seemed completely devoid of life.

Up ahead, I could see a soft glow coming from the bottom of a door on the left, probably too dim for the others to notice. It was a door that led to an interior room, which meant it had no windows to the outside. I gripped my sword even tighter, wanting to run down there and throw open the door and save Dakaran, but I held off the urge and kept the men at the same steady pace we'd been using. I didn't want the magistrate to hear me charging down the hall and have time to do something stupid like slit Dakaran's throat.

We passed several doorways on either side, most of them open to other adjoining rooms. One looked to be a simple reading room; another had a small pianoforte and some arranged seating. We passed a branching corridor on the left that led to what looked to be the kitchen.

I felt a tap on my shoulder, and Barthol pointed to the light ahead. I nodded that I'd seen it and kept going. We were only one door away when we heard the noise again. It was clearly coming from the room with the light. Whoever was inside was trying to speak or cry out but was being hindered. When we reached the door, I looked at the others and raised a finger to my lips.

They nodded, and I quietly reached for the handle.

With a deep breath, I focused on what I needed to do. Speed was going to be the most important. I was going to need to be quick if I planned on subduing the magistrate before he realized what was happening and hurt Dakaran. Taking a deep breath, I yanked the door open and rushed inside. My blade was up, ready to swing, my eyes darting about the room, but other than some man tied to a chair in the middle of what looked to be the home's pantry, there was no one else there.

The others flew in behind me, their blades up and ready for a fight, but when they saw that my sword had been lowered, they slowed.

"Is the see-through man here?" Stumpy asked, wisely shutting the door behind him to keep the noise down.

"No," I said. "At least, I don't see anyone. Well, other than him."

"Who is he?" Gellar asked, staring at the trussed up grey-haired man in the middle of the room.

"How should I know? I just got here."

Along with the ropes securing the man to his chair, he had a thick cloth tied around his mouth. He stared at us, eyes filled with tears of desperation as he tried to speak.

"Could be the house butler," Fipple said, moving slowly around the room, poking at everything with his sword.

"Or possibly the cook," Waylen added, doing the same but starting from the other side.

"How about we just ask him." I walked over and took hold of the gag. "You make a sound, and it will be your last."

The man attempted to speak but gave up and simply nodded.

I tried undoing the knot at the back, but it held fast. The cloth had begun to harden, same as my shirts would do when I didn't wash them regularly. Giving up on loosening the gag, I finally resorted to cutting it off with my sword, then proceeded to cut away the ropes that bound him to his seat.

Barthol held up the candelabra, adding its light to the single candle resting on the table by the man's chair. We all gathered around to hear what he had to say.

The prisoner tried working his jaw around for a moment, wincing as he did. There was a rash around his lips and cheeks where the cloth had been tied, making me wonder how long he'd been forced to wear it.

"Who are you, old man?" Gellar asked, growing impatient. "Where's Magistrate Nezrit hiding?"

"Where's Dakaran?" Waylen added. "What's he done to him?"

There was a moment of silence. "Well?" Gellar asked. "Speak, man!"

I held up my hand. "Give him a chance."

The man had tired brown eyes, a beard that hadn't been trimmed in some time, and a rather bulbous nose that looked to have been broken from repeated strikes to it. He was clearly on the verge of tears.

"I don't know who this Dakaran fellow is you're talking about, but I'm Nezrit."

Barthol raised his blade to the man's neck, doing his best not to tip the candleholder in the process. "What have you done to Dakaran? Where is he?"

When the man didn't answer, Barthol looked at me. "This is who you were fighting at the inn? His hair looks more grey than white, and his eyes are brown."

"The person I fought was much younger. White hair and—"

"Golden eyes?" the man claiming to be Magistrate Nezrit asked, his hands trembling. He glanced around the room, especially where the shadows were the darkest.

"That's right." I nodded. "It was as though I could see right through him."

An anguished scream from somewhere in the house sent the old man scurrying for the corner, where he crouched down and hugged himself

like a frightened child. I didn't have time to coddle him, so I walked over and lifted him to his feet.

"That came from a friend of mine. What do you know of what is going on here? The people in town believe you are the one responsible for all the killings. They say it started when you arrived."

The older man shook his head and sobbed. "It wasn't me. It wasn't—"

"Pull yourself together," Gellar said, grabbing the magistrate by the front of his shirt. "You tell us where you have our friend and maybe I won't hang you from one of the signs in town."

"It's not me, it's—"

Dakaran screamed, and this time it sounded like it was coming from underneath us.

"The cellar." I grabbed Nezrit and forced him out the door and into the hall. "Where's the entrance?"

He pointed back the way we came, then right at the hall leading into the kitchen. Once inside, he pointed at a door in the corner on the far side. "That's the way down," he whispered, and we started across the kitchen. "But don't make me go down there. Please!" He began sobbing once more, and Fipple quickly covered his mouth.

"Quiet, or I'll tie that gag right back."

I reached the door and grabbed the handle, then looked at the others. "Ready?"

# WILDFIRE

## Chapter 7

HE KNOB SPUN FREELY, and the door opened without a sound. My stomach lurched as the stench of death reached out and grabbed me from below. Whatever was happening down there, I was sure I was going to need a strong constitution to face it. Turning my head to take a breath, I slowly started down.

The stairs were walled on both sides with brick, the one on our left being the outside wall. The backs of the steps were boarded, so there was nothing I could see of the room beyond, only the faint glow coming from the open doorway at the bottom leading to the cellar on the right.

I could hear moaning below. I was almost afraid to look, afraid of what this see-through man might have done to my friend. I'd never be able to forgive myself if I let something happen to him, but as much as I wanted to rush down the stairs and save him, I couldn't risk it. If the white-haired man was there, it would only take a flick of his wrist to slit Dakaran's throat or stick a blade through his heart.

We were halfway down when someone below started talking. I didn't recognize the voice.

"Don't you worry, we'll take good care of you, won't we?"

*We?*

"When we're through with you, we'll make sure everyone will see our work. We'll find the perfect spot." There was a moment of silence. "The well! Yes, that's it. Why didn't I think of that? We can display you on the well. Everyone will be sure to love it." The man then began to hum softly to himself, and I continued down. I could feel Barthol's breath on the back of my neck. "Oh, feel free to scream as loud as you want. I promise I won't mind." The humming started once more.

Quickly, I moved down the next couple of steps, placing my feet near the edges to keep them from creaking and giving us away. I hoped the others were doing the same.

Someone on the other side screamed, and my heart leaped into my throat as I dove down the stairs and charged into the room.

I wasn't prepared for what I saw.

There were pieces of bodies hanging from every rafter, all surrounding a single table in the middle of the room. He had arranged them so they could be seen from the table like a gallery of his work.

I nearly retched.

The white-haired man startled and looked up, his body no longer see-through. His knife rested just above Dakaran's chest. From what I could make out between the pieces of hanging corpses, there were dozens of long cuts on Dakaran, running across his body in various patterns.

"You!" the man shouted, pointing at me with his blood-soaked knife. "How did you find us?"

By the time the rest of Room Eleven charged into the room, the man had vanished.

"Where'd he go?" Barthol shouted, raising his sword, as did the others.

"He's right there!" I said, pointing across the table. The white-haired man slowly backed away from the table and into the shadows, making it a little more difficult to see him, even with my eyes.

"Where?" Gellar asked, swinging his sword wildly at nothing. "We don't see him!"

I started for the table, then stopped. The man had said *we*. I looked around the room, studying every nook and corner and cranny not taken up with dead bodies—which wasn't much—any place someone else could be hiding, but there was no one there, at least not that I saw. I had a terrible thought. What if it was a fluke that I was able to see this one? What if I couldn't see the second? I quickly raised my own sword, holding it out as I made my way through the hanging corpses for Dakaran.

Dakaran looked up, and my breath caught in my throat. Even if I knew what to say, I don't think I could have. His face had been badly disfigured, to the point of being unrecognizable.

We were too late.

"Help me," he pleaded.

My heart skipped a beat. It wasn't Dakaran's voice.

I reached the table and started to cut the man free, where his arms and legs had been bound outward. As soon as my blade made it through the first piece of rope, the see-through man released an ear-piercing shrill and flew out of the shadows.

"No! He's ours!"

My roommates behind me shouted all at once and began swinging their swords in all directions.

I raised my sword as the white-haired man rushed me with his blade, his golden eyes almost catlike. I deflected his attack, and the world dimmed as our blades touched. I elbowed him in the face, and he flew to the side, bouncing off a piece of torso. He turned and swung, but I wasn't there. I spun to the left and kicked the man in the back, sending him sprawling to the bloodstained floor, where he scrambled back to his feet and charged once again.

The man was undeterred.

"No one disturbs our work!" He opened his jaw like he wanted to bite me and lunged.

If the man was looking to die, he'd normally have found the right person for it, except I couldn't risk killing him. I sidestepped his wild thrust and opened his arm with my blade, forcing him to drop his weapon. His dagger skittered across the floor, and he rushed to dive on top of it, apparently not affected at all by the deep gash.

I kicked the blade across the room before he could reach it, then kicked him in the head. He rolled over on his back, smiling up at me like a lunatic. I couldn't help but stand there and stare. It was like nothing affected the man.

"Where's Dakaran?" I demanded.

The man spit blood. "You won't stop us."

"I already did," I said, beginning to grow desperate. "Now where's the man you kidnapped last night from the inn?" *Please don't let any of these pieces be him.*

The white-haired man laughed as whatever had made him see-through dissolved and his body solidified.

Most of the others, seeing the man for the first time, cautiously walked over, their swords up, eyes darting about for any sign of an accomplice. Waylen stayed back with the magistrate.

The white-haired man began mumbling to himself as he stared up at my roommates.

Barthol placed the tip of his sword against the squirming individual's chest. "He asked you a question. Where's Dakaran?"

"We have him. Safely tucked away where no one can disturb him. He really needed his sleep." The man frowned. "Talks way too much."

I knelt beside him. "Where is he? Where is he sleeping? Is he in one of the bedrooms upstairs?"

The white-haired man shook his head and laughed. "Of course not. We wouldn't put His Highness in such a cramped space. He needed to see the stars. It is such a pretty night. The ground so soft."

He knew who Dakaran was. That wasn't good. I grabbed the man and jerked him to his feet. "Where is he? What did you do to him?" I shoved him toward the stairs. "Take us to him, now!"

The man stumbled forward, continuing to mumble to himself as he went, looking more confused than anything.

We made it out of the surrounding pieces of hanging flesh and started for the doorway. A shout brought me to a stop, and I quickly raised my sword, expecting an attack. But the attack wasn't on me. The magistrate leaped out of the stairwell in front of us and on top of the white-haired man. He grabbed the dagger I'd kicked toward the door and plunged it into his chest.

"No!" I shoved the magistrate aside and knelt beside the white-haired man. Blood was running from the corners of his mouth. "Where is he? Where's Dakaran? Please, you have to tell me!"

The man smiled and began to hum. His eyes began to flicker shut, then they didn't open again.

"You fool!" Barthol shouted and snatched the magistrate off the ground and held him about eye level. "We needed him alive. If Dakaran dies because of this, you'll be joining him."

The magistrate was shaking. "You have no idea what he made me watch, what he made me . . ." He didn't finish.

I stood and grabbed Barthol's arm. "Leave him. What's done is done. We need to see if we can find Dakaran."

"How?" Gellar asked. "If I may point out, the only person who could tell us is lying there in a pool of his own blood."

"He might have told us already."

Gellar's thick red brows shelved the tops of his eyes. "What?"

"Cut him free," I said, pointing to the injured man on the table, then charged up the stairs. Fipple was the first up behind me, since it seemed he was the one with the light. Apparently, he'd found a lantern and used Barthol's candelabra to light it.

"See if you can find more of those," I said, pointing at the lantern. "We're going to need them where we're going."

"Which is where, exactly?" Stumpy asked, walking over to grab a lantern off one of the kitchen shelves.

"The man said something about needing to see the stars."

"He also mentioned *soft ground*," Waylen added, the only one not holding a lantern, as his hands were already preoccupied with his sword and long knife.

Barthol was the last out of the basement, carrying the injured man, who didn't look in the best shape.

I left the kitchen and headed back through the house and out the same way we'd entered. The sky was still clear, the stars bright overhead. "Search the grounds. We might not have a lot of time. And pray he didn't decide to bury him."

"Here," Stumpy said, trying to shove his lantern into my hand.

I pushed it back. "You need it more than me." I turned to find Barthol laying the injured man down just inside the house. "We'll search in groups of two. Barthol, you and Gellar take the front of the house. Fipple, you and Waylen take the left-side woods and work your way toward the back. Me, Stumpy, and the magistrate will take the right and do the same. Shout if you find him."

"Or if you find something else," Gellar grumbled with a strong tug on his beard, which seemed even more fiery in the lantern's orange glow.

The three groups parted ways and began to search the surrounding yard and woods. Stumpy, Nezrit, and I didn't find anything on the right side of the house, so we crossed over the waist-high brick wall and began searching the trees.

"Dakaran!" I shouted, hoping the prince was still alive and capable of calling out to let us know where the lunatic had left him. I prayed he hadn't been buried. We'd never find him if that was the case.

"He might be gagged," Stumpy pointed out.

"True," I said, then shouted once more. "Dakaran, if you can hear us, make some noise! Kick a tree if you have to!"

Someone shouted in the direction of the woods near the back of the house.

"That sounded like Waylen," Stumpy said.

"Maybe they found him."

We rushed through the trees and surrounding undergrowth with some difficulty. The white-haired man had been right. The ground was soft. More than once, I nearly twisted my ankle when my foot sank too far into the wet soil.

We heard another shout, louder. This time it was Fipple. Breaking through some thick brush into a small clearing, I found Waylen on the ground, leaning against one of the trees with his hand on the back of his head. Fipple was standing in front of him, swinging his sword in all directions.

"I told you he was a shade!" Fipple bellowed angrily as he fought at nothing. "He's come back for us!"

Stumpy and I drew our blades as well, and I spun in a circle as Stumpy, too, began batting away at the air around him. The magistrate dropped to the ground and begged for mercy.

I clenched my teeth. The see-through man wasn't a shade. We'd seen

him die, hadn't we? He'd had a knife through his chest. No one could survive that. Which could only mean—

Another shout rang out on my right as Barthol and Gellar barreled through the underbrush, nearly on top of us, swinging their swords at everything in sight. Barthol had a slit in his sleeve and blood on his arm. They were going so fast they barely had time to stop before running into Fipple.

"He's back!" Gellar shouted, then noticed Waylen on the ground. "What happened?"

"The shade hit him in the back of the head," Fipple said, still swinging at every shadow."

"He's not a shade," I said. "The man we saw at the house is just that—a man. He must have been telling us the truth, though, when he said there was more than one of him."

"Over there!" Barthol shouted, pointing behind me.

I spun to see the white-haired man leaning out from behind one of the trees on our left. I was so stunned I could hardly speak. It *was* the same man. It wasn't just that he had the same white hair or was wearing the same clothing—he had the same face.

The man vanished, mostly.

"Where is he?" Barthol shouted, spinning around with his blade.

My roommates quickly formed a circle, back to back, even managing to get Waylen onto his feet to join them.

The man in front of me laughed and began to slowly make his way toward me. I kept my sword up and even swung it a couple of times at nothing, looking just to the right of where he was as though I couldn't see him either, hoping beyond hope that it wasn't indeed the same man and that he didn't know I could see him. He looked exactly like the other man, apart from the missing knife in his chest. Also, his clothing wasn't ripped from where the dagger had gone in, and there was no deep cut

on his arm from where I'd disarmed him. So either this truly was a spec-
ter of some sort, or the see-through man had a twin. Wouldn't that be
just our luck?

My eyes continued to dart about as I did my best not to look directly
at him. He seemed interested in me, cautious as he moved closer. He
had a long knife in one hand, blood on it, no doubt from where he'd
caught Barthol's arm. He didn't make any noise as he drew closer, careful
as to where he put his feet.

The others behind me had their swords up and moving, doing everything they could to clear the empty spaces around them. They
reminded me of blind Thorin, who could be seen most days begging in
front of the East Gate. He'd swing his staff in the same manner to keep
from hitting others and to let those around him know he was blind. Of
course, he wasn't blind, but the ruse worked well enough to keep his
pockets filled.

"Where are you?" I mumbled to myself, but loud enough for the see-
through man to hear me. I thought I caught him smile from the corner
of my eye as he drew closer. He was now within arm's reach, his knife
waist high but pointed in my direction. He took another step, and I
turned and looked directly at him.

"Oh, there you are."

He gasped, and I punched him in the face as hard as I could.

The man stumbled backward, too shocked to even remember he had
a knife in his hand, and by the time he did, I was already waiting.

Dropping my sword to free up my hands, I spun to the side as the
man lunged. The long knife just missed my stomach as it flew by, and I
grabbed his arm, twisting it so hard he spun with it. The world seemed
to fade as the colors dulled and the sounds grew muffled. It was a strange
feeling.

My roommates shouted behind me, wondering where I'd gone, but

I ignored them.

With his arm twisted around so his elbow was sticking straight in the air, I brought my arm down on top of it. The bone snapped.

The man screamed and dropped to the ground, and his magic, or whatever it was, disappeared.

"Where's Dakaran? What have you done with him?"

"Where's my brother?" the man spat, his eyes full of rage.

"Resting." I wasn't about to tell him that it was permanent. "You take me to my friend, and I'll take you to see your brother."

The man looked up and smiled. "We will have to spend some extra time on you when we get you on our table."

I smiled back. "Don't count on that happening anytime soon." I yanked him back to his feet. "Now show me where Dakaran is, or you'll never see your brother again."

The white-haired man sneered but turned and headed deeper into the woods.

"Are there any more of them?" Fipple asked as the others rushed over to catch up. Barthol was in the back, his arm around the magistrate, forcing him along. The poor man was probably never going to be the same. Whatever he'd witnessed had left him damaged. He looked on the verge of tears and was doing his best to stay at the back of the group and as far from the white-haired man as possible.

I kept my hand on the see-through man's arm as we walked through the trees, my roommates' lanterns lighting the way. We'd walked maybe a few hundred feet when I spotted Dakaran ahead, or at least his legs. They were sticking out from behind a large tree. I handed the white-haired man over to Gellar and rushed to see if the prince was still alive.

Dakaran was lying on his back, unmoving, his eyes closed. Beside him was a shovel, stuck blade down in a pile of dirt, where someone had been digging a shallow grave.

For the briefest of moments, I panicked. I was the one who had agreed to watch out for Dakaran. I should have known he wasn't ready for something like this. Why did I ever tell Tolin I could handle this? Just as bad was the thought of having the crown prince murdered by a couple of bloodthirsty lunatics while in my care. I'd never be able to show my face in Aramoor again. How would that affect my friends? The tribe? The orphanage? Master Fentin and Mistress Orilla relied on the royal stipend to keep the place running.

The blood rushed to my head, and I felt the world begin to spin. "No. He can't be dead." I turned and looked at the white-haired man, ready to bury him in his own hole, when Dakaran's boot suddenly moved.

I nearly shouted with relief and dropped into the dirt beside him. "Dakaran! Dakaran!" I worked on the ropes binding the prince's hands. Once they were free, I grabbed him by the shoulders and began to shake him.

"Is he dead?" Gellar asked, shoving the white-haired man forward as my roommates all gathered around.

"No, thankfully." I continued to shake Dakaran, finally resorting to a couple of stiff slaps to the side of his face.

His eyes jerked open. "What . . . what happened? Where am I?"

"You're safe," I said, hugging him as I helped him up to a sitting position.

Dakaran looked up and shrieked when he saw the white-haired man standing there. He skittered on his hands and knees to the other side of the tree. "Kill him! Kill him! Kill the monster!"

I moved to the back of the tree, where the prince was cowering in a ball against the bark. "You don't need to worry. He's not going to harm you."

"You don't understand. You don't know what they've done."

"Oh, I think we have a pretty good idea."

Dakaran's head shot up, and he quickly searched the surrounding trees. "There's more than one."

I knelt down beside him. "We know."

"I showed you where he was," the white-haired man called out from the other side of the tree where my roommates were waiting. "Keep your promise!"

I put my arm around Dakaran and coaxed him up, and we walked back around the tree and started toward the house. I had a promise to keep.

Dakaran and I kept to the front as we led the group back to the magistrate's home, where I left Dakaran with the others and walked the white-haired man inside. The rest of my roommates decided they preferred to stay with the magistrate and the injured man instead of going back down into the cellar. Barthol and Gellar were willing, but I only needed one, so Gellar stayed with the rest, and Barthol helped me escort the lunatic inside to see his brother.

Barthol held the lantern while I held the white-haired man. He continued to mumble to himself as we marched him through the house, into the kitchen, and over to the door leading down into their place of horror. The smell was pervasive, burning my nostrils the farther down we went. I tried breathing through my mouth, but I could almost taste what I was smelling, so I changed my mind.

We reached the bottom, and I had to really latch on to the white-haired man's arm to keep him from pulling out of my grip. "Brother! I'm back. And I brought some . . ." The man shrilled when he spotted his brother lying on the floor in his own blood, with a knife sticking out of his chest. "No!"

# WILDFIRE

## Chapter 8

HE WHITE-HAIRED MAN grabbed my arm, jerked me into the room, and then disappeared.

"Where'd he go?" Barthol shouted, dropping the lantern in an attempt to draw his sword. Thankfully, the candle didn't go out.

The man spun, fire in his eyes as he attempted to sink his teeth into my neck like an animal. I grabbed him by the scruff of his shirt to hold him back, but he was crazed. With a swift knee to his gut, he doubled over, and I quickly got my arm around his neck and squeezed.

His fighting slowed, then stopped altogether as his body went limp. As soon as it did, the colors grew more vibrant, the sounds more distinct.

Barthol lowered his sword. "I don't like it when you do that."

"Do what?"

"Disappear like that." He looked at the white-haired man. "Is he dead?"

"No. Just unconscious. Here, help me get him up the steps."

Barthol hmphed. "I say we put a knife in him and leave him here with his brother. Whatever he is, he's no longer human, and you don't let a rabid animal live." He glanced around the cellar. "And whatever was going on in here was way beyond simply killing for pleasure."

"I think this is something best left up to the citizens of Dorwall. They need to see who has been ravaging their town. Let them get closure by dealing with him themselves. That way, they will know for sure that the trouble has ended, and not just rely on the word of a group of traveling armsmen."

Barthol grabbed the lantern from off the floor and handed it to me so he could carry the unconscious man back up the steps. I took a few moments to blow out the candles around the room to make sure the place didn't burn down by accident. Although that might not have been a bad thing, considering the contents.

We made it back up the steps and outside where the rest were waiting.

"Killed him, did you?" Gellar said, looking at the limp body over Barthol's shoulder. "Good. Saved me from doing it." The white-haired man twitched, and Gellar reached for his blade. "Watch out! He ain't dead."

"No," I said, "he's not." I then explained my reasoning. Most seemed to understand; a couple, like Gellar, thought it best to bury the man in the grave he'd dug for Dakaran and be done with the whole mess. In the end, we carried the white-haired man back into town, along with the magistrate and the injured victim I'd mistaken for Dakaran.

By the time we reached Dorwall, the sky had already begun to lighten, the stars disappearing as a new day approached. We'd gone two nights without sleep, but even with the threat having been disposed of, I had no desire to stay in this town another night.

We reached the Spotted Pike Inn and found Tobar inside, straightening up the chairs and tables and setting out a line of new tankards across the bar in anticipation of his morning crowd. He started when the door opened and we walked in. In fact, he made a run for the kitchen but stopped when I called out his name.

"Can't be too careful nowadays," he said, dark circles around his eyes. He noticed we had three new people added to our group. Barthol dropped the white-haired man down on one of the tables, and I helped Fipple with the injured man. Tobar walked over to see who they were, but when his eyes caught Magistrate Nezrit standing just in back of our group, he shrieked and ran for the kitchen all over again. It took us several long minutes to coax him back out, assuring him that the magistrate wasn't the one committing the atrocities, and that it was the unconscious white-haired man and his brother.

I went on to explain to him what we had found at the magistrate's home and that the town no longer needed to live in fear. "Do you have a cell to keep him in until the town decides his fate?"

Tobar nodded. "The patroller office is around the corner."

"Good," I said. "We can take him there later, but right now this man needs some help."

"I can call a physicker."

"Good, I also need you to rouse the town and get everyone to the square as soon as possible so we can let them know that the terror is over, and those doing the killings have been either caught or killed."

"Aye!" Tobar said, not even bothering to take off his apron. "I can do that." He ordered a couple of the patrons to carry the injured man out, then rushed out the door himself, shouting all the way down the street.

"Best we get our things from our rooms and get ready to leave," I said. "I'll stay down here with the prisoner."

The others headed upstairs, all but me and Nezrit, who looked too exhausted to make it up a flight of steps. We sat in a couple of chairs and stared at the white-haired man on the table. I was surprised he hadn't yet woken, though I was glad he hadn't. The sooner we could turn him over to the townsfolk, the better. I also kept one eye on Nezrit to make sure he didn't try anything foolish like beating the unconscious man to death with his bare fists.

By the time I heard footsteps on the stairs behind me, the front door opened and Tobar rushed inside, out of breath. "It's been done. Word's spreading quickly. There's already a sizable crowd gathered at the well." He looked at the white-haired man and sneered. "What is he?"

"Not a shade is all I can tell you. Do you have some rope? Best to keep him bound and gagged until you decide what to do with him."

"Oh, I can tell you exactly what needs to be done to him. Replace poor Dreese's body with his."

I couldn't say I didn't like the irony of the suggestion—definitely fitting—but it wasn't for me to decide. Nor did I want it to be.

Tobar was in the back for a while before returning with a long coil of rope, which we proceeded to bind the prisoner with. He woke as soon as we got the first couple of loops around his arms in place, forcing Barthol to put him back out with a swift fist to his jaw. He hit him so hard, I was afraid he might pop the man's head clean off. Barthol was immensely strong and clearly didn't have any qualms with using every bit of it on *this* individual.

Barthol carried the prisoner out of the inn on his shoulder and headed straight for the center of town. Those on the streets stopped to see what was happening, then followed as we made our way to the covered well, where a very large gathering was waiting, most nervously casting about, seemingly afraid of their own shadows.

We pushed our way through to the center, Tobar doing his best to clear a path. I stood on the steps leading up to the well, which gave me enough of an advantage to see there were still more people coming from every street. I even spotted our illustrious ferryman pushing his way toward the front to get a better view of what was happening. When he spotted me with my head above the rest, he frowned but didn't leave.

I waited until the majority of those who were coming had arrived, and by then the sizable crowd had begun to grow impatient as furtive glances and upset mumbling spread through the ranks.

"Well?" someone near the back shouted out. "Are you gonna speak or just stand there staring at us? It's dangerous to be out here in the open like this."

I raised my hands to quiet the crowd, but it wasn't until Tobar hopped up on the well beside me and spoke that they quieted.

"You need to listen to what they have to say," Tobar shouted so that everyone could hear. "We have news about the killings." The townsfolk went deathly still, and Tobar turned to me and nodded. "I believe they're ready to hear you now." He stepped back down, giving me the makeshift podium.

"The killings are over. We have found the perpetrators and dealt with them. They weren't shades as many believed, but actual men. Very sick, very twisted men. Brothers, in fact. Twins. The magistrate was not the one committing these murders. He was just as much a victim as yourselves. We found him tied to a chair in his pantry, having been forced to witness some very horrific acts."

I paused a moment to judge the crowd's response. No one said a word, so I continued.

"We killed one of the brothers and have captured the second." I pointed over to where Barthol and Gellar held the bound white-haired man between them. "We'll leave him here for you to deal with. If you still have questions as to what they were doing, I suggest you visit the

magistrate's home, particularly the cellar . . . but only if you have a strong stomach. What you'll find down there will certainly turn it inside out and give you nightmares for weeks to come."

"And how do we know these are the ones who did the killing?" a woman in the crowd asked.

"Aye," another man said. "All we have is the word of a—"

Gasps spread through the crowd as the white-haired man suddenly woke and opened his amber-colored eyes.

"He's a faerie!" someone shouted.

"He's not a faerie," I said. Actually, I had no idea what he was. I probably wouldn't know a faerie if they walked up and shook my hand.

The white-haired man suddenly vanished, taking Barthol and Gellar with him.

People in the crowd shrieked, and some took off running down the street.

*Well, that was poor timing*, I thought.

"There's nothing to fear," I shouted, trying to calm the crowd before they all took off running. By the time I'd turned back around, I caught Barthol's see-through fist connecting with the white-haired man's face. All three immediately reappeared. "You see?" I said. "Nothing to fear. You will need to make sure he is kept locked up, though."

I was about to end my unprepared speech with a quip about finding a way to move on with their lives when a thought popped into my head. "Oh, and we will be leaving today." I passed a quick glance down at the ferryman, who crossed his arms, but for the first time he didn't tell us no. "And we would appreciate any assistance you could offer in the way of food for our travels."

"Aye!" Tobar said, hopping back up on the steps of the well. "Helping these men with provisions is the least we can do, don't you think?"

A slight rumble of agreement and head bobs passed through the crowd. Tobar turned. "Don't you worry, we'll have you stocked if I have to go house to house and pull it out of their pantries myself."

I hoped it didn't come to that, but at this point I didn't really care. I just wanted to be gone from this place. "Whatever you can do will be much appreciated. We'll wait at the inn for the next hour, then take our horses down to the ferry."

Tobar nodded and scurried into the crowd, shouting out specific names, probably those with shops he knew had provisions. Two men in uniform stepped forward to collect the prisoner.

"Make sure you keep him secured in a cell. As you can see, he has a tendency to vanish."

The two men hauled the white-haired lunatic off in the direction of the patrollers' office behind us.

I looked at my roommates as the crowd began to part. "I wonder if Tobar has any leftovers from last night. My stomach needs settling."

"Your stomach." Dakaran hmphed. "I was the one about to get chopped up into little bits and buried in the garden out back."

"But you weren't, thank the Creator," Stumpy said with a gentle pat on Dakaran's shoulder. "Still, I'm sure there's plenty you'd wish to forget."

Dakaran shivered.

We headed back to the inn and found the place empty, all except for Magistrate Nezrit, who I'd forgotten was even there, as quiet as he'd been. Gellar and Waylen helped themselves to some ale from the bar and poured drinks for everyone. I stared at the older man for a moment, wondering what he was going to do now that the turmoil was over. Would he continue to hold his position as magistrate, or had he been too permanently scarred by what happened? I wondered where he'd live, since I doubted that he'd be returning to his house anytime soon, if ever.

Whatever the case, I guessed it wasn't something I needed to dwell

on. A problem that thankfully didn't require any effort on my part to fix.

A few minutes later, several more patrons stepped inside, looking to knock back a tankard or two. One of the men walked in back and found the cook, who promptly came out and filled their drinks. The men passed cautious glances our way, but their mood seemed to have lightened from the previous night. One of the men even went so far as to raise a glass to our good health, which the others eagerly joined in.

"So, who do you think they were?" Stumpy asked.

Several of those at the table turned.

"The brothers," he said. "Where do you suppose they came from? Why do you think they chose this town of all places to stop? And why the magistrate?" He lowered his voice on the last word, what with Nezrit sitting at the next table over, still staring dead-eyed into his tankard.

I glanced over my shoulder at the magistrate. He seemed to be asleep with his eyes open. "I didn't get the feeling Nezrit had any more idea of who they were, or why they were here, than us." Whatever he'd seen and done, it had left him broken in more ways than I could understand.

"Why does anyone like that do what they do?" Fipple said offhandedly, taking a long pull from his tankard. "Don't think the same as the rest of us."

I nodded. "Most likely just a choice of convenience. Perhaps they needed a new place to stay, and the magistrate just happened to be in the wrong place at the wrong time. Or perhaps they'd been following him for days before he arrived." I shrugged. "Who knows." I pointed at the door with my tankard. "You can always try your luck and go ask him. Might not have long before the townsfolk get their hands on him."

The others didn't appear that interested, as they turned their attention back to their drinks.

My thoughts drifted more to where the two had come from. Why was it that I could see them and no one else could? It had to be my eyes. I wondered if all Upakans could have seen them or if it was just me. I sighed and set my drink back down on the table. Questions I would probably never get answers to. And honestly, right now, I didn't really care. I was too tired to even think straight as it was.

A good hour passed as we sat around the table and commiserated about our lack of sleep. My eyes were beginning to shut when the door at the front opened and Tobar stepped inside, a wide grin on his face.

"Gentlemen," he said with arms raised, "good news. We have supplies enough to get you to Ecrin and back if you so desire. We have a cart out front by the stables for you to load your horses from. I believe you will be pleased."

"I'll be pleased to put this town to my back and never step foot in it again," Dakaran said to himself. If Tobar heard him, he didn't show it.

"Wonderful," I said, standing from my seat. "Then I guess we'll be moving on. Need to get down the road while there's still light."

I started around the table and had barely made it to the other side when Nezrit hopped up from his seat and threw his arms around me. There were tears in his eyes.

"Thank you. Thank you for saving me."

Feeling uncomfortable with this elderly man squeezing the life out of me and soaking my collar with his weeping, I patted him on the back as I pried his arms from my shoulders. "No need to thank us. Just in the right place at the right time."

The man looked the worse for wear as he nodded and plopped back down in his seat, where he stared into his empty glass in silence.

Not knowing what else to say, I motioned to the door, and we left.

Outside, we found Tobar hadn't exaggerated the town's generosity. The cart was more the size of a wagon, and it was filled to the brim with food. I wasn't sure where it had all come from or where it was all going

to go, but it was a sight for some very hungry eyes.

"Gracious, man," Fipple said, swinging his topknot from his shoulder to his back, "we can't take all this. There wouldn't be enough room left on our horses for us."

Stumpy eyed some of the larger pieces of meat and smiled. "I'm sure we can make room."

We did the best we could at loading the supplies, but in the end, we left about half the wagon behind. One thing was for certain—we weren't going to need to worry about foraging along the way. As long as we could find clean water, we were set.

After Tobar shook each of our hands personally and placed our room and board payment back in mine at the finish, he bid us farewell and safe journeys and told us we had free meals at the Spotted Pike anytime we rode through. I waved from my horse as we started down the street and cast one last look back before cutting down the next.

By that time, Tobar was organizing some men to carry what was left of the food inside the inn. I guess he had no intention of trying to distribute it all back from where it had come.

I chuckled and turned back around, guiding my horse toward the river. We reached the end of the street just outside the docks, then turned right and started for the ferry. The ferryman was sitting on his front porch rocker, smoking his pipe as we rode up in front.

He pulled the pipe from his mouth. "Been expecting you."

"I would hope so," Gellar said with an irritated tone. "We've only been here three times in the last two days."

The ferryman smiled, then puffed out his cheeks and released another trail of smoke up into the porch's overhang. He stood from his rocker and walked down the steps, heading around the building as he made his way toward the large flatboat on the side. "Don't dawdle. I don't have all day."

Gellar looked like he was ready to hop off his horse and toss the man bodily into the river, but thankfully he refrained, and instead resorted to a few firm tugs on his beard.

"One at a time," the ferryman said as he lowered the ramp from the boat to the shore, allowing us to walk our horses up onto the large craft. Wooden rails lined two sides of the ferry, leaving the front and back open for loading and offloading. There was, however, a rope that was stretched across both the front and the back after everyone was aboard.

The horses were skittish at first, forcing us to keep a firm hand on their reins, but soon enough, they calmed as they found the loose hay the ferryman had left for just such a purpose.

"The water's down, but it will be a rough trip," the ferryman said. "And I'll need your help with the pulling."

All of the men, including Dakaran, started for the rope at the same time, but after some quick deliberation, Waylen, Stumpy, and Dakaran remained behind, leaving me, Fipple, Gellar, and Barthol to help the ferryman.

According to the ferryman, that was still too many, so we decided to take rotations.

Luckily, we crossed with little difficulty. I remembered the last time I'd been on a ferry, when me and my horse had to dive into the river to save Master Hobb. I wondered what my old friend was up to and whether he ever took Milly up on her offer of marriage. He certainly wasn't going to find better than the innkeeper of the Golden Tassel.

The sun was just reaching its peak when we unloaded on the other side and the ferryman started back across. We decided to go ahead and eat our lunch before starting back up.

The meal was consumed quietly—all of us still in shock at the previous two days' events—and washed down with watered ale before we

mounted and began our long journey across the western half of the kingdom. I figured, judging by the map, that it would take us a good four or five days to reach Ecrin, which was located on the western shores of Lake Nari.

I knew nothing of the city other than it was the capital of Cylmar and home to Overlord Saryn. One thing was for certain, though: By the time we were finished with our mission, the city and I were sure to become very well acquainted. How friendly that acquaintance might turn out to be was still yet to be seen.

WILDFIRE

*Chapter 9*

CRIN WAS BIGGER THAN I imagined, but unlike the white spires and golden domes of Aramoor, the capital of Cylmar looked more like Dorwall, except about ten times its size, minus the grisly decorations. The buildings were crafted of mostly stone, likely mined from the surrounding mountain ranges. They weren't much to look at, but they were solid.

The narrow streets smelled of rotten food and the discarded contents of freshly used chamber pots, and were lined with tightly packed buildings that made the Maze seem well thought out. The city rose and fell as it followed the natural curvature of the foothills between the Khezrian Wall to the west and the Ula Ree Mountains to the north. The broken and missing cobbles that paved most of the streets were moist underfoot as the light rain that had followed us for the last two days covered the city.

"Hang the ambassador," Dakaran said, keeping his horse close to

mine as we tried to navigate the compact streets. "I want out of this rain. I stink, my clothes stink, my horse stinks. This whole business stinks."

"I second that," Gellar said from behind us.

The sun had already begun to set, and the heavy clouds overhead didn't help matters as we tried to find our way through the city. A guard at the front gates had given us directions to a supposedly suitable inn. Many of the streets lacked proper signage, and those that were labeled were difficult to follow, as each corner seemed to branch off into multiple directions, and all with the same name.

In addition to the dingy streets and dingy buildings were the dingy people. Most looked like they'd rather be anywhere else in the Five Kingdoms than Ecrin. They kept their heads down, only peeking out from under their hooded cloaks when they thought we weren't looking. They all had the appearance of mice trapped in a cage with a large cat watching them squirm, which only reinforced the feeling that we were in Dorwall all over again.

There were very few patrollers keeping watch on the streets, but you couldn't spit without hitting a Cylmaran soldier. Their red-and-black uniforms were everywhere. It wasn't the nicest uniform I'd ever seen, but at least it stood out from all the brown, giving us plenty of time to steer clear.

"I've never seen so many soldiers," Fipple said, doing his best to keep his hood up, as it kept wanting to slide down his topknot.

"Are there not this many normally?" Barthol asked.

"How should I know?" Fipple shot back. "I've never been to Ecrin. Just because I was born in Cylmar doesn't mean I've traveled it. I was just referring to the number of soldiers in a single city."

"We certainly don't have this many in Aramoor," Waylen said, "at least not roaming the streets. Wonder if we picked a bad time to visit."

Barthol hmphed. "You reckon there's a good time?"

A couple of the others chuckled.

Another group of soldiers turned off the road ahead of us and onto ours, and I quickly took us down a separate branch, hoping to find another street farther down that would lead us around them. Sure enough, we found one that veered back into the one we'd been on earlier. By the time we were back on the main thoroughfare, the soldiers were nowhere to be seen.

"I don't like this," Stumpy said at the back. "All these twists and turns. How are we to ever find our way back out?"

"Luck," I said sarcastically, then pulled my horse to a stop in one of the lesser trafficked areas and twisted in my saddle to get a look at the others. "It's probably best we don't stay clumped together like this. Seven riders moving down the street is sure to draw attention. Best we break into groups of two or three and put some distance between each. We'll meet at the inn. If you get lost, ask someone for directions."

"And who do you suggest we ask?" Waylen said offhandedly.

I glanced around the street, noticing no one looking in our direction, and those who were there were staying as far from our side as possible. "Whoever you can find, I guess." I didn't have a better answer. "I'll take Dakaran with me. Barthol, you take Gellar. That'll leave Fipple, Waylen, and Stumpy."

There were no arguments, so I rode ahead with Dakaran. I glanced over my shoulder as we started to round the first bend and spotted Barthol and Gellar just beginning to urge their horses forward about thirty or forty feet behind us. The other three patiently waited their turn. This time when we came across a group of soldiers, I moved our two horses to the side in single file without attempting to find a different street to cut down.

I kept my head lowered, hoping Dakaran did the same behind me. Everyone else seemed to be doing likewise, especially when it came to

the soldiers. The townsfolk didn't look any happier than we were with the onslaught of Cylmaran troops filling their streets. Most turned away when they saw them coming, doing their best to keep from being noticed, some going so far as to press up against the walls of the nearest building or hide in a dark alley until they passed.

It was a stark contrast to the way Elondrian troops were treated by the majority of the citizenry. I had to exclude the street rats, since they still feared the Lancers, thinking them nothing more than glorified blue capes. The Sandstorm kids weren't quite as leery, considering one of their chiefs happened to *be* a lancer, but that didn't mean they wouldn't cut through a side street if they saw a group of them riding down the road.

In Aramoor, the Lancers were almost revered; people smiled and waved at us when we passed. Some even went so far as to stop and salute. I wondered why things were so different here.

As we drew closer to the center of Ecrin, I expected to see a notable improvement in the quality of the buildings and roadways, much like you would expect in most cities where the wealthier tended to build closer to the heart, but it seemed that no matter where we went, things were about the same. Perhaps we were nowhere near the center of the city.

We rode over the next hill and came across three or four red-and-black uniforms who'd stopped in the middle of the road to question a man struggling to pull a small vegetable cart up the street.

By the taunting way they were looking down at him and the crouched way the man was huddled back against his cart, it was clear they weren't there to help. I wasn't exactly sure what they were saying, but from the smirks on their faces, I didn't want to get involved, not with the crown prince riding beside me. It took everything I had not to go to the poor farmer's aid, but a single glance from one of the soldiers convinced me to direct our horses onto a side street. It left a sour pit in my gut, but I hoped my roommates had the same good sense.

Surprisingly enough, with help from a few willing citizens, we finally managed to find the Ram's Head Inn without incident. It didn't look that different from the Spotted Pike Inn back in Dorwall, apart from having a third story. The outside looked weather-beaten and worn, its stone chipped and its paint peeling, but it also looked like it had been built to last.

Dakaran and I waited outside the inn for the others to arrive. I breathed a small sigh of relief each time one of them appeared around the corner. Stumpy was the last, and as soon he arrived, we dismounted, huddling together at the front of the inn.

"Were those soldiers still hassling that farmer when you rode by?" I asked.

"Gellar and I had to go around," Barthol said.

I nodded. "We did the same."

"We didn't see any farmer," Fipple said. "We did pass several more groups of soldiers, though."

"Hopefully he got away in one piece, then." I glanced behind me at the buildings looming over my shoulder. "The sooner we get the ambassador and get out of this place, the better."

"Aye," Stumpy said. "This city feels wrong. Like there's a disease here that's eating away at everything and everyone."

I shivered. That was the perfect way to state what I was feeling.

"And that disease is Saryn," Fipple said, spitting off to the side.

Waylen nodded, then looked up at the somewhat dilapidated inn. "Doesn't look like much. At least we're sure to get a decent rate. Can't imagine anyone paying much to stay here."

I turned and stretched, stiff from sitting in a saddle for so long. All I wanted was a hot bath and a cool bed, both of which seemed doubtful

from the look of this place. Leaving the front, we walked our horses around the side of the building to a stable with a single open door at the front, where a young boy tipped his hat in greeting.

"You looking for lodging for the night?" he asked eagerly, holding out his hand as he hopped up from the barrel he'd been sitting on. He looked to be about ten or eleven, with short brown hair, a dirty face, and even dirtier hands. His nails were blackened, as though he'd spent the day cleaning soot from a chimney, and when he smiled, it was apparent he'd been in a scrap or two, as he was missing one of his front teeth.

"At least one night," I said, reaching out to hand him my horse's reins. "Most likely more."

The boy pushed the reins away when I offered and instead cleared his throat, leaving his outstretched palm in front of me.

Finally realizing what he wanted, I reached for my purse. "How much?"

He looked us over, his eyes passing over our outer cloaks, as they weren't much to look at. However, his eyes brightened when he caught our swords underneath. He smiled. "That'll be two coppers."

I was surprised by the extremely generous price. By the way he had eyed our weapons, I was afraid he was about to gouge us. I reached into my purse and pulled out the two coppers and handed it to him.

He looked down, then back up at me and shook his head. "Two apiece."

"One silver and four to stable our horses?" Gellar asked. "That's highway robbery."

"Feel free to leave them out in the weather," the boy said with a shrug as he stared past us out at the continual drizzle.

"For that price," Gellar said, "you better groom them, feed them . . . Flaming Pits! You better be in here singing them to sleep."

The young boy held his smile and waited.

I pulled out a silver and a couple more coppers and placed them in the boy's hand. "Thank you kindly," he said and took off running out the door.

A middle-aged man in a loose-fit vest, dark-blue shirt, and black cap came running around the side of the inn. "Hey! Get back here, you thieving little . . ." He stopped when he saw us standing there. "Sorry about that. Hope you didn't give him anything. He waits till I have to step away and then tries to con travelers out of their coin." He spotted my open purse and nodded. "Looks as though I got here just in time."

"Not hardly!" Gellar barked. "That guttersnipe just made off with a silver and four."

The man's eyes bulged. "A silver and four. Why would you pay a silver and four to stable your horses?"

I started to chuckle but bit my tongue. It sounded like a scheme one of my kids would have tried pulling. Whoever the street rat was, he was good. "We paid because he made it clear it was either that or leave them in the rain."

The man shook his head and took my horse's reins and walked inside.

"Aren't you going to give us the price before stabling our horses?" I asked.

The man shrugged. "If you're crazy enough to pay a silver and four to a street rat, I doubt you'll balk much at my price."

"Which is?"

"Five coppers for the night, including feed and water."

I looked back at the others and nodded, and we followed him in. There were several other horses stabled already, forcing us to double up on the stalls just to get them in. Thankfully, the stalls were large enough to fit two, and it seemed they had been freshly mucked. There was even a bucket of oats waiting and some dry hay to soften the floor. All in all,

it wasn't the worst stable I'd seen.

We took a few minutes to unsaddle the horses, all of which seemed to be as happy to be out of the rain as we were, whinnying and snorting and shaking their manes. After seeing to their water, we went about unpacking what was in our saddlebags. Besides our clothing and gear, our bags were mostly filled with leftover food from Dorwall.

"How's the crowd tonight?" Barthol asked, toting two large satchels over one of his broad shoulders. "Common room full?"

"About half," the man said, pulling off his cap to wipe his forehead and revealing a partially bald head, "but I expect it to grow if this rain holds out."

I pulled the last of what I was carrying from my saddlebag and met the others at the front of the barn. The rain had picked up a little, and the pale grey light of dusk had all but dissipated, leaving behind a depressing sort of darkness, one that not even the streetlamp at the front of the inn could hold back.

The stableman tipped his hat. "The name's Bosko. You need anything—drink, women . . ." He looked at me, seeming to catch a glimpse of my eyes for the first time. ". . . uh, weapons. Then I'm your man. In Ecrin, if you have the coin, anything is for sale."

"How about information?" I asked.

Bosko's eyes lit up, and he slid a little closer, but not too close. "Ah, I see you are after the most dangerous of gets. Information can be purchased for a price." His smile slid across his face like a snake. "What sort of information do you seek?"

"For the moment, why the streets seemed to be filled with soldiers."

Bosko spit off to the side at the mention of them. "It seems our illustrious lord and master Saryn has gone and kidnapped one of our neighbors to the east, apparently a person of some notoriety. Holding them for ransom, I suspect, but don't quote me on that. Seems foolish if you ask me, but what is there about Saryn that isn't foolish? The man thinks with his eyes and not his head, that's what I reckon—if he thinks at all." He chuckled. "You know—"

"Still doesn't account for the strong military presence," Gellar interjected while Bosko was taking a breath.

"It does if you suspect coming under attack from those same neighbors, especially when one of them happens to be the high king, with one of the largest military presences in the Five Kingdoms." Bosko shook his head and leaned in. "But whatever his reasons, I just hope they don't have anything to do with me."

I hefted my pack up higher on my shoulder. "I get the feeling that the citizens of Ecrin don't care much for their red-and-black protectors."

Bosko sneered. "Just because they wear the uniform don't make them protectors. Filchers and thugs, mostly. Don't give a copper toss for anything but themselves. We've learned it's best to steer clear of them when we can. And when we can't, it's best not to antagonize them." He looked as though he was about to say more, but instead took a closer look at the seven of us and frowned, most likely noticing our fairer skin. "You didn't say where you were from. What business do you have in Ecrin?"

"Our business is our own," Barthol said, a little too quickly.

"Fine, fine. Can't be too careful around these parts, I reckon." Bosko's eyes tightened as he continued looking us and our bags over. "Reminds me of a time—"

"We are looking for work," Stumpy said. "Know of any merchants looking to hire protection for their travels?"

"Work, you say?" Bosko relaxed a little, leaning back against the barn door as he pursed his lips in thought. "Come to think of it, I might know one, if only I could remember his name . . ." He cleared his throat and held out his hand.

I sighed but finally dug around in my purse and produced a couple of coppers and dropped them in his palm.

He smiled. "Yes, I believe Master Zivota is gearing up for a large shipment to Rhowynn. He has probably hired men already, but it couldn't hurt to ask. Besides, he might find hiring outsiders more beneficial. We Cylmarans tend to get looked at differently. Which reminds me—"

"That's very useful, thank you," I said, stopping him before he could continue what was sure to be another long-winded spiel about Cylmar, or the overlord, or the weather. I turned to the others. "We better get our rooms before they're sold out. It doesn't look like this rain is going to let up anytime soon." My bags were heavy, and I had a feeling if we stood there any longer, Bosko was going to start divulging his life story. The man clearly loved to talk.

"Yes," Bosko said with a smile, "if there's one thing you learn to live with as a Cylmaran, it's rain. Never seems to stop, only lighten, at least during these late summer months. Not that I'm complaining, mind you," he said, following us on around to the front of the inn. "It's better than baking in our skins. I much prefer this to being caught on the other side of the Khezrian Wall. Nothing over there but a barren waste from what I'm told."

"How interesting," Waylen said, trying to squeeze by the man, who was partially blocking the front door. "If you'll excuse me."

"My apologies." Bosko tipped his hat once more as he moved out of Waylen's way. "I'll just see to your horses, then. Remember, if you need anything—anything at all—I'm your man."

The door shut behind him, and I took a deep breath and slowly exhaled. His talking put me on edge.

"This place smells like wet dog," Dakaran said, his face puckered as he glanced around the darkened lobby. There were no chandeliers lighting the entryway, only a couple of sconces on the wall to the right, where a desk and chair had been set up to greet guests.

All of the others except Fipple pulled back their hoods now that we were out of the rain, but I planned to keep mine on at least until we'd gotten our rooms.

"You look to be well-traveled," a middle-aged woman said as she walked from the common room to the desk and sat down on the stool behind it. She had a stern look to her, emphasized by the deep creases around her eyes. Her black hair was streaked with grey and reached her shoulders. She might have had the faint traces of a mustache near the corners of her lips, or it could have just been a smudge from whatever she'd had for supper. The front of her clothes was dirt-stained, as were her hands and arms. She looked like she'd been cleaning the oven. For a moment, I wondered if she was really the innkeeper or someone pretending to be in hopes of cheating us out of our coin.

"Rooms for the night," she asked, though it sounded more like a declaration than an inquiry.

"Do you have any that sleep more than one?" I asked, thinking it safer for all of us if we at least doubled up.

She looked down at an open ledger on her desk, then at a display of keys hanging on the wall behind her. "I have a couple available."

"That's fine. You wouldn't happen to have a room that sleeps three, would you?" There were seven of us, so either one room slept three, or one of us would bunk alone.

She shook her head.

"Then I guess we'll take three doubles and one single."

She nodded and picked up her quill. "That'll be six each for the doubles and four for the single, which comes out to . . . two silver and four."

Stumpy cleared his throat. "I believe you mean two silver and two."

The lady frowned and then looked down at her ledger. "Yes, two silver and two."

I couldn't tell if her misquote had been on purpose or a simple miscalculation. Her face didn't reveal her intentions.

"I take it that includes our meals?" I asked.

"It does, so long as you're here when they're served."

I nodded and handed over her payment, which she took hastily and stuffed in her apron pocket. After glancing once more at the book, she grabbed four keys off the wall and handed them to me, three in one hand and one in the other. "You'll find your rooms on the second floor." She pointed to the stairwell on the left. "Evening meal is being served now if you care to eat once you see to your rooms."

"Thank you," I said, then lifted my bags and headed across the lobby for the stairs.

We made our way up to the second floor and stopped at the landing in front of a long hall that looked to run the entire length of the building. Unlike the Spotted Pike Inn, this hall wasn't against the outside wall, but directly down the middle, with rooms on either side.

"Who wants the single roo—"

"I do," Stumpy blurted out before I could finish. A couple of the others looked miffed for not having spoken up sooner, but no one argued, so I gave Stumpy the key. He took one look at the number and headed down the hall.

Barthol held out his hand. "I suppose Gellar and I can bunk together."

I handed him a key.

"I guess that leaves me to bunk with the recruit," Fipple said, giving Dakaran a strong look as he wrung the water from his topknot. "I hope you're not a light sleeper. I tend to flop about the bed."

Dakaran winced, then shook his head. "I'm with Ayrion."

Fipple took a deep breath and exhaled. "Fine." He turned and winked at Waylen. "I guess that leaves you and me." He took the key I was holding out, lifted his bag, and started down the hall. I caught a slight grin on his face as he left.

I lifted my bag and started down the hall.

There was another stairwell at the back. A young couple coming down from the next floor up nodded our way as they continued down to the main floor. I guessed the stairs ended at the back of the common room below.

Dakaran took the key from me and opened our door.

The room wasn't much to look at, similar to our room at the Spotted Pike. It was a little bigger, as it had to accommodate two beds instead of one, and certainly cleaner. Thankfully, the beds were on either side of the room, separated by a couple of windows that overlooked the next building and a fireplace with several pieces of wood stacked inside.

It was definitely too warm for a fire.

Dakaran tossed his bag down on the bed on the left, and I did the same for the one on the right, taking a minute to try out the mattress. The ropes underneath squeaked, and the feather filling was a bit lumpy, but it sure beat sleeping on the hard ground out in the weather.

Dakaran groaned as he lay prostrate on his bed, tossing from one side to the other. "Here I thought I couldn't find a worse bed than the ones in the barracks. Guess I was wrong."

We left our belongings in the room and joined the others in the hall to make our way down to supper. The common room was about three-quarters filled, with a few open tables near the center, as well as a couple around the outer rim. We found two near the back on the right that were close enough to push together.

By the time we got the tables situated and ourselves seated, a young woman, maybe a couple years older than me, walked over from another

table she'd been seeing to on our side of the room. She had long brown hair that fell halfway down her back, with soft green eyes and a strong hooked nose. She, like everyone else in the room, seemed hesitant at first to approach, as she gave us a quick looking-over.

Our hoods were down, all but Fipple's, and we did our best to offer polite smiles all around. It seemed the people of Ecrin were not used to seeing foreigners in their city. I guess if I were given the choice, Cylmar would be one of the last places I'd care to visit, unless I had business here. And from what we'd seen so far, the type of business that would have brought us across the border was probably not that reputable.

"What will it be, gentlemen?" she asked.

"A plate of whatever the cook is whipping up in the back," Barthol said, "and something strong to wash it down with."

The others nodded.

"But not too strong," I added.

The young woman paused a moment when she caught my eyes, then quickly looked away. "I'll be back with your drinks shortly." She made her way to a door at the front of the room just off the lobby.

"Anyone else get the feeling that we don't belong here?" Gellar asked, glancing over his shoulder at a table two down from ours, where the patrons had been keeping an eye on us until Gellar turned.

"It's not just you," Fipple said, staring at another table on our left.

"Best not to look like it bothers us," I said, casting a quick glance around the room myself.

We hadn't even begun a new topic of conversation when our server returned with a tray of drinks, quickly passing them out with practiced hands. "Your food will be out—"

Noise in the lobby caused the young lady to turn. Her face darkened when she spotted the red-and-black uniforms. "Not tonight," she mumbled to herself, her brows tightening. She looked at us and opened her mouth as if she wanted to say something, but then promptly scurried across the room and into the back.

"What do you think that was about?" Stumpy asked, his drink half-way to his mouth.

I frowned as I glanced over my shoulder at the men walking across the lobby toward the common room. "Got a feeling we're about to find out."

# WILDFIRE

## *Chapter 10*

HE UNIFORMED MEN LAUGHED and joked their way into the common room. There were ten, from my count. Several of the nearby tables emptied, and the occupants quickly filtered out of the room and up the back stairwell. There were still a few who remained, at least until the soldiers passed on their way to the back. As soon as the uniformed men were far enough away, several of those tables emptied as well, the people rushing through the lobby and out the front.

The soldiers laughed.

"You'd think they were afraid of us or something," one man said as he grabbed a tankard from one of the empty tables and downed what was left before walking over and taking a seat with the rest of the soldiers.

Several of the men began banging their fists on the table and demanding a wench come and fill them. Not exactly the way Elondrian

soldiers would have conducted themselves. One complaint from the local taverns and inns and those men would have been rooted out by their
captains and made to answer for it.

These men seemed more paid muscle than anything. That was a
dangerous way to run a military.

By the time all of the soldiers had found their seats, most of the
common room had been emptied, leaving me to wonder if perhaps we
should have done the same.

Dakaran started to turn around, but I grabbed his arm and shook
my head.

"Last thing we need is a confrontation. Let's just eat and get to our
rooms."

"Wench!" the same man from earlier shouted. "Where's our drinks?
Or do we need to come back there and get them ourselves?" He was one
of the taller men of the group, well-built, not on the scale of Barthol but
no doubt able hold his own. He had olive skin like Fipple, with dark
hair that hung to his shoulders and a large mole on his left cheek, nearly
the size of a silver.

From where I was seated on the end, I could just make out their
tables from the corner of my eye without having to actually turn my
head. The taller man's chair suddenly scooted away from their table, and
he stood. "Where is everyone?" He started for the front, but just as he
did, the kitchen door swung open, and he stopped.

A stout middle-aged woman with hair that was beginning to grey,
and a stern expression that said she wasn't going to take flak from anyone, stepped out and started across the room for the soldiers' tables.

The man who'd been doing most of the talking crossed his arms and
stared past her toward the kitchen door. "Where's the other wench? The
pretty one. One look at you and my thirst'll dry right up."

A roar of laughter resounded from the soldiers' tables, but it didn't

seem to deter the older woman, as she walked up to the big man and crossed her arms. "Your thirst, Ratko, is about the last thing I care about. Now, do you want your drinks or not? I don't have all night."

The man with the mole frowned. "I said we want the younger one serving us. I don't want to lose my appetite staring at your unhappy face."

The woman stood her ground. "You get me, or you get no one."

Ratko's face darkened.

"Flaming Pits," I mumbled and started to turn. Before I'd managed to get my leg out from under the table, the kitchen door opened.

"I can see to them, Mirna," the young server who'd taken our orders said as she slowly crossed the room.

The older woman turned. "You sure, girl? I don't mind. This lot don't scare me none."

Ratko laughed, then looked at the young server. "I said we wanted the pretty one. This one has a nose like a hawk." He looked at the young lady. "Where's that sister of yours, Jasna? Been looking forward to seeing her face all day."

"Kelsi's not feeling well. Afraid you're stuck with me tonight."

The soldier frowned but retook his seat. "Guess you'll have to do. Certainly better than this old hag."

Mirna gave the man a harsh look. If she'd had a rolling pin in her hand, the man would have been wearing it upside his head. "If they get too friendly, you let me know," Mirna said before making her way back to the kitchen, keeping an eye on the men over her shoulder.

"I'm starting to think we aren't going to get our food," Waylen pointed out, staring at the empty place in front of him.

"I'm getting that same feeling," Fipple agreed, his hands wrapped protectively around his tankard. "Perhaps we should retire for the evening."

"I think it might be better if we stayed," Barthol said, watching the way the men were eyeing the young server as she tried to get their orders.

I spared a glance at the soldiers' tables. "You could be right."

By the time Jasna had collected the men's orders and was halfway back to the front, the kitchen door opened, and Mirna came strolling out carrying a large tray, which she fought to balance in her arms. The soldiers looked excited by the quick arrival of their food, until they saw it wasn't heading in their direction.

Mirna headed straight to our tables and began to hand out the bowls of stew, which was still hot enough to have steam rising from the lips.

"You're going to serve them before us?" Ratko called out.

"They was here first," she shot back.

"They ain't even Cylmaran," another soldier said.

Mirna snorted. "What's your point?" She finished by placing a couple loaves of dark bread down between us. After a quick look at everyone's place to make sure we each had a bowl, she collected her tray and headed back to the front, ignoring the angry grumbling coming from the other side of the room.

I dipped out a spoonful of stew and blew on the top before stuffing it hungrily in my mouth. It was very salty, to the point it almost had me coughing, but still flavorful.

"This is just as bad as the Spotted Pike," Dakaran griped, making a face as he worked his first bite around in his mouth. "I've never tasted food this bad."

The rest of us looked at each other and shrugged as we continued to stuff our faces. It only showed how out of touch the prince was with the lives of common folk. His father had been wise to force Dakaran into the Lancers for a year. Not only would it toughen him up, but it would allow him to see how the vast majority of Elondrian citizens lived. It would make him a better ruler if he understood those he was ruling over.

I was reminded of the time the king and queen had graced our humble orphanage with their presence. They'd even gone so far as to take tea with Master Fentin and Mistress Orilla. Not once did they complain or look down on the refreshments or furnishings. Dakaran had a long way to go if he was to ever become like his father.

"Where are you from?" Ratko asked.

I turned my head slightly in their direction, just far enough to realize he was addressing us.

"Don't remember seeing you around here before."

"Just passing through," I said, taking a small sip of the very strong ale to wash down my latest mouthful. "Looking for work."

"And what sort of work would you be in the market for?"

"Transport," I said, still not turning.

"Where do you hail from?"

"Keldor," Stumpy said, having a difficult time with his food, as it wasn't something he could clearly separate in his bowl, though it didn't stop him from trying. He had the meat on one side, the carrots on the other, and the potatoes in the middle, all clumped together within the gravy.

"Keldor? Your accent sounds more Elondrian."

I looked at the others. Those at the back of the table had one hand on their weapons.

"Oswell, to be precise," I said.

"That's over near the Slags, isn't it?" Ratko asked. He sounded like he was testing us.

I nodded. "You know it, then?"

"Been there once when I was younger. Seemed a quiet place. There was this one inn . . . served the best dumplings."

I smiled. "The Golden Tassel."

"Yes, the very one. I guess it's still there, then?"

"It is. The owner, Milly, is quite the sergeant, but she keeps the place running smoothly." I remembered the way she and Hobb would go at it, arguing like an old married couple, too embarrassed to admit the way they felt about each other.

Before Ratko could say more, Jasna stepped out of the kitchen with a tray of drinks filled to the outer edge. She was quite nimble on her feet as she wove her way through the tables without sloshing a single tankard. She placed the tray down on a nearby table and began handing out the drinks to the soldiers, enduring the leering stares and unwanted comments.

One of the soldiers pulled her down on his lap. She pushed out of his arms and stumbled back as the others laughed.

The kitchen door opened, and Mirna stepped out, holding a large wooden peel in her hands. She held the flat shovel-like tool—normally used for pulling bread out of the oven—high, like she was ready to crack it over someone's skull. "You lay your hands on one of my girls again, and you'll feel this upside your heads."

The men laughed even more, and Jasna scurried across the room toward the front, barely managing to grab her tray on the way by.

The remaining patrons who'd stuck it out so far vacated their seats and made their way out, not wanting to get involved. I had half a mind to go in the kitchen, grab the next tray, and serve the soldiers myself just so the poor ladies wouldn't have to, but that would just force a confrontation.

"This isn't our business," Gellar said, obviously noticing the scowl on my face. He kept his voice lowered. "We've got a mission to complete. We can't go mixing it up with a bunch of Cylmaran soldiers and risk failing in our charge."

I ground my teeth because I knew he was right. Yet, how could we call ourselves men and do nothing? It was more than that, though. I had an itch in the back of my mind that needed scratching. And the answer to it seemed to be staring me right in the face. Well, staring at me from the corner of my eye. "We might be able to use this to our advantage."

"Are you drunk?" Dakaran asked, wiping the foam from his mouth after taking another long pull from his tankard. "Gellar's right. We don't need to get involved. In fact, I'm ordering you not to."

"Oh, stuff it. You can't order me to do anything unless you've somehow managed to earn an officer's patch somewhere between Dorwall and here." I was about to say more when the door at the back opened and both Mirna and Jasna stepped out, one carrying a tray of food, the other two pitchers of ale. While Mirna went to the soldiers to hand out their bowls, Jasna headed for our table to refill our tankards.

Jasna moved around the table, refilling our drinks. Every time I looked her way, I caught her staring, and it wasn't in a repulsive or even frightened way, at least that was the impression I got from her smile.

The soldiers complained from the other side of the room about not having Jasna there to dish out their food.

This was perfect, I thought.

"Do they come in often?" I asked her as she made her way to my end of the table.

Jasna's smile turned to a sneer as she spared a passing glance over her shoulder at the soldiers. "At least two or three nights a week." She finished Dakaran's tankard and started on mine, her smile returning.

"Would you be willing to help us if I said we could make sure they never bothered you again?"

Her hand stopped halfway through pouring my drink. "What do you mean?" She looked me in the eyes, not flinching at all.

"What are you doing?" Barthol asked.

I smiled. "Trust me, I have an idea."

Gellar shook his head. "Blood and ash. Every time he says that, my bladder wants to empty itself."

I looked at Jasna. "Will you help us?"

"I don't know you."

"You know them," I said, nodding to the other side of the room. "Would you prefer us to leave you with them?" I knew my question was harsh, but I really needed her help.

She finished pouring my drink, her hand shaking. "What do you want me to do?"

"I want you to sit down on the bench beside me and look friendly. Real friendly."

Her eyes widened. "Are you crazy? I'm not going to do that."

"Do you want them gone or not?"

She looked at the tables behind her. By now, Ratko and half his men had been served, and Mirna was already heading back to the kitchen to collect the rest. Several of the soldiers, including Ratko, were looking our way.

"Fine." She nodded and set the pitcher down on the table in front of us and sat down beside me on the bench, which was at the head of the table. "What do you want me to do?"

"Laugh," I said as I leaned over and whispered in her ear. "Pretend you're having a good time."

She giggled at first, then suddenly leaned back and bellowed out a hearty laugh. I was honestly a little startled by how real it sounded. For a moment, I actually thought I'd said something funny. I laughed as well, then pretended to whisper in her ear again, and she laughed some more. She was really good at this.

More of the soldiers turned, but unfortunately, none of them seemed to be taking the bait, though I could see Ratko's fists balling. He looked as though he'd swallowed a lime.

"It's working," I told her. "I'm going to put my arm around you.

Don't flinch."

She gulped. "Okay."

I put my arm around her waist, and Ratko scooted to the edge of his seat. I continued to whisper in her ear, and she continued to giggle and laugh, but it wasn't enough. "Come on. Take the—"

Jasna suddenly wrapped her arms around my neck and kissed me hard on the mouth. I nearly lost my breath. My entire table stopped what they were doing, spoons and tankards halfway to their mouths, eyes bulging.

Ratko flew to his feet. "What do you think you're doing? Unhand her immediately!"

Jasna released her embrace with a smile. I couldn't tell if she was smiling because of the kiss or the astonished expression on my face.

It took me a moment to gather my thoughts. Keeping my arms around her waist, I spared a glance over at Ratko. "Why would I unhand her? She kissed me. Besides, I believe I heard you complaining that she wasn't the sister you wanted. I don't know why. She's absolutely stunning."

Jasna's cheeks reddened.

Dakaran groaned.

"I hope you know what you're doing," Fipple whispered on my right, his sword already halfway out of its sheath.

Ratko started forward. "No foreigner is going to put his hands on our women."

The soldiers at the front of the table stood and followed him across the room in our direction, the others looking ready to. So far, none of them had pulled a weapon.

"I think it's time you left," Ratko said, stopping a few feet away. "Pack your things. If you know what's best for you, you'll leave the city tonight."

"Oh, I think we rather like it here," I said, giving Jasna another squeeze as I finally turned and looked Ratko in the eyes.

He took a step back and reached for his sword. "Upakan."

Clearly, my people's reputation was known here.

I smiled. "No. I believe we'll stay. Where else could we find such flavorsome food, such fine accommodations, or such beautiful women?" I leaned forward and kissed Jasna playfully on her cheek, which was enough to force Ratko's hand.

He drew his sword, as did his men, and I quickly moved Jasna to the back of the table. "Go to the kitchen and stay there," I whispered.

I nodded at my roommates, and they all stood at the same time, weapons in hand.

Barthol rose to his full height and turned to face Ratko.

Ratko's eyes widened, and he and his men took another step back. Those still at the soldiers' tables rushed to join the rest.

Out of the corner of my eye, I caught Jasna bounding through the kitchen door, pulling Mirna and her peel in with her. I reached up and grabbed my sword from off my back. "Trust me when I say: surrendering is your safest option."

Ratko snarled. "The day Cylmaran soldiers surrender to a pack of Keldoran dogs is the day they lay us in the ground."

"As you wish." I reached for my magic, and the two groups collided. They had ten to our seven . . . well, six, since Dakaran hung back by the tables unless needed, but it still wasn't enough to slow us down. I swept through three before they knew what hit them, dancing between their blades to the point they were swinging at themselves trying to hit me. I had them disarmed and on the ground before they knew what had happened.

The others had disarmed, killed, or severely wounded the rest by the time I had turned back around. It was one of the quickest and easiest battles we'd fought.

Ratko was the last man standing as he and Barthol continued to lock blades. The rest of us moved back to give them room. Barthol seemed to be toying with Ratko, retreating, then countering at the last moment to put the soldier back in his place. After seeing the rest of us standing around waiting for him to finish, he batted another attempted thrust away and then reared back and punched Ratko in his face, sending the man flying backward with a few less teeth.

Ratko hit the floor with a heavy thud and didn't move, though he did release a mournful wail as the breath slowly released from his throat. We quickly dragged him over with the other men, who were now huddled or lying on the floor between our respective tables.

The kitchen door creaked, and Mirna, Jasna, and a man, who I guessed was the cook, stuck their heads out. I wondered what had happened to the innkeeper. Come to think of it, I hadn't seen her since the soldiers first arrived.

When those in the kitchen saw the soldiers had been disarmed, they walked out.

"Fine mess you've put us in," Mirna spouted on her way over, stopping about halfway. Her arms were crossed once again as she stared us down. "What exactly are we supposed to do now?"

I smiled. "Take their clothes off."

Mirna gaped. "What?"

"You heard me. Strip them down."

Waylen turned from where he'd been holding his blade on a couple of the men. "As funny as it would be to see them dancing around in their nothings, why exactly is it that we—"

"He wants their uniforms," Barthol said with a smile, seeming to understand what I was planning.

Dakaran sheathed his sword and grabbed his tankard. "And why is it we would want their smelly old uniforms?"

Stumpy looked at Dakaran and shook his head. "We'll let you think on that while we undress them. I'm sure if you give it enough time, it'll come to you."

I looked over at Mirna and Jasna. "Well, are you going to help us or not?"

Mirna took one look at the unconscious Ratko—blood running from his mouth—and smiled. "I'd love nothing more."

It took us a little while, especially with those still conscious and un-injured enough to struggle, but eventually we managed to strip the men down to their long underwear. I had no intention of taking those. Last thing I wanted to see was a bunch of naked Cylmarans.

"Do you have a cellar here?" I asked. "Some place out of the way where we can tie them up and keep them from being found?"

"We do," Jasna said, trying her best not to smirk at all the men in their undergarments, especially Ratko, as his were well-worn with holes around the backside.

"But we can't just keep them there indefinitely," Mirna said. "You promised they wouldn't step foot back in here again. How do you plan on making that happen?" She pulled me to the side. "We can't release them. They'd have us all hanging by morning. And we can't just leave them here."

"As soon as we finish our business, we'll come back and deal with them."

"And all we have is your word on that? Sorry, but I'm not about to put all our lives on the line just because you say so. Your word might be good wherever it is you come from, but here, it doesn't mean nothing."

She had a point. Keeping the soldiers prisoner would be quite risky for them.

"How about if we leave a couple of our party here to keep an eye on

the prisoners until we get back?"

"I volunteer to stay," Dakaran said with a smile and a raised glass.

"No need to volunteer," I said. "I'd leave you here whether we needed assurance or not." I looked at Stumpy. "Can you stay with him?"

"Why me? Because of this?" He raised the arm with his missing hand.

"You should know better than that by now. This doesn't have anything to do with your hand, but if we are going to try impersonating Cylmaran soldiers . . ." I cleared my throat. "You might stick out a bit."

He looked down at his dark skin and laughed.

I turned to Mirna. "Do you have rope?"

"Plenty enough for these pigs. If not, I'm sure I can find a host of people willing to donate some for a good cause."

"Don't let people know what it's being used for."

She gave me a stern look, and I didn't press the issue further.

It took us about an hour, but we did manage to get all the half-naked men down into the cellar, bound, and gagged before heading back up to the common room to clean up. Surprisingly, the innkeeper, who had been sitting at the desk when we first arrived, was back at her desk again. She started when we stepped out of the door to the cellar. "What happened? Where did everyone go? I stepped away for just a moment and now everyone is gone." She looked at the seven of us. "Well, almost everyone."

"I ought to conk you over the head," Mirna said, the peel still in her hands, "leaving us alone with those ruffians. I have half a mind to quit right here and take the rest of your staff with me. I'm sure there's much finer establishments in town who'd appreciate hard workers."

The innkeeper's eyes bulged, and she flung her hands up to stop her. "No, don't do that! I . . . I'm sure we can work something out."

Mirna pursed her lips and stood there in silence for an uncomfortable moment, no doubt to make the innkeeper feel her resolve. She finally nodded. "Very well. We'll discuss those arrangements before I leave."

The innkeeper lowered her hands and breathed a sigh of relief as she nodded and quickly scurried back behind the front desk, where she went about organizing the keys to make herself appear busy.

"Any chance you still have some stew warmed in the back?" I asked the short cook, who up to this point had been fine with letting the women do all the talking.

The cook had a bald head with thick brows and an even thicker mustache that curled upward on the ends. "I'm sure I can heat you up a few bowls," he said with a smile, then disappeared into the kitchen.

"And I can get you some refills," Jasna said, taking a moment to walk over and kiss me on my cheek before scampering toward the kitchen herself.

Mirna gave me a warning look that said I better not get any ideas. She then walked over to the desk, where she and the innkeeper conversed quietly.

I looked at my roommates, then out at the empty common room. "Looks like we have the place to ourselves tonight."

# WILDFIRE

## Chapter 11

FTER SUPPER, WE STABLED the soldiers' horses to keep them from being spotted on the street as we waited for Mirna and Jasna to clean up and head home for the evening. Once the innkeeper had locked up for the night, we made our way up to our rooms. We had piled all the soldiers' uniforms and weapons in my room, deciding we would wait until the next morning to disperse them.

The Cylmaran uniforms didn't fit us very well. Either they were too long or too short, too slender or too wide. You would think with ten men to choose from and only five of us that needed to be outfitted, we'd be able to come up with something close. Barthol's was the worst. His sleeves rode well above his wrists, and his pants ended halfway down his shins. Thankfully the pants were dark, so his boots could help hide the gap.

In my case, the uniform was too baggy. But I could live with that better than it being too snug, like Waylen's. The rest of us tried not to laugh, as it took two of us to get his tabard on. If he bent over too far, it was sure to split.

"I can hardly breathe," he said, panting. "I'll never take a beautiful woman in a fancy dress for granted again if this is what they have to go through."

The sun had yet to rise, but the faint traces of grey seeping through the windows said it wasn't far off.

"I'm hungry," Dakaran said, yawning, which caused me to do the same. He'd kept me up for hours with the constant squeaking from the ropes under his bed as he tried to find a comfortable position.

Now that those of us going into town had our uniforms on, we thought it best not to eat with everyone else in the common room. We didn't want a repeat of last night with people rushing back up to their rooms, especially since many of them missed their supper from the previous night already. We did, however, send Stumpy and Dakaran down to order our food, since neither of them were wearing a uniform. The rest of us waited in Waylen and Fipple's room, discussing what to do next.

"This is the best way to remain unseen," I said. "Did you see the way the people looked at the soldiers when we rode through town?"

"They didn't," Fipple said.

"Exactly. No one is looking at the soldiers. They seem to have free rein of the entire city. And they aren't confined to their barracks either, wherever that is."

"What do you mean?" Waylen asked, stroking the long, thinly braided beard dangling from his chin.

"I mean, ten soldiers are missing, and has anyone come looking? Has anyone even noticed that they're gone? If Jasna's correct, and these men frequent this inn a couple times a week, you'd think this might be one of the first places the other soldiers would look. So far, we haven't heard

a peep. If we were sent out on patrol and never showed back up, how long do you think before Tolin had half our barracks out looking for us? Apparently, no one is really keeping up with the soldiers' comings and goings, which is good for us."

"Are you saying you want us to just spend the day walking around the city?" Gellar asked, tugging nervously on his own beard.

I nodded. "If the soldiers can move about the city freely, that will make our job easier. Most citizens are going to stay as far away from where the overlord lives as possible, which is probably where they are keeping the ambassador and his wife. If we have any hope of rescuing them, we need to know where everything in the city is, including where the overlord resides. We need to know the fastest routes back to the main gate, and whether there are any other ways out of the city. Where's the garrison? Who's in charge? Are the soldiers permitted entrance into the overlord's estate?" I stopped to take a breath. "One of the first rules taught to every Upakan is that failure comes from not being prepared."

Before I could say more, there was a tap on the door. Barthol stood and opened it. Stumpy, Dakaran, and Jasna were in the doorway, holding trays of drinks and plates of food.

The men quickly stood and grabbed the trays from them and placed them wherever there was free space available, mainly on the two beds.

Jasna smiled shyly when she saw me. "I made sure the food was hot. Did you sleep well?"

"I did, thank you."

She looked beyond me toward the beds. "I know they're not the most comfortable. I should know. My sister Kelsi and I have had to sleep over several times when Father stays out drinking."

"Is your sister feeling better?"

Jasna smiled. "She is, but I think she's going to take one more day to recover. I hope you'll still be here when she returns. She says she wants to meet you."

I chuckled. "She might regret that decision."

Jasna stepped forward and laid a hand on my arm. "Don't say that. Any girl would be lucky to know you."

"That's kind of you to say." I glanced back at the men, who were already stuffing their faces and trying to act as though they weren't listening in. "Well, thank you for the food, Jasna. It looks delicious. Perhaps your sister will be feeling better tomorrow, and I can meet her then."

Jasna nodded and stepped out of the room. She waved as she shut the door behind her.

There were a few snickers from my roommates, but they stopped when I took my seat.

"What? She's a nice girl." I took the plate Stumpy offered. "You never know when a kind word will come in handy."

"Looked more than kind," Fipple said.

Dakaran chuckled. "That kiss last night might have had something to do with it."

"Personally, I think it's the eyes," Waylen said, trying to catch his breath in his extremely tight tunic. "Women love a good set of eyes, and there's none quite so unique as yours."

I could feel my face heating up. "Enough. We've got more important things to worry about." I stuffed a spoonful of eggs, sausage, and gravy in my mouth and tried not to notice the amount of pepper. My eyes were watering by the second bite. I finished what was on my plate and washed it down with a single swallow of watered-down ale. It was rather on the vinegary side and left a tart taste in my mouth. I placed the plate and mug back on the tray and stood, not knowing whether I felt better or worse for having eaten. "The sooner we start, the sooner we find what we're looking for."

"A map of Ecrin would be useful," Barthol said.

"There's bound to be a shop somewhere in the city that sells them," Gellar pointed out. "Or perhaps a cartographer."

Stumpy looked at the door. "Jasna or Mirna may know where to look."

I slung my new red-and-black cape around my shoulders. It hung almost to the floor. It did have a hood, but the inside smelled like sour Cylmaran, which was a ripe mix of sweat, ale, and something else I didn't want to guess at, so I left it down.

"Let's divide into two groups," I said. "Barthol, you, Gellar, and Waylen try seeing if you can find the garrison and any information you can gather about the numbers there, the patrols, the best times to move about the city . . . whatever you think might prove useful. Fipple and I will see if we can find that map. He stands a better chance of walking into a shop and making a purchase than the rest of us."

Fipple grumbled something too soft to hear, but the frown on his face told me enough.

"Depending on how long it takes us to find a map, we might try searching out the overlord's dwelling . . . castle, palace, whatever. We'll meet back here for lunch."

The others nodded, and we headed down to the main floor. There was an exit behind the stairs leading to a blind alley between the inn and whatever building was directly behind it. While the others made their way out the door, I remained in the cubby of the stairwell and waited for Jasna, who I spotted filling drinks for a table near the front.

As soon as she finished, I waved, and she smiled and walked over.

"Do you know where we can find a shop that sells maps of the city?"

Her lips pursed. "Jkovis sells maps . . ."

"And how would I find this Jkovis?"

She frowned and scratched her head. "I don't know if I can explain it." She pondered a moment more, then her face brightened. "Wait here."

Before I could ask why, she rushed back across the common room and disappeared into the kitchen. A few minutes later, she reemerged, this time without her apron and wearing a thin cloak.

"I will come and show you."

I shook my head. "You've already done enough. I don't want you to get into any trouble."

"It's no trouble. Mirna says she will cover my tables." Jasna smiled. "I think she will be happy to see you gone."

I sighed, catching Mirna's glare from the crack in the kitchen door. "I think perhaps you are correct." I couldn't argue the fact that having Jasna along would make things much faster. "Fine, you can come. But," I said, putting a hand on her shoulder to hold her back, "if anything happens, I want you to run and not look back."

"What would happen?"

"I don't know. I'm just saying if something does, I don't want you anywhere near it."

She nodded and I followed her out the back door.

We made our way around the side of the inn to the stables. The others were already there and mounted, with one of the horses saddled for me.

"What's this?" Gellar asked, spotting Jasna.

"Couldn't leave without her, aye?" Dakaran remarked with a grin. He'd walked out to see us off.

"She knows where we can get a map to the city."

"She couldn't just tell you?" Fipple asked.

"It's not well known and difficult to get to," Jasna said. "I will need to show you."

Fipple frowned but left it at that.

"I didn't know to saddle two horses," Barthol said, looking unsure as to whether he should climb down and get another.

I waved it off as I put my foot in the stirrup and swung up onto the Cylmaran's horse. "No need. She can ride double with me."

"I bet she can," Dakaran teased.

I gave him a harsh look, and he shrugged, then walked back inside. Leaning over, I offered Jasna my arm, and she swung up behind me and wrapped hers around my waist. I could almost feel her smiling.

With a nudge of my boot, we started down the street. As much as I didn't want to, I did eventually raise my hood, more worried with keeping my eyes hidden than the smell. We all rode in the same direction toward the center of town, at least until Jasna pointed Barthol's group down a converging road to the west that led in the general direction of the city garrison. She gave them a rough idea of how to get there along with some landmarks, which was more information than what they had to begin with.

Fipple, Jasna, and I kept on the same road, veering left and right as it wound itself along, stopping at the most illogical of places, forcing us to skirt around a building or two before the road would pick back up again. It was by far the most confusing city I'd ever been in. There didn't seem to be any coherent flow to it, and I wondered if there had been any kind of design when it was built. We eventually reached what I thought should have been the heart of the city, though there didn't seem to be any castle or fortress or palace marking where Overlord Saryn resided.

Instead, we were in the main shopping district for Ecrin. The road that ran around the square was lined by buildings with faded signs hanging over their doors. I could see a butcher shop to my right, and on either side of it, a vintner and a weaver.

Even though those in the streets gave us a wide berth, we kept our hoods up. I knew why I did; I just wasn't quite sure why Fipple did as well, considering he was Cylmaran. Though, I had to admit, I didn't remember seeing any other Cylmarans with topknots.

I asked Jasna where the overlord lived, as well as what was the easiest way to reach the lake and were there any decent shops in town where one might pick up a coat. I was hoping not to give away our true intentions by asking too direct a question. Then again, with us riding around town impersonating Cylmaran soldiers, it might not have been too difficult to figure out if common people like Jasna had any inkling what their overlord was doing.

I didn't believe Jasna would turn us in. She would have had just as much to lose, considering she helped us capture the soldiers. I was more worried she might be taken and questioned.

"The overlord's keep is on the top of Rodon Hill. It's the highest point in Ecrin. I've heard you can see the whole city from its upper parapets."

"Wow, then it must be quite large."

"I would imagine so."

I twisted in my saddle. "Don't you know?"

"I've never been there," she said.

"But you've at least seen it, right?"

She shook her head.

"How long have you lived in Ecrin?"

"My whole life."

I stared at her in shock. "You mean to tell me you've lived here your whole life and have never once seen the overlord's estate?"

"I've never had any need to go over there. Papa always said there were three places in the city that me and my sister were never allowed to go: the overlord's keep, the garrison, and the docks."

I sighed. "Well, I'm sure if he told you that, he had good reason." The reason was quite obviously to keep his girls as far away from the castle guards, the common soldiers, and the sailors as possible. After seeing the way these soldiers had behaved, it was no wonder.

"Which way to this Jkovis's shop?" Fipple asked.

Jasna pointed to the right, and we headed in that direction. The people were quick to move out of our way as we moseyed through the shopping district. We passed a few other groups of red-and-black capes, but none seemed too worried by our presence. A couple nodded as they passed. Most simply ignored us.

We left the town's square and the shopping district behind and once more headed back into the maze of streets that was the capital city of Ecrin. Jasna was correct: There was no way she could have pointed us in the right direction. As many twists and turns as we had taken, I had no idea how she had ever found the place.

We finally pulled to a stop outside a small two-story building that appeared to be connected to three others, with only a door and window dividing each store from the next. The sign, which was posted to the door and not hanging over it, depicted a half-open scroll with squiggly lines running throughout. If it was a map, I had no idea what it was a map of. I hoped the man's work was more legible than the imagery on his door.

"That's Jkovis's shop," Jasna said, sliding off the horse before I could offer her my hand.

I dismounted and joined Fipple in tying my horse to one of the porch posts, seeing as how there didn't seem to be a hitch rail anywhere nearby. There was a faint light inside, and the curtains were open, which I assumed meant the shop was open for business.

"How did you ever find this place?" I asked. "It seems quite out of the way."

Fipple grunted. "You could wander these streets for a year and probably never lay eyes on it."

Jasna smiled and pointed down the cobbled lane. "We used to live a couple of streets over."

"What does your father do for a living?" Fipple asked.

"He was a lakeman. He owned several boats that trawled Lake Nari every day, bringing in fresh catches for many of the local inns and eateries."

"He doesn't do it anymore?" I asked.

Her face darkened. "No. His business was stolen from him by Dovan, the head of the Fisher Guild. He didn't like that my father's boats were continually out-fishing his, so he levied higher and higher dues on him, threatening that if my father didn't pay, he would be forced out of the guild and no longer allowed to work." Jasna balled her fists. "It was unfair. My father was forced to sell his boats just to keep a roof over our heads. We lost our home and were forced to move over to the south side."

"That is poor luck, indeed," Fipple said. "And did none of the other captains stand up for him?"

"They're all afraid of Dovan."

"Where does this Dovan live?" I asked.

"Down near the lake." She brightened. "I can show you if you want after we get your maps. You said you would like to know the quickest route to the water."

"I thought you said you weren't allowed to go near it?"

Jasna grinned, then turned and opened the shop's door.

I looked at Fipple and shrugged, and we headed inside after her.

Lanterns hung around the room, though there were no candles or open flames in sight, giving the shop a warm glow. It was darker than expected, even at this time of morning. The light didn't make it much farther than the first foot or two through the window. There were two shelves in the middle, spaced so that they split the shop into thirds. Each shelf was built in honeycomb fashion, with stacks of rolled parchment sticking out from the individual cells. Along the outer walls were tables displaying dozens of maps and charts, as well as an assortment of illustrations of small ships and sea creatures, elements the cartographer no doubt placed within each of his creations. These works of art made the simple painting on the sign out front look like a child's doodle. I supposed the sign's simplicity was to make it easier to read from a distance.

Fipple pulled his hood back a little to better see one of the maps. It looked like a map of the southern half of Cylmar.

"Can I help you?" An older gentleman with a stoop shuffled out of the back and into the main shop. He had a long white beard that covered most of his face and a large pair of spectacles balanced on the bridge of his angular nose.

"Master Jkovis, it's me, Jasna."

"Jasna? What are you doing . . ." He finally got a better look at me and Fipple, and his eyes widened. "Are you safe, my dear?" Before she could answer, he moved her back behind him with his cane, then addressed us. "I don't wish any trouble, sirs. I am but a humble cartographer, and I'm sure that whatever she's done, it can be made right."

Jasna laid a hand on the old man's arm. "Master Jkovis, there's no need to fear. It's not what you think. These gentlemen are here to purchase." She moved around to the front of the cartographer and crossed her arms. "And why would you immediately assume I was the one causing trouble?"

He glared at her over his spectacles with a knowing look.

"Fine." She turned and motioned for us to join them. "This is . . ." She looked at me and giggled. "We've kissed, and I have no idea what your name is."

Master Jkovis's mouth opened in shock. He looked like he'd choked on a cherry pit. "You did what?"

She smiled. "It's a long story."

I walked over but kept my hood in place. "My name is Ayrion. This is Fipple."

Fipple turned to greet the man.

"A Southern Watcher," Jkovis said reverently, peering at the bit of Fipple's bald head visible beneath his hood.

Fipple quickly slid his hood back into place.

"Don't see your kind this far north. Haven't met one in years."

"Believe me," Fipple said, "it's not by choice."

"Still, you honor me with your presence, sir."

Fipple nodded but said nothing more.

I had no idea what a Southern Watcher was, but I definitely wanted to know.

Jkovis looked at me. "My eyes might be dimming, but my ears certainly are not. Your accent is foreign. Where are you from?"

"Keldor," I said, going along with the story Stumpy had given the previous night. It wasn't exactly a lie. I was originally from Keldor, just a part of Keldor that no one ever visited.

"Strange to see a Keldoran and one of the Southern Watch sporting the overlord's colors." He waited for us to answer, and when we didn't, he continued. "Don't get me wrong. I have no love for Saryn, so whatever your business is, I needn't know. What is it I can do for you, gentlemen? Young Jasna here says you are in the mood to purchase. Is there a specific item you are looking for?"

"A map of the city," I said. "Our business requires us to be able to move about unhindered, but I've never seen a place so perplexing." And I'd been raised in a place called the *Lost* City. "If you have such a map, that would be extremely helpful."

"Ah, yes, it is one of my best sellers. You won't believe how many travelers find their way here for that very reason." He chuckled. "You wouldn't believe how many of those living here need them as well."

"I can imagine," Fipple said.

The cartographer walked over to one of the shelves and grabbed a roll from a stack near the middle. He then made his way over to one of the tables and placed the parchment on top of another and opened it, using an inkwell and a couple other items to hold it in place.

The map was rather extensive, covering a large swath of area. The cartographer had even placed part of the lake against the far-right side, no doubt to help people see which side was up.

"That's the city square, is it not?" I asked, pointing to what looked like the shopping district we'd traveled through earlier.

The cartographer nodded and adjusted his spectacles a little higher. He ran his finger to the east and then south and stopped. "This is us here."

"And that is the Ram's Head," Jasna added excitedly, her little finger tapping on a spot much farther south.

"I take it that is the garrison, then?" Fipple asked, steering us to the far western side of the map where a wall had been depicted around several buildings that looked to be barracks. There were tiny drawings of men carrying spears and swords inside the wall.

"Yes, that is the Ecrin garrison," he said.

I was surprised he didn't ask why we didn't already know that, considering the uniforms we were wearing.

"What's this here?" I asked, pointing to a spot farther north. Apart from the city's square and the barracks and perhaps the docks, it was the only other large construct shown on the map.

"Ah, now that is a place you don't want to visit," the cartographer said. "That is Rodon Hill."

I spared a passing glance at Jasna, who was staring wide-eyed at where my finger was resting.

"That is the home of Overlord Saryn . . . the most fortified place in all of Ecrin. The outside is guarded by Cylmaran soldiers, and the inside by the palace guard."

I stared at the stone keep, which was depicted as being on the top of a small rise. "You're right. That does sound like a place to stay well clear of."

The cartographer grunted, then moved the objects holding the corners of the map in place and rolled it back up.

"Would you have more than one for purchase?" I asked.

The old man smiled. "But of course. How many do you need?"

"Two would be nice."

The man's eyes brightened, and he hobbled over to the shelf where he'd pulled the first and grabbed another, carrying both over to his desk near the back. "That'll be a gold and five."

After we paid, the cartographer placed each map in its own protective tube with an attached strap, making it more convenient for toting. Fipple and I thanked Jkovis and headed back outside, while Jasna stayed behind to chat.

"I have to ask," I said as we waited for Jasna in front of the shop. "What was the man saying about a Southern Watcher?"

Fipple didn't say anything, but his fingers tightened around the post he was leaning against. I waited, but when no response came, I thought I might have offended him and figured it best to just let the matter drop. Fipple was the one member of our group who seemed the most distant. He wasn't hard to talk to, but he wasn't exactly open either.

"The Southern Watch was a volunteer unit of overworked and underappreciated warriors."

I turned, surprised that he'd answered.

Fipple hmphed. "I say *warriors* because, unlike the soldiers, we weren't paid to do what we considered was our duty, which was to protect the southern border. We didn't have fancy uniforms, and we weren't given a monthly stipend, but we kept our kingdom safe nonetheless, and for the most part, the people recognized it.

"We were farmers and tradesmen, fishermen and merchants; we were the everyday people giving our all to keep our families safe. About ten years ago, Cylmar came under attack. Bristonian ships, sent by the newly appointed Overlord Meyrose, tried to breach our kingdom by attempting to sail up the Ryne River to reach Ecrin. We stopped them."

Fipple smiled, his back straightening. "They outnumbered us five to one, and for nearly a week, the Southern Watch held off the Bristonian brigades. We fought them from the Rhunarin all the way to the marshlands, but we couldn't hope to defeat them. There were just too many. When we sent word to Ecrin to warn them and plead for their help, we received no reply." Fipple's jaw clenched. "There were no reinforcements, no supplies, not even the hope that some were on the way. There was nothing but silence from our capital, and the Southern Watch was nearly killed to a man.

"My father was one of those that died. His body was never recovered. Killed because the overlord couldn't be bothered to send word that a counterattack was on the way. If we had known this, we would have adjusted our strategy, pulled back our attacks, but believing that we were the only line of defense, we continued fighting. We were nothing but fodder for Saryn to use, warriors that valued something other than gold. We represented the one thing he hated most—people he couldn't control."

Fipple spat to the side. "He did eventually drive them back off of our shores, but only because of what the Southern Watch did. Saryn never once even acknowledged our sacrifice, and took all the credit himself." Fipple turned and looked at me. "I swore I'd never step foot in

Cylmar again after that." He sighed. "And now here I am in the very heart of it."

I glanced around the vacant street before speaking. "At least this time you have the backing of the king himself."

"A lot of good that'll do us, way over here in the middle of this Creator-forsaken kingdom. A lot of good it did our ambassador."

I didn't say anything. Wasn't much I could say. He wasn't wrong. If something did happen, there wasn't anyone there to rescue us.

Jasna stepped out of the shop and closed the door. "Are you ready to go to the docks?" she asked with a bright smile.

I turned to look at Fipple and found him already in his saddle. "I guess so."

# WILDFIRE

## Chapter 12

ITH A COUPLE OF HOURS still to spare before we needed to meet with the others, Fipple, Jasna, and I headed for the docks. Jasna seemed to know her way around the eastern side of Ecrin fairly well. If her father had been a lakeman, then she would have come down to the docks on occasion to meet him.

I smelled the fish long before I saw the water. It was a strong smell, carried by the breeze off the lake. Before reaching the water, we had to first pass through Fishtown, as she called it, which was located just above the docks. The streets were lined with booths where the lakemen would bring in their hauls for sale, most supplying the local eateries and inns.

"Those used to be my father's booths," Jasna said, pointing to several prominent stalls ahead on the right. They were some of the first in line, making them the most easily seen.

We dismounted and walked our horses slowly through the market. The street was busy with shoppers, moving from one booth to the next as they picked up fish, looked them in the eyes, sniffed them, slapped them, wiggled them about, then either set them back down on the table and moved to the next or purchased them.

"Jasna, what are you doing here?" a man called out from one of the first booths on the right. He was middle-aged, with curly brown hair that stuck out from the sides of his cap and thick whiskers on the sides of his face. He had dark circles around his eyes and a long pipe that hung from his mouth all the way to his chest.

Jasna smiled and pushed her way through the people to give the man a firm hug. He smiled back warmly until he noticed who she was with, and then his smiled disappeared as Fipple and I moved in behind her. "What are you doing in Fishtown? Your father would kill me if he knew I'd let you walk around down here, and with the likes of them, nonetheless." He spat off to the side, not afraid in the least of offending me or Fipple.

Looking around, I couldn't help but notice Fipple and I seemed to be the only red-and-black capes about.

"Doesn't appear to be much love for the soldiers down here," Fipple said. "Perhaps coming here wasn't the best idea."

"Coming here is a good idea," I said. "Coming here in uniform, perhaps not so much. I want to see how accessible the docks are. It's another avenue in and out of the city if we need it. Best we take a look while we can."

Jasna waved me over. "Ayrion, I want you to meet Pradjic."

I handed Fipple my horse's reins and walked over and held out my hand.

Pradjic sneered. "I shake no hands with the likes of him."

I lowered my hand. I wouldn't have shaken hands with a Cylmaran soldier either.

"But, Pradjic, he's not—"

"Not here to get in the way," I said. "My friend and I had a hankering for some fish, and this young lady was kind enough to show us where to purchase from. She claims your booths have the best in the city."

Pradjic held his sour expression but stepped aside to let me take a look at the day's catch. He might not have cared for soldiers, but it didn't look as though he was foolish enough to try stopping us, not with the way the soldiers seemed to be overrunning the city.

"How many boats come in from the Ryne?" I asked.

"Several," Pradjic said, trying to catch a better view of my face under my hood. I wondered if he noticed my accent like Jkovis had.

"Any of them taking passengers?"

"Some," he said, looking at me curiously, "at least as far as the marshlands. Few travel through there."

"We've heard boats have quit stopping at Dorwall."

Pradjic rolled his pipe around in his mouth. "That town is cursed from what we've been told, if you believe that sort of thing. People down there too scared to come out of their houses."

I picked up a few of the various kinds of fish, mimicking what I'd seen the others do. They didn't seem to have as strong a fishy smell as others. I wondered if that meant they weren't as good. I even went so far as to slap a couple, not really knowing what that was supposed to do except cover my hands in scales and slime. Eventually, I turned to Jasna. "What do you suggest?"

She bit her lip to keep from smiling. "The salmon," she said, pointing to the end of the table. "A few coppers more and they'll fillet them for you."

I looked at one of the men standing behind the table and nodded. He grabbed one of those on top and plopped it on a table to the side and began to cut off the meat. I hoped my roommates liked fish, because apparently that was what we were going to be eating tonight.

I thanked the man and paid him, then took the rather large fillets that they had kindly wrapped for transport and stuffed them in my saddle. I motioned to Fipple, and we continued down the street toward the waterfront. Jasna stayed behind to talk with Pradjic, who didn't look happy at all with her being there, less so with her being there with the two of us.

I just hoped she didn't accidentally say too much about who we were . . . or more importantly, who we weren't.

The crowded street ended at the docks, which, though filled with people, wasn't as tightly packed as the market, giving me a chance to feel like I could breathe. A stone bulwark had been erected along the edge of the city, holding back the lake. It had two tiers. The top being the city itself, which was connected to the street we were presently standing on, and the second, a stone roadway that ran from the street down below, with wagons coming and going, either loading or unloading supplies to and from the ships.

Long wooden piers stretched out from the dock to meet the ships. Most of the vessels there had at least a single sail, reminding me of the *Wind Binder*, but none were quite so sleek or beautiful.

There were also several shorter piers along the outer edges, where the single-manned boats were tied off, boats small enough to confine their business to within eyeshot of shore.

I looked out over the lake, its bluish-green waters stretching across the horizon. It moved to its own rhythm, rising and falling at will, sending small waves lapping against the piers and the sides of the bulwark.

"Beautiful, isn't it?" Jasna said, appearing out of nowhere beside me.

"Did your father ever take you out on his boats?"

"Of course. I was going to be a captain just like him one day. We would have sailed Nari together, father and daughter."

"What about your sister?" I asked.

Jasna shook her head. "She couldn't stomach the motion. She prefers her feet on dry land."

"And your mother?"

Jasna sighed as she leaned against the waist-high stone wall fronting the top tier of the shipyard. "She passed several years ago."

"Oh, I'm sorry."

"It was a mercy. She'd been sick for a long time."

"What's that building over there?" I asked, noticing a large stone construct just off the water, at the edge of the dockyard. It was by far the grandest of the buildings I'd seen surrounding the docks so far, almost like a miniature castle. It even had a few turrets rising high enough to be seen across all of Fishtown.

"That's where Dovan lives."

"Seems these fees that he has been demanding have done him no harm. How's he able to keep up the gouging without the rest of the captains complaining?"

"Because those who complain tend to disappear . . . Boating accidents, they call it. Those captains that stand with Dovan get the better routes. They also seem to have less accidents and problems with their boats. The only reason my father's boats didn't have these kinds of accidents was because he was smart enough to keep a constant watch on them day and night."

"What happened to your father's crews when he sold?" Fipple asked.

"You just met some of them," she said. "Pradjic was my father's first mate. Now, he's a common crewman aboard one of the very ships he used to be in charge of."

"Who purchased your father's boats?" Fipple asked. "Wait, let me guess . . . Dovan?"

She nodded.

"What does your father do now?" I asked.

Her expression soured even further. "Drink."

I wished now I hadn't asked. "Probably best if we start back toward the inn."

After taking one last good look at Dovan's residence, I led us back up the street. The fish market was just as busy as it had been on the way through. Most of the fish, however, had been picked through by the local eateries and the wealthy, who'd sent their servants, leaving the smaller, less-meaty fish behind for those not having risen quite so early.

We were nearing the first booths, where Pradjic and the rest of Jasna's father's crew were busy washing down their tables, when the crowds on the other side of the street parted as several colorfully clad lakemen forced their way through. Behind them was a small entourage being led by a large man in a white tunic with rolled-up sleeves, a brown leather vest, and a bright red sash around his waist. By his demeanor and the way the others deferred to him, he was clearly a man of some importance around here. And if I were to guess, I'd say I was looking at—

"It's Dovan!" someone at a booth on our left called out. "He's coming to collect."

Several booths down the street began scrambling to gather their belongings and get out of there.

"Get her out of here," Pradjic said when he saw us coming. Unfortunately, it wasn't soon enough, and the crowds blocked our horses in.

I grabbed Jasna and spun her around, hoping to keep her from being seen as we tried to push our way through the throng. I motioned at Fipple, and we edged the horses over to the side of the street, wondering if we should leave them and make a run for it, but as soon as I started to swing out of the saddle, a booming voice behind us called out.

"Jasna!"

My heart sank. They'd already seen her. Or perhaps someone from the market had snitched.

The look of rage on Jasna's face as she turned was enough to let me know whose voice it was.

Fipple looked at me and sighed but turned with me to watch the small parade of figures move up the street in our direction, stopping a few feet away. I dismounted, helping Jasna down with me. It was pretty clear that if we needed to make a quick escape, we weren't going to be able to do it from the back of a horse.

The crewmen with Dovan moved the people aside, letting him and four others pass unhindered. The other four, by their similar dress, were captains as well: three men and one woman. Dovan was by far the largest, with dirty-blond hair that hung to his shoulders, and a single small braid tied with a leather cord on the side of his head. His beard was thick and hung to his chest. At his waist was a sword, along with a hefty coin pouch.

It was quite obvious why he was the head of the Fisher Guild. He was nearly as big as Barthol, and his face hard as flint, which, with the right disposition, would make him not a man to be trifled with.

Dovan got one look at me and Fipple and frowned, especially with Jasna hugging close to my arm. He turned to Jasna. "You know better than to be down here. You and your father were banned from the docks."

Out of the corner of my eye, I could see Pradjic and several other lakemen moving around to the front of their booths. I couldn't tell if they planned on apprehending her if Dovan demanded it, or helping her. Hopefully the latter. If we were to fight our way through, we were going to need to make a run for the side booths and hope to lose them inside if it came down to it.

I moved Jasna closer to me. "And why would a beautiful young lady like this be banned from Fishtown?"

"Our affairs do not concern you," he said, looking the two of us over. "And what business do you have here? The docks are off-limits to soldier patrols. Our arrangement with your commander is still in good standing."

"Our business is that of filling our bellies, and Jasna here was kind enough to point us to where we could find the best fish on the market." I opened my saddlebag and pulled out one of the fillets for them to see. "Of course, if you're saying the soldiers are not welcome to purchase here, then I will be sure to relay that information to the commander." I held my place. His response would let me know all I needed to when it came to the relationship between the lakemen and the soldiers.

He stared at me a moment, as if trying to determine whether he should press the issue or not. Eventually, he smiled. "But of course the soldiers are welcome to purchase what they will. Fill your bellies to your heart's content." He locked eyes with Jasna and sneered, then headed back down the street in the opposite direction.

I breathed a small sigh of relief as I watched Dovan and his followers melt back into the crowd. "Clearly, he has no love for you or your father."

"Nor us him."

I had a feeling that if Dovan ever caught her in Fishtown again, they'd probably find her body floating face down under the pylons.

"Was it smart to call him out like that?" Fipple asked.

"I needed to know where we stood. Now I do."

"Wonderful. Now how about we get that fish back to the inn before it goes bad."

Jasna hugged Pradjic, and he even gave me a half-friendly nod before we turned and led our horses back up the street and away from the market.

With two maps to the city and two thick cuts of fish, we headed back to the inn, feeling like our trip was time well spent. We hadn't yet gone by to see the overlord's estate as planned, but our detour to Fishtown

was hardly a wasted trip. We now had a better understanding of how the docks worked and who ran them. As my instructors had drilled into me, knowing the political hierarchy of a place was always a first step toward knowing where to go, and where not to. The docks could likely be our best choice for getting the ambassador and his wife out of the city.

Back at the Ram's Head, we found the others' horses already in their stalls. I wondered how long they'd been back.

We left ours saddled since I planned on heading back out immediately after we ate. Fipple handed Jasna the fish as we left the stable and walked around to the back of the inn so as to not disturb those eating.

"I'll have Cook whip up a nice chowder with these," she said.

I thanked her for her help, and she offered me another kiss on the cheek before heading back into the common room.

With maps in hand, Fipple and I headed up the stairs to our rooms. We stopped by my room first, but Dakaran wasn't there.

"Sounds like they're in Barthol and Gellar's room," Fipple said, already making his way down the hall.

A door on our left opened, and the young couple inside took one look at us and our Cylmaran uniforms and quickly shut it.

Fipple chuckled when we heard the latch being thrown, then walked over and opened the next door down on the right.

"Ah, there you are," Gellar said, sitting in one of the chairs on the left.

"Where've you been?" Dakaran asked, relaxing on the bed beside Stumpy.

"We've been exploring the city," I said. "Taking in the sights."

"I hope those are what I think they are," Barthol said with a smile, eyeing the rolled parchment in my hands.

"If you think they are fully fleshed-out maps of the city, then you'd be right." I walked over to the table that sat in the middle of the room and unrolled the parchment, grabbing a bar of soap from the wash table and the candlestick from the desk to hold it in place as the others gathered around.

"Here," I said, tapping on a location southeast of the center of the city. "This is us." I moved my finger up toward the middle. "This is the city square and the main shopping district. We took this route to the east and then south here to find the cartographer." I tapped once more on the narrow street where the mapmaker had been. "From there, Jasna took us northeast through Fishtown to the docks."

"Why the docks?" Waylen asked. "I thought you were supposed to be scouting the overlord's estate." Waylen didn't look quite as flushed as he had earlier, but that was probably due to the fact that he had taken his uniform off and unbuttoned the borrowed trousers, which hung partly open around his belly.

"We went to the docks because Jasna's father is a lakeman . . . or was," I added. "He used to own several boats that ran daily hauls for the fish market." I went on to explain what all had happened during our visit to Fishtown and our run-in with Dovan, the head of the Fisher Guild.

"Sounds like a problem we don't want to get involved in," Gellar said.

I shrugged. "Perhaps. Or it could be an opportunity."

"An opportunity to bring trouble down on our heads."

I looked across the table. "And if you had the ambassador and his wife right here in this room, what would you do?"

Gellar spared a passing glance at Barthol and the others before answering. "I'd get them out of Ecrin as fast as I could."

"Would you go right now or wait until dark?"

He thought a moment. "I'd wait till dark."

"But if you wait, don't you risk their escape being discovered? Once

they realize the ambassador is gone, they'll sound the alarm and the city gates will be shut."

"Then we would leave immediately."

"How far do you think you will get with the Cylmaran army on your tail? Will you be able to cross the entire kingdom before they catch you?"

Gellar's knuckles pressed against the top of the table. "What's your point?"

"My point is that these are all aspects we have to consider before we rescue the ambassador and his wife. It won't take Saryn long to realize they're gone, and when he does, we will be running for our lives. Personally, I think we stand a better chance of catching a boat down the Ryne than trying to keep ahead of the Cylmaran army on horseback. And if we plan on getting passage, we need to know who to ask. We wouldn't want to ask the wrong captain and get sold out for our troubles."

"Fine," Gellar said, raising his hand in submission. "I get your point. I just don't see how getting involved with this girl's problems is going to help us."

"Our visit to the market showed us a couple of things for sure. First, Dovan's a thug and runs Fishtown with a heavy hand."

"Not too different from the way Saryn seems to run Cylmar," Stumpy said.

Fipple sneered. "That's not surprising. When you have corruption at the top, it tends to breed more of the same. Get rid of Saryn and his ilk, and you'd probably see a whole new Cylmar."

He was right. I just had to look at Rockslide and Avalanche as examples of corruption seeping down from those in charge. Were all the kids living in those tribes thugs and bullies, or was that a product of how they were being raised? Obviously, it was their upbringing. We had taken in numerous members from each of these tribes and found that they could function within our larger extended family without reverting to old habits.

"Second," I said, "even though it's clear Dovan and the rest of his circle of captains fear the soldiers enough to not push a conflict between them, it'll be best if we don't wear our uniforms around the lake. Last thing we need is a full-blown conflict, which means we will need to split our group once again. While some of us scout the overlord's estate, the rest can visit the docks to see how difficult it'll be to barter passage downriver."

"I vote to go to the docks," Waylen said eagerly as he undid the rest of the buttons on the front of his trousers and released a heavy sigh. "I can't wear this thing a moment longer." With that, he shot from the room, holding the front of his pants closed with his hands, not even bothering to close the door on his way out.

Barthol and a couple of the others chuckled.

There was a knock on our door frame, and we turned to find Jasna and Mirna standing with trays of food and drink. Mirna was staring rather wide-eyed after Waylen.

"Come in, come in," I said, quickly gathering up the parchment to get it out of the way as Barthol and Gellar rushed to take the trays from the two ladies and place them on the table.

"Cook says it was one of the finest fishes he's prepared," Jasna said with a proud smile as she wiped her hair back from her face.

"It certainly smells that way," Stumpy said, leaning over the bowls to take a whiff.

"Nothing fancy," she said, "but there's plenty of meat in the chowder."

I turned to Mirna, who was standing quietly by the door. "How are the soldiers behaving?"

She hmphed, though I could sense her discomfort as she looked at

my eyes. "As well as you can expect. I fed them their lunch earlier. I hope whatever business you have is finished quickly. We need those men gone from here."

"We're doing our best."

"Well, do it faster. If they are ever discovered, our lives won't be worth a pinch of salt."

"I promise you, when we're through, you'll never have to worry about them again."

She didn't exactly look relieved, but she did leave us to our meal.

"Is there anything else you need?" Jasna asked, moving out of the doorway as Waylen found his way back in, now dressed in his regular garb.

I looked at Jasna. "I think we have what we need. Everything looks delicious. Thank you."

She nodded with a smile and shut the door on her way out.

I listened for her footsteps down the hall before turning back around. "That does smell good." I returned to my seat, and we finished off our meal. The chowder was quite excellent. Best meal we had eaten since leaving the tinkers.

Afterward, we placed the dishes back on the trays and left them on one of the beds while I unrolled our map once again. I pointed to a spot in the northwestern section. "This is the overlord's keep." It was represented by a small depiction of a stone tower. "It's located on Rodon Hill, the highest point in Ecrin. Jasna says that you can see the entire city from the upper ramparts."

"It's also heavily guarded," Fipple added. "Cylmaran soldiers on the outside and Saryn's personal guard on the inside."

"That sounds like a lovely place to visit," Gellar grumbled, his face pinched tight as he studied the map.

Barthol crossed his arms. "A great place to get yourself captured."

"Regardless," I said, "we need to see it for ourselves." I turned to Stumpy.

He sighed. "Yes, I know. You want me and the recruit here to go with Waylen to Fishtown."

I smiled. "You read my mind."

Dakaran smiled as well.

"And I guess you'll want me with you?" Fipple said.

I nodded. "You are the one Cylmaran among us." I looked at Barthol and Gellar. "I'll let you choose who wants to go where. One of you can go with me and Fipple, the other can go to the docks. Just remember, whoever goes to the docks needs to leave their uniforms behind." I started to turn but then stopped. "Oh, I almost forgot. How did it go at the garrison? Anything we need to know?"

"Nothing to speak of," Barthol said. "Using Jasna's directions, it wasn't too difficult to find. We didn't go inside, but from what we could see through the gate, it looks as though the majority of the troops are out roaming the city."

"Or assigned to border watch," Waylen added. "The border patrol on the Elondrian side did tell us that there was an unusually high number of Cylmaran troops moving up and down the Pyruvian. And the tinkers told us they'd seen several clusters of troops heading up and down the main roadways."

"The point is," Barthol said, "that the garrison looked about as sparse as our dining hall on an Eighthday evening."

I frowned. An empty garrison only reaffirmed what we already knew, and that was that the soldiers were everywhere, which would make it difficult for us to move about the city unnoticed. I rolled the map and handed it to Stumpy. "Your group can have this one. We'll take the other." I took one last look around the room to see if I was missing anything, then headed for the door. "Those coming with me, grab your gear."

WILDFIRE

## Chapter 13

HE STREETS WERE JUST as crowded as they had been earlier this morning. I was starting to wonder if it would have
been more advantageous to have remained on foot. I was used
to blending in with the crowd, moving through the city with the natural
flow of the people. I didn't like sitting so high above everyone, making
myself an easy target. The benefit, however, was that we were easy to
spot, and most did their best to get out of the way.

Fipple, Barthol, and I reached the center of Ecrin with little trouble,
only having to refer to the map twice. From there, instead of heading
east toward the docks, we kept north on the main road.

"The city's bigger than I would have thought," Barthol commented
as we passed the last of the merchant shops and headed into what appeared to be a residential area.

"Too big for its own good," Fipple mumbled.

The streets on the north side seemed to be fewer in number, or maybe it was just that they were wider and less traveled. It reminded me of the differences between the north and south quarters of Aramoor. The buildings were definitely in better shape, clearly belonging to those of the upper classes, if there was such a thing in Cylmar. Most people were dressed about the same. From what I could tell, unlike Aramoor, there was no high fashion. The people of Ecrin didn't seem to see a need in dolling themselves up, something I could respect. Many of those in Aramoor took caring about their appearance to the extreme.

The one main difference from the poorer quarters was that the people in the northern half of Ecrin didn't seem quite so hesitant in our presence. No one smiled or tipped their hat, but neither did they take off running.

The buildings grew in height the closer we got to Rodon Hill, and the streets began to slant upward. We stopped in the shade of a building on our right to get a better look at the map. My nerves began to prickle. It was pent-up energy buried deep in my gut that always swelled whenever I was about to undertake something dangerous. Needless to say, it was a feeling I had grown quite accustomed to.

"We're close," I said, leaning far enough over for both Barthol and Fipple to see where I was pointing. "We can't be more than five or six streets away."

"I'd say closer," Barthol said, motioning with his head to a troop of Cylmaran soldiers marching their way down the street toward us. "Either that or there's another garrison around here that's not listed on the map."

I quickly rolled up the parchment and stuffed it back in the tube tied to my horse's saddle. With a nod, I nudged the horse with my boot, and we started forward. We passed the soldiers from the opposite side of the street, doing our best not to look in their direction.

Pretty soon the topmost bulwark of the overlord's keep came into

view. The ramparts were dotted with guards in solid black uniforms, very different from the red and black of the soldiers patrolling the front of the keep, which meant I was going to need a different outfit.

We stopped on the side of the road that fronted Overlord Saryn's estate. It was nothing like the sprawling palace at Aramoor. It was built more like a medium-sized castle, though the wall surrounding the keep was barely higher than the wall surrounding the Temple back home. In fact, if I stood in my stirrups, I could make out most of the buildings on the other side. At the heart of the estate, surrounded by towers, was a tall rectangular block building with a crenelated roof. It was made entirely of the same grey stone used for the buildings along the waterfront and was very similar to Dovan's house, though built on a much grander scale. I was delighted to see that the stonework was offset, making it much easier to climb.

Fipple pointed toward the front gate and the company of mounted soldiers passing through as they made their way back out to the road. They turned in our direction and slowly rode down the street, passing us without so much as a glance. Standing at attention in front of the gate was a row of footmen holding long halberds similar to the ones carried by the palace guards back in Aramoor.

The place seemed well-guarded. Even from this distance, I could still see the heads of the black-uniformed men looking out over the crenelated ramparts.

"Not the easiest place to break into, it appears," Fipple said with a sneer as he stared up at the overlord's estate.

Barthol glanced my way. "It's like you keep reminding us. As long as we act like we belong, they'll think we do."

I smiled at the reference, though it made me want to sigh. I didn't feel much like a leader at the moment. In fact, I felt like that same thirteen-year-old who'd made his way into the royal palace to save his tribe without having the first clue where to go or what to do when I got there. We had no idea if the ambassador was even being kept in the castle.

Unfortunately, other than the uniforms we had garnered, Ratko and his men had been of little help. They had no idea where the ambassador was being held, and not a single one of them had ever stepped foot inside the overlord's keep.

"We need to get some information."

"And how do you suggest we do that?" Fipple asked. "Walk over there and strike up a conversation?"

Barthol grunted. "If you want to join the ambassador and his wife."

"Perhaps we could wait until some of the castle guards get off duty," I suggested.

Barthol smiled. "Put a tankard in their hands and they'll prattle on like a fishwife."

"It's a good idea in theory," Fipple said, "but have either of you seen one of these guards walking about the city? The only time I've ever seen them is here on the castle grounds. What if they don't leave?"

"Surely they have to leave at some point. What about their families?"

Fipple huffed. "Knowing Saryn, he could have chosen them specifically for the fact that they don't have any."

I looked up at the bulwarks once more. If Fipple was correct, that was going to be another big wrinkle in our effort to save the ambassador.

"What do you want to do now?" Barthol asked, twisting in his saddle to get a look at the road behind us.

"Get a better look while we can."

We turned down the street that fronted the overlord's estate and started around the outer perimeter. I studied the layout—where the windows were, which ones were closest to the ground, and which had lights on inside. The latter was a little harder to determine, as the sun was still high enough in the sky to keep the towers bathed in light.

I was able to see which windows were open and which were shut, a good indicator as to which rooms were being used. I studied the walls all the way around, looking for the best entry point, one that was tucked away enough to be hidden in shadow and had architectural designs that would make for better hand- and footholds.

After two complete passes, I decided that the tower on the western side was the best option. Not only was the back side of it nestled against the rest of the castle in a way that would be mostly hidden from the road, but its windows were the closest to the ground and had no glass or shutters. There was a slight ledge running just underneath, certainly wide enough to grip if I could find a grapple. And that particular portion of the wall was covered in thick creepers, which would make it easier to scale.

Yes, that was definitely the spot.

The problem, however, was going to be the grapple. I had no idea how difficult it might be to find one, or worse, get one commissioned to be made. I was sure any smithy worth his salt could forge one, but how long would it take and how much would it cost? I could have kicked myself for not thinking to bring my own, but Overcaptain Tolin hadn't exactly given us a chance to grab equipment before we left Aramoor.

I hopped off my horse and took a small piece of cloth from my saddlebag, which I cut even smaller with my belt knife. I waited until no one was coming and quickly walked over to the wall and tucked it in between a couple of the offset stones, where the mortar was thinnest, to mark the location for later. Hopefully no one would spot the material and take it out. Mounting, we made our way back to Canal Street.

"See what you needed to?" Barthol asked as we finished our second round and stopped at the road we'd ridden in on.

"I believe so." I twisted in my saddle and took one last look at the front gate.

The hairs on the back of my neck suddenly rose, and I spun back around. I scanned the street ahead, staring at each house, the windows, doors, alleyways between, looking for something, anything as to why I was feeling a sense of warning. But no matter how hard I looked, I couldn't find the reason. There were a few pedestrians walking along the sidewalk, but not a soldier in sight.

"What's wrong?" Barthol asked as he and Fipple stared down the street. "What are you looking at?"

"Ever get that feeling like you're being watched?"

Barthol shivered. "I'm feeling it now."

"To be honest, there's been few times since crossing into Cylmar when I *didn't* feel like I was being watched." With a shrug, I nudged my horse, and we started back down the road. "Let's get back to the Ram's Head. We've got some soldiers to question."

It was a fairly quick trip back across town, or at least it seemed faster now that we were better acquainted with the city and knew more of where we were going. We were the first back to the inn. The others were no doubt still working their way along the waterfront, looking for possible passage out of Ecrin.

"You look thirsty," Jasna said, meeting us at the back stairs after she saw us come in. She was holding a tray of empty mugs.

The common room was barely a quarter filled, which wasn't too unusual, since it was the middle of the day, and we still had a couple hours until supper. Those that were inside were busy sipping on their ale and chatting quietly amongst themselves. Most were probably travelers who, like us, had gotten rooms for the night and didn't want to take the chance of getting lost in Ecrin, which wasn't hard to do. Just step outside and you'd be lost before you made it around the block.

"Any peep from the soldiers?"

Jasna shook her head, but I could see the worried look in her eyes at

the mention of the men tied up in the cellar.

"I can make them peep," Fipple said with a surprising hint of eagerness.

All three of us turned and stared.

"What?" He shrugged. "You want information. I'm sure there's something they haven't told us yet. If so, I can get it."

"Fine, but don't take it too far. I don't want to go down there and find you've been cutting them or something." I turned to Jasna, suddenly anxious for her to leave before she started getting that same worried look about us. "I believe we'll have those ales after all. Oh," I said, catching her before she left. "Do you happen to know where we might find a smithy who crafts odd equipment like large hooks?"

"How large?"

I spread my hands apart to give her an idea.

"You mean like a grapple? Every boat in the docks has one. Best way to hop from one ship to the next. Also good for larger catches."

I smiled. Well, that was easy. "Yes. Where could I purchase one?"

"There's a couple smithies that service Fishtown. I can show you which are the best."

"After the welcome we received from Dovan, I think it best you stay as far away from there as possible."

"But if you don't let me go, they'll rob you blind. Fishtown doesn't have much love for the soldiers, as you saw, so if you try purchasing from them, there's no telling what you'll get and for how much."

The last thing I needed was a softly forged grapple that would split while I was halfway up a wall. I sighed but eventually gave in. "Fine. But only if we stay off the main roads." If I asked her to just tell me which one I needed to see, she would have come up with another reason why she had to be there, or she might have just outright refused to tell me.

"I know a back way through the market."

"Do you think Mirna will be able to spare you?"

She turned and looked at the mostly empty common room. "I think she can handle it. Besides, Kelsi is planning on being here for the supper crowd."

"Is she feeling better?"

Jasna nodded. "Wait here. I'll go tell Mirna." She took off across the common room before I could stop her to tell her I needed to change out of my uniform first.

I turned to Barthol and Fipple. "Think you can handle questioning the prisoners on your own?"

"We're Room Eleven," Barthol said with a raised brow.

Fipple simply smiled and patted his belt knife.

I looked at Barthol. "Keep an eye on him."

Barthol smiled and put a hand on Fipple's shoulder. "I won't let him get too carried away."

Conversations inside came to a halt as the patrons watched Barthol and Fipple make their way over to the door on the left, leading down to the cellar. It wasn't until they were inside and the door shut that talking resumed. A couple of tables cleared out as their occupants headed for the stairs at the front of the common room.

It didn't take long before Jasna shot out of the kitchen and scooted across the room with a bright smile, her apron no longer tied around her waist. "Mirna said I can go."

"You'll have to wait for me," I said. "I need to change out of this uniform. Don't want to walk around Fishtown wearing it."

"Good idea. I'll wait for you here."

I nodded and headed up the stairs to my room, which was a bit of a mess, as Dakaran's stuff was scattered across half the floor, the chair, and the table. Hurriedly, I pulled off my uniform and redressed into my common street clothes, then headed back down to the first floor, where

Jasna was patiently sitting on the bottom step waiting.

She stood when she heard me coming and gave me a quick looking-over. "That's nice," she said, pointing at my ring.

"It was my father's. It's the symbol for my clan."

"Oh? What clan is that?"

I smiled. "One you've never heard of, I'm sure."

When she saw she wasn't going to get more out of me, we headed out the back, through the alleyway, and over to the stables. The afternoon sun was warm, but I raised my hood, regardless. This time, I saddled my own horse. No sense in riding one of the soldiers' horses when I wasn't in uniform. Leaving the inn, we headed toward the center of Ecrin, but before we reached the main merchant district, Jasna had us taking a street to the right. She said it would get us into the market without walking through the center of Fishtown.

The narrow road wound through a small residential community with buildings close enough to string clotheslines between. Each line was filled as the residents sought to dry what the rain had soaked the previous day. Before long, I spotted the water ahead, and the road ended against the far side of the docks.

"We can tie up here and go the rest of the way on foot," she said, alighting from the horse before I could offer her my hand. "It's too small for a horse to fit through anyway."

I climbed down and tied the reins to one of several metal rings fastened to a stone wall that divided the upper docks from the lower. A glance over the side showed it was at least a six- or seven-foot drop down to the cobbled lane below. I thought about grabbing the map from the saddlebag to keep from losing it or having it stolen, but then I remembered I hadn't brought it, since Jasna was with me. So, with nothing else of value to lose except the horse itself, I followed her across the street and into the ramshackle buildings, tents, and booths that was Fishtown.

She was light on her feet and certainly knew her way around the half-thrown-together stalls, as she ducked under tarps, skirted fallen sections of plank boards, and hopped across overturned barrels of something that had me holding my breath as we passed. Pretty soon, I was completely turned around and doing everything I could just to keep up. If I lost sight of her, I'd never find my way back out.

Above the ruckus and clamor of vendors calling out for customers to buy their catch, I could hear the familiar clanging of metal against metal. The noise grew the closer we got to a large stall at the end of one of the rows. Sparks flew as the smith bent over a piece of long steel on top of his anvil. I had no idea what it was to become, but it looked like it had a ways to go yet.

The walls around his stall were lined with a variety of nautical items, like pieces of metal rigging, small boat anchors, harpoon tips. There were also several buckets of fashioned nails of various sizes, along with a row of hammers and mallets. A table on the right was filled with knives, axe heads, and scythes, all ready for peening and whetting. There was even a piece of what appeared to be the undercarriage of a wagon just beside his shop. I didn't see anything that resembled a grapple, though.

As soon as the man spotted Jasna, he smiled and struck a few more blows to the rod he was shaping before tossing it in a bucket on the side. Steam shot into the air, and the metal hissed as it made contact with the water.

"You shouldn't be here, Jasna. If your father caught me letting you anywhere near the market, he'd hang me from the yardarm by my toes." He lifted one of his sandaled feet, revealing he was missing some toes. "And you know I've only got a few good ones left."

She folded her arms. "And if you don't start putting on some boots while you work, Stanis," she countered, "you're going to lose the rest. You'd think you'd have learned your lesson the last time you dropped a

piece of hot steel."

The smith smiled and lowered his leg. His smile dropped, however, when he noticed me standing in the shadows of the booth beside his. "Is he with you?" His eyes narrowed. "Does your father know?"

"Know what?" She turned and looked at me. "Oh, it's not like that. He's a guest at the Ram's Head and was looking for a smithy. I told him you were the best. He's looking for a large hook."

"A grapple, actually," I said, taking a step forward but keeping my hood raised to cover my eyes. I scanned the nearby stalls, looking to see if anyone was coming this way, also looking to see if I spotted any of Dovan's men. Not that I would have recognized them, apart from them being better dressed than the rest of the people working here. It also helped that most of the workers tended to vacate their booths in a hurry if they were around.

Stanis pursed his lips. "I might have a few fishing grapples in the back. I'll check." He looked hesitant to leave me alone with Jasna, which I guess was only natural. I did look like a rather shady character, standing in the shadows with my hood raised. He walked into a small stone building just off his work area.

Looking around, we appeared to be a few rows over from the main street that ran through the center of Fishtown. There was a lot of foot traffic moving up and down the thoroughfare, and some even broke off in our direction as customers moved from one booth to the next, looking at wares. Most of the booths on the larger streets were for selling fish, while those on the outskirts were for other things like rigging and supplies.

"He's a good man when you get to know him," Jasna said, walking over to stand by me while we waited for Stanis to find a hook. "Just protective."

"Nothing wrong with that. Good to have people who—"

"I have two left," Stanis said, stepping out of his shop.

I kept my head lowered to try hiding my eyes as he walked over and held the two grapples out for me to inspect.

"That one there," I said, pointing to the hook on the left. They both had four teeth, but while the one on the right had its hooks bent inward to a very fine point, the one on the left was spread in a way that stood a better chance of snagging a stone lip and holding. I took the hook and felt its weight. It was a little heavier than I was used to, but certainly workable. "Do you have a coil of rope I could purchase?"

Stanis looked at me like I'd lost my mind. "This is Fishtown. Of course I have rope." He walked over to the door of his shop, leaned in to grab something off the wall, then came back out with a coil of rope. "That'll be eight coppers."

"*Eight* coppers?" Jasna hmphed.

"Fine. Six. And that's my final offer."

I tried not to smile as I dug around in my pouch and produced the payment.

"Now, I suggest you get home, young lady, before Dovan or any of his ilk spot you."

"Yeah, had a run-in with him earlier," she said hesitantly.

"And you came back?" He looked at me. "I hope that hook is worth it."

"So do I."

We started to leave, but a small commotion near the main road had us turning back around. Someone was apparently yelling at one of the vendors. I couldn't see who it was, since we were several booths away, and their words were garbled.

"That sounds like . . ." Jasna shot forward, but Stanis grabbed her by the arm and held her back.

"It can't be," Stanis said, a worried look on his face as they both tried

to see through the crowded aisle. "Your father knows better than to come down here."

After another round of shouting, both Jasna's and Stanis's faces darkened.

"It *is* Father."

# WILDFIRE

## Chapter 14

ASNA TRIED PULLING OUT of Stanis's grip, but she was no match for the smith's powerful hands.

"Stay here while I go have a look," he said to her. "If it is your father, you aren't going to do him any good if Dovan's men grab you too." He looked at me. "Keep her here."

I nodded and started forward, but before I could get close enough, she kicked Stanis in the shin and took off running down the side lane for the main road.

Stanis shouted and chased after her, and I ran after them both. The main street was packed with people crowding around to see what was going on. I shot past Stanis and through the crowd, just managing to get my hands on Jasna's cloak before she reached the street.

I stopped her as we broke through the throng, catching a glimpse of the scene ahead.

"Father!"

I put my hand over her mouth.

A tall man with a thick brown beard, circles under his bloodshot eyes, and clothes that looked to have been slept in for several days, turned in our direction. He staggered forward a step or two, scanning the crowd. He had a half-empty bottle in one hand and a long belt knife in the other. He blinked several times as though having a hard time seeing who was standing in front of him.

I kept my hand over Jasna's mouth and pulled her back into the crowd. The last thing we needed was for Dovan and his men to catch both of them.

"Zlatin, you shouldn't be here." Pradjic, her father's former first mate, rubbed his hands nervously as he glanced cautiously about.

"Where's Jasna?" Zlatin asked, his speech slurred. "What have you done with her?"

"We need to get your father off the street," I said, "before Dovan shows up." I knew the best chance we had of making that happen was Jasna. "If I release you, can you bring him over here?"

Jasna nodded.

"All right. Bring him over here so we can sneak him out the back." I started to release her, but a familiar voice broke through the crowd.

"I thought I recognized that voice," Dovan said. The head of the Fisher Guild, along with three other men—all armed—made their way out onto the street from the opposite side.

Zlatin turned, and when he caught sight of Dovan, he raised his knife with a shaky hand. "Where's my daughter? I heard she was here."

Dovan smiled. "Yes, and I told you both what would happen if I were to catch you here again."

Pradjic walked over to Zlatin and put his hand on his shoulder. "Zlatin, you need to go. Jasna's safe. She isn't here."

Zlatin pushed Pradjic back. "I don't need no help from you." He turned back to Dovan. "You're a coward and an oath breaker, and it's high time someone put you in your place."

Pradjic tried to pull Zlatin back toward the booth, but Jasna's father shoved him backward with enough force to nearly send Pradjic on his backside. Zlatin then turned to face Dovan.

At this, Jasna jerked free of my grasp and darted through the crowd before I could grab her.

"I told you to hold on to her," Stanis hissed, watching as she broke out into the street and ran over to where her father was standing. "Is that your knife she's holding?"

My hand went to my side. Sure enough, my dagger was gone. "Stupid girl."

A small voice in my head wondered if she hadn't planned this all along to force me to help.

Dovan grinned. "Well, what do we have here? Father and daughter at last." He and the other three captains drew their swords. "You two have been a hook in my side long enough."

"You got another blade on ya, son?" Stanis asked, having left his shop in a hurry without grabbing anything useful.

I handed him my boot knife.

He stared at it a moment. "Got anything bigger?"

Zlatin tried to push Jasna away, but when she refused to move, he turned to Dovan. "What's wrong, Dovan, too scared to face me on your own like a man?"

"Fool's going to get himself killed," Stanis said. "Going to get us all killed."

I glanced over at Pradjic, but he and the men didn't seem to be willing to make a move. From what Jasna had said, if they did, they'd likely lose their positions, which meant their families would go hungry.

Zlatin, who was standing rather wobble-legged in the middle of the road with his knife and bottle, waited on the other three to come to him, Jasna right beside him.

I reminded myself I hadn't come to Ecrin to right a wrong done to some local fish captain. I was here to rescue the Elondrian ambassador and his wife. I sighed and reached for my sword. Who was I kidding? With Jasna out there, I didn't have much choice.

The three captains spread out in front of Zlatin and Jasna. Her father was a big man, but he was also outnumbered, outweaponed, and drunk. If I didn't do something now, they were going to cut him down before he even realized the mistake he'd made, then turn on her. I grabbed Stanis by the front of his tunic and dragged him out onto the street.

"What are you doing?" he hissed as I pulled him toward Jasna and her father.

The three captains stopped, and Dovan pointed at me with his sword. "Who's this?"

Zlatin turned his head and startled when he realized I was standing beside him. "Who are you?"

"Someone trying to keep you alive." I snatched my knife back from Jasna and handed her over to Stanis. "Get her out of here." I couldn't stay focused if I was being forced to worry about both her and her father.

"Keep him safe!" she shouted at me as Stanis quickly hustled her back off the road and into the crowd.

Zlatin sneered. "I can fight my own battles."

"You couldn't fight your way out of bed in your state."

"Who do you think you are?" Dovan bellowed. "This is none of your affair."

"I beg to differ."

Dovan's mouth tightened. "Do you know who I am?" Before I could answer with a clever quip, he roared, "I'm Dovan. I run Fishtown. How far do you think you're going to get, you and this pathetic excuse for a boat captain? Look at you, Zlatin, a midday drunkard who lost his daughter." Dovan laughed. "It's a wonder you didn't lose your trousers on the way over here."

"I'm right here, Dovan!" Zlatin spat. "You gonna fish or cut bait?"

Dovan sneered and looked at his men. "Kill them!"

The three captains raised their swords and started forward once more, slower than before, but still determined.

Beside me, Zlatin raised his long dagger and quarter-full bottle. "I've been waiting for this a long time," he shouted and charged straight at the first man.

The other two men and I were so amazed at Zlatin's tenacity that none of us moved as we watched the other two clash. I don't know how, but Zlatin managed to hold the other man off with nothing but his long knife and bottle, and eventually cracked it over the man's head, momentarily stunning him enough to stick his knife in the man's gut. The man screamed and went down.

The other two attacked while my attention was distracted. With a slight nudge from my magic, I shifted positions, and the first blade missed as I deflected the second. I wasn't in the mood to play around, so I sliced the wrist of the first man and stuck my dagger through the leg of the second.

Both hobbled backward, cursing and spitting.

This was our chance to go for Dovan. I had only intended to keep Jasna's father alive, but if I was able to take the head of the Fisher Guild down, it might open up doors for our mission.

Before I could do anything about it, Dovan grabbed a whistle from around his neck and blew. The high-pitched shrill echoed off the booths around us, and within seconds, more than a dozen men pushed through the crowd to form a protective line in front of Dovan.

My hopes of finishing Dovan off quickly were flung overboard. Now it was all about getting the two of us out of there with our heads still attached.

The people who'd been watching from the sides of the street quickly moved back, not wanting to get swept up in what appeared to be our execution.

Zlatin spat. "You're a coward, Dovan! You don't deserve to be the head of anything."

The man was surprisingly articulate for someone who could barely stand. He turned and looked at the surrounding booths and those inside. "Well, are you just going to stand there?"

"Kill them!" Dovan shouted, and I jumped in front of Zlatin, who still had his back turned as a dozen men with swords and cleavers and boat pikes charged straight for us.

"Turn around, you fool!" I shouted at Jasna's father as I dodged and ducked and wove my way around the first four or five attackers, cutting and slashing and stabbing at everything that came within my sword's reach. My movements were precise. They had to be. One wrong step and I wouldn't get a second chance, even with my magic.

I ducked under another sword and stuck mine through the top of a man's foot. He squealed and fell backward, knocking another aside. Beside me, Zlatin took a knife to his arm but then headbutted the man in the face. Blood shot from a broken nose, and the man hollered as Zlatin kneed him between the legs, and he went down.

I cut the legs out from under two more as I darted back and forth between their swings, their swords whooshing by my head. Even with my magic, I could see it wasn't going to be enough as more of Dovan's cutmen poured into the street around us.

I dodged and spun, blocking as fast as I could. If I'd had just a spare second, I would have replaced my dagger with one of the fallen men's swords, but I didn't have the chance. I took a cut to the left arm. The pain was sharp, but I couldn't lose focus. It wasn't bad, but it was either that or spin the other direction and take a pike to the chest.

This battle was lost before it had begun. Me and my stupid sense of honor. I wouldn't have been in this situation if I hadn't been trying to help Jasna. And now her problems were going to get me killed.

Zlatin took a knife to his shoulder and hollered.

I tried to reach him, but I was pinned down. It was taking everything I had to keep from joining him. I could feel the warm blood running down my arm, which meant sooner or later my movements were going to slow, and I was going to make a mistake. There was another shout on my right, and I turned. It wasn't Zlatin.

It was . . . Pradjic! He was fighting to reach Zlatin, several of those from his booth rushing in to help.

Suddenly, the entire fish market erupted as men and women charged out from their booths to fight alongside us. The crowd ran, scattering into the booths and empty lanes between to keep from getting killed as more of Dovan's men joined the fight, which was now a full-on battle.

It was all I could do not to laugh. I'd been in Ecrin two days and found myself in the middle of a street war. What were the odds?

I kicked a fisherman in the gut and buried the top of my sword halfway through his thigh while using my dagger to block another man's swing for my head. I was nearing the far side of the street but found myself completely surrounded. I had no idea who was who; they all looked the same. The only difference being the direction the people were standing. Those facing me, I fought, while those facing the general direction I was, I left alone.

I fought my way to the right, trying to reach Jasna's father. I'd barely managed to get within ten feet when I saw he was locked in battle with Dovan himself. Both men's faces were filled with rage, but Dovan's

seemed to be mingled with a sense of desperation that Zlatin's didn't have. There wasn't much left of Zlatin's bottle but the neck, which came to a jagged edge.

My magic struck, and I spun to the left just as the tip of a fisher's pike flew by. I grabbed the end and yanked the man holding it forward off his feet. With a swift jab, I rammed the butt end back into his gut, forcing him to double over, then kneed him in the face, and he went down.

Those around moved back to give the two captains space. Both sides seemed to pull back at the same time, seeing as how all of this hinged on these two men in the first place. It was clear only one was going to be walking away. I only wished Zlatin had been in better form, but drunk or not, the man was going toe-to-toe with the head of the Fisher Guild with nothing but a long knife, a broken bottle, and the determination to get justice for what had been done to him and his family.

Stanis appeared out of nowhere beside me, with Jasna in tow. This time she wasn't fighting him. She seemed to realize the importance of letting her father finish what he'd started.

The two men fought back and forth, blood on both from several cuts and stabs, but neither was willing to give in. Zlatin staggered and lost his footing and went down to one knee, managing to grab a fallen sword before Dovan could finish him.

Jasna started forward, but Stanis held her back. "You'll get him killed, young missy. Best let him be."

I wanted to jump in myself and put a quick end to it, but if I did, Zlatin would never forgive me. This was a fight he needed to finish himself, drunk or not.

Dovan caught Zlatin's forearm, forcing him back a couple of steps. Surprisingly, Zlatin managed to hold on to his sword, but the blood on his arm said he wouldn't be holding it for long.

Dovan smiled and lunged.

Zlatin staggered to the right, bringing the sword up high enough to keep from getting skewered. With one swift motion, he spun and rammed what was left of his bottle into Dovan's gut.

Dovan gasped and staggered backward, the neck of the bottle sticking from his waist. Dovan pulled the bottle from his stomach. It was covered in blood. He looked around at all those staring at him, realizing, perhaps for the first time, that he was standing alone. He snarled and raised his sword. It was clear he wasn't going to quit until one or both of them were dead. He lunged, but his feet were unsteady.

Zlatin slapped Dovan's sword away with his hand and buried his own in Dovan's chest. Dovan's eyes widened, and he stumbled back, staring down at the hilt as though not quite believing what he was seeing. He dropped to his knees, blood dripping from the corners of his mouth. He opened it to say something, but then his eyes went lifeless, and he slumped over.

Dovan's men turned and ran, disappearing back inside the booths on the other side. Some of those in the market gave chase, but I had a feeling they wouldn't be seeing their faces around these parts ever again.

Stanis released Jasna, and she ran for her father, catching him as he, too, dropped to his knees, his legs too weak to hold him up any longer. The captains and crew of the fish market gathered around.

"Stand back," Pradjic said, still holding a bloody sword in one hand, as if expecting more of Dovan's men to come rushing in at the last minute. "Give the man room to breathe."

I wasn't sure how Zlatin was supposed to breathe with Jasna's arms wrapped around his neck like a vise, but he didn't seem to mind. In fact, he was beaming as he sat there with his arms around her.

"You might want to get these bodies out of here before the soldiers arrive," I said, looking around at the dead and wounded. "A skirmish

this big is going to draw attention."

Pradjic turned. "He's right." He looked at those gathered around. "Let's clear the street, and quick."

The people spread out and began lifting bodies and weapons. The dead they toted to the right, down one of the larger passageways off the main road. The wounded, they took left. Perhaps there was a physicker nearby.

I started to walk over to help Zlatin to his feet, but Pradjic and Stanis beat me to it, each grabbing an arm and hefting him up. He winced, blood from his wounds soaking his tunic. There was also a nasty gash above his left eye. Jasna was there with a moist cloth, doing her best to clean the wounds, even as he tried reassuring her that he was fine and there was nothing to worry about.

They carried him over to the booth Pradjic had been manning and placed him in a chair under a canvas overhang.

Zlatin looked up and put his hand on Pradjic's arm. "Forgive me, old friend, for what I said. I—"

Pradjic waved him off. "It is nothing. I only regret it took a stranger to force us to do what should have been done a long time ago." He looked over at me, where I was standing at the edge of the booth, my hood still raised, and nodded. "Though it cost us dearly," he added, glancing out at the road, where those who had survived the conflict were still collecting bodies.

The sight of the dead ate at me. Perhaps all of this could have been avoided if I had simply tried kidnapping the man in the middle of the night instead of causing a bloody street war. However, the more I thought about it, the more I realized there really wasn't any other outcome I could have created. One way or the other, it would have come to bloodshed. It was as if fate had pushed me here. I only hoped it had a reason.

"A high price, indeed," Zlatin said with a heavy sigh, then leaned forward to look past Pradjic over to where I was standing. "I owe you my life, sir, and I don't even know your name."

Pradjic took a step back to give Zlatin a clear view.

"You owe me nothing. I just happened to be in the right place at the right time."

"Fish guts," Zlatin said. "No one puts his life on the line for someone they don't even know. Who are you?"

"He's with me, Father," Jasna said, drawing a whole different kind of look from Zlatin, who suddenly found the strength to stand.

"With you?"

I groaned inwardly. She certainly had a way of intensifying a situation. "My companions and I are guests at the Ram's Head. Your daughter was kind enough to show me where the docks were, as we might be looking for passage. We were purchasing some tools from Stanis when the fight broke out."

Zlatin looked at Stanis, and the smithy nodded. "He speaks the truth. Jasna brought him to me for a boat hook."

Zlatin looked at Jasna, his face tightening. "You know better than to be coming down here."

Jasna lowered her head slightly. "How did you find out?"

"Your sister went by the inn earlier, and Mirna mentioned something about the fish market."

Jasna gritted her teeth. "I told her not to say anything."

"Don't blame Mirna. She was worried."

Jasna started to say something, then thought better of it.

Zlatin sighed. "What's done is done." He looked at me. "It seems I owe you my life. How can I repay such a debt?"

My head lifted. I knew the honorable thing would be to release him from that debt, but this was the opportunity I'd been hoping for. "Do

you think me, and those traveling with me, might secure passage down-river?"

"I'd say it's the least we can do," Zlatin said, then looked at his daughter and the way she was looking at me, and his eyes narrowed. "How soon do you wish to set sail?"

I looked at Zlatin. "We have some business here in town, but I expect it will be a swift transaction, and then we will need to set sail immediately. To be honest, depending on how the meeting goes, it might need to be sooner rather than later." I glanced down the street toward the docks. I hadn't thought about it until then, but I wondered if my roommates had been at the docks when the fighting broke out. I had a feeling they would have come looking if they were. They must have already gone back to the inn.

Zlatin stared at me a moment, his eyes seemingly no longer glossed over from whatever he'd been drinking. "I see. And where is it you will need passage to?"

I looked around at all the curious faces, not feeling safe with divulging our destination in front of a crowd. "South."

He looked at me and frowned. "That's not much to go on."

"I'm afraid that's all I have to give at the moment."

Zlatin looked at Pradjic, who shrugged in response, then back at me. "Very well," he said, his face suddenly brightening. "I'd have sailed you around the entire coast of Aldor if it meant getting my ships back." He looked once more out at the main street running through the heart of Fishtown. "You've done more good here than you know."

Stanis took a step forward and put his arm around Zlatin, whose legs were beginning to wobble. "Let's get you to a healer before you bleed to death."

"Aye," Pradjic said. "We can look after things here till you return. I'm sure the captains are going to want to hold forum on setting up a new council now that Dovan and most of his captains are no longer around."

"And I have business to attend to," I said, taking a step toward the booth's entrance. "I promise to do my best to give you notice before we leave."

"Are you going back to the inn?" Jasna asked, leaving her father long enough to walk over.

"I was planning on it."

"Here, let me take a look at that."

I looked down, spotting the run of blood down my arm. I'd all but forgotten about it.

Jasna grabbed a wet cloth, some wrapping, and a knife from one of the tables. Walking over, she cut back part of my shirt and cleaned the wound. I tried not to wince as she ran the cloth over the cut. It wasn't deep enough to need sewing, but it was enough to burn. After wiping up what she could, she wrapped the arm tight, which seemed to stop the flow.

"Thank you."

"It's the least I could do."

Seeing the torn sleeve reminded me of one of the reasons I'd come into town in the first place. "I'm looking to find a good coat if you know of any decent tailors."

"I can take you to some shops," she said, but then paused and glanced back over her shoulder toward her father, who was watching us with a scrutinizing glare.

"No. You need to stay with him. Just give me the names of the shops and where they are, and I can find them. I'm starting to get a better feel for the city now."

She smiled. "Are you sure?"

I nodded, and she told me where to go.

# WILDFIRE

## Chapter 15

I LEFT THE FISH MARKET feeling rather good about myself. Not only had I survived a street war I had no business being in the middle of, but I had walked away with the promise of passage downriver for me and my roommates, and hopefully the Elondrian ambassador and his wife . . . not to mention a small company of Cylmaran soldiers that I didn't know what to do with. Zlatin was probably going to regret having made me the offer.

After finding my way back to my horse, this time taking the main streets instead of working my way around the maze of booths, I spent a couple of minutes staring out over Lake Nari and its greenish-blue water as the sun sparkled across the surface. It was a very lovely spot, even if it did smell strongly of fish. Not wanting to linger, I mounted and started back toward the center of Ecrin where Jasna said I would find most of the prominent clothing shops.

I had just reached the city square when the hairs on the back of my neck stood once again, and I spun in my saddle, quickly scanning the street behind me, along with the buildings on either side. It was the second time I had felt someone watching me. I waited a few minutes, wanting to see if anything stuck out, someone who didn't belong or was trying too hard to appear to belong, someone doing their best to blend in with the shoppers and merchants lining the sides of the street, someone looking in my direction. If there was someone there, they were doing a good job of keeping themselves hidden. After Dorwall, everything was making me jumpy.

Moving on, I stopped at the first of two shops Jasna had told me about. This one was just off the main street before reaching the heart of the shopping district. By the number of people walking up and down the cobbled lane, it was clearly more heavily shopped than the map maker we'd visited earlier, but not as busy as those merchants whose shops faced the main square. I hoped I was able to find what I needed here. The thought of visiting one of the busier shops on the next street down had me anxious.

The door to the shop was open, so I tied my horse out front. There was a sign over the entrance, but it didn't have any lettering, only the depiction of a pair of trousers and a tunic.

Walking toward the door, I happened to catch part of a conversation between several men who were standing in a circle between shops. I couldn't hear much, since they quieted as I walked by, but what I did hear was about the battle at Fishtown. I frowned. Word was already spreading.

I stepped inside, thankful to be out of the sun.

"Welcome," a gentleman at the back called out. "Is there anything we can help you with today?" The man and what looked to be his wife were busy working behind a long table. He was short and plump, and she was tall and skinny, a very strange pairing, but they seemed to work

well together as they passed materials and tools back and forth, seemingly knowing what the other needed without having to ask. The man was deftly mending one of the buttons on a suede jerkin.

"I'm looking for a leather coat."

The man thumbed his chin. "Not quite the time of year for those, but I might have a few in the back that I can show you, if you give me a moment to finish up here."

I nodded and, leaving my hood raised, began to work my way around the room, keeping to the shelves on the opposite side from the other shoppers as I waited for the owner.

Once I had made it about halfway around the shelves of clothing, I glanced over at the front workstation and noticed that the shopkeeper was no longer there. The door behind the table was open, revealing a darkened room beyond. Light suddenly washed across the room on the left from what I gathered was a window whose curtains had just been pulled. I could see shelves laden with folded clothes.

I continued my perusing, finding a pair of black leather trousers I rather liked. I looked around to see if anyone was watching, then pulled them off the shelf and held them up to see if they would fit. The legs looked perhaps a little long, but the waist seemed the right size. I wondered if they'd allow me to try them on.

I folded the pants but didn't stick them back on the shelf. I just hoped I could find a coat that would suffice. Ecrin wasn't exactly Aramoor, and the selections here were going to be limited.

After several minutes of rummaging through the back room, the owner reappeared with several coats under his arm, which he began to drape across the table for me to see. He waved me over, and I went to take a look, keeping out of the way of an older couple who were in the process of purchasing a couple of summer tunics.

"See anything that grabs your interest?" the shopkeeper asked as he finished placing the final coat down on the table with a friendly smile.

I walked over to take a look, and the man froze, his eyes bulging as he stared at my chest in shock. I looked down and realized for the first time that my shirt underneath was streaked with blood. I quickly pulled the front of my cloak closed.

"My apologies. If you haven't heard, there was a scuffle that broke out in the fish market earlier. I stopped to help some of the wounded. Afraid I haven't had time to go change."

The man's smile reappeared, and he gave the waist of his trousers a quick tug. "It was only a matter of time. Fishtown's been on the verge of erupting for years, surprised it took this long." He looked at me a moment, a worried expression lowering his brows. "Are you affiliated with the docks or those working there?"

"No. Just passing through town."

The man seemed to relax and then shook his head. "Don't care much for the way Dovan runs the docks. Quite the slave master from what I hear."

"So, you haven't heard?"

"Heard what?"

"Dovan was killed during the fight."

The shopkeeper tugged his trousers. "Can't say I'm surprised. Wonder who'll take his place. No doubt someone just as ruthless as he was."

I smiled, not that he could see too well, what with my hood still raised. "I have a feeling things are going to get better for Fishtown."

"I hope you're right."

I scanned the row of coats on the table, taking my time with each as I picked them up, feeling the leather and judging the size and weight. Two of them were similar to my old coat, which had really been more of a jacket, tapering off just below the waist. I was hoping to find something longer this time, something that would allow me to hide larger

weapons than a dagger underneath, though truth be told, I just liked the way a longer coat looked.

The one longer coat he had was unfortunately the wrong color. It was a textured brown, and the leather was a bit rougher than what I would have liked, not to mention heavier. With a deep sigh that the shopkeeper took as me beginning negotiations, I pursed my lips and stepped back from the table.

"I'm sure we can work out a fair deal on the price," the merchant said as he rubbed his hands together.

Sadly, my mind was made up. I didn't see anything here that I wanted, which meant I was going to have to try the other shop after all, and if they, too, didn't have a longer black leather coat, I might be forced to make do with a jacket. I walked over to the shorter jacket on the left and lifted it once more.

The shopkeeper smiled. "I can alter it to fit, no problem. High-quality leather, well treated, keeps the rain and snow off for sure."

"I was hoping for something longer. I had one similar to this for a couple of years but grew out of it. I'm really hoping for something different this time."

The shopkeeper's expression soured as he stared down at the row of jackets and one coat, and his possible loss of sale. "Are you sure you wouldn't prefer the jacket? More maneuverable. Lighter." He lifted it up. "See here, the stitching? It's very strong. Won't rip. And the leather has been treated with a special blend of my own making. Won't find its like in all of Ecrin."

"I don't doubt it." I stepped forward to feel the leather once more just to satisfy him. "But I believe my mind is made up. I really am looking for something longer."

"And you won't consider the brown?" he asked, dropping the black jacket to pick up the brown rough-leather coat in the middle.

"Afraid not." I smiled. "Black is my color."

The shopkeeper sighed but nodded. "I understand." He began gathering up his selection. "When you have your heart set on something, not much I can do to change it. I wish you the—"

"Are you looking for something like this?"

I turned. The shopkeeper's wife, who was standing in the doorway leading into the back, was holding up one of the most beautiful black leather coats I'd ever seen.

"But dear," the man said, "we aren't finished with that one, or I would have brought it out. I thought you were wanting to spend more time on the front."

She smiled. "I had planned on adding some decorative stitching around the collar to sell to one of the nobles, but this young man doesn't look the type. And I'd prefer selling it to someone who actually needs it to giving it to some hobnob that will stuff it in his closet only to forget about it as he purchases five others."

I walked over and took the coat carefully from the woman's hands. The leather was soft but with a good grip, and much lighter than I would have expected for a coat so thick and long. Just having it in my hands felt right, like it had been made with me in mind. I spared a quick glance over my shoulder to see if anyone was looking, then took off my cloak, keeping my head down as I did. I spun the coat around my back, and the arms slipped straight in . . . a perfect fit. I looked down. The bottom hung below my shins. It was exactly what I wanted.

"Would you happen to have a—"

"There's a standing mirror right over there," she said, noticing the way I was trying to see what it looked like in the back.

I walked over to a thin mirror in the right corner. It wasn't as large and grand as the one in Dakaran's room, but it would suffice. I stared at myself in the glass. My heart was racing. I'd never seen a coat so . . .

perfect. I checked the insides to find it had been fitted with several pre-made pockets. Perfect again.

The front fastened with buckles at the top and buttons below. There were even buckles on each of the sleeves, moving up the forearm. I couldn't tell if they had been added just for looks or for an extra layer of protection, much like that of an armguard. Regardless, they made the coat stand out, and I loved it. The buckles and buttons were not the more popular silver or copper ones that would reflect light. These were black, exactly what I would need when wanting to move about unseen. The bottom of the coat widened out from the waist down, making movement easier. It also had a wide textured lapel and collar, and a hood for keeping the rain off my head and hiding my face.

I raised my arms over my head to mimic reaching for my sword and winced as I did, forgetting once more about the cut on my arm. I even went so far as to take a quick spin. This coat seemed to have been made for me. I pulled the hood up before turning to face them. "I'll take it."

I had no idea if I had enough coin to actually purchase such a work of art, but I knew I had to have it. I had brought along a few extra coins from my normal pay as a chief of Sandstorm. Along with them was the purse the king had given us to use in our endeavor to rescue the ambassador, which I could easily justify using some of, since the black coat would no doubt aid me in my attempt. There were also the coins we'd taken from the Cylmaran soldiers while stripping their uniforms. One way or another, I wasn't leaving this shop without the coat. I didn't care if I had to trade my horse in the bargain.

Thankfully, the price was quite reasonable—or perhaps the clothing in Aramoor was just that much more expensive—and I was able to purchase the coat and the black pants with some coin left over, though not much. I did end up using most of my pay from Sandstorm, but it was worth it.

"I've never seen a coat look so good on a customer," the shopkeeper said, standing back to admire the way it hung on my shoulders.

"I've not seen a coat that looked this good, not even in Aramoor."

The shopkeeper's wife smiled at the compliment. "I hope it will serve you well."

"I have no doubt it will." I waved my thanks to the couple and stepped back out into the heat, and somehow I thought the leather was cooler than my cloak, if that was possible. But by the time I reached my horse, my back was sweating, and I changed my mind. Nope, it was just as hot.

The ride back through town wasn't too difficult, with those on the street giving the man in the hooded black leather coat a wide berth. I rode up to the Ram's Head stable to find the same young street picker who'd been there to greet us on our first arrival sitting on the barrel in front of the stable.

He hopped up when he saw me coming. "Looking to stable your horse?" Clearly, he didn't recognize my new coat. But one look at it, and his price went up. "That'll be four for the night," he said with his hand out.

I grabbed his hand and yanked him over to me and pulled back my hood. "Did you think to steal from me again?"

He squealed when he saw my eyes. "I'm sorry, mister. I . . . I didn't know who you were. Here, you can have your coins back." He dug around in his pocket to pull out a few of the coppers he'd taken. I didn't see any of the silvers.

I smiled. "Keep them. I respect someone who can con me the way you did. And that's coming from someone who came up on the streets himself."

The young boy looked up at me. "You're a street rat?"

"I am. Chief of my own tribe."

His eyes widened.

I smiled. "I gather you know the city pretty well."

"Like the back of my hand."

A grumbling noise had us both turning as Bosko walked around from the side stable. He spotted me and the boy and started for us. "I see you caught the young guttersnipe finally!" He looked at the boy. "Ought to hang you by your toes."

I raised my hand to stop him, pulling my hood back into place. "I'll deal with our little thief, if you can restable my horse and pat him down." I took the grapple out of the saddlebag before he did.

Bosko looked upset at not being able to get his hands on the little picker, but he finally nodded and walked my horse into the stable.

I turned to the boy. "How familiar are you with the overlord's keep?"

He shivered. "That's Forang's territory. We don't pick there. I'm part of Vulkina's tribe. We run the streets east of Rodon Hill all the way down to the fish market."

"Are there a lot of soldiers out at night?"

"Not as many as there are during the day." His eyes narrowed. "Why?"

If there was information one needed to know about a city, the street tribes were the best place to go. "Have any from the tribes ever been inside the keep?"

"Those that've been caught by the soldiers, but we never see them again. Oh, and Vulkina, of course."

"And she's the head of your tribe?"

He nodded. "She's the only one who's been inside, and that's because her mother used to work in the keep as one of the cleaners." He looked at me and shook his head. "Best you stay as far from that place as possible. You get caught around there, and you'll never be heard from again either."

I smiled. "I wish I had a choice. What's your name?"

The boy rubbed his nose with the dirt-smudged sleeve on his arm. "I'm Neven."

"Well, Neven, how would you like to earn some more coin?"

His face brightened at first, then turned dour. "What would I have to do?"

"Set up a meeting with me and Vulkina tonight. Do you think you could handle that?"

"I don't know that she'll come."

"Tell her it would be a favor from one chief to another."

He stared at me a moment, then nodded. "I'll see what I can do. Where and when do you want me to tell her to meet you?"

"You said your tribe's territory stretches to the docks, correct?"

Neven nodded.

"Then tell her I'll be there tonight at ninth bell."

"How will she know it's you?"

"I'll be the one in the black leather coat."

He looked at my coat and smiled. "Yep, no one else is crazy enough to wear something like that in this heat."

Some noise from the stables had Neven scurrying off down the road. I stared after him until he vanished around the corner, then headed inside.

# WILDFIRE

## Chapter 16

I STOPPED BY MY ROOM, but no one was there. I could hear some faint noises coming from Barthol and Gellar's room, so I headed down the hall. Thinking to get a rise out of them, I pulled up the hood on my new black leather coat and yanked open the door with a start.

All of them came out of their seats, reaching for their swords.

"It's just me," I said, pulling back my hood as I shut the door. I couldn't help but laugh as they, one by one, began retaking their seats.

"Are you trying to scare us to death?" Gellar asked, holding a glass of water to his forehead. He'd poured half of it in his lap when the door opened.

"Where'd you get that?" Dakaran asked, walking over to admire the new coat.

"I purchased it on the way back from the fish market."

Gellar cleared his throat. "Did you happen to purchase the one thing you went there for?"

I smiled and reached into my coat and pulled out the grapple and rope.

"Well, at least you got that. Certainly took you long enough. We were about to go looking."

"I got a lot more than that," I said, and took off my coat so they could see the blood on my shirt.

Barthol came out of his seat once more. "Are you injured? What happened?"

"Quite a lot, actually. And no, this isn't my blood. Well, not all of it." I proceeded to tell them everything that had happened, from getting the grapple, to Jasna's father showing up, to the battle that had brought about a shift in power at the docks.

"You get all the fun," Gellar grumbled. "All we did was sit here and sweat."

"I got to question the prisoners," Fipple said with a smirk.

"Did we learn anything new?" I asked.

"Not unless you count a few choice curses I'd never heard before."

"So, nothing helpful." I sat down in the empty seat between Barthol and Fipple, enjoying the cool breeze blowing in from the windows on the other side of the room. I didn't realize how hot I had been wearing that coat until I took it off. "I might have found someone who can tell me more about the inside of the overlord's compound."

"Oh?" Stumpy asked. He was seated next to Dakaran on the edge of one of the beds. "That would be extremely helpful. Who is it?"

"Her name is Vulkina, and she is the head of one of the city's street tribes." I told them of my run-in with Neven.

"You want us to come?" Barthol asked.

I shook my head. "It'll be best if I go alone. Street kids can be very skittish when they feel threatened. A group of armed men waiting for

them won't send the right message."

Barthol nodded, and the others went back to whatever conversations they were holding prior to my arrival, which consisted heavily of complaining about the heat.

The rest of the afternoon and evening passed slowly as we moved about the rooms, walking down to the common room every so often to order another pitcher of ale or plate of cheese and bread. By the time eighth bell had rung, I was up and dressed in my new coat, this time carrying not only the sword at my waist but the one on my back as well. I wanted to leave early and get there with time to scout the location to make sure there were no surprises waiting. Any good chieftain would no doubt do the same, and I was at a disadvantage, not being familiar with the terrain.

"I'm going to take another look at Saryn's compound after I meet with Vulkina. I want to see how they station the patrols at night. I don't want any surprises." I smiled as I opened the door and turned to those in the room. "If I don't make it back by morning, you better come looking."

Dakaran grunted. "If you don't make it back by morning, then you're likely at the bottom of the lake."

"Then I guess it'll be up to you to rescue the ambassador and his wife. Too bad. I'll miss watching you try to shimmy up the side of the keep."

"That'll be the day."

I took one last look at my roommates before stepping out and shutting the door. They were too busy ribbing Dakaran about climbing up the side of a building to notice me leave. I needed to hurry if I was going to reach the docks in time, especially since this time I was going on foot. The last thing I wanted was the heavy clop of horse's hooves echoing down the empty streets, announcing my arrival. It was stealth and cunning I needed now.

Making my exit out the back door, I cut down the side alley, past the stables, and started at a light jog up the street. The sun had set, and the evening wind off the lake was already beginning to cool the air, which made my run across the city easier. In fact, it was one of the only things about this place I found tolerable. No matter how hot it was during the day, the evenings cooled quite comfortably.

The city looked different at night. With no one out on the streets, it seemed almost eerie. Up ahead, I could hear horse hooves coming my way, so I ducked between two buildings and pressed against the one on the right, letting my black outfit blend with the shadows. I watched as a group of soldiers on patrol passed by, not in a hurry to get anywhere, simply sauntering down the road, chatting idly as they did. I waited until they had moved down the street far enough to not be seen before continuing.

I took Jasna's back way to the docks, even though I was less familiar with this route, hoping to keep from running into more patrols. Thankfully, I only got lost once and was able to backtrack and find the correct street before pressing on. I couldn't afford to miss the meeting. If this girl was the only person who'd seen the inside of Saryn's keep, I needed that information. It would likely make the difference between us rescuing the ambassador and his wife and us failing.

Dock lights ahead let me know I was nearing my destination. Stopping at the corner of a narrow lane between residences, I stared out across the three-tiered platforms leading down to the water. I spotted some fishermen just getting in and unloading their haul, while another group looked to be getting ready to set sail. There were a couple of night watchmen moving about the place, keeping an eye on the docks.

Quietly, I worked my way down the fronts of the closest buildings,

keeping to the shadows as I made my way along the front of the port. Once I reached the other side, I began the slow task of working my way around the surrounding buildings, looking for scouts, watchers, or a hidden group of beaters that might be waiting just out of sight to attack the moment I showed my face.

It took me a while, but I managed to completely scout the northern half of the docks, and from what I could tell, there were no surprises to be found. I was a little disappointed at the tribe's lack of preparation, but thankful I didn't have to contend with a possible ambush, which left me to focus on what I would say to convince the chief to give me what I needed. I found a good spot that was just out of sight but afforded me a clear vantage of anyone coming, and took a seat.

Of course, no one being here could simply mean this Vulkina wasn't planning on coming. Perhaps Neven didn't talk to her after all, or perhaps she didn't listen or think it worth her while to talk with me. All were valid explanations for why I was sitting there alone in the dark, staring at an empty street. *Come on, you have to show up.*

The northern side of Fishtown seemed almost dead. Apparently, the dock patrols didn't come this far north. A clanging noise behind me had me spinning and reaching for my weapon. How had someone managed to sneak up behind me? My sword had nearly cleared its sheath when I spotted a hungry tabby. The cat stiffened and hissed when it saw me, but after realizing I wasn't there to stop it from eating, it meowed softly and went about its business.

Eventually, the cat tired of its search and came over to inspect the lump of black leather leaning against the side of the brick building. It purred and worked its way around my legs in a circular fashion. I finally reached down and petted the top of its head. It purred some more.

*Well, this was a waste of time.* I was really hoping to have talked with this girl. Any information she could have given me on the layout of the overlord's keep would have been vital. It seemed I was going to be forced to search it myself, which was much riskier and would take a lot more time, perhaps several days, depending on how guarded the inside was. From everything else I'd seen, Overlord Saryn was someone who erred on the side of caution.

With a disappointed sigh, I ran my hand down the tabby's back and tail one last time. No sense waiting around any longer. I stood and was about to step out when I spotted movement on my left. I quickly slid back into the shadows as several larger kids moved cautiously up the street. Just behind them was a girl who looked about my age, with short brown hair and a faded yellow dress with black boots underneath. She carried two knives, reminding me a little of both Sapphire and Red.

There was a strength to her presence and a resilience in her eyes that said she had to be Vulkina. There were four older boys at the front, no doubt her guard, each with a sword in their hand and a look in their eyes that said they were ready to fight. Behind her, bringing up the rear, were a couple of beaters. Neven, who was walking just behind her, looked a little out of place, as he was the only one not carrying a weapon, at least that I could see.

Neven was busy scanning each building they passed. "I told you we shouldn't have waited so long," he said, earning a hiss from Vulkina. "He's already done come and gone."

They stopped two buildings down. They looked around for a moment, and I waited to see if there were any others behind them before revealing myself, but it didn't appear anyone else was coming. Soon enough, the girl said something angrily to Neven, but before they turned to leave, I stepped out and walked to the center of the street.

"That's him, Chief!" Neven said, no doubt recognizing my coat. "That's the one that says he's a chief as well."

Vulkina and her entourage started toward me, their weapons raised.

I made sure to keep my hands at my sides so they could see I wasn't threatening. They stopped about ten feet from where I was standing, her guard a few feet in front of her, watching me with scrutinizing glares.

"Who are you and what do you want?" Vulkina asked. "My picker says you claim to be a tribal chief. Where from?"

"Rhowynn," I lied. I didn't want to take the chance that someone in their tribe might spread word that I was from Aramoor, and somehow have that word get back to the overlord. "And I heard that you have knowledge about the inner workings of the overlord's keep."

"And what do you intend to do with that information?"

"I'm afraid that's my business."

She stared at me a while, her lips pursed, eyes narrowed. "What's in it for me?"

I knew I didn't have enough coin to tempt her, but I couldn't turn back now. "What do you want?"

She smiled, which had me wishing I hadn't asked. "A locket."

"A locket?"

"If you'll promise to retrieve my mother's locket while you're in there, then I'll give you the information you seek. And don't think you can simply sneak in and out without getting it. My people will be watching every exit. We will know when you leave, and you better have it with you, or you won't be leaving Ecrin alive."

"And where will I find this locket?"

"It was stolen by the mistress of the robes. You'll find it with her. And if you happen to walk away with something else of hers," she said with a grin, "all the better."

I thought a moment. "If you can give me as detailed a layout of the keep as possible, including the kitchens, the dungeons, the overlord's bedchambers, and the sleeping quarters of this mistress of the robes, then I will do my best to get you your locket."

"You better do more than your best. Either you come out with my locket or don't bother coming out at all."

My fists tightened, but I agreed, nonetheless.

"When do you need this map by?" she asked.

"Tomorrow night, if possible. I can let Neven know if anything changes by tomorrow afternoon at the latest."

"Fine. We will meet back here tomorrow evening." With that, she turned, and they started back up the street the way they'd come, Neven included.

I waited until they were out of sight before melting back into the shadows and heading back the way I'd come, eventually reaching the main road leading through Fishtown. There was probably a shorter way to get to Rodon Hill, but I only knew the most direct, which was to take the main road back to the city's square and head north on Canal Street all the way up to the castle. I wasn't planning on attempting anything tonight, not without first having our transportation and escape route planned and ready, but I did want to see how difficult it would be to get past the patrols surrounding the keep at night.

The streets were quiet, with only the occasional passerby who kept to themselves as they hustled along. The road steepened the closer I got to my destination, leveling off slightly as I reached the top of the hill. Torches lit the castle in front of me as I settled down to wait in the deeper shadows of one of the buildings across the street.

There were two mounted patrols that slowly circled the overlord's estate, not to mention the guards standing at the front gates, and the men in black uniforms watching from the upper bulwark. The wall encircling the estate would be easy to slip over, as it wasn't all that tall, and the mortar around the stones was inset far enough that it would allow for a decent grip. Thankfully, my earlier scouting trip with Barthol and Fipple had allowed me to find the best place to cross. Not only was it

the least guarded from the street—a section far enough away from any entrances that those standing watch wouldn't see—but it was also a part of the keep where the upper parapets didn't quite connect, which meant if there were guards watching from the top, it would be difficult to lean over far enough to see someone scaling the side of the main wall.

Instead of trying to walk down the street and risk exposing myself to all the guards, I backtracked to a small side lane that ran in the same general direction. I followed the route taking one back lane and side alley after another, until I was close to where I needed to be. Squeezing between buildings, I stuck my head out to find that I was only a few houses down from the section of wall I was hoping to reach. I spotted the piece of material I'd stuffed between two of the stones and cautiously made my way down the fronts of the residences till I was standing across the street from where I wanted to be.

I stared at the wall a moment and was about to cross the street when the sound of horse hooves had me backing back up into the crevice and waiting as two mounted soldiers rode past. They chatted quietly, the one closest to me holding a torch, its light barely missing my hiding place between the two homes. I ducked down, nonetheless, and waited until they had completely passed and rounded the corner before making my way out.

I quickly ran across the road, using one solid kick off the stone wall to leap up to grab the upper lip, which jutted out far enough for me to get a good fingerhold. I pulled myself up, rolled over the top, and dropped onto the other side, then pressed against the wall as I studied the space between me and the section of the castle I was looking to climb. The climb up had my arm hurting from where Jasna had wrapped it, but I did my best to ignore the pain. It wasn't like I could wait for it to heal.

There didn't look to be all that much in the way of guards on the inside. This particular section of wall was only a stone's throw from the keep proper. There was a steep incline from the outer wall to where the keep rested at the top of the hill. It almost seemed as though the wall had been built to keep the hill from eroding.

The turret I needed to reach was just to my left up the incline. Taking a moment to scan the dark windows above me as well as the crenelated bulwark on my left, I climbed up the grassy mound, stopping in the corner where the turret connected with the outer wall. There was a long patch of creepers growing up the sides. The greenest and healthiest of the vines were those closest to the corner, where the turret kept them shaded during the day.

I grabbed a handful and gave a tug. They were firm, possibly firm enough to climb if I needed to. Not wasting any time, I pulled out my new grapple and the coil of rope tied to it. It wasn't an overly long coil, but it looked long enough to reach the lower window. Judging the distance, I took aim and swung.

The hook flew upward, clipping the underside of the lip with a notable clang and bouncing off. I sidestepped to keep from getting hit when it came back down. *Drat!* I quickly moved into the corner of the wall and pressed myself against the creepers, waiting to see if anyone stuck their head out a window or the crenelation above. After waiting longer than I probably needed to, I finally decided to come out and try again. Taking aim once more, I swung.

This time the grapple flew over the lip instead of hitting it, and I pulled down to force the hooks to grab the edge. They did. Again, I moved back into the corner to wait and see if the clang of the metal would attract anyone. So far, it hadn't seemed to. Keeping the rope taut, I slowly pulled myself up to see if it would hold my weight.

The grapple held.

Taking a quick look around to make sure no one was watching—

which would have been difficult given the dark shadows I was currently standing in—I slowly started up the rope, cautious at first as I continued to test the grip of the hook. The further I went, the more secure I felt and the faster my hands and feet worked. Soon enough, I was reaching for the window's sill and pulling myself up. It wasn't a large window, not much wider than a typical arrow slit, but wide enough for me to wriggle through.

With part of the grapple's rope wrapped around my arm to keep from losing it, I made my way inside, dragging the rope with me, which I quickly wound and stuffed inside a very large pocket in the inner lining of my coat. The weight of it continued to pull my coat off balance as it shifted to the right, but there was nothing to do for it now.

For a brief moment, I wondered if I should turn back and not risk getting caught, but I wanted to gather as much information as I could about the place, something my father would have demanded before risking a mission like this. Besides, there was no telling if Vulkina would come through with her map, and if she did, how reliable it would be.

Keeping next to the window, I took a quick look around. The room was mostly empty, save for a couple of shelves on the right, filled with neatly stacked piles of cloths and scrub brushes. Several racks lined the left wall, each laden with brooms of all shapes and sizes. I looked to have crawled into one of the cleaners' supply closets. If I were to have picked an entry, I couldn't have found a better one. This was probably one of the last rooms I needed to worry about running into anyone in the middle of the night.

I walked over to the door and was happy to find it hadn't been bolted from the outside. The door squeaked slightly as I slid it open a crack, just enough to see if anyone was on the other side. Other than a dark, empty corridor, this part of the keep looked vacant, so I slid the door open, just far enough for me to slip out.

I was in a small corridor. To my right was the outer wall of the tower I had just climbed, and to my left was an archway that opened into the main keep itself. Directly in front of me was a circular stairwell I was guessing led down to the bottom floors, as well as up to the ramparts.

Keeping to the shadows, I crept along the wall to the left, stopping at the entranceway to get a closer look out into the main part of the keep. The corridor ended at a balcony that ran four-square around the heart of the keep, which looked down onto an open hall two floors below. Above me, I could see at least one more balcony before the walls eventually reached the top. There were guards in black uniforms posted on every level, mostly keeping to the landings closest to the stairs.

It appeared there were extra guards posted on the balcony above this one. I wondered if that was where Overlord Saryn and his family slept. Getting down on all fours, I crawled out onto the balcony to take a peek. My guess was that somewhere down there was a door leading to the dungeons, and that would be where we'd find the ambassador and his wife. The good news was that getting in the castle seemed easy enough. However, getting down to the bottom floor was going to prove difficult, considering all the men in black standing watch.

Leaving the balcony, I moved back down the hall toward the door I'd entered from, stopping only long enough to take a look down a circular stairwell across from it. Unfortunately, unless I started down, I'd never really know where it went. It might prove the best option for reaching the lower levels without being seen, though.

The way the guards were positioned in the main hall seemed to be protecting against intruders breaking in from the front, not from someone scaling the outside wall and working their way down.

There wasn't much more I could do right then, so I left the stairs and headed back inside the storage room and climbed onto the window. With the grapple firmly back in place, I shimmied out onto the rope and

when I was forced to leave home. It had been almost five years since I'd seen either of them.

"What are you doing here?" I asked, still too in shock to know what else to say.

My father finally released me and took a step back to stand beside Jorn. "We're here on a contract. The bigger question is: What are you doing here? I thought you were going to Aramoor. The last time I talked with Hobb, he said he booked you passage south on one of the riverboats."

"He did . . . or I did. I went to Aramoor. In fact, that's why I'm here. I'm here by direct request of the high king." If my face wasn't beaming before, it certainly was now. Just to see the look of shock on my father's and brother's faces when I mentioned the king was worth it all.

"You know the king?" Jorn asked, looking skeptical.

"I'm here with his son." My heart was pounding. I had no idea where to even begin. I looked at them both, memorizing every line and curve of their faces. "I can't believe how much you've grown," I said to Jorn. "Pretty soon, you're going to be taller than me."

My father leaned forward and pinched my chin. "I like the new look."

I rubbed the short growth around my face and smiled.

My father spotted something else and grabbed my hand. He smiled with pride as he stared at his ring on my finger.

"It fits," I said.

"That it does," he said with a nod. "That it does."

"So, what's been happening back home? How's Mother? How's Rianna? Is Brim still leading the clan?"

My father laughed and put his hand on my shoulder. "Best we find some shelter first. We have a lot to catch up on."

He was right, of course. We didn't need to be holding a lengthy conversation just outside the overlord's castle with constant patrols riding by.

"Come," I said. "You can meet my men, and I can fill you in on everything that's happened since I left the Lost City." My hands were shaking with excitement as I guided them down the alley, and from there, back to the main road. I couldn't wait to introduce them to my roommates and hear about everything that had happened while I was gone. I kept looking back over my shoulder just to make sure I hadn't imagined it. The thought of seeing my family again was more than anything I could have ever dreamed or hoped for. Unfortunately, I couldn't think of a worse time for it to happen. Or maybe this was the perfect time.

# WILDFIRE

## Chapter 17

ITH NO HORSES TO STABLE, I directed my father and brother around to the back entrance of the Ram's Head Inn, and we headed up the back stairs to our rooms. Even with the moon out, it was still early enough that I doubted my roommates had already turned in for the night. They were no doubt huddled around the city map, planning our escape. At least, I hoped they were.

I stopped by my room first to find it empty, as I expected. My legs were shaking, I was so giddy at the chance to introduce my friends to my family. To have my father and brother meet the prince. I just hoped Dakaran didn't stick his foot in it by saying, or doing, anything stupid.

I could see light under the third door on the right, which was the room we had dedicated to taking our meals and discussing our plans. I took a deep breath and turned the handle.

Those inside hopped to their feet, several drawing their swords. I felt a sense of pride at their readiness. Made me look good in front of my family.

"It's me," I said, my father and brother standing in the shadows be-hind me. "Though, I do have a surprise."

"Did you get the map?" Dakaran asked.

"Even better," I said as I stepped inside and motioned for my father and brother to join me. "I want to introduce you to Narris and Jorn . . . My father and brother."

The men all turned, shuffling toward the front to get a better look as my father and brother stepped into the candlelit room and removed their hoods.

"Your father and brother?" Stumpy stared, like all the rest. "How is that possible?"

I couldn't help but grin. "I have no idea." I walked over and shut the door, then turned to my father and brother. "Let me introduce you to my friends. They are Elondrian Lancers in the king's service."

"I'm not a lancer," Dakaran huffed before I could start giving names.

"You got that right," Gellar chided with a wry smirk.

I rolled my eyes. "I'd like to introduce you to His Highness Dakaran, the crown prince of Aldor."

My father and brother looked at me as though unsure if they were supposed to bow or not. My father did manage a slight bow, my brother following suit.

"It is an honor to meet you, Your Highness," my father said.

"It won't be once you get to know him," Fipple said, earning a few chuckles from some of the others.

Dakaran balled his fists, but he did his best to retain his composure as he nodded his appreciation for my father and brother's deference. "It is an honor to meet the one responsible for raising such an incredible talent," he said, "though I hear it is a trait shared by most of the Upaka."

I turned to the others, who were waiting anxiously to be introduced

as well. "This is Barthol," I said, going around the room, "and Gellar, and that's Fipple and Waylen, and Stumpy, there beside Dakaran."

The group waved or nodded or smiled when their names were called.

"It's an honor to meet you," my father said, then turned to me. "So, you are a lancer?"

"I'm . . . whatever I need to be."

He gave me a curious look.

"I'll explain later. I have a thousand questions of my own." I turned to my roommates. "Were you able to secure passage for tomorrow night?"

They looked at me, then at my father and brother.

"You can trust them," I said.

"No offense," Gellar said, "but how do we know? We are risking more than just our lives if the wrong people were to find out about this."

I started to say something, but Father put his hand on my shoulder. "It is a wise precaution, and a wiser man willing to speak it, especially knowing who he stands in front of, but family is more important to us than any contract, and you can be assured that our business here will not interfere with your own."

Gellar hmphed. "Well, you can't be too careful."

Barthol turned. "Jasna took us to meet with her father. It looks like he will have a boat and crew ready and waiting on us."

"Did you tell him about the prisoners?"

Barthol nodded once more. "I thought it only right. They could be risking their lives as well."

"Now if only we knew what to do with them."

"Actually," Waylen said, after finishing off what was in his tankard, "Jasna's father had a good suggestion. We—"

"We can take them all to the Isle of Delga," Dakaran blurted out as if the idea had been his all along, "and drop them off at the salt mines."

"Which is about as much as they deserve," Fipple said with a sour face.

"Would Zlatin be willing to transport them that far?" I asked.

Barthol scratched at his lengthening beard. "Says he will. I reckon if he'd be willing to transport us all the way back to Aramoor, the king would more than compensate him for his efforts."

It was a good idea. It would certainly get the soldiers out of our hair, with little effort on our part, except for figuring out how we were going to transport them all from the Ram's Head over to the docks.

"Perhaps we can rent a wagon or something and tote them under blankets from here to the water."

Gellar rubbed at the split in his brow. "Might work. I'm sure Jasna or Mirna could direct us to someone willing to rent out their wagon, that is, if we still have enough coin." He cleared his throat and made a point of glancing at my new coat. "Me and Stumpy can look into that in the morning."

"What exactly is it the king has asked you to do?" my father asked, looking a little out of place.

"We are here to rescue an Elondrian ambassador and his wife. They're being held by Overlord Saryn as a bargaining chip in his negotiations with the king."

"Not exactly the smartest way to get what you want," my father said dryly.

"No one has ever been accused of calling Saryn smart," Fipple added.

"You never answered my question," Dakaran said. "Did you get a map of the overlord's castle?"

"I will by tomorrow tonight."

Dakaran frowned. "You will?"

"I found someone who used to work inside the keep and is willing to draw me a layout for what I need."

"Sounds like there's a *but* coming," Stumpy said.

I smiled. "But . . . she wants me to find her mother's stolen locket and steal it back, or, from the way she talked, she will alert the castle guard to our presence."

The room grew quiet.

Waylen gulped, and this time not from his tankard. "You don't think she would actually do that, do you?"

"The impression I got was that she meant what she said."

"Well, that's a serious hiccup," Gellar stated. "It's one thing to try sneaking into the overlord's palace and rescue some people from the dungeon—which, honestly, sounds ridiculous saying aloud—but it's quite another to demand you go sneaking into someone's bedchambers and filch their necklace while they lie fast asleep in their bed."

"I don't see as I have much choice. Last thing we need is a confrontation with an entire street tribe while we are trying to find a way to move about the city unnoticed."

Barthol chuckled. "I'd say we were doing a pretty poor job of the latter, considering what happened in Fishtown."

I sighed. "That was unfortunate, but it did open the opportunity for us to secure passage downriver."

Stumpy looked at my father and brother, then me. "I think we can handle the preparations from here. You look like you have some catching up to do that doesn't need to get put off any longer."

I glanced at my father and brother and smiled, then turned back to my roommates. "We'll be in my room if you need anything."

The others nodded and waved us on, and I escorted my family down the hall and into my rather messy room. I shut the door and quickly tidied up Dakaran's clothing.

"Sorry about that," I said as I cleared a space on the bed and the chair in the corner. "I don't think the prince has ever had to clean up after himself before." I took a seat on the chair while my father and brother paced the room a minute before sitting down on the bed.

"You know why I'm here," I said, breaking the silence with a simple question. "Why are you? You mentioned a contract?" I looked at Jorn and smiled. "I can't believe how big you've gotten."

Jorn didn't exactly smile. He seemed very hesitant. "You look different."

I rubbed my chin where my jawline beard met my goatee. "I guess I do. It's been nearly five years. A lot can happen in that time."

My father dropped his pack down on the floor in front of the bed. "We were contracted to deal with the leader of the Fishtown guild, a man named Dovan. In fact, we had just learned who he was and where we might find him when all Pits broke loose, and the entire community erupted into a battle zone. That's when we first spotted you. We didn't know who you were at first, but we could tell by the way you fought that you were different. I've only ever seen one person fight with that kind of accuracy. However, I didn't want to approach you until we knew for sure, so we've been following you around town. Thought you'd spotted us a couple of times."

"I knew someone was watching me, but I never saw you."

My father turned and smiled proudly at Jorn as if to say: *Your old man still has it.* He looked back at me. "It seems you fulfilled our contract before we had a chance to deal with it."

I smiled. "Seems it couldn't be helped. But I don't care about contracts right now. How's Mother, how's Rianna? She has to be, what, nineteen?"

"Twenty," Jorn corrected.

"Twenty." I shook my head. I couldn't imagine my sister so old.

"She is bonded to Lorn," my father added. "I don't know if you'd remember him. He was a couple of years older than you and in his final

year of training when . . . Well, when you left."

I shook my head. "I don't remember him." I might have known the name, but I couldn't put a face to it.

"He's a good man," my father said, "a good provider. He treats her very well. They have a daughter, and another on the way."

Tears formed in my eyes. I couldn't help it. My sister was married and a mother. I was an uncle. Would I ever get the chance to meet them? "And Mother?"

My father smiled. "As beautiful as ever. We still live in the same house. Thought we'd lose it for sure after what happened with Flon, but the rest of the Peltock talked Brim down, not wanting to cause an even greater stir amongst the tribe. But enough about us. What about you? I want to know everything. I can't believe you are friends with the crown prince. Have you actually met the king?"

I laughed. "Where do I begin?"

We talked long into the night as I revealed the incredible tale that was my life since I left the Lost City. I told them of my journey down the Shemoa River with Captain Treygan and his crew aboard the *Wind Binder*, how we had fought river pirates and Cylmaran slavers, and had even rescued Magistrate Sirias and his family. I told them of my life within the great walls of Aramoor, leaving nothing out. I told them of the hardships, the battles, the constant struggle to keep our tribe alive. I told them of my time fighting in the Pit with Flesh Eater. I told them of my friendships, those within the tribes and those without.

I told them of my first meeting with the king and how I had broken into the palace to steal the royal signet and ended up fighting the palace guard. I told them of my relationship with the king and queen, and Dakaran. I told them of Master Fentin and Mistress Orilla and our work with the orphanage. I told them of my time spent in the Lancers and my place as a chief amongst the tribes. I told them of my accommodations within Sandstorm Manor and the luxury that position afforded.

I even told them of the time I snuck into two different senators' houses in the middle of the night. My father seemed especially proud of that feat. I told them everything I could think of. I couldn't believe how badly I had wanted to tell them of all I had accomplished, how far I had come, the names I had made myself.

Death's Shadow and Protector.

In all the time we spoke, only once were we interrupted, and that was when Dakaran came in to get his blanket and pillow, having decided to sleep in one of the other rooms, since he figured we'd be up the rest of the night talking.

"It's quite the life you've made for yourself, Ayrion," Father said with a proud smile on his face but with a hint of sadness in his eyes. "I wish . . . I wish things could have been different, though."

"Don't."

My father looked surprised by the declaration.

I took a deep breath and released it slowly. I'd put the anger of what had happened to me aside a long time ago, but seeing my father and brother and hearing them discuss the goings-on at home, I couldn't help but feel a twinge in my gut as some of those old feelings seeped back in. "What's done is done. I really like my life now. Besides, what Upakan can say they have accomplished what I have? What Upakan can say they have the ear and respect of the high king?" I shook my head. "I wouldn't trade what I have for a hundred Lost Cities. Though, I would like to have my family closer."

Jorn didn't look so impressed. In fact, he looked a little angry.

"Enough about me," I said, turning to my little brother. "What about you? You would have to be in your, what, third year now?"

"Top of his class," Father said with a wink. "Takes after his older brother for sure."

"And quite the heartbreaker, I bet," I added, trying to rib Jorn into a smile. "Just look at those dark curls."

Jorn almost grinned but got control of himself before it actually broke the surface. "Getting to where I am wasn't easy," he said. "Not when your brother is Ayrion."

I leaned forward. "What does that mean?"

"It means I have to work twice as hard as everyone else. When your brother is one of the banished, you don't make friends easily."

I sighed. *Great. Something else for him to resent me for.* "So, if I stay, you're angry, and if I leave, you're angry. Seems like I lose either way."

"It's not that bad," Father said.

"Sure, that's why you only get the leftover jobs and why the council hasn't let you have your seat back."

Father smiled halfheartedly. "We get by. Would you rather us leave the Lost City? You think you have it hard now, imagine how hard it would be for me to get work as an Upakan out here. Our family would have probably starved by now."

"He's not wrong," I said, more to Jorn than just to agree with Father. "People with eyes like ours aren't looked on favorably. At the least, they think you have some sort of sickness and try to stay away. At the worst, they know your heritage and either run or call for the blue capes."

"Blue capes?" Jorn looked confused.

"What we on the streets call the patrollers."

"Your eyes haven't seemed to hurt you none," Jorn pointed out snidely.

"That's because I've earned their respect, and trust me, it wasn't easy. Even now, I have to be careful who I show my face to. Do you think I enjoy wandering all over the city in the heat of summer wearing a thick coat and pulled hood?"

I didn't mention that I planned on changing that. One day I would walk through Aramoor with my head held high, where everyone would know who I was and not run in fear. One day I would have their respect.

"Clearly, you've found a way to get past the stigma," Jorn added, wanting to get in the last word.

"Something more easily accomplished when there is just one of me. I don't know how feasible it would have been for an entire family of Upaka." I looked at Father. "I gather Brim is still heading the clan?"

Father hmphed. "Unfortunately, and as Jorn pointed out, he hasn't made it easy on us. The man has no forgiveness in his heart, only vengeance." There was a short moment of silence before he scooted forward and started speaking again. "Well, as you have fulfilled our contract for us, it seems only right that we help you fulfill yours. What are your plans for getting the ambassador and his wife out? There was some mention of a map to the inside of the castle? How much did you see during your excursion this evening?"

A cock crowed somewhere off in the city, and we all turned and looked at the windows. A faint stream of grey lit the sill.

"I guess it wasn't this evening but last evening," Father said with a smile. "Where has the time gone?"

I told them what I'd seen of the inside of the keep, which wasn't much. I also told them what I'd seen of the outside, and the rotation of the guards, mentioning that those on the inside weren't the same as those on the out. And that by the way they carried themselves, they were no doubt chosen because of their skill, which meant they would be more difficult to deal with.

My father thought a moment, rubbing his chin like I remembered him doing. "If you hope to get in and out in a timely fashion, you'll need more than one person inside. From what you've mentioned, you have two separate goals: the ambassador and his wife, and the young lady's locket. If we were to work this commission together, you'd stand a

greater chance of success."

I stared at the two of them a moment. "I can't ask you to get involved. If something were to go wrong, it wouldn't just be imprisonment, not with what I've seen of Saryn. Hang it, he wouldn't even do you the courtesy of killing you outright. Most likely he'd torture us for as long as possible, or until he got bored of hearing us scream, then kill us."

Father smiled. "Then I guess we need to make sure nothing goes wrong."

I leaned back in my chair and yawned. "I can't believe we've talked the entire night away." My mind was groggy as I tried focusing on what all needed to be done. This was a really bad time to be missing sleep.

By the time the thought of trying to catch a few winks had filtered into my mind, I could hear those in the room next to ours stirring around. A knock on our door let me know they were ready to go down to breakfast.

"It's open," I said, and Stumpy stuck his head in.

"Good, you're awake. I thought you might have still been asleep. How late did you stay up?"

I smiled, which ended up dragging another yawn out of me. "We never went to bed."

"Oh, well, we're all heading down to breakfast if you care to join us." He passed a quick look at my father and Jorn.

I nodded. "We'll be right down." I stood from my seat and stretched, only now realizing how stiff I was from sitting for so long. My head felt heavy. I took a moment to wipe my eyes, which had begun to cloud, then strapped on my sword, leaving my new coat for last. A couple of swigs of Mirna's ale and my head was sure to clear. Leaving my second sword and its sheath under the bed, I headed out the door, where the others were waiting in the hall.

Greetings were hurriedly passed, and we all started down the stairs for the common room. We were the first to arrive. A girl who looked a little older than Jasna, with dirty-blonde hair, moved about the tables, lighting candles as she went. This had to be Kelsi, Jasna's sister. There was a definite resemblance around the eyes and cheeks, though Kelsi was a fair sight prettier.

After we maneuvered a couple of tables together and all found our seats, she came over to take our orders.

"Is Jasna around?" I asked, surprised not to see her, figuring she might be in the kitchen helping Mirna. "I take it you're Kelsi, her sister?"

Kelsi nodded with a smile and walked over to where me and my father and brother were sitting. "You must be Ayrion. Jasna won't stop talking about the handsome man who saved our father." She tucked a long strand of hair back behind one ear. "She's not here today, too busy helping Father get the boats ready. It's been almost a year since they've been on the water together." She shook her head. "Never really cared much for it myself; got sick every time they tried to take me out."

"You're not the only one, my dear," Waylen said with a smile from the other side. He patted his waist. "Never was one to handle the rock of a ship."

"So, what can I get you?" she asked, looking down the row of hungry men.

"Something strong enough to wake me up," I said with a chuckle.

Kelsi pursed her lips a moment, then her face brightened. "I've got just the thing."

"And a plate of whatever the cook is whipping up in the back," Gellar added, taking a quick whiff.

The smell of bacon filled the room, which was enough to get my stomach grumbling.

Kelsi headed back across the room for the kitchens, passing the

owner, who looked to have just crawled out of bed herself. There were dark circles under her eyes and a sudden frown when she spotted us on the other side of the room. I had no doubt she was counting down the hours till our departure. She wrung her hands as she sat stiffly on her stool in the lobby, waiting to greet customers, though one look at her gloomy face and they'd probably turn around and head right back out the door.

The bacon was mushy, the eggs over-peppered, and the bread chewy, but it was hot, and I was happy to have it, especially the tankards of Cylmaran wine. One sip of the spicy red drink and my eyes had no problem staying open . . . my mouth either, as it felt like my tongue and throat were on fire.

"Now that's the good stuff," Fipple said, seemingly not bothered in the least.

The one swallow I had was enough for me. You could have lit soggy driftwood on fire with that stuff.

As soon as our plates were cleared, we headed back upstairs, gathering once more around one of the maps of Ecrin as we began to talk through our plans for getting the ambassador and his wife out of Saryn's castle and across town to where Zlatin would be waiting at the docks to transport us all downriver. Not forgetting, of course, the added chore of getting the Cylmaran soldiers from the Ram's Head to the docks and stowed on board with no one seeing. And of course, the addition of retrieving a stolen locket.

Even with the help of my father and brother, things were certainly not looking in our favor. But when did they ever? We were Room Eleven, after all, and Room Eleven never quit. Of all the people the king could have picked to send in to rescue his ambassador, he chose us. Well, Overcaptain Tolin chose us . . . but the king agreed. We couldn't let them and our reputation down by failing.

"Fipple and I will look for a wagon to rent," Barthol said, "to transport the soldiers down to the waterfront tonight."

"See if they have some tarps to cover them with, as well," Gellar added. "The dead ones are already beginning to stink."

"We'll make sure they get a watery grave somewhere far enough downriver that we won't risk them being seen," Barthol said.

Gellar nodded. "Good idea. Waylen and I will go down to the docks and see how things are progressing there. No sense in us doing all this planning if the boats aren't going to be ready when we need them."

I turned and looked at Stumpy, and he sighed.

"Yes, I know. Dakaran and I will stay here with the gear and keep out of sight."

I chuckled. I felt bad for Stumpy, but like it or not, Dakaran was the crown prince, and we couldn't take any unnecessary risks, not in a city like Ecrin, when going to look for a grapple had led to a full-blown fish market war.

Barthol turned to me. "What are your plans? Any chance of getting some additional help?" He passed a quick glance at my father and brother. "Nothing like having a couple more master mercenaries around to get a job like this done, especially ones known for moving about unseen."

I smiled at the compliment. "My father and brother have agreed to help me get the ambassador and his wife out of the castle while the rest of you work on getting the soldiers over to the docks. With any luck, we'll get in and out and across town before anyone realizes they're gone. If we can make it to the docks before any alarms are rung, we should be safe."

"Famous last words," Dakaran grumbled.

The others quickly nodded.

only seeing a horse when you pop your head up for a contract, it was easy to remain distrustful. It didn't help that contracts only came a few times a year.

If I hadn't been there to witness it, I would have never believed a battle had taken place in the middle of the fish market the day before. As we rode down the street, customers filled the main roadway as they walked from booth to booth, inspecting the latest catch. The street was so tightly packed, we decided to walk our horses through instead of riding them. Also, I didn't trust my brother's ability enough to keep him from accidentally trampling someone.

Once through, we remained on foot, tying off the horses at the docks and taking the stairs down to the next section of cobbled roadway, where the wagons came to load or unload their haul. After we climbed down to the piers, I studied the ships along the boardwalk as we passed, hoping to see someone I recognized to know which one was the ship I was looking for.

Thankfully, I spotted my roommates in front of the third pier from the end. The docked ship was one of the larger vessels. It had a single sail rising from the middle, similar to the *Wind Binder*, and though it wasn't as sleek as the *Wind Binder*, it looked like it had a deep enough hull to store our prisoners.

"We were beginning to wonder if we needed to come looking," Barthol said as we walked down the dock to join them.

"Getting through the fish market took longer than expected," I said, then turned to Gellar and Fipple. "Were you able to find a wagon?"

"It's not the prettiest thing you'll ever see," Gellar said, "but it's large enough to haul the soldiers' ornery backsides from the inn to the water, as long as we don't run into any patrols on the road."

"There's a less-traveled way that Jasna showed me. We'll take it on the way back."

"Still," Fipple said, "best if she can trace it on one of our maps. Riding one way down a street can look different from the other, especially in a place this convoluted, and at night."

I nodded. He had a point. Every time I'd come into town, things had looked different. "I'll see what I can do." I left the men and led Father and Jorn down the pier toward the ship's gangway.

Jasna saw us coming and rushed down the docks to greet me. "Ooo, I like the new coat," she said with a smile, going so far as to hug me before stepping back to inspect my new purchase. She paused when she saw my father and brother, whose hoods remained up to keep their eyes hidden, which I knew was just as much for their benefit as for those they met. Their eyes hadn't spent years like mine adjusting to the brightness of the sun. Even now, I still found times when it overpowered me, especially in the mornings when Reevie would rush into my room and yank back the curtains without warning.

"I'm sorry," I said to Jasna, turning. "This is my father, Narris, and my brother, Jorn." I looked at the two of them. "This is Jasna. Her father is the captain of the boat that will be taking us downriver. Jasna has been an incredible help since we've been here." I smiled at her. "My personal guide. If there's anything you need to know about the city, she can likely tell you. Which reminds me, do you think you could sketch out the back route we traveled to get here from the Ram's Head? I need to get it marked on one of our maps."

"Of course."

Before I could thank her, Father spoke up. "It's lovely to meet you, Jasna," he said with a bow.

"Same," Jorn chimed in, bowing as well. He seemed to be smiling giddily, but with his hood up, I doubted she could see.

"It's nice meeting you," she said with a curtsy, then took my arm. "Come, let me show you the *Osprey*. We named her that because of the

way she glides across the water."

I smiled. The ship did remind me of the large bird. The bow even came to a sharp point, much like a beak.

We passed the rest of my roommates on the pier as they stood off to the side, chatting with Pradjic, Zlatin's former first mate. My roommates looked a bit out of place as they watched the swift hands and feet of the crew move about the ship unimpeded. The fishermen never had to look at what they were doing, their hands automatically maneuvering the lines as though by magic. It was a routine I remembered all too well with my time spent on the Shemoa River. And to think I could have still been there if I had made different choices.

"Permission to come aboard," I called out from the gangway, having spotted Jasna's father, who was making his way down the port side of the ship. He stopped and looked over the side and smiled. "Permission granted."

We shook hands at the top. His were strong and callused, the hands of a man who'd seen hard labor.

"Well, what do you think of her?" he asked, slapping the ship's rail.

"I think she lives up to her name," I said. Not knowing what else to say, I turned and introduced my father and brother.

They shook hands, and then Zlatin rushed off, barking out orders all the way to the aft.

"Will there be room enough for the prisoners?" I asked Jasna.

She smiled and started for a door on the left, dragging me along. "Come, I'll show you."

The four of us headed across the deck and through the doorway, which had a set of stairs leading down to the lower hull. It was quite roomy, as most of the crew slept there. There were hammocks strung around the room, leaving plenty of space for storage. Unlike the *Wind Binder*, the *Osprey* smelled strongly of fish. It wasn't the most pleasant of smells, but I was hardly in a position to complain.

"We can keep them over there," she said, pointing to the far side of the ship, where several rings had been hammered into the sides, perfect for tying off barrels and crates—or Cylmaran soldiers on their way to the salt mines.

"Does your father have a problem with us bringing the soldiers on board?" I asked.

Jasna shook her head. "The fewer of them around, the safer he feels."

My father took a moment to test the strength of the rings, and once satisfied, we headed back up the stairs to breathe in some fresh air. Well, fresher than what could be found down there.

"Seems you have things well in hand," Father said with a clap to my shoulders. "Best we leave Miss Jasna to her duties."

Jasna released my arm, looking none too happy about it, and watched from the deck as we walked down the plank to the dock, passing Pradjic on the way, who nodded when he saw me.

Jorn's footing was shaky as we stepped back onto the pier. "That was not pleasant," he said, glancing back over his shoulder at the ship. "I'm glad we will not be traveling by water as well."

I smiled. "It can take some getting used to. I spent the first couple of days aboard the *Wind Binder* hanging over the side of the ship."

Jorn shook his head and frowned, but I caught him glancing back across the lake every chance he got. It was probably the first time he'd seen a body of water like it. I remembered my first time seeing the Rhunarin Ocean and how captivated I had been at so much water in one place. I'd spent days wondering what kept it from rushing into the city and drowning us all. Come to think of it, I'd never really gotten a satisfactory answer as to why that was.

I led Father and Jorn back to the front of the pier where the rest of my roommates were waiting as they chatted quietly amongst themselves.

Father made a point to check their cords and gags. The dead were wrapped in old sheets and laid in the far corner. If we didn't get them out of here and soon, the smell was going to start driving away customers and raising questions.

As soon as Father was finished, we headed back up the stairs. We only had the afternoon to talk through strategies on how we planned to get the ambassador and his wife out of the castle, then we had to prep for my meeting with Vulkina and hope that her map was detailed enough to be of use. So many threads were still left to be woven, and if any of them snapped or came undone, the entire thing could collapse on our heads.

I didn't feel like we'd accomplished half of what we needed to when I glanced out the bedroom window and realized the sun was no longer there. In fact, I'd somehow missed its entire setting. So far, there had been no sign of Neven, even though I had gone down to the stables periodically to check. I wondered where the little picker had gotten off to and hoped that his chief hadn't changed her mind.

My stomach was too unnerved to eat any supper, and apparently I wasn't the only one, as none of the others bothered going down either. There was a knock on the door, and I stood, half-expecting to find Kelsi standing there with a pitcher and some drinks. She was very good about checking in on the guests. I opened the door, and sure enough, the pretty blonde-haired girl was standing in the hallway, but she was not holding a tray of tankards.

"Does this belong to you?" she asked with a frown as she reached beyond the doorway and grabbed something and dragged it into view.

It was Neven. He got one look at me and smiled. "That's him."

She looked at me skeptically. "He says you wanted to speak with him."

I chuckled. "That's true. I do."

"He also says that he was collecting coins to help with—"

"Don't give that little thief a bent copper." I gave the little picker a harsh look.

Neven shrugged. "A boy's gotta eat, don't he?"

I shook my head, then looked at Kelsi. "You can release him. I'll make sure he doesn't bother the other guests."

Kelsi stared at Neven a moment, as if judging whether letting the little boy loose inside the inn was a good idea or not, but eventually let go of his collar. As soon as she did, he turned and stuck his tongue out at her.

She crossed her arms and looked at me. "Will you be wanting anything before I close up? Cook's already gone home, and I'm sure Father will be along shortly to pick me up."

I shook my head. "We'll be fine for tonight. Thank you for all your help." I wanted to say a proper goodbye since this might very well be the last time I ever saw her, but the fewer people that knew our plans, the better, so I simply smiled and waved as she walked back down the hall.

"Get in here," I said, grabbing Neven's collar and dragging him through the doorway before shutting it. "Now, where've you been? I've been up and down these stairs all day, checking to see if you'd shown up."

Neven feigned a look of shock. "Vulkina had me running errands all day. I just now finished."

"Are we still set to meet?"

"Are you still planning on getting her locket?"

"Do I have a choice?"

"Not really." He looked at my father and brother. "Who are they? Are they coming? Vulkina won't like it if you don't come alone."

"Don't worry about them. You won't even know they're there."

"Well, of course I'll know they're there. You just told me."

I sighed. "Are you ready?"

He looked at me and scratched the top of his head. "Are you?"

I walked over and lifted my coat from a peg on the wall and flung it around my shoulders, then snatched my two swords and put them on as well, taking a moment to adjust the one on my back so it was balanced correctly. I finished by lifting my coat's hood.

My father smiled when he saw me. "I might have to look for a coat like that myself. Very fashionable."

"The inside is also lined with wide pockets." I patted the side with the grapple and rope. Turning back to Neven, I nodded toward the door. "Let's get this over with." I was the last one out of the room. Stumpy and Dakaran met us in the hall.

"You be careful," Stumpy said.

I looked at Dakaran. "Don't forget my travel sack when you're packing yours." I'd already taken my coin pouch and stuck it in my new leather pants. Didn't want to lose that.

Dakaran rolled his eyes. "Yes, we certainly wouldn't want to leave your smelly clothes behind. That would be tragic."

The other two doors on our side of the hall opened, and the rest of my roommates stepped out.

"Thought I heard voices," Gellar said as he and the other three walked over.

Barthol clapped arms with me. "May the Creator guide your steps . . . and keep them silent." It was the first time I'd heard Barthol mention the Creator before, except the few times in dire circumstances when he'd desperately asked for His help.

I smiled. "If our luck holds out, we will meet you at the docks around midnight."

"Let's hope it does," Waylen said.

"For all of us," Fipple added.

I took one last look at my roommates, memorizing their faces, not that I really needed to, having spent the better part of two years sharing everything from sleeping quarters to washing facilities. It was one thing to sneak into a senator's home, but it was quite another to sneak into an overlord's fortified castle. Then again, I reminded myself, it wasn't like this was the first time. I'd found a way into the royal palace and the king's own study, though admittedly I'd been captured in the process. The difference was this time, if captured, I wouldn't wake up on a soft bed in the king's chambers.

With a deep inhale and a slow release, I looked at my father and brother and nodded, and with Neven in hand, we headed down the stairs.

# WILDFIRE

## Chapter 19

T HE STREETS WERE DARK, as the moon had yet to rise high enough to provide any substantial light. There were no lamplighters or even lamps on this side of the city, but our little guide pressed on, his pace never slowing. He knew his way around the city like any good street rat, their lives depending on knowing where they were at all times and the quickest way to find shelter or escape the grasp of the patrollers.

The closer we got to the docks, the stronger the smell of fish became. Rounding one final curve, the road opened beside a large warehouse, revealing the lake ahead on the right. We passed the docks and even the old stone keep on the northern side, where Dovan had previously made his dwelling. This section of the city was lit with street lanterns, making the way ahead easier to follow.

I recognized several of the buildings, including where I'd hidden while waiting on Vulkina the first time. Behind us, a bell rang out in the harbor, signaling the ninth hour. Normally, I would have arrived at least an hour early to scout out the location, but this time I wasn't here to surprise anyone. They knew I was coming.

The cobbled street ahead was empty. Vulkina and her guards had yet to arrive.

"There's a good vantage point between those buildings there," I said to Father, pointing to the spot I had hidden the last time. "Best you and Jorn stay out of sight. I don't want to make Vulkina nervous and risk losing her map."

My father nodded and motioned for Jorn to follow as he moved to the left side of the street and into the shadows of the surrounding buildings.

"Is she coming?" I asked Neven, who stood quietly beside me, casting furtive glances back over his shoulder as he tried to see where my father and brother had vanished to.

"Vulkina arrives when she wants to," he said.

"Well, if she wants me to recover her locket, she better show up soon. I don't have all night to wait, map or not."

Neven stared up the street, as though willing his chief to appear by how hard he was concentrating on the dark cobbles ahead.

I spared the boy a passing glance but kept most of my attention on the road ahead, as well as the surrounding buildings. "How long has it been since your chief has been inside the castle?"

"I don't rightly know. She's been—"

Noise ahead signaled Vulkina's arrival. They didn't seem all that concerned with remaining quiet as they marched down the street. She had a few more guards with her this time. I remained in the middle of the road with my arms hanging loosely at my sides. The closest street-lamp was behind me on my right, leaving my hooded face in complete shadow.

I could hear Neven fidgeting beside me, his hands rubbing together as he watched the approaching entourage. He licked his lips nervously, making me feel just a little unsettled. What did he have to be so worried about? He wasn't the one about to sneak into Saryn's castle and abscond with the overlord's one bargaining advantage.

Vulkina and her guard stopped about twenty feet away, keeping a safe distance but making it difficult for me to communicate unless we planned on shouting back and forth. I looked at Neven. "Go find out if she has my map."

Neven hmphed, clearly not wanting to run over there, but he did, the armed guard in front letting him pass once they saw who it was. Neven and Vulkina convened a moment, then Neven turned and rushed back through the guard and over to where I was standing.

"Where's the map?" I asked, noticing his hands were empty.

"Vulkina says she demands to know whether you intend to retrieve her locket before she hands over the map."

I groaned. "I already said I would."

Neven sighed. "That's what I told her." He threw his arms in the air and ran back up the street. Once again Vulkina and he spoke back and forth. This time, however, she handed him a rolled piece of parchment. He ran back through the guard and handed the paper to me. "Here's your map."

I took the parchment and unrolled it. It was too dark for Neven to see clearly, even with the streetlamp's help, but I was able to get a good look at the drawing. It seemed to be broken down into four levels. Some of the rooms weren't named, obviously rooms Vulkina was unfamiliar with, while others were clearly marked. She even had a red X beside one room on the second floor. No need to guess whose room that was. Clearly that was where she thought we would find her locket.

I scanned the rest of the map thoroughly. "I see the kitchens and the bedrooms, but I don't see the dungeons."

Neven groaned but took the map and ran back up the street once more, handing it to Vulkina. I couldn't see what they were doing, as he had his back to me, but a few minutes later, he came scurrying back through their guard to hand me the parchment. This time there was an arrow drawn toward a passageway on the first floor, but no other markings as to what the dungeon looked like. Not surprising. When would a young girl working in the castle ever have need to go down into them?

I rolled the parchment up and stuffed it into one of my inner pockets. "This will be helpful, depending on how accurate it is."

"It's accurate," he said.

Either way, I didn't have much choice. It was more than I had started out with. I just wished it wasn't costing me the time and risk of trying to burgle something else while I was there.

"And what exactly does this locket look like?"

"She said she drew it on the map."

She had? I pulled the map back out. Sure enough, there was a small depiction of a round locket with some sort of designs around a blue oval stone. Hopefully, it wouldn't be too hard to find. I rolled the parchment and stuffed it back in my coat, then held out my hand to Neven.

"Thank you for your help."

He smiled as he shook it. "Good luck. You're going to need it. I hope whatever it is you're after is worth it."

"Me too."

With that, he rushed back over to Vulkina's side, and the group marched back up the street. I waited until they had made it over the rise before walking over to join my father and brother. They stepped out, and we started back in the direction we'd come toward the docks, stopping at the main road that led through the fish market. There was a lamppost on the side of the street, and we opened the map there to better

examine the layout.

"I'm guessing the X is where you will find Vulkina's locket," I said, keeping my voice lowered, even though there was no one around to hear. "We can only hope that the woman who took it still sleeps in the same room." I pointed to the depiction of the locket. "Apparently, that's what it looks like."

My father pursed his lips but nodded. "Seems straightforward enough, depending on how well-guarded each floor is."

"Where's the dungeons?" Jorn asked, staring at the map.

I pointed at the quickly placed arrow Vulkina had added. "I think that marks the entrance, but other than that, I'm afraid we're on our own."

"The sooner we get inside, the more time we'll have to figure things out," Father said, already starting up the main road, leading back to the center of town. We didn't really know our way around the city enough to risk taking side streets, so we kept to the most direct routes that guaranteed we didn't get lost or run into dead ends that would force us to waste time backtracking.

If a patrol rode by, we melted into the shadows of the nearest buildings until they passed. The city was all but silent, which was strange for this time of night. In Aramoor, the taverns would still be half-full, with the other half of its occupants stumbling down the street for home. It seemed in Ecrin, the only people still out were the soldiers, and the occasional patroller, though there weren't many of them. In a way, it almost felt like Dorwall all over again, the people fearing to step foot outside after dark.

Saryn certainly kept a tight leash on his subjects, using the fear of the soldiers to keep them in line.

Canal Street, like all the others, was void of life. The climb up Rodon Hill left me wondering if we shouldn't have brought some horses along and hidden them a few streets away. It would have made for a faster getaway if the need arose, and probably would've made travel from one side of the city to the other easier on the prisoners. There was no telling what sort of condition the ambassador and his wife might be in.

I wished I had thought of it sooner. Unfortunately, I wasn't exactly given much time to prepare, so my choices were limited. The innkeeper at the Ram's Head was beyond impatient for those soldiers in her cellar to be gone, and if we waited longer, I wouldn't have put it past her to up and try setting them free herself and saying she had been coerced. Besides, the longer we waited to rescue the ambassador and his wife, the greater the chance they'd be dead by the time we did. Even now, I had no idea if they were still alive. We could be going to all this effort to rescue a pair of corpses.

We stopped before the end of the street, which fronted the castle, and took one of the side lanes to the left, leading to the narrow alley across from where I had climbed over the wall the previous night. Crouching just inside the opening between buildings, we waited for the first of three patrols.

The horses' hooves on the stone cobble was the only warning we received before the next pair rounded the bend. It was one reason we were on foot. Horses, though swift, were also very loud and much easier to track. Perhaps silence was safer than speed when it came to rescuing our people.

Father motioned to my coat, and I pulled out the grapple and made sure the rope was loose and ready to throw. We would need to be quick and precise if we were to get all three of us up and over before the next patrol arrived. While waiting, I double-checked my swords and sheaths, especially the one on my back, making sure they were good and secure.

We heard the clop-clop-clop of the horses and pressed against the side of the building. The two horses and their riders passed slowly, the one closest to us carrying a torch. Father and Jorn pulled their cloth masks up to their noses. I wasn't sure what the purpose for the masks was, other than to maybe keep the glare from their faces from being noticeable, but wasn't that what the hoods were for? Of course, I was hardly one to judge. I'd covered my entire body in black paint before sneaking into Senator Gerrick's home.

After a tap on the shoulder from my father, I slid out from between the buildings and ran across the street. My father and brother stayed behind as I dropped the rope into place and took aim. The last time I'd come, I'd been able to run up the wall, but I had no idea what kind of shape my brother and father were in, so I opted for the grapple.

The hook left my hand and snagged the top on the first throw. I smiled inwardly, feeling pretty good about my aim as I motioned them out. They rushed across the road, and Jorn was the first up. I kept the rope taut to maintain the hook's grip as he shimmied up.

As soon as Jorn grabbed hold of the top of the wall, my father took the rope and motioned for me to go next. I didn't argue. There wouldn't have been much use. I quickly made my way up the rope and lay down on top, as did Jorn, to stay as inconspicuous as possible. The windows in the buildings across the street were dark, but that didn't mean someone might not be up using a chamber pot and looking out the window at the same time we were sitting there.

I kept a tight grip on the grapple to keep it secured against the back of the stone where it was fastened. As soon as my father reached the top, I pulled up the rope and reversed the grapple to grip the other side of the wall. As soon as the hooks had dug into the top, we quickly slid down the rope to the bottom, and I flicked it hard enough to release.

Jorn caught the grapple before it hit the ground and handed it to me. With rope and hook in hand, we made our way up the steep ravine to the castle wall, keeping a close eye on the surrounding windows, and more importantly, the upper parapets where the tops of guards' heads could be seen walking by.

Once we reached the walls at the top, we hid within the thick creepers that clung to the dark side of the stone near the corner of the tower. It was the perfect place to catch our breath. I looked up and spotted the sill just to the left of where I was standing. Hopefully I would be able to catch it on my first throw.

Lowering the rope to make sure it didn't tangle, I loosened my grip on the grapple and took a couple steps back from the wall. The window was too high to simply just throw the hook up and hope it hit the mark, so I gave it a couple of good swings, then released.

It snagged onto the sill with a clang, and I quickly shot back up against the side of the tower in case someone above heard. No heads appeared, so I stepped back out, rope in hand. It wasn't a thick rope, which would have made it easier for climbing, but it was thick enough that it didn't require me to wrap it around my hands.

Before I let them climb, I made sure it was secure by giving the rope a firm tug. As soon as I did, the hook slipped with a noticeable scraping noise as the metal dug into the stone before plummeting over the side and dropping straight for my head. I hopped out of the way, and it thudded in the dirt beside me.

Once again, we pressed against the wall and waited, and to my surprise, no one appeared to have noticed. Biting my tongue, I started to try again, but Father stopped me and took the grapple himself. Suddenly feeling thirteen all over again, I relinquished my claim on the tool and took a step back to give him room. Three swings and the hook flew into the air, this time fastening around the back side of the sill.

For the third time, we all moved back into the shadows of the wall and waited. When no one came, I decided to be the first up. As Father held the rope, I ascended as gracefully and swiftly as I could, hoping to

earn back some of the confidence I'd lost just a moment ago. I reached the sill and pulled myself up and over, taking a quick moment to look around the room and make sure I was alone before leaning out the window and waving them up.

It didn't take long before my brother and father were inside the keep, and we were pulling up the rope. Father went about winding the coil and placing it on a nearby shelf for easy access as I headed across the room for the door. I had thought to take the grapple with me in case I needed to use it to climb something else, but if anything happened to me, that would leave them without a way to escape.

"Through this door is a small corridor," I whispered, explaining as best I could what I'd seen on my first visit, since none of this was detailed on Vulkina's map. "The right leads to the edge of the tower. Left leads out to the heart of the keep. Just across from this door is a circular well that leads down to the main floor and up to the ramparts. At least, I think it does, since the tower we're in reaches that far."

"Let's look at that map once more," Father whispered as we huddled near the window for a little extra light.

I unrolled the parchment, and we took a few minutes to go over it, memorizing every facet. My father studied the first X located on the floor above the one we were on, which Vulkina had marked as the location of the locket. Jorn and I took a moment to look at the squiggly arrow on the main floor, but other than getting a basic idea of which direction we should be looking, it was going to be up to us to find it.

"We can take a quick look at the main keep before parting ways," I said. "The stairwell should get us to the correct floors."

The other two nodded, and I rolled the map and stuck it back in my coat.

Father thumbed his chin. "I've said it before, and I'll say it again. I don't like how little time we had to prepare for this."

"I don't like it either, but each day we wait, the greater the chance of us getting caught or the ambassador and his wife dying."

The one and only contract I'd been on with my father had been to Oswell, where we'd displaced Magistrate Sirias and his family. We had spent days preparing beforehand, and that job hadn't required us entering an overlord's heavily guarded castle to do it, especially not an overlord known for his ruthlessness.

Taking a deep breath, I slid open the door slowly and peeked outside. I was about to step out when I heard voices coming up the stairs. Quickly, I scooted back in and eased the door shut, leaving only a crack large enough to listen through. This would be my luck. I'd pick the one room where an overly anxious cleaner had decided to do their sweeping in the middle of the night while everyone was asleep.

I positioned myself to grab whoever came through the door first. My heart pounded in my ears as I waited for the handle to turn. The voices grew louder, and I stared at the handle. *Three, two, one . . .*

But then the voices began to fade and eventually disappeared altogether.

I took a moment to release a heavy sigh of relief. Whoever they were, they hadn't stopped. Waiting a moment just to be sure, I finally slid the door open once more and stepped out.

Quietly, we scooted down the side of the narrow corridor to the archway that led out to the main part of the keep. There were guards posted on the other side of the balcony, where the stairs led to the floor below. No other guards could be seen. Father pointed to a spot on the next floor up, where the map had marked the room where Vulkina thought we would find the stolen locket.

I nodded and then got down on my hands and knees and crawled out to the edge of the balcony. From there, I peered through the railing down to the bottom floor. There were guards posted at every landing, making me very thankful for the stairwell in the tower behind us. Father and Jorn studied the layout below as well. Apart from using the grapple and trying to hang over the side of the rail and lower ourselves down to the bottom, I couldn't see any way down that wouldn't require us fighting through armed men and raising the castle's alarm.

Slowly, we made our way back to the tower archway and down the corridor to the stairs on the left. "Mine is the simplest task," Father said, "so I will wait for you here once it's done. If something goes wrong, just remember, your life is more important than the contract. You do whatever you have to do to get out."

It was a typical Upakan statement, but this was more than just a contract to me. Still, I nodded, and we parted ways.

Father headed up; Jorn and I went down.

The stairwell was surprisingly cool this early in the evening. The stone did a great job of making my new coat bearable. The steps were quite shallow, forcing me to focus on where I was placing my feet. With my luck, I'd miss a step and go rolling down the well. I kept my hand to the wall for balance as I moved on the balls of my feet to keep as quiet as possible.

We reached the first landing down, and I slowed, holding my arm out to stop Jorn. I peeked around the opening only to find another empty corridor, very similar to the one we'd just left. With a nod, we continued on to what I was sure had to be the first floor, leading out to the main gallery.

I counted the number of spirals to determine how close we were getting to the bottom, slowing as we reached the final turn. Quietly, I pressed against the left wall and peeked around the corner. My heart sank. There were two more guards posted at the entryway. Overlord Saryn was certainly taking no chances.

The black-uniformed men had their backs to us. If I leaned out a little further, I could see other armed men beyond them guarding the grand staircase in the main hall. We wouldn't be able to subdue these two without the others seeing. I balled my fists. Maybe grappling down the balcony wasn't such a stupid idea after all?

I turned and motioned for Jorn to head back up the stairs, then stopped him on the next landing up. Hopefully it was far enough away to safely speak without being heard, and we stepped out of the well and into the narrow corridor.

"I don't see how we're going to get past those guards," Jorn whispered. "This place is too heavily watched down here." Jorn paused a moment, his lips pursed. "We could lure them up the stairs, then take their uniforms."

I shook my head. "It'll take too long. If both guards leave their post and we take the time to subdue them, gag them, and then strip them, the other guards are going to come looking. And even if we managed to get their uniforms before the others came to look, what then? We can't just leave our post and head for the dungeon. That would certainly raise brows. Not to mention, those standing watch on the other side of the hall probably know these guards and would clearly see that we aren't them."

I took a deep breath and exhaled in frustration. How were we going to make this work? To get across the grand hall, it was clear we were going to need uniforms, and we couldn't use the uniforms from any of those standing watch down here. I walked down the hall to the archway and glanced up at the upper levels. We needed uniforms, but there were too many guards watching on each floor to manage it without being seen. That left only one place.

Jorn moved up beside me to see what I was looking at. "Why are you smiling?"

"I have an idea, but we need to switch towers."

# WILDFIRE

## Chapter 20

QUIETLY, WE CRAWLED ON OUR hands and knees out of the tower and into the main part of the keep. We kept close to the balcony rail around the back so we could see down to the first level easily enough to make sure no one was coming. The guards on the second floor, which was the floor we were presently on, were located on the far corner of the balcony where the stairs led down to the main gallery. The large stairway leading up to the third floor, where Father was, was located about thirty feet to the right of the tower entrance we'd just exited. Thankfully, the guards watching it were positioned at the bottom of the stairs and not the top, which would have given them a direct line of sight down to us.

We kept our heads lowered as we crawled along the back wall to the opposite side, where there was another similar archway leading into an adjoining tower. I could only hope there were stairs in it as well, leading to the next floors. I wondered if the tower stairs were used by the staff and the guards, while the much larger and far grander staircases around the balcony were reserved for the use of the overlord's family and his guests.

I edged up to the corner rail of the balcony and peeked around the right to see if the guards at the end still had their backs to us. They did. Quickly, we left the cover of the railing and rushed into the next tower, pressing against the wall as we waited to make sure no one had spotted us. When no warnings came, I started down the corridor, releasing a sigh of relief when I spotted the winding staircase ahead on the right.

"Where are we going?" Jorn whispered before I stepped into the well.

I turned and pointed. "Up."

After taking a moment to listen, we headed into the stairwell and started winding our way up the narrow corridor toward the top, passing a few window slits that provided just enough moonlight to keep our feet from faltering. My head remained cocked as I listened intently for any sounds above, but so far there had been nothing but the soft scraping of our shoes on the worn stone. I slowed at each landing, taking a moment to look around, then with a simple nod, we continued on. As luck would have it, there didn't seem to be anyone guarding these side passageways.

The hollow echo of our feet against the stone changed as we started around the last spiral. I could hear wind seeping down through the well from above. Holding out my hand to stop Jorn, I pressed against the left wall and crept slowly forward. The landing at the top ended in an open doorway, which led out onto the upper battlement. I figured if a couple of guards were to go missing, it would be less noticeable up here in the dark than down in the main keep, where all the guards were practically staring at each other.

I started to turn to let Jorn know what I was doing when a vision had the hairs on my back of my neck standing. I snatched the sword off my back and spun just in time to stop a sword from taking my head. It

was a single guard. How had I missed him? He must have been standing in the crook between the edge of the archway and the crenelation. Our swords struck, and I grabbed the front of his uniform and threw myself backward, kicking out with my legs as soon as I hit the ground to send him flying over me.

The guard landed on his back with a thud, and before I could spin around to clamp his mouth, Jorn had kicked the man in the side of the head. I caught a flash of steel above me and barely got my arm up in time to stop Jorn before he plunged the blade into the guard's chest. Shoving my zealous brother back, I hopped to my feet and quickly dragged the guard back into the stairwell and out of the open.

As soon as we were back within the safety of the tower, I spun on my brother. "What do you think you're doing?"

"Making sure he doesn't let anyone know we are here."

There was an anger in his eyes that worried me. Had Father not been training him the way he had me? Had he not been showing Jorn how to do this job without killing everyone who got in their way? "He's just doing his job. You don't kill a man for that."

"You killed those men in the fish market."

"They also didn't leave me any choice. There's a big difference between fighting an opponent face-to-face in a battle and slitting someone's throat in the middle of the night for no more reason than they were in your way."

"He was going to kill you."

"I had the situation completely in hand. I . . ." I shook my head. "I don't have time to argue about this. Here, help me get his uniform off. But from now on, no killing."

My brother snarled but didn't say anything further. He'd clearly been spending way too much time training with the wrong sort of people back home. I wondered if my leaving wasn't partly to blame. Could I have kept him from this if I had been around?

As fast as we could, we stripped the guard of his clothing, using some of his undergarments to tie his hands and feet and gag him if he woke.

"Keep watch while I put his uniform on," I said, all but pushing Jorn toward the doorway.

The guard was about my height, though maybe a little thicker in the chest. I ended up keeping my own boots and pants, since they were the same color anyway, and used the guard's tabard and cloak as the main concealer. There was no need to swap everything. I doubted very highly anyone was going to have me drop my trousers just to make sure I was indeed wearing the proper uniform.

"Psst."

I turned, and Jorn waved me back. Someone was coming. Two guards stopped just outside the tower on their way by, close enough to hear them talking. I kept to the shadows but still had the vantage of seeing the two men. What were they doing?

"Where's Egert?" one of the guards asked, turning to look at the tower doorway.

My hand slid slowly toward my sword.

"Probably headed down to the privy," the other said with a chuckle. "Last time he tried going over the side, he nearly fell off."

The two men laughed.

I couldn't help but think this might be our best opportunity to get another uniform, though I would have preferred taking only two. The more men that disappeared from the wall, the more suspicious it would look. I pulled my hood over my head and started to step out of the shadows to see if I could draw them over to the door when one of the men started over on his own.

"I might just join him. Been holding it for too long as it is. I'll catch up with you on the next round."

I quickly moved back into the shadows, thankful for our unexpected turn of luck.

Jorn was standing just to the left of the opening, a blade in his hand. I shook my head, hoping he saw me and didn't do anything rash.

The guard that remained on the battlement didn't wait for the one approaching the tower and instead continued on around.

I inched my way forward, getting as close to Jorn as I could in case I needed to stop him from opening the man's throat.

As soon as the guard broke the entrance, I leaped into action. I practically kicked off the wall behind me and dove on top of the man before Jorn could bring his knife to bear. I hit the guard full on, throwing him backward onto the stone with me directly on top. I landed on his chest, forcing the air from his lungs. He couldn't have cried for help had he wanted to.

The man was so shocked he didn't even have time to try defending himself before I had him in a choke hold with one hand over his mouth. A few moments later he was unconscious, his head drooping to the side.

We rushed to get his uniform off like the first, then cut up his undershirt to use as a gag, and for binding. We dragged the two men back down the stairs to the next landing, and I checked the doors on that level, finding several open, but only one with a room that looked like it would be a good place to keep the two men from being seen. It, too, seemed to be some kind of storage room.

We dropped them inside, and I reached into one of the inner pockets of my coat and pulled out a bottle of dwale that Reevie and Physicker Saban used during their surgeries. It wasn't as strong smelling as the ether but just as effective. Having a friend that trained with an actual physicker was proving extremely useful.

Shutting the door, I used my lock set, which I never went anywhere without, to snap the lock back into place. Hopefully, the two men would be unconscious long enough for us to get the ambassador and his wife out.

There was no time to waste as we slipped back into the tower stairwell, but this time we took the stairs *down*. It made no sense to crawl all the way back across the balcony to the other tower when this was the side of the keep we needed to be on anyway. According to Vulkina's map, the entrance to the dungeons was located approximately thirty or forty feet from this tower. It was still a lot of open ground to cover.

We reached the bottom in quick order, but like the tower on the other side, this, too, had armed men guarding it. We raised our hoods. Now to find out if our uniforms would be enough.

Taking a deep breath, I started down the last couple of steps to the bottom landing. "I don't care what time it is," I said to Jorn. He looked at me funny, then seemed to understand what I was doing and nodded. "When the overlord tells you he wants something, you go get it."

The two guards standing just outside the open doorway turned.

"You two know what I'm talking about," I said to the men, including them in the conversation. "Saryn isn't a man you say no to, or question. When he wants something done, you do it. You don't ask why." I looked at the two guards, and they slowly nodded, clearly unsure as to what was happening. "Ol' Grouchy Pants up there demands we bring him the Elondrian prisoners."

The two guards looked at each other quizzically. "Which ones?"

"What do you mean, which ones? The only ones that matter, of course. Why do you think we're all missing our beds tonight? You can't spit off the balcony without hitting half a dozen men on the way down."

"Ain't that the truth," the one on the left said as they both nodded in agreement. "Never seen Ecrin this strongly protected before. He's got the soldiers patrolling the streets night and day. You'd think we'd kidnapped the king's own son."

The guard on the left laughed.

If only they knew how close to true that statement was.

"We haven't been sent on dungeon patrol yet," I said. "What's the best way down?"

The two guards paused a moment.

I bit my tongue. Admitting I wasn't sure where the dungeon was might not have been the wisest choice. My hand slid for my belt knife behind my waist, but as soon as my fingers found the handle, one of the guards motioned us out of the stairwell. He then pointed down the hall on the left.

"The entrance is just down there. Take three flights down, and you'll reach the duty station. Moric is on duty tonight, I think." He turned and looked at the other guard, who simply shrugged. "I think it's Moric."

I nodded. "Much appreciated. Next round's on us."

The two guards smiled, and we quickly left before they realized they had no idea who was supposed to be buying them a round.

We passed a couple of doors on our left, leading off the main part of the keep, but they were closed. The bottom of the grand staircase was coming up on the right. We had to pass it and the guards in front in order to reach the entrance to the dungeons, which was just beyond. We kept as close to the left wall as possible as we made our way past the stairs and the two sets of guards standing there. Not too far past the bottom of the staircase was a large passageway on the left that led off the main keep, with stairs heading down. That had to be it. We left the main keep and started for the stairs leading down. Another set of guards stood watch at the top. I'd never seen so many guards in a single house. Not even the royal palace had this many.

*Please don't let them stop us*, I thought as we headed in their direction. There was one guard on either side. Jorn's hand started to slide toward his sword, and I elbowed him.

"Where're you going?" the guard on the left asked.

We didn't stop, didn't even slow. "The overlord wants to talk with the prisoners."

I kept my eyes on the upcoming stairs like it was the most natural thing to go walking into the dungeons in the middle of the night to fetch prisoners for the overlord to question. If we were stopped, there wasn't much more I could say, and we certainly couldn't take the chance of trying to fight our way in. One drawn sword and we wouldn't be making it back out, not with this many guards. Once again, I found myself holding my breath and counting the stairs down; each new step meant a greater chance we'd make it without being stopped.

Halfway, I took my first breath. I didn't bother glancing over my shoulder to see if the two at the top were still watching. It was one thing to learn how to blend in, but it was quite another when you found yourself in the heart of one of the most dangerous castles in Aldor, walking through an army of black guards.

The landing at the bottom of the stairs was lit with a couple of torches on either side of a large wooden door. The jailer, Moric, or whoever the guard thought was Moric, sat watching us from behind his desk, a quill resting in one hand. He seemed to be waiting to jot something down on one of the parchments in front of him.

Now came the real test.

We stopped a few feet from the desk, keeping back far enough that our hoods blocked the majority of our faces from the torchlight. "We've come for the ambassador and his wife," I said, doing my best to sound as relaxed as possible.

Moric leaned forward, resting his elbows on the desk as he looked us over. His gut pressed against the side of the desk, shifting the legs ever so slightly. "I've heard nothing about a prisoner transfer."

"It's not a transfer. Saryn has asked to see them personally."

The jailer stood from his desk, the legs of his stool scraping the stone floor. He looked bewildered. "In the middle of the night?"

"The overlord gets what the overlord wants," I said, using nearly the same line I'd used with the last two guards. "Who are we to question?"

He looked the two of us over one more time, clearly not as easily convinced as the last two men. "Do you have any papers?"

I cleared my throat. My palms were sweating. *Papers?* Was he wanting a written order? I could see Jorn fidgeting beside me from the corner of my eye. His arm was slowly moving downward. "Why would we need papers to take the prisoners to the overlord? His bedchamber is right above us. Are you saying you want me to walk all the way back up those stairs and tell Saryn that we were unable to get him the ambassador because his jailer refused?"

Moric gulped as he worked his tongue around in his mouth.

I continued. "Are you saying you want me to tell our overlord that he needs to crawl from the comfort of his bed to write you a personal notice?" I looked at Jorn and motioned for us to head back up the stairs. "Guess we'll be dealing with a new jailer tomorrow. This one isn't long for the world."

"Fine, fine," Moric said before we'd reached the second step. "Don't get yourself so worked up. Can't be too careful these days. If you was to abscond with the prisoners, it'd be my neck in the noose." He turned and snatched the keys off the wall behind him, and I frowned. I hadn't thought about it, but we were practically sticking the man's neck in the noose.

Moric walked over to the large door and turned the key, its hinges groaning under the weight as he pulled it open. He grabbed a torch that was resting on the inside wall and handed it to Jorn as we made our way inside. As soon as we were through, he locked the door again, stowing the key in his trousers as he then took the torch back and started down the first of several long dark corridors.

The dungeons stank of wet stone, unemptied chamber pots, and death. Not a pleasant place for the ambassador and his wife to be. I couldn't imagine how scared they must be right now. We followed Moric for quite some time, even taking another flight of stairs down to a lower level, where the rats ran free and the stone was wet, as though having been underwater recently.

"Watch your footing down here," Moric said as we stepped off into ankle-deep water. The rats remained on the stairs, not wanting to get any closer to the flooded area than they needed to for drinking. I was thankful for my good boots.

How close were we to the lake? Surely we were far enough away that there wouldn't be seepage this far underground. Anyone left down in this cesspool would be dead of disease in no time. I was beginning to wonder if perhaps we'd made this entire trip for nothing.

"This place reeks," Jorn mumbled.

Moric chuckled as he glanced back over his shoulder at the two of us. "I take it this is your first time to the dungeons."

"You would be correct," I said. "Where is all the water coming from?"

Moric turned and pointed behind us, down the long stone corridor we were in, back far enough that even our Upakan eyes couldn't cut through the shadows. "There's a fissure in the rock that water pours through every few hours. They say it runs all the way to the lake. Gets bigger every year. Pretty soon the lower dungeons are going to be unusable." He said it like that was a bad thing, lessening my earlier guilt for the possibility of putting his neck in a noose by absconding with his prisoners.

"Then why don't you just seal it up?" Jorn asked.

The jailer chuckled. "Wouldn't work. The water would eventually wear through." He turned and started back down the tunnel. Eventually, he stopped outside one of the last few doors remaining before the passageway ended at what appeared to be the back of the lower dungeon. Other than a few sad wails seeping down from the upper levels, there didn't appear to be anyone left alive down here.

"How many other prisoners are they keeping here in the lower dungeon?" I asked. "The place sounds empty."

"Mostly corpses, I reckon," Moric said. "Those the overlord has a particular fondness for hurting, he keeps down here." Moric shivered slightly. "We have to come in every so often to clean out the bodies." He handed me the torch and pulled out his ring of keys, sifting through till he found the one he was looking for. He placed it in the rusty lock, and it clicked. The door squealed on its hinges as he pulled it open, then he snatched the torch back and stepped inside. "You still alive in here?"

I looked at Jorn and frowned. It was a bad sign when your jailer had to ask if you were still alive. I heard a faint groan and followed Moric in, bending to keep from hitting my head. Jorn remained out in the corridor. I didn't blame him. The smell inside was worse than anything I'd smelled before. Even worse than Tubby after we first pulled off his mask and had been forced to bathe him from head to toe.

Unlike the rooms upstairs and even the corridor just outside the door, which were fashioned with stone blocks, the cells themselves were nothing more than chiseled-out hulls in the rock. The floors were uneven and would be nearly impossible to sleep on, even if they weren't layered in ankle-deep water.

The prisoners were huddled in the far corner, the man with his arm around his whimpering wife. Dark circles around red eyes said they hadn't slept in days, and if they had, it was a fitful sleep. They were nothing but skin and bone. I wondered if they would even be strong enough to walk. I didn't know how we would get them out if we were forced to carry them.

"Still alive, I see," Moric said, sounding a bit relieved. "It seems the overlord is desiring of your company this evening." He looked them over, then lifted the collar of his tunic over his nose and mouth. "Best we wash you up first. Don't want Saryn losing his supper while trying to question you." Moric chuckled. Somehow the thought of the overlord gagging at the couple's smell struck the jailer as humorous.

The ambassador was a short man, and about as frail-looking as a man twenty years his senior. His hair, or at least what was left on the sides and back of his head, had whitened.

"Well, come on, we haven't got all night." Moric paused as he turned for the door. "Actually, I guess we do." He laughed and stepped back out into the corridor, taking the light with him.

He turned and raised his torch to say something to Jorn but stopped. Then he cleared his throat and glanced back at the cell door. "I think I'll go on ahead and see about getting a tub ready and someone down here to help us carry them up."

Jorn grabbed Moric's arm before he left.

"What?" Moric asked, spinning around.

Jorn snatched the torch from the jailer and turned and lit one of the dead torches mounted in the hall, then handed it back to Moric.

Moric didn't say anything, just turned and headed back the way we'd come. I could hear the splash of his footfalls down the corridor.

"Help me get these people back to the stairs," I said to Jorn, who was standing in the hall, staring after Moric.

Jorn turned, then hesitated. I could see the disgust on his face, but he did eventually step inside the cell after taking a quick breath, not that it smelled that much better in the corridor beyond.

"What does Saryn want?" the ambassador asked, doing his best to

try to help us carry his wife over to the doorway. "Haven't we suffered enough?"

We helped them to the exit, and I stopped and listened. There were no more splashing footsteps, which meant Moric was already heading back up the stairs to the upper level. With a heave, we helped the ambassador's wife through the door and into the stone corridor beyond. The torch on the wall behind us crackled and flickered against a slight breeze, which I guessed was either coming down from the upper level or from wherever the water was seeping in.

I turned to the ambassador. "We aren't here to take you to Saryn. We're here to rescue you."

The two prisoners looked up, and I pulled my hood back. Their faces went slack. "You're, you're—"

"Upakan?" I smiled. "Yes, I am. But don't hold it against me. King Rhydan sent me and my team here to get you and your wife out."

The ambassador's wife suddenly found some strength in her legs as her eyes brightened. "The king? The king sent you?" She turned and clung to her husband. "You see? I told you he wouldn't abandon us. He wouldn't do that."

I grabbed her arm to keep her from tipping over. "We need to hurry."

"But how are you going to get us past the guards?" the ambassador asked as we struggled to make our way back toward the steps leading out of the lower level.

"Hopefully, we walk you right past them."

The ambassador and his wife looked confused, but I didn't have time to stop and explain our plan, especially since I wasn't quite sure of it myself.

"What's your name, young man?" the ambassador asked as we continued down the long damp corridor. "I'm Gorman, and this is my wife,

Neina."

Neina tried to smile, but it came off more sad than anything.

At this point, I didn't see any harm in giving my name. Even if we were captured, knowing my name wouldn't make any difference. What was important, they would already know—the fact that I had been sent there by the king.

"My name is Ayrion."

The ambassador turned and looked at my brother, who was presently carrying the torch.

My brother sighed. "Jorn."

The ambassador smiled. "Thank you, Ayrion and Jorn. You have our undying gratitude. If there is anything you ever need, don't hesitate to ask."

I smiled. It seemed a sincere gesture, though somewhat hollow, since this would be the one and only time Jorn would ever lay eyes on the man, and even with my connection to the palace, it was likely to be my one and only time as well. "Let's just focus on getting the two of you out of here safely, shall we?"

We reached the steps and started up.

"Where are those men Moric was going to get?" Jorn complained. "We could really use some help right about now."

Both Neina and Gorman were struggling to make it up, especially Neina. Her legs gave out on nearly every step, slowing our ascent drastically. Finally, I maneuvered myself around so that I could lift her up into my arms completely, while Jorn used one shoulder to help stabilize Gorman. I was beginning to wonder where that promised help was as well. They should have been here by now.

"I'm getting a bad feeling," Jorn said, stopping for a moment as I lowered Neina back down to catch my breath.

I looked at Jorn, trying not to let the others see how worried I was.

"Did Moric say anything else to you while we were in the cell?"

Jorn shook his head. "But I think he might have seen my eyes."

"What? Why didn't you say anything?"

"Because I couldn't really tell if he had, and you needed my help at the time."

I suddenly had a chill run down my back, and I took the torch from Jorn. "Stay here." Hoping with everything in me that I was wrong, I ran up the stairs, leaving them alone to the darkness. I reached the upper level and still found no sign of Moric, not even a hint that he or anyone else was coming down to help us.

I rushed through the dungeon corridors, forced to backtrack after I had taken a wrong turn, before finally coming to a stop outside the dungeon door. It was locked. I started to bang on the door to get Moric's attention and see what was happening, when I heard shouts coming from the other side. If Moric had seen Jorn's eyes, he would have known that we weren't who we said we were. I shook my head. "I'm going to kill Jorn." He should have stopped Moric as soon as he thought the jailer had seen him.

I opened the peephole, located about two-thirds up the door, and the breath caught in my throat.

Guards were beginning to gather up in the main hall, and they were all looking in my direction. There was no doubt in my mind. Moric had alerted them to us, and now we were trapped.

# WILDFIRE

## Chapter 21

I RAN BACK THROUGH the dungeon as fast as I could. This time, I reached the stairs leading down without taking a wrong turn. For a moment, I wondered how Father was doing, whether he could see what was happening. I hoped that our bad luck didn't reach him, as I was sure the castle was now on full alert.

Below me, Jorn was standing in front of the ambassador and his wife, who were plopped down on the steps with their backs leaning against the wall. They looked on the verge of unconsciousness but revived when they saw me coming.

"What's wrong?" Jorn asked, seeing the look on my face.

"Moric must have seen your eyes after all. They've locked us in, and from what I can tell, half the palace guards are waiting in the main hall to rush down here and take us."

"I should have just killed him," Jorn said, "but no, you had to insist that I don't harm any of your precious guards."

"They'll torture us for sure," Gorman said, his hands trembling as he tried standing, only to collapse on the step once again.

His wife started to sob, too scared to move, not that she had the strength.

Jorn drew his sword and his knife, his face tightening. "Then we fight our way out."

"Through a hundred guards?" I asked.

"With these uniforms on, in the dark, we'll blend in. They won't be able to tell who they're fighting. It'll be chaos." He actually looked excited.

"And what about the ambassador and his wife? You plan on carrying them while you're doing all this fighting? They don't have uniforms. How do you propose we hide them?"

Jorn looked down at the two, then back up at me. "You heard what Father said." I could see it in his eyes. He had no intention of taking them with him. "You have a better idea?"

"Maybe." It wasn't a good idea, but it was the only one I had.

"I hope it doesn't involve us waiting around for your roommates to show up."

I shoved the torch back into Jorn's hand, forcing him to sheathe one of his blades to hold it, and bent to lift Neina off the steps. "We don't have time to wait for anyone. They'll be rushing the dungeon at any moment."

"Then what are we going to do, oh great one?" Jorn asked as he yanked Gorman back to his feet.

I looked back up the stairs one last time. I couldn't hear anything from above yet, but that didn't mean they weren't coming. "We head back down." Hefting Neina higher in my arms, I started back down the damp stairs toward the water-filled tunnel below.

"Great," Jorn said. "What next? You want us to lock ourselves in one of the cells? I'm sure Saryn will show us great mercy seeing how cooperative we've been."

I ignored him and kept my focus on my footing. One slip and both me and the ambassador's wife would likely snap our necks rolling down the stone steps.

Neina and I were the first to reach the bottom, rats scurrying around my feet. I didn't have time to bother with kicking them out of the way. If they were too stupid to move, they deserved getting stepped on. We splashed down in the water, which had somehow risen since we had last left it. It was now almost shin deep.

"This place is flooding," Jorn said.

"Thanks for pointing out the obvious," I shot back and started us down the tunnel to the right, the opposite direction we'd taken the last time.

"I hope you're not thinking what I think you're thinking," Jorn said.

"What's he thinking?" Gorman asked.

My foot slipped on a loose bit of stone under the water, but I righted myself before Neina and I went down. "I'm thinking I want to get out of here before the palace guards show up. I only hope it's large enough."

"What's large enough?" Gorman asked, his words hesitant, as though he was just realizing what I had planned.

We came to the end of the passage, and Jorn held out the torch as we all stood there staring at the gaping crevice in the rock. It wasn't much to look at. The jagged edges were barely wide enough for a person to fit through and started about a foot up the rock wall and ended not much higher than my head.

I wondered how long it had been there, and how far in it went.

"You don't expect us to go in there, do you?" Neina asked, halfwhimpering as she did.

"We'll drown," Gorman added.

I turned. "You stay here and you're a dead man for sure, and it won't be quick. You want to stick around and see what new and inventive forms of torture Saryn can come up with for his entertainment?"

Neina practically pulled herself out of my arms as she tried stumbling toward the fissure, which was seeping water into the tunnel at a very swift pace. I guess I had my answer.

"We don't even know where this comes out," Jorn pointed out. "We don't even know if it's large enough to fit through." He huffed. "We don't know anything."

I helped Neina the rest of the way through the split and started in myself ahead of Jorn and Gorman. Once inside, I removed the second sword that I had kept hidden under the Cylmaran uniform and strapped it to my back to better free up my hands. Keeping it hidden now was pointless. "We know that if we stay, we're as good as dead." I slid the rest of the way into the crevice. The bottom was lower in the fissure than what was in the dungeon, which put the water up over our knees.

Behind me, I could hear faint shouting from the dungeon passageway above. Gorman and Jorn practically fought to be the next in. "Hurry," Jorn said. "They're coming."

I put my arm around Neina's waist, and we started forward as fast as we could manage. Unlike the stone block of the lower dungeon behind us, or even the chiseled cells used to hold the prisoners, this place was completely of its own making—larger crevices, wide enough for two to fit through, emptied into smaller cracks barely wide enough for one to fit sideways, and only if they sucked in their gut to do it. There were times when the top of the stone lowered to the point we had to crawl through with our heads barely above water.

Panic overcame the ambassador and his wife more than once, forcing us to stop to encourage them to keep going. Jorn and I were much more familiar with the concept of crawling around in underground tunnels, though it had been years since I had spent any length of time in one, and I would be lying if I said I wasn't worried, what with the water rising at the pace it was. We had no way of knowing how fast the tunnel would fill, not to mention the guards were sure to have discovered where we had disappeared to by now and were likely in pursuit.

The water was quite cold, cold enough to numb my fingers and toes. I wasn't sure if it was pouring in from the lake or from some underground spring. I reasoned that if it had been a spring, the lower dungeon would have remained filled with water. This acted more like the rising and lowering tides of a larger body of water. I wish I knew how much farther the crevice went. At the rate the water was forcing us upward, if we didn't find an exit soon, we were going to drown.

I hadn't seen my family in nearly five years, and not one day after I did, it looked like I might manage to kill not only myself but my brother. I shook my head. I had to quit thinking like that. We were going to make it. We had to. Too many people were depending on me. What would Sapphire and Reevie do if I ended up just like Noph and never showed up again?

Neina cried out and went down, and I grabbed her before her head went completely under.

"What happened?" Gorman asked, trying to push forward to get to his wife. "Are you all right?"

She held up her hand. "I'm fine. I tripped."

The water was now past our waists. "Hurry," I said. "We've got to move before it traps us in here." The guard's uniform over my other clothes was really weighing me down, and I ended up stopping to try pulling it off. After untying the cloak, Jorn helped me yank the tabard over my head, then I did the same for him. My new coat was heavy enough without the weight of the guard's uniform to restrict my movement.

Wrapping my arm around Neina, I pushed forward. We crawled through another narrow slit in the rock that looked like it led to a larger chamber, and as soon as I turned to pull Neina through, I stepped back and went under.

I kicked out with my feet to stop myself on the floor, but my feet never touched the bottom, which scared me even more, and I swam back to the top. My head broke the surface, and I paddled over to the edge.

"What happened?" Jorn asked, his belt knife in his hand as he used the torch to cast about the small cavern I'd crawled into.

"I don't know," I said, spitting water. "The floor just gave way. And I didn't feel a bottom when I went under." I turned and looked at the open room. "I have no idea how deep it goes."

"It can't be all that deep, surely," Gorman said, his arm around his wife as they stared into the chamber. "That would mean this place would have to fill before the water could leak into the fissure and back to the dungeon." He glanced around. "Does anyone see where the water is coming in from?"

I swam over to the crack where they were all standing and pulled myself up to the narrow shelf on the side of the drop-off. Getting my footing back under me, I turned and looked at the room, and more importantly, the edges around it. Gorman was right. I didn't see any water seeping through, or any other gaping holes for us to crawl into.

That was what I had been afraid of.

"Where's the water coming from?" Neina asked, her voice shaking under the chill, or the lack of strength, or maybe just plain fright.

As soon as her voice finished bouncing off the stone around us, she got her answer. Bubbles broke the surface on the other side, lasting for a few moments, then disappearing just as fast.

Jorn turned and looked back down the passageway we'd just entered from. "Maybe they'll be gone if we go back, figuring we'd drowned or something."

"Don't count on it." I looked up at the ceiling, but like the rest of the chamber, I didn't see any holes or passageways leading up or out, nothing but solid stone. I gritted my teeth. Being back underground should have felt at least a little comforting, considering my upbringing, but comforted was the last thing I was feeling right now. I removed my sword from my back as well as my new coat and handed them to Gorman. "Don't lose those."

"Where are you going?"

"I'm going to see where those bubbles are coming from."

"Probably from some water creature that's going to eat us all," Jorn said with a slight grin.

"There's no water creature in here," I said, giving Jorn a harsh look. "Quit trying to scare everyone." I turned and pushed off the rock and headed across the chamber to the other side, where we had spotted the bubbles. Of course, I had no idea if there was anything living down there or not. If I'd been smart, I would have edged my way around the outside of the room instead of swimming across the open hole. My hands started shaking, and not from the cold. Jorn's comment got me thinking about what might be lying in wait below me, which I suddenly found very, very disturbing.

Something touched my right leg, and I yelped. I grabbed my dagger from behind my back and spun in a circle with my legs tucked up under me as close as I could get them. I waited, spinning slowly in the water as I stared down at the blackness below.

Nothing appeared. Had it just been my imagination? I didn't have time to find out.

"Why'd you stop?" Jorn called out.

I almost told him but thought better of it. If I frightened them now, they'd go back for sure. "Just being careful," I said, somehow managing

to sound mostly calm. I turned and continued on, reaching the other side without incident. As soon as my hand touched the stone and I found a grip, another cluster of bubbles broke the surface, startling me into raising my feet once more as I clung to the side of the wall. With my luck, the bubbles were from some kind of sea monster at the bottom. One way or the other, I had to find out where they were coming from on the off chance it led to a way out.

*Here goes nothing.* Releasing the wall, I sank into the water, pulling myself down using the side of the stone. It didn't take long to find the bubbles' origin. There was another fissure farther down, larger than the one we'd entered from. I could feel the force of the water coming through, but just before I started back up to the surface, it stopped, and the water calmed.

Quickly, I swam back up, my teeth chattering. The water seemed to be getting warmer, but that was probably just the numbing of my body. If we had to stay in this much longer, our arms and legs were going to stiffen to the point of not being able to swim.

"What did you find?" Jorn called out from the other side.

I wiped the water from my eyes. "I found another passageway, but it's underwater, and I have no idea how far it goes, or if it rises high enough to find air."

"Clearly, it does," Gorman said, sounding rather desperate. "Where else would the bubbles be coming from?"

"Yes, but like I said, I have no idea how far in it goes first. I'll see what I can find."

"Be careful," Jorn said.

I nodded, then took a couple of deep breaths and dove back under. I pulled myself down to the opening as fast as I could and started in. The torchlight above barely broke the surface. It certainly did nothing to light the tunnel ahead. I kicked as hard as I could, using one arm to pull my-self through the water, while the other I used to feel what was in front of me.

The passageway was fairly open, and I found places to grip and pro-pel myself forward. I was reaching the point of not having enough air to get back when the tunnel started to angle upward. I didn't know where it went, but at this point, I was too afraid to keep going, so I swam back as fast as I could. I broke through the tunnel entrance, my head pound-ing as I fought to hold the air in. I reached the surface and took a huge gulp, thankful to have made it back.

"What happened?" Jorn called out. "We were getting worried."

I didn't answer right away, still trying to catch my breath. I let the pounding in my ears slow, and when I did answer, it was in choppy sentences between breaths. "The fissure goes . . . on for . . . some dis-tance . . . before angling upward. I didn't have time . . . to see where it went." I treaded water a little while longer as I continued to calm the beating of my heart. "I'll try again. Now that I know what's down there, I should be able to swim through it faster."

At least, I hoped I'd be able to.

Still feeling out of breath, I sucked in another large gulp of air and pulled myself below the surface. Feeling more confident about where I was going, I swam faster, keeping one arm out in front just in case. I reached the fissure easily enough and headed in, not bothering with feel-ing around the surface for where I was going.

I reached the part of the tunnel that angled upward sooner than be-fore, but my breath was waning. If I went too far, I risked not being able to make it back. Pushing the fear aside, I swam upward as hard as I could, keeping my arms out in front to keep from hitting my head on a jutting piece of rock and knocking myself unconscious.

Pretty soon, I'd reached the point of no return, but I kept on swimming. There had to be an opening somewhere, there had to be. Where else would the bubbles have come from? I chanted it in my head over and over as I swam.

*There is an opening. There is an opening.*

My lungs were on fire and my head was beyond throbbing. I could feel myself losing consciousness, and the fear was debilitating. This was it. Ayrion the warrior, Death's Shadow, was going to die alone and forgotten in some underground pit that no one would ever—

My head broke the surface, and I sucked in a huge lungful, inhaling just as much water as air as I desperately clung to life. It was several long moments before the throbbing pain in my head lessened enough for me to even open my eyes. Surprisingly enough, I could see. Moonlight flooded in through the front of what appeared to be some sort of cavern on the edge of the lake. I could see the shimmer of the water farther out. There was a stream that ran from the lake to the mouth of the cave, filling the inside. This had to be the reason for the rise and fall through the day.

After catching a few more breaths, my head began to clear. I needed to get back. Jorn was probably already trying to find me, or, more likely, had figured I'd drowned and was trying to take them back to the dungeons. I didn't have time to let the pounding ease completely, so I took a couple of deep breaths and dove back in.

This time I knew where I was going. I knew that the tunnel was clear nearly straight through, so I kicked and paddled and pulled myself down with both feet and hands, now confident that I didn't have to guard against striking jutting pieces of rock. I reached the bottom and started through the tunnel back toward the open chamber, my legs kicking even harder the closer I got. My head was pounding, but I finally broke the surface.

Jorn yelped. He was swimming just to the side of where I came up. "Where did you go?" he shouted, looking like he wanted to hit me. "We thought you'd drowned for sure. Couldn't find you anywhere."

I held up my hand to let him know I needed a second to catch my breath before answering. Once again, the pounding in my head slowly faded as the beating of my heart calmed. "I found a way out," I said between gulps of air.

"You found a way out?" Gorman called out from the other side of the chamber. He was sitting on the edge of the fissure with the torch held in the air.

"Yes," I answered, and started back across the room, Jorn right behind me. We pulled ourselves up on the lip, and Gorman moved to give us room to sit. Neina was sitting to the right, her face pale as she shivered against the cold. Gorman had tried putting my coat around her to keep her warm.

"There is another tunnel below the surface that leads to an open cave that shares a stream with the lake. That stream is no doubt what keeps filling the tunnel throughout the day." Sitting there, I began to shiver myself, my teeth chattering against the cold. "The problem is that it is quite a swim." I didn't want to look at Neina, but I couldn't help it.

"You don't think I'll make it, do you?" she asked.

I sighed. "I think it's going to be very difficult. The good news, besides there being a way out, is that it seems to be a straight shot from the opening under the water to the opening in the cavern. I didn't come across any major obstacles, but like I said, it's quite a distance to swim. Best chance we have would be for one of us to swim with each of you and try pulling you through."

Gorman wiped grey hair from the front of his face. "I don't see that we have much choice. Either we try, or we wait for Saryn's guards to show up." He looked at his wife and smiled. It was a sad sort of grin.

"We can do it," she said with a nod as she placed a quivering hand on his. For a brief moment, I was reminded of Mistress Orilla. She and Neina looked about the same age, and Neina's determination suddenly struck me as familiar.

"The question is, can *we* do it?" Jorn said, turning to look at the other side of the chamber. "If it was that difficult for you swimming alone, imagine how much more difficult it will be trying to pull them through as well."

"Like the ambassador said, we don't have much choice. Going back would mean certain death, and possible torture beforehand—"

"We choose to go forward," Gorman said, his wife echoing his sentiments with a firm nod. "If we don't make it, better this way than to have our deaths stretched out for weeks at the hands of that sadistic monster upstairs."

I slipped back into the water. "We need to go now, if we are. The water is—"

Something hit my leg, and I yelped once more as I reached in and grabbed whatever it was and threw it up into the fissure. Gorman and Neina shrilled at the same time as the creature went flying past their faces. Jorn simply jumped back, his knife raised from being startled.

We all turned and looked at the monster and started laughing. It was a large lake trout that had been nibbling on my leg. Most likely it had followed the stream out of the lake and had gotten caught in here once the tide went back out.

I shook my head, feeling a little embarrassed by having been startled by a fish. Turning back toward the other side, I motioned for Gorman and Neina to climb down into the water. I took my sword and flung it over my back, then took my coat from Neina and knotted the sleeves around her chest, just under her arms.

"I can use that to try pulling you through without losing my grip."

I didn't want to use her top, as it would have likely ripped off in the struggle. I was wishing now that we hadn't tossed the guards' uniforms away. I could have cut one of them up for rope. No sense thinking about it now. It wasn't like we had time to go back and look.

Jorn held the torch while he and Gorman helped Neina down into the water I was presently treading. I held her hand as she slipped in and let her put her arms around my back. Gorman was next in. Jorn held one of the ambassador's hands as he dropped into the water. I grabbed him before he went completely under and helped him over to the side to hold on to the rock while we waited for Jorn.

"Keep the torch until we get to the other side," I told him. "We need to make sure we get to the right spot before going under."

Jorn nodded and for once didn't argue or offer a snide remark as he climbed down the shelf and slipped in at the side, keeping the torch over his head.

I looked at Gorman. "Can you make it over?"

He looked at the other side and nodded. "I can make it, young man. Don't you worry about me."

I wanted to laugh. "You're the reason we're here, Ambassador. It's my job to worry."

I spun in the water, Neina clutching me as tightly as her frail hands could manage. However, instead of swimming straight across, I decided to go around the perimeter, letting Gorman use the juts in the rock as leverage to keep from winding himself completely before the big underwater swim. There were plenty of formations along the way to grab hold of, and he seemed appreciative of it as he quickly moved from one to the next, trying not to overexert himself. As weak as he was, swimming across the chamber might have been about all he could manage, and he was going to need every ounce of strength he had to make it through the underwater passageway.

I had Neina use the rock as well, as much as possible, to keep from having to hold her entire weight on my back. It also kept her from squeezing the life out of my neck when she got nervous. Getting around the chamber took longer, but we reached the other side without incident and with quite a bit more strength remaining than if we had tried swimming across.

"How far down is it?" Jorn asked, lowering the torch to try to see beneath the surface, but only managing to blind himself with the reflection off the water.

"Not far. Using the wall will help get you down faster. Inside, it's a straight shot forward before the tunnel begins to angle upwards. Once it does, kick as hard as you can and don't stop. Your first instinct is going to be to turn back. Ignore it. If you stop, you won't make it."

Gorman and Neina both shared a look that said they were wondering how *they* were going to make it.

"The most difficult part of this is to keep from panicking," I said, mainly addressing Gorman and Neina, who were still sharing doubtful looks as they clung to the side of the rock. I kept a tight grip on my coat. "Panicking will get you killed, as well as the one trying to help you. Whatever you do, don't fight to break free. Let us pull you through. You will only slow us down and cause us all to drown."

Neina gulped.

Gorman nodded slowly. "Are you trying to scare us to death before we even go down there?"

I smiled. "No, but I am trying to let you know what to expect and what to do when it happens. This won't be easy, but we can do it. Just think: On the other side of this tunnel is your freedom. You can do this, I promise." I held an encouraging smile, though I was all but smiling on the inside. I glanced at Jorn.

He wasn't smiling.

"Go ahead and swim down there," I said. "That way you can get an idea of where the entrance to the tunnel is."

Jorn handed me the torch and dropped beneath the water. Jorn was only thirteen, but he was taller than I had been at his age, and if he'd been keeping up with his training, I knew he had the strength to make it. I only hoped he was able to do it while helping Gorman.

A few moments later, Jorn's head broke the surface, and he wiped his face.

"Did you find it?" I asked.

He nodded. "It's not that far down."

I turned to Gorman and Neina. "Are you ready?"

The ambassador kissed his wife and then nodded. "As ready, I guess, as we'll ever be."

I looked at Jorn and hoped it wasn't for the last time. "I'll take Neina in first. You and Gorman follow right behind."

He didn't say anything, just nodded. I felt a sense of pride. There was strength behind my brother's eyes, determination. Then again, he was a teenager, and we teenagers tended to think we could do anything.

"All right," I said, suddenly feeling the weight of what we were about to do on my shoulders. I looked at Neina and smiled. "Take a deep breath."

As soon as I sucked in a mouthful of air, Jorn dropped the torch, and everything plunged into darkness.

WILDFIRE

## Chapter 22

ITH ONE HAND CLUTCHED TIGHTLY to my coat and the other to the rock wall, I dragged myself and Neina down into the cold depths of the pool. A dozen different scenarios began to play in my head, most ending with everyone drowning. I'd barely reached the mouth of the tunnel and was already panicking, not so much because I was running out of air but because it was my brother's life I had put in jeopardy. If something happened to him, I'd never be able to face my family again.

That unexpected fear had me pausing for a split second at the entrance, but Neina's squirming broke through, and I quickly grabbed hold of the nearest rock and pulled us in, kicking my feet with everything I had in me. I stroked through the water with my one free arm, the other held fast to the sleeves of my leather coat. The water was black and cold, and the tunnel felt as though it were closing in, though I couldn't actually touch the sides.

I had no idea how far we'd gone. Without the vantage of sight and sound, distance became irrelevant. Time was measured by the beating of my heart, which was increasing by the moment, with every additional stroke of my hand, each new swish of my feet. I could feel the pressure in my head building.

Behind me, Neina began to jostle about, her arms hitting the side of my legs. Surely she hadn't already run out of air? If she did, there was no way we were going to make it. I kicked and stroked through the water even faster, desperation driving me forward. My head was aching by the time we reached the backside of the tunnel, where it began to angle upward.

For a brief moment, I wondered how Jorn and Gorman were doing. Had they started into the tunnel yet? Were they right behind us? Were they overtaking us? I needed to hurry. My coat began to thrash in earnest. Neina was running out of air. I hoped she fought to keep her mouth shut and didn't give in to the temptation of trying to breathe.

With all the strength I had to muster, I swam upward. My body was numb from the cold and the exertion. I couldn't feel my arms or my legs. I just had to trust they were still moving. My head felt like it was about to explode. Neina convulsed and then suddenly went still. Once again, the thought of Mistress Orilla flooded my mind. What if she had been the one to place her life in my hands? I gripped the sides of the tunnel and yanked us upward as fast as I could. *Please don't let her die*, I called out to any higher power that might be listening.

It's said you think of the strangest things when you're about to die, one of which is the question of whether there is a Creator or not. I hoped if there was, He was listening. As soon as I had finished my rather sad little plea for help, my head broke the surface, and I sucked in a lungful of air, nearly passing out as I did.

With what energy I had left, mostly fueled by fear, I shoved Neina's

unresponsive body up onto the stone and crawled out. I knelt down, ignoring the throbbing pain in my head, and put my ear to her mouth. She wasn't breathing. I quickly turned her over to see if it would drain the water. It didn't. Not knowing what else to do, I grabbed her legs and lifted her upside down. As soon as I did, she spat and coughed up a mouthful as she half-gasped, half-wretched what was inside.

After laying her back on the stone, I unhooked the sword on my back and plopped down beside her, thankful to see her eyes beginning to open. I quickly turned over and stared down at the water. "Come on, Jorn. You can do it." They should have been right behind us. Each moment spent staring at the pool felt like hours. Where were they? Had something happened? Had they not left as early? Did they get stuck?

Fear flooded my body, breaking through the chill and numbness, sending a searing flame of panic racing over me. Something was wrong.

I didn't hesitate. Jumping to my feet, I sucked in another lungful of air and dove into the blackness, pulling myself down as fast as I could. They had to be here somewhere.

I reached the bottom, and they were nowhere to be found. About the time I started into the passageway leading back to the cavern, I hit something.

It was Jorn. He was pulling on something. Gorman. The ambassador wasn't moving. Why wasn't he moving? I quickly felt down his back and found his belt had snagged on one of the small rocks on the tunnel ceiling. As fast as I could, I yanked it off, and we started into the second tunnel leading up. I didn't know if we could make it.

Jorn was barely moving himself, and I fought to keep all three of us going. My head was pounding, my heart throbbing, my chest on fire. I felt the life draining from me. We weren't going to make it. I willed my arms and feet to keep moving. Where was the top? I had no idea how far we still had to go. Everything around me began to fade; even the sound of my heart seemed to slow. Was this what it felt like to die? Then I remembered what I'd told them. Don't stop! Whatever you do, don't stop!

Grabbing another jut in the rock, I yanked upward with what little strength I had, then again. My mind seemed to have left me, and the only thought I could muster was to grab another rock and pull. Suddenly my head broke through the water, and I gasped and choked and sucked in air and water all at the same time.

"Gorman!" Neina cried for her husband as soon as she saw him pop up between us.

My eyes and head cleared just enough to force the ambassador's limp body up onto the rock, and then Jorn, before crawling out myself. I wanted to drop down and die right there, but I couldn't. I hadn't come this far, gone through this much, to see the ambassador die when I was this close to accomplishing what had seemed an impossible task.

I spun around, taking only enough time to see that Jorn was moving, and grabbed Gorman's legs. I didn't know how I was going to manage it, but one way or another, I was going to yank the man off the ground and get him breathing. I jerked up with everything I had in me, barely managing to lift much more than his knees off the stone.

Nothing seemed to be happening.

"Why isn't he moving?" Neina cried, jerking on her husband's arm, urging him to wake up.

This couldn't be happening. Not after what we'd gone through to get this far. Not after what we had risked. I couldn't return to Aramoor having failed my first, and what was sure to be only, mission. I flipped Gorman over. The only thing I could think to do was something I'd seen Reevie do once after one of our kids had swallowed a cherry pit and had begun to choke.

"Here," I said to Jorn, "help me sit him up."

Jorn, who was still struggling to catch his own breath, turned over and helped me pull Gorman up, grumbling as he did. "Can't you see the man's already dead? What do you think you're going to do?"

I moved behind the ambassador and wrapped my arms around his chest and squeezed, then did it again, but apart from a slight wheezing noise and some water draining from his mouth, he didn't move. "Come on!" I tightened my grip and jerked again and again.

"Ayrion, what in the flaming—"

Gorman's eyes flew open, and he retched all over the front of Jorn.

I nearly shouted with excitement.

"Yuck!" Jorn stumbled backward, crawling on his hands and knees as far from the ambassador's mouth as possible. He moved over to the pool and dunked his body in.

I was too elated by the fact that we had defied all odds and made it out to care about the vomit. As soon as Gorman had finished emptying everything he'd swallowed, I helped him over to the side to wash his mouth and face. Neina clung to him like a tick, not wanting to let go of her husband's arm, even when he tried using it to wash himself.

"I thought we were dead for sure," Jorn said, crawling back out of the water and lying on his back to stare up at the cave's ceiling. He was still breathing heavily but doing his best to slow it by taking measured breaths. It was a technique taught to all Upakan trainees, a way to calm the mind during difficult situations and direct your focus to what was important, instead of panicking. It was also a great way to put your body into a state of rest, to save strength.

"I'd be lying if I said the thought didn't cross my mind once or twice, but we didn't." Hooking Noph's old sword over my back, I stood, my legs wobbling under me like a drunk sailor. I walked around for a bit before enough of the numbness had worn off that I could feel a thousand little pinpricks rushing up and down them. "We need to get going."

Both Gorman and Neina groaned from their spot near the water.

Jorn did as well, but he managed to get to his feet.

"We might have made it out of Saryn's keep, but we still have to find our way to the docks, where we have a boat waiting to take us down-river." I looked at Jorn. "I wonder if Father made it out. I hope he isn't still inside trying to figure out a way to get down into the dungeons to help us."

Jorn shook his head like a dog, flinging water droplets in all direc-tions. A worried look crossed his face. "I hadn't thought of that. What if he gets captured trying to rescue us and we aren't even there? We can't exactly break in all over again."

"We can't think about that right now. Let's get the ambassador and his wife to the boat first and see where we're at. Father knows that the plan is to reach the docks. Perhaps if he can't find us inside, he'll go there to let the others know what's happened."

Jorn nodded, though not enthusiastically.

"Here," I said, walking over to where the older couple sat next to the pool, "help me get them on their feet. We need to keep going. The docks can't be too far."

With Jorn's help, we managed to get the ambassador and his wife on their feet and moving. I was all but carrying Neina, as she had no strength left to walk on her own. She could barely stand without collaps-ing. We reached the mouth of the cave and stopped beside a small creek that was feeding the cavern well inside. It hardly seemed large enough to have caused so much damage below, but as I'd seen growing up in the Lost City, just a single drop over time could dig out a large hole in the stone.

Neina untied my coat from around her chest and handed it back to me. I shook the water from it as best I could before removing my sword and flinging the coat around my shoulders and thrusting my arms

through the sleeves. Surprisingly, it didn't weigh all that much more than before, most of the water rolling right off the thick leather, though the lining and inside pockets were thoroughly drenched. As soon as I managed to get my sword back on, we started forward once more.

We crossed through the water to the other side, where there was an embankment wide and flat enough for us to climb up. At the top was a small copse of trees that opened into the back of what looked like a milling yard for lumber. The place was empty, and we made our way through the piles of stacked wood as quietly and quickly as possible, not wanting to be caught by a night watchman and have them alert the authorities to our presence.

We reached the far side of the property without anyone seeing but found ourselves standing in front of a ten-foot wall that fronted the establishment.

I groaned as I looked up at the top of the ledge. "Now I'm wishing I'd brought that grapple after all."

I gave Jorn a boost up to the top, since he seemed almost too exhausted to climb up himself, then turned to give Gorman a hand as well. With my shoulder under him, he made it up high enough to grab the top of the wall, and Jorn helped him the rest of the way up and over. Neina was another matter altogether. She didn't have the strength in her legs for me to boost her up, so I ended up having to grip her legs and lift her high enough for Jorn to reach her hands. Between the two of us, we managed to push and pull her up and over the side.

Jorn had a difficult time lowering her down the other side. He eventually dropped her partway, though I had to believe Gorman was there on the other side to catch her, or at least break her fall.

I got a running start, and with what strength I had left, I kicked off the stone, leaping high enough to grab the top lip, barely managing to pull myself up with Jorn's help. With a nod to let Jorn know I was fine, we quietly slid over the back side of the wall and dropped down onto the cobbled street below. I could see the lake on our left and had to guess that we were north of Fishtown, since the castle was north of the docks, and the tunnels we took out led from the keep to the lake.

"Which way?" Jorn asked.

I pointed straight ahead, as the road seemed to run along the side of the lake with houses between. As long as we kept the water in view, we had to eventually reach the docks. We started down the street, mostly hobbling. I finally ended up lifting Neina and carrying her in my arms, my own legs wobbling when I did. I could have really used a pushcart right about now. The road meandered for some distance, occasionally cutting away from the lake and toward town before turning back in the direction of the water once again.

There were very few streetlamps in this part of town, which I was thankful for. It was nice to not have to worry about people spotting us from their windows. I glanced up at the moon, which wasn't above us but instead sinking below the horizon. Morning was just around the corner.

We had to hurry.

I thought I recognized a couple of the buildings and picked up the pace. We turned the corner and ran straight into the back of Vulkina's tribe. Too surprised to know what to do, I stopped and quickly put Neina down, handing her to her husband, who was barely standing himself.

"Who are they?" Gorman asked, his voice quivering.

"They are here to collect a debt that I can't pay right now."

"Is that you?" Neven called out, stepping away from the others to walk slowly in my direction.

"Yes, Neven, it's me."

Neven perked up and rushed over, looking hesitantly at Jorn first,

then at the ambassador and his wife. He pursed his lips. "I see you found who you were looking for. Why are you all wet?"

"We decided to take a swim."

He cocked his head. "Huh?"

I glanced past him toward Vulkina, who was standing in the middle of her entourage of beaters and guard. "I'm afraid I don't have her locket."

Neven frowned. "That's not good. No telling what Vulkina will do. How did you get out? We had watchers posted around the castle for hours. Then the whole place went on alert, guards and patrollers and soldiers scurrying like rabbits. Rodon Hill is a madhouse. When you didn't show, we figured you was caught for sure, but Vulkina insisted we wait at the docks just in case. She didn't want you . . ." He cleared his throat. ". . . trying to sneak off in the night."

"We aren't trying to sneak off . . . Well, not really. We were trying to hide from the palace guard. We had another man with us inside the palace. He was the one looking for Vulkina's locket. Did you see anyone coming out?"

Neven shook his head. "Only people in and out of the overlord's keep were wearing black uniforms." He looked up, and his face paled. "Just like that," he said, pointing over my shoulder.

I turned to see one of the palace guards running down the street in our direction. My heart sank. I had the worst luck.

Before Neven had a chance to even call out to warn Vulkina, I had both swords out of their sheaths and in my hands. Something about the way the guard was moving seemed off. He didn't appear hesitant. No single guard would have been running through Fishtown in the middle of the night without looking at least a little cautious.

"Wait!" I said, stopping Neven before he took off running for his tribe. "That's not a guard." I breathed a huge sigh of relief when the guard passed by the next streetlamp. "That's the man I told you about."

Both me and Jorn smiled when Father came to a stop in front of us.

"I thought you four were gone for sure," he said, hugging both me and Jorn as he did. "How in the name of Aldor did you get out of there? I watched from the balcony for as long as I could to see if you made it out of the dungeons, but when I saw the guards assembling around the front, I knew something was wrong, so I found a stray guard and borrowed his uniform."

"We did the same," Jorn said, pointing at what was left of his.

"There was a fissure in—"

"Where's my locket?" Vulkina demanded as she and her entourage marched over, weapons in hand.

Father dug around in one of the inner pockets of his black uniform and handed the piece of jewelry over to Neven, whose eyes lit up when he saw it. He rushed it over and into the awaiting hands of his chief. Vulkina barely had time to look at it before several kids came running down the road, shouting that the palace guards were heading our way.

We all turned to see at least two dozen armed men cresting the top of a hill on one of the side streets. They were still some distance away, but close enough to see that some wore the palace guard uniforms and the rest were Cylmaran soldiers.

"I might not have made it out as unseen as I would have liked," Father said.

Vulkina shouted, and her tribe scattered, leaving us to face the men on our own.

"What are we going to do about them?" Jorn asked, pointing at Gorman and Neina, who were barely standing upright, holding on to each other for support.

"Run!" Father said, grabbing Neina and throwing her over his shoulder. I hoisted Gorman's arm over my shoulder, and we took off running

for the docks.

We didn't make it past the first house before I knew this was a bad idea. The last thing we wanted was to lead them straight to the boats; then they would know how we were planning on escaping. Worse, that would put Jasna's father and all his crew in jeopardy.

"Stop!" I shouted to Father, steering Gorman away from the docks and over to one of the buildings on the right side of the street. "In here." The soldiers hadn't yet reached our road, but it wouldn't be long, and as fast as I could, I shoved Gorman into a narrow cubby between two of the taller residences. My father and Jorn ducked in as well, lowering Neina down beside her husband, who was leaning against the side of the house, panting.

"What are you doing?" Father asked.

I looked at Gorman and Neina. "Wait here until the soldiers pass, then run straight for the boats. We'll try to lead them away from you. Do you think you can make it on your own?"

Gorman nodded.

"Tell them Ayrion sent you, and if I'm not back by the time the sun rises, leave." I bolted out of the passageway, not having time to say anything else, my father and brother right behind me. We barely got back on the cobbled road when the first of the soldiers poured into the street behind us. As soon as they caught sight of us, they shouted and ran in our direction.

I spared a quick glance over my shoulder to see if any of them stopped or made a move toward the ambassador's hiding place, but it seemed our ruse had worked, as they never slowed in their chase. I pointed toward the next street up that led back toward town, and we ran all the harder.

A bell rang in the harbor, signaling fifth hour. It wouldn't be long before the sun started to rise, making our escape all the more difficult.

There was movement on our left at the loading area, leading down to the piers. Knowing my roommates, it was probably them, waiting on us to arrive. Unfortunately, that was the last place I needed to be right now. I just hoped Jasna's father didn't get spooked by seeing all the soldiers running through Fishtown and take off without us, though I doubted my roommates would let him if he tried.

My legs were shaking. The chill of the water and the hard swim through the tunnels had taken its toll, but I pressed on. We couldn't stop now, not with the soldiers so close. I remained in the lead, with Jorn and my father on my heels. We took the next street to the right and away from the docks.

Behind us, the soldiers shouted as they fought to catch up. Lucky for us, Fishtown was a maze. I wasn't very familiar with it, but I knew enough from my last two visits to get around. Once inside the hundreds of booths and shanties, there would be no way the soldiers could follow or keep up.

I cut left toward the main road leading through the center of the fish market. I knew right where I needed to go. Seeing Pradjic's booth up ahead, I started for the left side of the street. The soldiers spilled out behind us, not slowing in the slightest. I had a feeling it was their heads on the chopping block if they failed to catch us. At this point, that was on them. If they wanted to work for a tyrant like Overlord Saryn, then they deserved what they got.

My father and brother didn't say anything, trusting I knew where I was going. I ducked into one of the narrow alcoves just past Pradjic's booth that led to a small passageway on the left. I recognized the spot where me, Jasna, and Stanis had stood watching the face-off between Jasna's father and Dovan. Forcing my legs to keep moving as I fought through the weariness, I wove between shanties and tents, pausing when I finally reached Stanis's smithy. Now if I could just remember the back

WILDFIRE

*Chapter 23*

ONE OF THE SOLDIERS spotted us and started to shout our position. He barely got three words out before my father flicked a knife, and it buried itself in the unsuspecting man's chest.

The soldier looked down in shock, then crumpled. Before he hit the ground, I had drawn both my swords and was running straight at the remaining men. I could feel more than see my father and brother on either side of me as I rushed the soldiers, my magic roiling inside me, burning away any last vestige of chill still in my bones.

The heat was welcoming, like an old friend who came to visit. Except this friend seemed to show up more often than I would have liked. And being the decent host that I was, I opened the door. I hit the front row of soldiers and tore through the first three, barely giving them time to react as I spun and ducked and cut my way through their initial attack with little effort. My father and brother were somewhere behind me, neither having the magic to see them through the wall of soldiers and steel.

Another group of palace guards appeared from the shanties on the right and joined the first, cutting me off even further from my father and brother. There had to be at least a dozen men now, maybe half the group that had been chasing us, and it wouldn't take the rest long to catch up. We had to get out of there. For a moment, I lost sight of my father and brother as the ranks closed around me. My magic was fighting to take over, but I managed to hold it to a trickle as I danced between my attackers.

"Ayrion!" Jorn's voice sounded scared. He was in trouble.

I spun, blocking two swords at once as I did. Dodging another swing, I cut the sword from the guard's hand, then stuck one of mine through his leg and kicked him backward, knocking two more aside. I ducked, deflected another blade, and cut the legs out from two more, leaving them to writhe on the cobbles as I fought to reach my brother. He was barely managing to fend off three much larger men who were determined to cut him down. I caught a glimpse of my father on the left about ten feet away, moving and striking like an adder. Two men were already down, but I could see red staining one of his sleeves.

I focused on the men between me and Jorn. The fear of losing my brother bolstered my magic, and what had felt like a crackling fire on a cold night now roared with the heat of a forge's flame, burning away the last vestiges of my control. Panic washed over me, and I let the magic take over. It felt like I'd lost all control, as though it wasn't actually me fighting, almost a dream, where I watched as a mere spectator.

My swords moved with incredible accuracy, cutting down everything in their path as I pressed forward. I blocked and parried with one while using the other to cut and chop and stab my way forward. One of the remaining two men opened a deep gash on my brother's arm, and

Jorn dropped his dagger. The second managed to kick Jorn to the ground, but before he could finish him off, I broke through and slammed my blade through his back. The man stiffened, then went limp and fell on top of Jorn. The second turned, but not fast enough, and my second sword relieved him of his weapon and his hand at the same time. He screamed, grabbed his arm, and ran.

I kicked Jorn's weapon back to him as he clambered to his feet and then turned to fight off another wave. My father was holding his own, his hands moving nearly as fast as mine as he cut his way toward us.

Blood was pouring down Jorn's arm, but he managed to keep his blade up and moving.

Behind me, I could hear shouting coming from the direction of the docks. I didn't know if it was more guards coming, or worse, my roommates. I needed to get us out of here. Every moment we lingered near the water was another moment the guards might figure out that there was a reason we were here in the first place and search the boats.

Cutting off part of the flow of my magic in an effort to gain control, I forced Jorn behind me, holding back two men as I did, their attacks falling short of my abilities as I used the visions to anticipate every swing and thrust and lunge. It didn't take much, just a swift jab and a well-placed twist of my wrist, and both men were on the ground, and I was once again beside my father. The soldiers were now down to only a handful. Seeing their numbers rapidly dwindling, they retreated toward the side of the street, no doubt to regroup and wait for their fellow soldiers to arrive.

We didn't have time to waste.

"This way!" I shouted, and we took off down the road and away from the port. We'd barely made it to the first corner when the rest of the soldiers barreled out of the shanties behind us, joining those still remaining, and the chase started once more.

The fire of my magic continued to fade the farther we got from the docks, but exhaustion kicked in, and I was finding it hard to run, harder even to catch my next breath. I couldn't imagine how bad it was for Jorn. Not only was he weak from the underwater escape and the fight moments ago, but he was losing blood as well.

I kept up our pace as best I could, moving from one street to the next. I knew I was lost, but I had to keep us moving, keep ahead of the sounds of pursuit. I only hoped we didn't end up in a blind alley or a dead-end street, which was likely, considering how many there were. We ducked into a narrow crevice between two buildings just as a group of soldiers rushed by the lane we were on, then quickly scooted our way toward the other end. It was a tight squeeze with all the rubbish they had piled between the two buildings, as though the residents had simply opened their windows and tossed out anything they no longer wanted.

We reached the far end of the passageway and ran headlong into a group of men carrying long staves. I raised my sword, surprised that my visions hadn't warned me.

"Ayrion?" said a surprised man with a baggy patchwork cloak and white beard.

I lowered my sword. It couldn't be. "Brishad?"

The leader of the Sil'Rhivanni we had rescued smiled, which looked more out of relief than being happy to see me. "I was wondering if we'd run into you here. Though, I must admit, I presumed that your urgent business would already be completed by the time we arrived." He looked around the darkened lane. "What are you doing running around Ecrin in the middle of the night?" He glanced at my father and brother, clearly not recognizing either of them. "Where is the rest of your band? Nearby, I imagine?" He glanced over my shoulder toward the passageway we'd just exited.

"They're at the lake, and by now, hopefully setting sail for home."

He looked surprised. "Without you? You are staying in Ecrin?"

I smiled. "Not if I can help it." I looked at the men with Brishad, recognizing a couple from our evening spent in their company. "Why are *you* out wandering Ecrin's city streets at this hour of the morning?"

Brishad smiled. "Safest time for tinkers to move about, especially with the city on such high alert."

"Speaking of," I said and glanced over my shoulder, straining to see if I could hear any sign of our pursuers. "We need to get off the streets. Do you have a safe place to go?"

"Why? Are you in trouble?"

I nodded. "We need to get out of the city, but they are going to be guarding the gates."

Brishad blew out his beard and looked at the four men beside him. "The market can wait. We can collect what we need in Pirn. Besides," he added, taking a step forward and laying a hand on my shoulder, "we owe a debt." He looked at me. "Come, our wagons are nearby."

"Are you sure?" I wanted to slap myself for asking and giving him a chance to back out, but I also didn't want to put their people in danger.

"If it were not for you and your friends, we would not be here today," Brishad said. "It is the least we can do. The Sil'Rhivanni always make good on their debts."

"My brother is wounded—"

Brishad waved his hand. "Say no more. We have healers that can see to him."

We headed back down the street and reached the first intersection. Crossing that, we came to another street, which we took left, then crossed two more before finally reaching an empty yard next to what looked like an abandoned warehouse. There was a single wagon parked beside it. I looked around for the rest of the wagons, but then felt foolish for doing so. They wouldn't have driven their entire caravan into the city. They would have had nowhere to park them, not to mention all the unwanted attention it would have drawn.

We climbed in the back of the wagon with Brishad and two other men while the remaining two members of the clan climbed up onto the driver's seat. Before I knew it, the wagon lurched, and we were heading down the road.

"The palace guard and the Cylmaran soldiers are looking for us," Father said, no doubt wanting to be upfront with our hosts.

Brishad pursed his lips, then looked at me. "You have a knack for finding trouble, my young friend."

Father chuckled, then rubbed the top of my head. "Truer words . . . truer words."

It was an awkward gesture for someone my age, but somehow having my father's hand rustle through my hair was one of the best things I'd felt in a long time, as though no time had passed since we'd been together.

"They are going to check the wagons at the gates," Father said, looking around for a possible place to hide, stopping on a large trunk in the corner. "Best we not be seen when they do."

Brishad waved again. "No worries. We can hide you in here." He pointed to the floor of the wagon between the cot on the left and the bench on the right.

One of the men leaned down and moved a small rug, then grabbed a metal ring and lifted. A hatch in the floor opened.

A memory flashed across my mind of my first meeting with Master Fentin in his bookshop and the time he had hidden me and Reevie from the patrollers in just such a fashion. I held back a smile.

Brishad grabbed a piece of cloth from off one of the shelves and tied it around Jorn's arm. Jorn gritted his teeth as the old man tightened the knot. Hopefully it would help slow the loss of blood before we managed

to get to wherever it was they were taking us.

"Right," Brishad said, finishing the knot, "in you go."

I climbed down into the hidden compartment, then helped my father with Jorn. Without saying a word, we squished into a prostrate position and waited as they lowered the door and rolled the rug back across. This was a much tighter fit than what I remembered enduring with Reevie. The wait felt like hours. Each new bump of the wagon on the loose or missing cobbles jostled us, smashing me into the wagon's planks on one side and jabbing me with the hilt of my father's sword on the other. I gritted my teeth but kept my mouth shut. If discomfort was the extent of our worries, then we were lucky indeed.

The wagon began to slow and then stopped altogether. I wondered if we'd finally reached the gate. I couldn't see anything through the wooden slats. I could hear several voices, though. The clap of boots circling the wagon had me sweating. It had to be the watchtower at the main gate. The back door of the wagon opened, its squeaky hinges setting my nerves on end. If they caught us, there would be no escaping. It wasn't like we could outrun the entire Cylmaran army in an old tinker wagon. My only consolation was that with us to distract the pursuing soldiers, chances were good that the ambassador and his wife had been able to reach the boats.

I could hear Brishad's voice above the others, and the wagon rocked gently as though someone was either getting out or coming in. Another couple of voices joined those above, voices I didn't recognize. I held my breath and lay as still as possible. It seemed the harder I concentrated on not doing something foolish like sneezing, the more I wanted to.

I needed to focus on something else, anything else. I settled on my weapon readiness. The sword from my back I had unsheathed, and it was resting against my chest since it rose too high above my head for me to fit in the cramped space. The sword at my waist would have been impossible to draw from this position, but my belt knife was within reach and could be easily pulled if the need arose.

The voices above us grew agitated, especially one in particular that I did not recognize, and the boards under his feet creaked and groaned as he moved about. Suddenly, I heard the clanging of pots and pans and other items as though being tossed around the wagon. Whoever was up there was either determined to search every nook and cranny, or just wanted to cause the tinkers a little grief. I hoped they didn't kick back the rug in the process.

I tightened my grip on my sword as one of the men above stepped right on top of the latch. If only we had been faster back at the docks, we could have made it down to the piers without being seen. If only I hadn't gotten us lost. I gritted my teeth. I needed to focus on what was happening right now, and right now we were about to be—

The wagon rocked once more, and the voices faded as whoever had been in the wagon left. My father exhaled, and Jorn squirmed for the first time since the back door had opened. I loosened my grip on my blade but didn't let go. The wagon bounced again as someone climbed back inside. I had to assume it was Brishad. Pretty soon the wagon lurched, and I nearly smacked my head on the trap door as we began to move once again. The back door of the wagon closed, and a few moments later the rug was pulled back and the hatch opened.

Brishad stood over the compartment and looked down with a smile. "That was a close one, I don't mind admitting. When they started going through the stuff, I thought we were going to be discovered for sure. But a few bottles of our Rhivanni mead seemed to dampen their eagerness for continuing the search."

I smiled and handed Brishad my sword so I could crawl out. The wagon was in disarray—the table overturned, shelves emptied, goods strewn across the floor. A stool leg had been broken and tossed in the

corner. I turned and helped my father and brother out, then stepped out of the way for one of the tinkers to shut the door and roll the rug back overtop.

"It's a mighty fine weapon," Brishad said, running his finger along the side edge of my blade. "Wouldn't be interested in trading, would you?" He smiled and handed it back to me.

I placed it in its sheath and shook my head. "Afraid not. It was a gift. Don't plan on parting with it."

Brishad shrugged. "Didn't have much to trade anyhow." He motioned for us to sit down on the bench, but we insisted on first helping undo the mess that the soldiers had left in the wake of their search. When we finally sat, Father took the time to inspect Jorn's wound. It was deep, but the wrapping seemed to have stopped the bleeding, though he was looking quite pale. We needed to get him to a healer.

Sunlight was just beginning to sift through the window on the side when the wagon slowed. There were several large jolts that nearly tipped me out of my seat as we pulled off the road and eventually stopped.

"Looks like we've arrived," Brishad said as he stood from his chair in the corner. He pointed at Jorn. "Best we see to that wound before you end up losing an arm."

Jorn paled even further. His hands were shaking, and he was having a difficult time standing. Father and I each took an arm and carried him out the back. Father raised one hand over his eyes as the early light from the rising sun blinded him. Jorn, too, squinted, but since we held his arm, there wasn't much he could do.

"This way," Brishad said as he walked through the opening in the circle of wagons. Those gathered moved aside to let us pass. I got one quick look outside the circle before entering and noticed we were far enough away from the city that I could no longer see it, which was good news. Still, I wanted to be even farther away. Once they realized we were no longer in the city, I wouldn't put it past Saryn to send his forces out searching the roads out of town. Hopefully, he wouldn't consider us leaving by boat, though eventually someone was bound to notice Jasna's father being gone for an extended period of time.

I turned back to the surrounding wagons. I couldn't dwell on it now. I had other things to worry about. Namely, my brother's injury and then me finding a way across the kingdom of Cylmar on foot.

"In here," Brishad said, pointing with his staff to a wagon on our right. "Our healer can see to his injuries."

Father and I helped Jorn over to the wagon, and I started to carry him up the stairs, but two of the Sil'Rhivanni stopped us at the back, wanting to carry Jorn up themselves.

Brishad laid his hand on my father's shoulder. "You can trust them. They will take good care of your son."

Father looked at the two men, clearly not wanting to let go of Jorn, but finally nodded, and we handed him over. The men carried him up the back steps and into the wagon, where a woman, who looked to be about my father's age, with thick wavy chestnut hair, stood waiting. She had a long white apron tied around her front.

"You can put him there," she said, pointing at something inside the wagon, no doubt a cot. Before I got a chance to move around to the other side to take a look, she ushered the two men who had carried Jorn in out and shut the door.

"Don't worry," Brishad said with an encouraging smile. "He's in good hands. Come. The two of you look like you could use a cup of Rhivanni mead."

I looked at Father and shook my head. "You'll be taking your life in your hands if you do."

Brishad bellowed out a hearty laugh.

Leaving their healer to her work, we joined Brishad on some seats

facing the fire, which were nothing more than cut timber that had been turned up for sitting. There were several others already gathered, as breakfast appeared to have just been made. A steaming bowl of oats and honey had my weary bones singing once more. I wasn't quite ready to jump up and lock steel, but I found I wasn't having to force my eyes to stay open either.

The oats came with two very thick slices of bacon, which turned out to be the perfect blend of saltiness to offset the honey. What I appreciated the most, however, was the fresh mug of cream, dosed with the slightest bit of mead to give the milk just a hint of sweetness. Best meal I'd eaten since the last time we'd stayed with the Rhivanni some weeks back.

"Where are you headed next?" Brishad asked Father, chomping down on one of the strips of bacon. The crunch of the crispy fatback had my mouth watering all over again, and I took another bite of my own. "Back to the Lost City?"

I hadn't thought about my father and brother going home until right then. I'd been so taken with the excitement of seeing them again that I didn't even stop to consider the fact that we would be forced to part ways, perhaps for the last time.

Father pointed toward the healer's wagon. "My younger son and I will be heading back, but Ayrion walks another path." He put his hand on my shoulder. "One much greater than my own, I see." He said it with a proud smile that made me smile as well. Hearing those words meant more to me in that moment than anything Overcaptain Tolin, or even the king, could have said. "But," Father continued, raising his mug in Brishad's direction, "that is what we want for our children, is it not? To see them grow and exceed our expectations."

Brishad raised his mug to my father's, and they clapped them together. "It is indeed. Family is everything to the Rhivanni. Our children

are our heritage. We want to give them every opportunity to suc-
ceed . . ." He paused a moment. "Not by doing it for them, of course,
but by raising them to do for themselves."

My father nodded. "Aye. It seems the Rhivanni and the Upaka have
much in common."

"I'll drink to that," Brishad said with another raise of his glass. "Then
again, there's not much I won't drink to." He bellowed out another
laugh, and I couldn't help but join him, as did Father.

As soon as breakfast was consumed and our places cleared, Father
and I went to check on Jorn. Surprisingly, we found him sitting up in
the bed with a hint of color coming back into his cheeks. His hands were
no longer trembling, and the hasty wrapping on his arm had been replaced with clean bandages.

"Whatever she gave me has dulled the pain," Jorn said with a smile,
something I wasn't used to seeing. "I feel great."

I looked at the healer and she shook her head with a smirk. "I dosed
his tea with some tellareen mushrooms. He'll be fine in a few hours."

I frowned. We didn't have a few hours. We needed to get on the
road before the Cylmaran soldiers were sent out. Hopefully that didn't
happen until they felt certain we were no longer hiding in the city, and
if our luck held up, that would take at least a day or two.

"Is he fit for riding?" Father asked, evidently coming to the same
conclusion I was.

She looked at Jorn and nodded. "Should be. You might want to keep
an eye on him at first, just in case. Don't want him falling out of his
saddle."

Father nodded. "What do we owe you?"

The healer looked at me. "The debt was ours to pay."

Father looked at me as well, then leaned down to give me a hand
lifting Jorn back to his wobbly feet. Jorn tried pushing us off, but as soon

as he did, he tipped backward right back down on the cot. He took a couple of deep breaths and tried again, this time making it to his feet on his own.

"I think some fresh air will help," Father said, directing my brother toward the door. He helped Jorn down and over to the fire, where they had a warm bowl of oats and honey waiting for him.

"He's looking stronger already," Brishad said. "Petrija knows her stuff. Has a way of tending to wounds that cuts the time of healing by half." He looked at Jorn. "How are you feeling, son?"

Jorn looked up and smiled, then stuffed a spoonful of oats into his mouth. He clearly had no idea where he was.

I tried not to laugh, but the silly grin on Jorn's face and the oats sliding out the side of his mouth had me chuckling. I finally turned to Brishad. "As pleasant as your people's company is, we really need to be going. As soon as Saryn realizes that the Elondrian ambassador and his wife are no longer inside Ecrin, he's bound to send soldiers out to search."

Brishad's brows lowered over his eyes. "The Elondrian ambassador?"

I sighed. "It's a long story. Short version is that we need to be leaving." I looked at Father. "Unfortunately, our horses were left back in Ecrin."

Brishad tugged his beard. "Then I guess it is good for you that we kept the horses of those bandits you sent packing. By rights, they would be yours anyway. You were the one to dispense of their riders, so the claim would fall to you."

"Then I guess I will claim three of them. Feel free to do with the rest what you will."

Brishad stood from his stump. "I shall." He turned and whispered something to one of the men sitting nearby, and that man promptly made his way over to a bright blue wagon on the left. "I'll make sure you have provender to get you to where you are going. And that should expunge our debt, should it not?"

I nodded. "I would say that would more than cover it."

Brishad nodded and left, leaving Father and me to help Jorn finish his breakfast.

"I wish we had more time," I said, wiping the leftover oats on the side of Jorn's mouth with his napkin.

"Aye." Father stood in front of me and smiled. "You have no idea how proud it makes me to see the man you've become, despite your circumstances . . . or perhaps, because of them. It sounds as though you've made quite the name for yourself, and I'm glad to see you have been able to find those who care about you."

"I wish you could come back with me to Aramoor," I said, "and meet everyone, see the places I've lived. I could probably even get you an audience with the king."

"And to hear you say that brings me more joy than I have words for. My son, friends with a crown prince." He shook his head. "It's almost too incredible to believe. And don't think I won't rub it in Brim's face every chance I get."

Somehow, I didn't think that Brim, the head of our clan and father of the boy I'd killed, was going to give a toss about me being acquainted with the high king, but it wouldn't stop Father from gloating.

"I have a feeling your destiny has only just begun, my son. Seize it. There's no telling how far you can go."

"He can go to the Pits," Jorn said with a loud belch as he tried to stand. He would have toppled over if not for Father being there to catch him. "Ayrion this, Ayrion that, Ayrion's got a such a great destiny, Ayrion's friends with the king."

"And I wouldn't be standing here if it weren't for you," I said, trying to aim some of my father's praise in Jorn's direction. Father hadn't seen

me in five years; it was only natural he would want to celebrate my accomplishments, but it wasn't helping my relationship with my younger brother. "I would never have gotten the ambassador and his wife out of those dungeons without you. I might be acquainted with the king and queen, and friends with their son, but I'd trade all of that in a heartbeat to have my brother back."

Jorn looked like he'd wanted to say something more, but whatever he'd been going to say seemed to wither in his mouth. He stared at me a moment, then to my amazement, held out his hand.

I pushed past it and engulfed him in a hug, my arms wrapping tightly around his back. Jorn even managed to hug me back, though maybe not as strongly. As awkward as it felt, I didn't want to let go. After a prolonged moment, Jorn did finally manage to wiggle free, the corners of his mouth curling slightly.

Father pointed behind me, and I turned to see that Brishad and his men had three horses saddled and waiting on us just outside the wagons. Several women were there as well, toting wrapped bundles, which they were busy stuffing into the saddlebags on the sides. We walked out to join them, Jorn a little more stable on his feet than earlier. As long as he was able to sit ahorse, he would be fine.

"I believe this is where we part ways, my friends," Brishad said, leaning against his staff. He looked the three of us over, stopping on me. "It has been a pleasure and an honor to have made your acquaintance, young man. Our fires are always open if you find yourself in need of a stout drink and some good company. The women have prepared provisions for your journeys and have placed them in your bags." He offered us each his hand, and we shook it in turn.

I'd never met the Sil'Rhivanni before this trip, but they certainly seemed a friendly lot—the kind of people that let you still have faith in this world.

"It has been an honor meeting you and your wonderful people," Father said. "I hope we get the chance again."

Jorn offered a polite smile and a head bob.

"I will not forget your kindness," I said.

"Or I yours," Brishad countered with a long stroke of his beard as he turned and ushered everyone back within the wagons, giving the three of us a moment alone to say goodbye.

I hugged Father for what seemed like an eternity, trying to remember his smell, the feel of his arms, the sound of his voice. We finally parted, and he took my hand and lifted it to look at his ring. "Wear it proudly, Ayrion. Always remember from where you come."

"I will." My voice cracked. There were tears forming, clouding my vision until I blinked, and they rolled down my cheeks as I watched my father and brother mount. I did the same, and we all sat in our saddles a moment, staring at each other.

"Tell Mother and Rianna I love them and miss them. Tell Mother she doesn't need to worry about me."

Father wiped his eyes, one of only a few times I'd ever seen him cry. "I will."

I looked at Jorn. "Next time I see you, you'll be bigger than me. Try not to break too many of my records during training."

Jorn huffed, but in the end he smiled.

We sat there a moment longer, then finally nodded, and with a simple wave, we parted ways. I watched them ride off from over my shoulder as they headed north for Keldor and me south for Elondria. I wished I could have seen Rianna and Mother as well.

My father and brother melted into the distance, and I kept watching over my shoulder until they vanished altogether, my tears flowing freely when they did. As miserable as this trip had been, it had all been worth it to see them again. I still couldn't believe it had happened.

Turning back in the saddle, I faced south and kicked my horse into a full gallop. I needed to get as far from Ecrin as I could. I had two other families awaiting my return.

# WILDFIRE

## Chapter 24

I T TOOK ME LONGER to reach the Pyruvian River than I expected. The rains had picked up once again, slowing my progress, and when I reached Dorwall, Tobar the innkeeper at the Spotted Pike insisted that I stay the night to wait it out and catch up on some much-needed sleep. I took him up on the offer, especially considering the room and meals were on the house. The townsfolk were glad to see me, many recognizing my face from our last visit. They didn't even seem all that put off by my eyes.

Dorwall was a different place from the first time I'd ridden through. Yes, the rain was still coming down in sheets, leaving the roads a muddy mess, but the aura of darkness and gloom seemed to have dissipated. People tipped their hats in the street, even waved as I passed. After a full day of waiting and a full night of rest, I decided to be on my way. I couldn't wait for the rain to pass. If Saryn had sent search parties out, they were sure to be heading this way.

I thanked Tobar for his hospitality, and he made sure I knew that there was always a room for me at the Spotted Pike if I was ever back that way. With my saddlebags refilled with the town's generosity, I hit the road and started southeast for the Pyruvian.

It took at least a week before I caught my first glimpse of the water. The rain had finally let up three days out from Dorwall, leaving me and my horse more than a little thankful to see the first rays of light popping through the grey clouds overhead. It took another two days for the sun to dry out my clothing completely, though I had discovered that through the deluge, my coat had done a remarkable job of keeping most of me dry. Unfortunately, now that the sun was out, it was leaving my back slick with sweat.

I did eventually take it off, along with my swords, though I kept those within easy reach. Once I made it to the river, they were quickly put back on. I had no idea where I was in relation to the bridges. I had done my best to stay as far away from the main road as possible, not wanting to risk running into Saryn's soldiers, since I was sure they were going to be making a run straight for the border.

My roommates and the ambassador were probably back in Aramoor by now. Even if they'd stopped at the Isle of Delga to drop off Ratko and his men at the salt mines, they would have still had plenty of time to reach the Bay of Torrin by ship. I would have really liked to have been there to see the king's face when we came walking into the palace with his ambassador. Honestly, I would have been more interested in seeing my roommates' faces if they had been allowed an audience with the king. Most of them still got nervous whenever we had our training sessions over there.

I waited for the cover of darkness to make my way down to the water. Unfortunately, there was nowhere for me to cross. The rain had clearly hit the Black Hills north of me, and the runoff was swelling the river's banks. There was no safe way to attempt a crossing.

I stood there for a while, staring out at the moonlit shimmer off the fast-moving water, trying to decide what to do next. As I saw it, I only had one option: find a bridge, the one thing I had been hoping to avoid. Climbing back up into the saddle, my tired horse and I made our way south.

Not knowing where I was along the river, the safest direction I could take was south. The crossing at Belbridge was the closest to where I needed to go, but I had no idea if I was north or south of that location, and I couldn't waste days of riding north just to discover I was already north of it.

If I was already south of Belbridge, at the very least I could find another crossing down at Laneer, which was a small port town just off the Rhunarin Ocean. From there, I could book passage aboard a freighter heading to Aramoor.

The air was crisp after the rain, leaving the night a touch brisk, which was strange for this time of year in the southernmost regions of Aldor. But after days of scorching heat, I was thankful for it. The moon had just slipped past its high point when I caught the first signs of people ahead. Flickers or torchlight, like tiny glow worms, dotted the night, and I quickly put my black coat on. Soon enough, I could hear voices and see that I was indeed reaching what I assumed was the crossing at Belbridge. It certainly looked like the bridge we had scouted upon our arrival in Cylmar.

On the other side of the water, I could see similar dots of light, but smaller. Those had to be the Elondrian Lancers guarding their side of the crossing, keeping a close eye on the Cylmarans. Every now and then, I would hear of skirmishes that had taken place out here along the border between the two kingdoms, some growing to the point that a larger military campaign had become necessary to force an end to the conflict.

Thankfully, it had never been large enough to require our help. Up until recently, Room Eleven had always been the last ones called into any sort of action.

Most of those battles, though, tended to happen around the passes into the Black Hills and the mining communities there, as Cylmar continued to demand rights to the mines, threatening the miners and forcing the Lancers to keep a year-round barracks on the premises.

I remembered my first encounter with Cylmarans not long after leaving the Lost City, back when I was sailing south on the Shemoa River with Captain Treygan and the crew of the *Wind Binder*. We'd fought a large band of slavers inside the Black Hills and rescued former Magistrate Sirias and his family. It hadn't exactly been a great first impression of Cylmarans.

That seemed a lifetime ago.

It didn't take long before I was close enough to see movement. I breathed a small sigh of relief to find maybe a dozen men guarding the Cylmaran side, which meant I'd beaten Saryn's search party here. Still, there were plenty of men in uniform milling about the front of the bridge to make the crossing more difficult.

Moving closer to get a better look, I noticed they had brought in a wagon to block the front. Disappointing. I had been hoping to make a break for it and gallop through. That was now out of the question, leaving me with only two options: talk my way through or fight.

I hoped I could manage the first.

Nudging my horse into a slow trot, we headed for the front of the bridge. "Evening," I called out, letting them know I was riding into their camp, not wanting to startle them.

Everyone turned, some near the fire stood, and a couple sitting near the outskirts closest to me drew their weapons.

"Lot of rain we've been having," I said, keeping my hands on the reins where the soldiers could see them. "Water's up so high, I couldn't find a safe place to cross." I pulled my horse to a stop a few feet from the first of the men and pointed at the wagon blocking the road. "Is the bridge out of order? I'd planned on crossing here."

"State your business," one of the four guards closest to me demanded. He was one of the few who'd felt the need to draw a weapon.

I scratched the top of my head, keeping my eyes lowered, since my hood was down. "As I said, my business is crossing that bridge. I'm heading to Terhi to look for work. Heard they were hiring on the boats down there." I hoped I'd pronounced the name of the city correctly. I'd only ever seen it printed out on a map, never heard it named.

"What kind of work you looking for?" the man asked, staring at the sword rising over my shoulder. "Mercenary?" He spit to the side. "Don't have much use for sellswords. You want a real job, join the Cylmaran ranks." He patted the front of his uniform respectably.

I almost chuckled. If my dream in life was to become a thug for hire, then sure.

"I've always been one for the open road," I said. "Not too good with being cooped up in a barracks. Besides, I prefer to do my business in private, not share a stall with a hundred other men."

Several of the men laughed.

The soldier pointed his sword at me. "Why are you looking for work in Elondria? Much better places here in Cylmar."

I didn't answer right away because I wasn't sure if he was joking. When I realized he wasn't, I continued. "I tried, even went so far as Ecrin, but the head of Fishtown . . . Dovan, I believe his name was, said they weren't looking to take on any more workers. Been the mantra every place I've passed through."

The man doing all the talking spat to the side once more, and his face contorted like he'd sucked a lemon. "Dovan and his guild ain't

nothing but a bunch of cowards. Treats us soldiers like something he squashed under his boot. You couldn't pay me enough gold to go work for him. Count yourself lucky."

"I got the same impression," I said. "Wish I'd come by here earlier. It would have saved me from making a wasted trip." I glanced beyond them to the wagon. Some of the other soldiers near the bridge had already retaken their seats and had gone back to their previous conversations. "So, is the bridge out of order, or is there some sort of toll that needs paying to cross?" I didn't want to bring up the toll as I was running very low on funds, especially with the clothes I'd purchased, but I needed to get across without a fuss.

I turned to reach for my purse and spotted what looked like a small cloud in the distance floating across the ground behind me. It took me a moment to realize what it was. Dust from a group of horses, and it was coming this way.

Saryn's search parties had finally caught up.

"I don't have much," I said, digging out my purse and bouncing it in my palm, hoping they'd take pity on me and just let me cross. *Come on. Let me pass.*

The guard stared at my purse a minute, then glanced over his shoulder at the other guards, who had all but gone back to their own business. What was he waiting for? I was about to toss the purse at them and make a break for it when the man finally turned and waved me off.

"Nah, you're fine." He looked at the wagon. "Let him through."

I raised my hood so the light from their torches didn't reflect off my eyes when I passed, then nudged my horse forward. "Wish me luck."

"You'll need it over there," the man called out.

I passed through the encampment slowly, keeping my eyes straight ahead, too afraid to glance over my shoulder to see how close the riders were. I grabbed the reins and watched as the men in front of me slowly began to work their way around the wagon to push it out of the way.

"Wait," the soldier behind me said.

I acted like I hadn't heard, or didn't realize he was speaking to me, and kept going. The men hadn't moved the wagon yet, and there wasn't enough room between the wagon and the sides of the bridge for a horse to pass.

"You, there, stop!"

I bit down on my tongue and pulled back on my reins. A couple of the men near the wagon turned and drew their swords, wondering what was going on.

I twisted in my saddle. The cloud was close enough that I could see horses and riders at the front. "I really need to be going," I said. "What is it?"

The soldier walked over, keeping his voice lowered. "Come to think of it . . ." He looked almost embarrassed. "I really do need to charge a toll. If the others report I was letting people pass without it, they'd take it out of my pay."

I gritted my teeth. "That's fine." I quickly dug my purse back out with nervous fingers and opened the strings. Sweat was dripping down my back, and my palms were slick. "How much?"

"Three coppers."

I pulled out three coppers and leaned down to hand it to the man when someone shouted.

"Riders coming!"

I looked up, the coins still sitting in my hand. The soldier's attention was momentarily diverted. The cloud parted on the road, and there was no mistaking who it was. At least two dozen men in Cylmaran uniforms pulled up just outside the camp.

I had to get out of there. I had to reach the other side of the bridge.

"Here's your coppers. How about letting me through?"

The man turned and took the coppers half-heartedly, but instead of telling the men to move the wagon, he turned back toward the soldiers to see what was happening. As soon as he did, a couple of the men on the far side of the camp, who were presently conversing with the new arrivals, turned and pointed straight at me.

I couldn't wait around to find out what they were saying. I was sure it wasn't good, and there were too many of them to fight on my own. I had to reach the Elondrian Lancers on the other side.

The man who'd just taken my coin turned, and as soon as he did, I kicked him backward and then dug in my heels. The horse reeled as I jerked him around, and he bolted straight for the wagon. The men standing around it quickly reached for their swords, those that didn't already had theirs out.

I knew the horse couldn't jump the wagon, which left me with only one choice. I climbed up in the saddle, holding on to the horn to keep from completely tipping off. As soon as the horse turned to keep from hitting the wagon altogether, I leaped from its back and drew my swords in midair—a definite first.

I landed on top of two men, swatting aside their attempts at skewering me. Both went down as my weight plowed into them. I stabbed the first in the leg, rolled over, and punched the second in the face before he could raise his sword, then stabbed him as well. Shouts from behind had me scrambling to my feet as I cut down two more.

Behind me, I could hear soldiers shouting for me to stop. What fool was going to stop and let Cylmaran soldiers torture and kill them? I climbed up and over the wagon and leaped off the other side and onto the bridge. I could see tiny spots of firelight ahead.

"Help!" I shouted as I ran.

Shouts to move the wagon rose behind me. I didn't take the time to look. I already knew what I would see: mounted soldiers charging across the bridge, hoping to run me down before I reached the soldiers on the other side.

"Help!"

I ran as hard as I could. The bridge was even longer than I had thought, or maybe it was just the urgency that made it seem that way. One thing was for certain: I wasn't going to reach the other side before their horses reached me. Still, I kept running and shouting for the Elondrian soldiers to help. I did see what looked like movement on the other end, dots of torchlight heading my way, but they were still a long way off.

The bridge shook with the force of the charge behind me. The sound of the horses galloping across the wooden planks had my heart racing. I couldn't run any faster, and if I didn't get out of the way, they were going to trample me under their hooves. Quickly, I veered to the side of the bridge to keep from getting plowed under and jumped onto the railing just as the first of the horses reached me.

I turned and leaped on top of the closest rider, burying one of my swords in the man's chest as I deflected an attempted swing for my left arm with the other. The soldiers pulled to a stop to keep from running each other over, giving me a chance to fight them two or three at a time instead of the entire company.

The problem was that I wasn't half the horseman they were, and I was finding it nearly impossible to keep the horse I was on under control. My visions kept me from getting my head lopped off when my horse suddenly decided to spin, leaving my back completely open. I ducked another swing and dug in my heels. I needed to reach the oncoming lancers.

The horse reared and then took off, breaking through the mounted soldiers blocking my way. There was nothing standing in my—

A whistle shrilled from someone behind me, and the horse stopped

in mid-gallop and sent me flying. I hit the floor of the bridge and rolled, keeping a tight grip on my swords. My knuckles were bleeding from where they had scraped against the wooden planks. So much for my quick escape. I hopped to my feet and ran for the halfway point on the bridge. I could feel as much as hear the sound of the horses behind me as the Cylmaran soldiers charged once more.

The lancers on the Elondrian side were nearly to me. Their numbers could have held off those sent to guard the Cylmaran side, but now there was an entire company of mounted riders to contend with as well. I hoped the lancers were seasoned enough to help me fight them off. Maybe I'd get lucky and the Cylmarans would pull back, not wanting a confrontation.

Who was I kidding? That was all the Cylmarans ever wanted.

I was nearing the halfway point on the bridge, close enough to make out faces in the oncoming torchlight, but not close enough to reach them before being trampled. "I'm an emissary for the king!" I shouted to the oncoming lancers, then spun around as the first of the horsemen flew past. I took a glancing blow to the arm from the horse on the left, which sent me careening into the one on the right, but neither was bad enough to make me drop my swords.

Not seeing any other option, I used my lower height to its small advantage and sliced open the first two horses' legs. Both went down, sending their riders tumbling overtop. I didn't like hurting the horses. It wasn't their fault they were there, but I wanted to live more. As soon as the two men hit the bridge, I planted my blades in their legs as well, leaving them to writhe on the ground next to their mounts.

The rest of the horsemen pulled to a halt and dismounted, not wanting the same to happen to them. The bridge was proving too tight to maneuver anyway.

I took the momentary distraction and ran. The full company of Cylmaran soldiers were just behind me, and the lancers were just ahead. But for some reason the lancers had stopped. What were they doing? They seemed to be yelling at me to run. Idiots! Couldn't they see I was already doing that? Why weren't they coming to help?

My legs were aching. I could hardly feel them after weeks in a saddle, but I fought through the weariness, my heart pounding, beating to the rhythm of my feet on the planks below. I was almost there. Twenty feet. Fifteen. The lancers shouted, and I dove to the right to keep from getting a sword planted in my back, as one of the Cylmarans had managed to catch up.

The two sides collided. Whatever unseen barrier was keeping the Elondrian lancers from moving past disappeared in a wave of arms and swords and battle cries.

I rolled to my feet and spun, swords in the air, but with this many bodies on top of each other, they weren't proving as effective. There was no room to spread out, with the railing at the side keeping us all bunched up together. I was blocking and weaving and dodging just as many blows from the Elondrians as from the Cylmarans.

With quarters this tight, two swords were proving difficult, if not impossible. I was hardly able to get the one up and around without smacking it against those fighting beside me. I quickly sheathed my lancer sword at my waist and pulled my belt knife from behind my back, sticking it into the closest gut I could reach that wasn't wearing the Elondrian crimson and gold.

Several of the lancers beside me went down, others pushing forward to take their place. Unfortunately, the other side had far more bodies available to refill their gaps than we did, and soon our gaps widened far enough to let some of their numbers through. I fought my way to the side. If we didn't close the breaches, they were going to have us flanked.

Throwing myself in the middle of the largest opening, I forced back three of the soldiers trying to break through. They were clearly skilled with the blade, but I wove through their attacks, deflecting what I could and countering to keep them from spilling through. They killed a lancer beside me, who'd turned his back just for a split moment to defend a fellow brother in arms. An unexpected thrust went to his side before I could stop it, and he went down.

Another dropped. Pretty soon there were only a handful left and still plenty of Cylmarans to go around. I delved deeper with my magic, feeling its heat building in my chest. I had to do something. My arms moved as though on their own as my sword and dagger blocked and parried and deflected the three pieces of sharp steel looking to bite into my flesh. One of the attackers went down with a swift slash of my dagger to his gut.

Beside me, another cry, and another lancer down, a sword through his chest. There were only three of us left, but I didn't have time to see how they were doing as I was fighting to keep from going down myself. My face was dripping with sweat, beads flying from my hair with every spin of my head.

I heard another cry to my right, but I couldn't turn to see if it was one of ours or theirs. I pulled back as two more took the place of the one I'd killed, leaving me four on one, which wouldn't have been too terrible if I didn't know there were still more to take their place.

My hands were cramping, my legs wobbling. I hadn't slept much since leaving Dorwall for the second time. Fear of dying and my magic were the only things keeping me on my feet. With two injuries already, I knew I wasn't going to make it. If the other lancers went down, my only option would be to attempt a jump from the bridge, which would no doubt lead to me being sucked under.

I turned to readjust my stance when an unexpected shout on my right had me nearly jumping out of my skin. Several bodies suddenly appeared out of the night around me like wraiths. I couldn't turn to see if they were Elondrian or Cylmaran, as I was too busy keeping the soldiers and their swords in front of me occupied. I was just waiting for that piercing sting from one of their swords to finish me off.

"Couldn't let you have all the fun!" a very familiar booming voice said, forcing me to turn and look anyway as the men I'd been fighting suddenly pulled back from the newcomers.

Barthol had a wide grin on his face as he swung his massive sword around, nearly taking off his opponent's entire arm in an attempt to, quite literally, disarm him.

"How did you—"

"Thought you was a goner for sure," Gellar bellowed on my left as he jumped in to hold off at least one of the men trying to get to me. His battle-ax pounded into the man so hard it threw the Cylmaran off his feet. My time spent with him in our weekly sessions in the palace had woven the gruff man into quite the skilled armsman. Which could be said for all of my roommates, including Dakaran, who was surprisingly not standing at the back this time with Stumpy, but at the front alongside Fipple, his sword moving with accuracy and speed.

I stumbled back, as it was getting to be too many fighters in one clump, and nearly tripped over Waylen, who was waiting with the horses, sword in hand, ready to cut down any of the Cylmarans who made it past the rest. It was my first chance to get a solid look at the battle, or what was left of it. With the arrival of an extremely skilled group of fighters, the Cylmarans, what few remained, were now pulling back into a full retreat.

Fipple shouted something at them as they fled. I couldn't quite make out what it was, but he certainly seemed excited to say it. No doubt something to do with them being cowards, and a well-placed slight

against their familial upbringing, something about their father and a milk cow.

Beside Fipple, Stumpy had his special-made shield strapped to his bad arm and a bloody sword in the other. "Looks like we got here just in time."

"I'm sure our young swordmaster could have handled it," Fipple said with a wink as he walked by, his topknot holding the back of his hood off his head.

"Yes," Waylen agreed, walking over, dragging the horses with him, "but why let him have all the fun?"

"Did you see the way I dispensed of that soldier?" Dakaran said proudly.

I smiled. "He didn't stand a chance." I took a deep breath and slowly exhaled, releasing the tension that had built up in my chest and neck and shoulders. I could feel the heat of my magic slowly dissipating as I leaned against the side rail of the bridge and stared at the worn-looking faces of the men in front of me, faces I hadn't been sure I'd ever see again.

# WILDFIRE

## Chapter 25

NLY TWO OF THE ORIGINAL lancer party remained on their feet as we searched through the remains for other wounded, removing the dead for a proper Elondrian burial, or at least as proper as we could muster under the circumstances.

Every inch of me ached with exhaustion. Looking over the bodies left me aching in a different way. A heaviness settled over me, like a vise was squeezing my chest, stealing my breath. I hated to think that these soldiers had been forced to give up their lives to save mine. I didn't think mine worth the cost of so many, but that was the unfortunate lot of a lancer. It was also what earned us the respect of our kingdom. Most were more than willing to give up a seat, tip their hat, or offer to buy a round for a lancer. Sure, you had some bad apples in the barrel, like you did everywhere, but on the whole, Elondria wouldn't be what it was today if not for the Lancers.

I smiled as I thought about how scared of the Lancers I had been as

a street rat. Some days I still felt like a street rat, at least at heart. It had been nearly two months since I'd been home, since I'd seen Reevie and Sapphire and all the others. What was supposed to have only been a part-time stint with the Lancers was quickly becoming something much more permanent. The strange thing was that even though I missed my tribe, I didn't miss them as badly as I used to. I didn't know if I liked that idea or not.

My life was changing. I wondered where that change would lead me.

I looked at my roommates, sitting with me around one of the fire pits on the Elondrian side of the bridge, sharing some dried meat and biscuits while waiting on the sun to fully rise. We had spent what was left of the night burying the dead, since we were definitely still too far away from Aramoor to try shipping bodies back.

"How in Aldor did you find me?" I asked.

Barthol swallowed what was left in his waterskin and wiped the remaining drops from his beard. "We figured if you did make it out of Ecrin, you were most likely to try heading back the way we came, with it being the most familiar. Couldn't see you trying to head north around the Black Hills. And with the Pyruvian having flooded her banks, we didn't figure you were crazy enough to try swimming across."

Gellar cleared his throat.

"Fine," Barthol added. "Most of us didn't think you would."

Gellar leaned forward from where he was seated on the other side of Barthol and smiled.

"But how did you get here so quickly?" I asked. "And where is the ambassador and his wife? I thought you would have taken them straight to Aramoor."

Barthol nodded. "Instead of going on to Aramoor after we dropped the prisoners off at Delga, we had Zlatin take us upriver at Laneer and head toward Belbridge. We figured you'd be coming through here at some point, might as well be here to greet you."

"Not everyone was sure that you'd make it," Waylen said, twisting his long, thin beard around one of his plump fingers.

Everyone turned and looked at Dakaran.

Dakaran lifted his hands. "What? I wasn't the only one."

Barthol turned to me. "Jasna talked her father into giving us a few more days to see if you'd show up, but time was running out."

"Are you saying they've already left?"

"No, I'm saying you were lucky. Zlatin was planning on giving you one more day, and then we would have been stuck finding alternate transportation."

Fipple wiped his bald head back toward the topknot. "Apparently, his debt to us only goes so far, or lasts so long. Typical Cylmaran."

"He's done right by us," Waylen said. "Taken us this far when no one else would have, and at the risk of his own crew. I only hope Overlord Saryn doesn't find out where he's been."

Stumpy leaned forward. "From what we've seen of the love between the soldiers and Fishtown, I'd wager those in the community will do their best to protect him."

Barthol stood and stretched, staring off in the direction of the brightest part of the grey sky as it slowly turned to a soft blue, letting us know the sun was about to breach the horizon. "Time to be going." He turned to the two remaining lancers. "We'll send back replacements as soon as we reach Aramoor. Do you have any other men to stand watch?"

"There are more," the older of the two guards said, "but they are making their rounds through the passes." He pointed north toward the Black Hills. "Won't be back for several days, but I'm sure we can find some folks in Belbridge willing to come out for a night or two. Might cost us some of the king's gold, but better that than being overrun by another raiding party."

"I don't think you'll have much trouble with the Cylmarans," I said. "It'll take a while for them to get word back up the line to Ecrin for replacements."

I thanked each of them for my life and for their service, promising I'd mention them by name to the king if I got the opportunity. The younger lancer, who was still at least five or six years my senior, handed me a slip of paper with the names of each of the fallen, instructing me to make sure Commander Goring received it and notified the families.

With that, my roommates and I mounted and headed south until we spotted a sail in the distance. I rode double with Dakaran since we were down one horse, which he didn't care for but also didn't gripe about. I guess they thought I would have been riding one across, which I almost did, but for the Cylmaran's wagon blocking my way.

We left the horses in Belbridge and took a boat out to Zlatin's ship. It took us two trips to get everyone on board, but as soon as we did, we started south down the Pyruvian and from there headed east toward the Bay of Torrin and home.

Hurricane   Avalanche   Rockslide   Wildfire   Sandstorm

The water remained calm for our voyage, which I was quite thankful for. After my time on the *Wind Binder*, I knew what rough water could do to an untrained stomach. Sailing into the Bay of Torrin hit me harder than I was expecting. Seeing Aramoor's white walls glistened in the midafternoon sun, the towers, steeples, and domes rising up like flowers in the tall grass, had my emotions reeling. I found myself tearing up, but I managed to hide it with a well-timed wave that struck near where I was standing, dousing my face. I wiped the salty brine and tears from my eyes and took a deep breath, slowly exhaling with a smile.

I was home.

I no longer found it strange to think of Aramoor that way. It *was* my home. The Lost City was my past. Even after the incredible reunion with my father and brother, I truly had no desire to return to the underground tunnels of the Upaka, other than to see my mother and sister.

Aramoor's skyline was breathtaking from this view, seeming to rise as high as the Sandrethin Mountains, which encircled this small portion of the world.

It was certainly a busy day for the Aramoor docks. The port was teeming with ships of all shapes and sizes flying a collection of colors that encompassed all of the Five Kingdoms. I even spotted several ships flying the orange-and-yellow Keldoran flag, which wasn't as common, since Keldor was the only kingdom that was completely landlocked with only the Shemoa and the Taloos Rivers capable of handling trade shipping.

We waited for a free pier and then quickly made our way in before it was taken by one of the many other vessels in the bay.

"I'm going to miss you," Jasna said, waiting on me as I headed down the steps of the top deck to join the rest of my roommates, who were all anxiously waiting to disembark.

"I'm going to miss you as well," I said, stepping off the stairs and onto the main deck. I passed the ambassador and his wife, who were green from their time on the high seas. Sick or not, they both wore bright smiles as they made ready to once again step foot inside their beloved city.

"Will you ever come back?" Jasna asked.

"I don't know," I admitted honestly. "Don't take this the wrong way, but I hope not. However, if I do, you'll be the first person I come to see."

She smiled and, taking a quick peek to see if her father was around or looking, leaned forward and kissed me. "Something to remember me by." She turned and sauntered off toward the gangplank.

Pradjic, her father's right hand, frowned from the side rail.

I tried not to smile.

"Some men have all the luck," Waylen said as he jokingly slapped Dakaran on the back. "Aye?"

Dakaran scrunched his nose, but he did seem to be staring pretty hard after Jasna when she left. Personally, I was just glad Sapphire was nowhere around to witness Jasna's goodbye. The sudden thought of Sapphire had me pushing my way to the side of the ship, where Captain Zlatin was waiting.

"It's been quite the adventure we've had, you and I," he said to me with an outstretched hand.

I took it. "Adventure is putting it mildly."

"Let's not do it again anytime soon," he said with a smile.

I laughed. "Sounds like a good plan. I appreciate your help getting us out of Ecrin. We'd be in the tower dungeons for sure if not for you."

"And if not for you, I'd be drinking myself into a pauper's grave. Now . . ." He put his arm around Jasna and kissed her on the forehead. "Now I can hold my head high when I walk through town." He smiled. "I believe I came out the better for this arrangement. If any of you ever find yourselves back in Ecrin with need of transport, you know where to look. Let's just keep the palace guards out of it next time, aye?"

My roommates nodded.

"I think we can do that," Barthol said.

Fipple stepped forward and shook the captain's hand. "It's good to see that not all Cylmarans have lost their way."

Zlatin nodded. "And I never thought to meet one of the Southern Watch. It is an honor, sir. What they did to your people was a disgrace to Cylmar. I'm glad to see you've found a place for yourself here."

Fipple nodded and turned to help the ambassador and his wife down the gangplank. The others shook the captain's and Jasna's hands before disembarking. I was the last off, and I waved farewell as we started down the pier for the docks. Walking on solid ground felt strange, and I knew it would take some time getting used to once again.

The sun was beginning to lower as the afternoon waned toward evening. It wasn't low enough for the lamplighters to be out, but enough for them to be getting their wicks ready. My stomach grumbled when I caught a whiff from the Wooden Leg Tavern. It was hardly reputable enough to eat at, mostly used for sailors to drink away their hard-earned pay, but whatever was wafting from their chimney stack smelled divine.

"Where can we escort you, ambassador?" I asked, turning to our esteemed guests.

"Home," his wife was quick to say. Her clothes had been marred beyond repair, and all that had been available on ship was an extra pair of trousers and a tunic from those on board. She seemed to be looking around to see if she spotted anyone she knew, clearly self-conscious by her state of dress. She pulled on her husband's shirt. "Order us a carriage."

"With what?" he asked. "The shoes on our feet?"

"I believe we can cover a carriage for you, milady," I said.

She smiled. "Son, you've done enough for us already." She looked at my hand, which was halfway in my coat. "But if you could see fit to order one, my husband will repay you tenfold once we reach our estate."

Gellar nudged me in the side, letting me know he could really use the extra coin.

"We will be more than happy to see you safely home," I said. "And there's no need for the restitution. It will be our honor."

Gellar coughed.

"Nonsense," Ambassador Gorman said. "I don't know what a lancer's salary is, but I'm sure it isn't enough. Anyone willing to travel halfway across the Five Kingdoms and risk their lives breaking an old man and his wife out of an overlord's dungeon deserves compensation." He looked at all of us. "You have our undying gratitude, sirs. You make sure to come by the estate tomorrow, and I will have that payment ready."

I handed Stumpy my purse, and he left to fetch a carriage.

"I can't wait to go home and crawl into my bed and sleep for the next week," Dakaran said.

Barthol hmphed. "We'll be lucky if Overcaptain Tolin gives us the day off tomorrow."

Dakaran's eyes widened. "After what we've just been through, he better."

"Tolin's a fair man," Gellar said, winking at Barthol. "I'm sure he'll give you an extra hour in the bunk before morning duties."

"An extra hour!" Dakaran looked ready to explode.

My roommates laughed.

Gorman and Neina stood to the side and smiled politely, not knowing which side to take but political enough to know better than to choose. In all honesty, I was hoping Tolin would give us the day off as well. Not only was I looking forward to sleeping in, but I wanted to get back to Sandstorm Manor. I couldn't believe how long I'd been away.

The sound of hooves coming down the street had us all turning. Sure enough, Stumpy had managed to find a carriage to escort the ambassador and his wife home. It wasn't anything extravagant. For the little money we had left, that was a good thing.

The carriage pulled alongside, and Stumpy hopped down from the front seat. The driver, on the other hand, climbed down slowly, clearly not as spry or lean as Stumpy. Apparently, we weren't able to afford a carriage with a footman, so the driver walked around and tipped his hat as he opened the door, giving us all a good looking-over, stopping at the approaching older couple.

"Afternoon, gents, milady," he said politely with a South Aramoor accent most notably heard around the docks. "Can I help the lady inside?" He stared at her worn trousers and tunic.

Neina gave the driver her arm, and he helped her in. The driver even started to offer the ambassador the same courtesy, but a quick wave from the ambassador let the man know his help wasn't needed. The driver tipped his hat once more as he waited for the ambassador to take his seat.

"Any other takers?" the driver asked, turning back to us. "Last chance." When we didn't make a move toward the carriage, he shut the door. "Well, don't complain to me when you reach the barracks with blisters." He climbed up on the seat, the carriage rocking back and forth. He gave us one last look, then tipped his hat and snapped the reins softly, calling out to his horses to get a move on.

The carriage started forward and pretty soon disappeared around the first bend as it made its way out of the shipping yards toward Bay Street. As I watched the carriage vanish behind a large warehouse, a thought occurred to me.

"Did anyone find out where they live?"

Gellar's eyes widened. "What? We don't know where they live? How are we going to get our money?"

Fipple laughed. "Guess it wasn't meant to be." He yawned and started to pull up his hood to hide his topknot but, seeming to remember where we were, changed his mind and left it down. "I'd trade all my gold for a good night's sleep."

"Hang your sleep," Gellar said. "I want the gold." He looked at the empty street where the carriage had been. "We should have taken the driver up on his offer. At least that way we could have found out where

the ambassador lived and saved us a long walk back to the barracks."

"Afraid we didn't have enough coin left over," Stumpy said, handing me back my pouch.

I looked inside. There was nothing but a few coppers clinking at the bottom, barely enough for a single cheese tart from Master Endle's bakery. My mouth began to water at the thought.

Gellar hmphed. "Rotten luck, this is. This whole trip has had the Defiler's hand on it."

"And yet, we're still here," I said with a smile.

"And we're the stronger for it," Barthol added, his towering frame blocking the late-afternoon sun from my face.

Waylen twirled his long, thin braid as he, too, stared after the carriage. "A hot bath and a warm meal, and I'll be ready to sleep till winter."

Dakaran was uncommonly quiet beside me, his eyes seemingly glued to the cobbles below his feet.

"What's got your tongue?" I asked him.

He looked up. "What?"

I chuckled. "It must be pretty important to keep you from adding in your two coppers."

Dakaran frowned. "I was just thinking. I've only been a lancer for about three months, and I've already almost died at least half a dozen times. At this rate, I'm not going to make it to my eighteenth birth year."

Barthol leaned over and slapped Dakaran on the back and nearly sent him to the ground. "But just think what a year that will be. Besides, weren't you the one who insisted on coming in the first place, even over Overcaptain Tolin's objections?"

Dakaran frowned. "Yeah, I'm definitely regretting that choice.

WILDFIRE

*Chapter 26*

THE TRIP ACROSS TOWN was a long one. No one really had much to say other than to complain about the heat, or the soreness of our feet, or our current lack of funds. I kept my eyes open, hoping to catch a glimpse of someone from my tribe, but being this close to Bayside, the likelihood of that happening was slim. We finally reached King's Way West and picked up our pace as we headed down Lancer Avenue and caught our first glimpse of the garrison's stone wall.

One look at our state, and those lancers meandering up and down the street were quick to get out of the way. The rest of my roommates were wearing their travel garb, while I remained in my black leathers.

"Thought you was dead," one man called out.

"Thought you'd deserted," another said.

Pretty soon, we'd built a steady following of lancers trailing us toward the gates to see what was happening, probably out of sheer

curiosity. I doubted it was because they were concerned with our well-being.

By the time we passed through the front gate, we had quite the crowd surrounding us, enough to make moving forward difficult. Many wanted to know where we'd been, others wondering why we looked like we'd just come off a month-long pilgrimage through the Wengoby Desert. Apparently, no one had been informed of our mission.

"Move aside!" a familiar voice shouted from the direction of the main building, where the senior officers kept their offices.

The men in front parted as a short but broad-shouldered man with a red ducktail beard pushed his way through. Captain Asa looked as astonished to see us as the rest of the lancers. "I see you made it back, and in one piece no less, by the look of ya. Not that there was much to look at in the first place."

Several of those closest snickered.

He took in my black leathers and the sword riding on my back and pursed his lips. "This way. You'll need to brief the commander and the overcaptains before you do anything. That includes changing your clothes, which by the smell of ya needs to be done immediately."

More chuckling sifted through the crowd, though after a growl from Barthol, it quickly faded.

"As luck would have it, the senior officers are in a meeting this very moment. You can catch 'em all at once." He looked us over again and shook his head. "This ought to be quite the briefing." Asa turned, but the circle of lancers had closed behind him, so he waved his arms. "Move aside, or I'll have you cleaning privies for a month!" Those in front nearly broke out in a fight to get out of the way, opening a clear path to the entrance of the building.

I couldn't help but walk a little taller. This was quite the welcome we were receiving—not something Room Eleven was used to. Our private training sessions had raised the level of my roommates' proficiency to the point that it had become apparent, earning us some regard, especially when those of Room Eleven were now considered some of the best swordsmen in the garrison—but it hadn't earned us this much.

Captain Asa led us up the stairs and through the front doors into the open lobby. Instead of heading up the central staircase leading to the second floor where the offices were, he turned right and marched us down a brightly lit corridor, where he stopped in front of a set of double doors at the end. I'd never been inside the officers' meeting room. My time in this building had mostly been spent upstairs in Overcaptain Tolin's office or in the surrounding hallways while on cleaning duty.

Asa knocked.

"Come in," a high-pitched voice said. I recognized it as Commander Goring.

Captain Asa opened the door. "Sorry for the interruption, Commander, but I thought you would want to know: Room Eleven has just returned."

I heard a seat scooting back from the table. I didn't need to see into the room to know whose it was.

"Where are they, Captain?" Tolin's voice boomed.

Asa smiled. "Just outside the door."

"Show them in, man," Goring's voice called out from the other side of the room.

"Yes, sir."

The door on the right opened before Asa could get to it, and Overcaptain Tolin stepped out. He had a wide grin on his face as he looked us over and nodded, breathing a very notable sigh of relief when his eyes found Dakaran. The king was no doubt riding Tolin hard with the crown prince having been gone for so long with no word.

"It appears you are all in one piece. That is something, I guess."

Asa chuckled. "That's exactly what I said."

"You can stand over there," he said, motioning to the end of the table on our right, opposite where Commander Goring was sitting. There weren't enough places left around the long table for all of us to sit, not that we would have felt comfortable doing so in the officers' presence, so we moved around to the end and stood at attention.

Goring leaned forward in his seat and rested his elbows on top of the table. "I'd be lying if I said we weren't growing worried." He looked us over and waved his hand. "Stand at ease. You look like you're nearly ready to fall over. Tell us: Was the mission successful? Did you find the ambassador and his wife still alive?"

Some of the officers scooted forward in their seats. Tolin, who hadn't yet retaken his chair, turned and waited for our answer.

I looked at my roommates, and they all looked at me. I was the nominated spokesman. I nodded to Commander Goring. "Yes, sir. We found them alive . . . but barely." I proceeded to fill the officers in on every detail of our journey, even including the strange occurrence we came across in Dorwall with the invisible killers running around town carving people up. I made sure to mention the aid my father and brother had given in the rescue of the ambassador and his wife, as well as that of Jasna, her father, and the members of his crew, and, of course, the timely arrival of the Sil'Rhivanni.

My roommates, mostly Dakaran, chimed in when they thought I had forgotten some bit of interesting detail, and by the time we had finished unveiling our harrowing experience across the Cylmaran border, the room had been stunned into silence. Even Overcaptain Tolin, who had finally managed to find his seat, had nothing to say.

I did leave out the offer of payment by the ambassador for our help. I didn't see the need to bother the officers with such a trivial detail.

Goring was the first to speak. "That is quite the tale. If half of what you say is true, it's a miracle you're here at all. I'm sure as soon as the ambassador and his wife are rested up, they will share their experience with the king."

The others in the room seemed to have been waiting for the commander to speak before pelting us with a barrage of questions, which mostly centered on the two white-haired lunatics and their collection of bodies. I also received several questions about our escape from Saryn's castle and any details we might be able to share as to the interior of the fortress. Overcaptain Tolin asked for a copy of the map that Vulkina had drawn, which I thought was a prudent question.

We did our best to answer each and every one as briefly and respectfully as possible, no matter how ridiculous.

Henzlow, who had somehow managed to earn a promotion over the last two years, and no doubt wanting to prove himself, asked why I wasn't wearing proper uniform. How he had managed to get promoted, I didn't know. He clearly had some powerful friends or family in his corner, because he certainly couldn't have earned it on his own merit. There were few in the garrison who could stand the man, even fewer officers it seemed, as they all turned and looked at him with the same amount of disgust. The man had had it out for me ever since my first day. It was Henzlow who had sent me and my roommates into the Warrens, where we were nearly killed.

I answered that it was because I had to infiltrate the overlord's castle, and I couldn't do so while wearing Elondrian colors, and that by the time I was finally reunited with my roommates after crossing over the Pyruvian, my uniform was nowhere to be seen. Of course, that wasn't exactly true. It might have been in one of the carry packs my roommates had toted with them onboard the ship, but I hadn't checked.

Henzlow crossed his arms and grinned proudly as he looked around

the table, as though hoping for some sort of pat on the back for having discovered a perceived misbehavior on my part. In reality, all it earned him was a harsh look from his fellow officers and a roll of the eyes and a shake of the head from the commander.

Henzlow slouched in his seat and didn't open his mouth again.

"You were certainly missed," Commander Goring said, "and I'm sure there will be a letter of commendation added to each of your files for your bravery. But for right now, I suggest you kindly leave this room and find the closest watering hole to dunk yourselves in. You could ward off the entire Cylmaran army with stink like that."

"Yes, sir," we all said at once, coming to attention.

"And take the rest of the week to rest and get your things in order. I'm sure some of you have family that will be anxious to see you haven't gone and died on them."

"Yes, sir!" We saluted, banging fist to chest, and filed out of the room.

This was even better news than what I had expected. It gave me four days to try smoothing things over with Reevie and Sapphire and to catch up on some much-needed sleep. But if I knew Reevie and Sapphire, they probably had a list of chores as long as my sword waiting on me.

On the way out, I decided my bath could wait until I got back to Sandstorm. The washroom connected to my bedchamber was much better than anything here. I started after the others, but a hand on my arm stopped me, and I turned. Overcaptain Tolin pulled me to the side. By the look on his face, I figured I was about to be reprimanded, no doubt for having let Dakaran come with us on this mission. He'd probably heard the same from the king, and now it was my turn.

"I just thought you should know there was some sort of trouble between the tribes while you were gone. I'm not sure which ones, but from what I've heard, it was bad. You might want to check on your friends as soon as possible."

Trouble with the tribes? Had Sandstorm been attacked? I was almost too stunned to say anything, my heart pounding so hard I could barely hear anything else.

"Thank you," I managed, and before he could say more, I took off running down the hall, passing my roommates along the way.

"What's going on?" I heard a couple calling after me, but I didn't have time to stop and explain. My feet wouldn't let me. I raced through the hall and out the lobby to the open yard. I was halfway across before I heard my roommates leave the building, calling after me, but I didn't stop. I had to get home.

If I had been thinking straight, I would have run to the stables and commissioned a horse, but all I could think about was getting back to Sandstorm and praying my family was still alive. Had Rockslide attempted coming after us again? After what I had done to Kore the first time, we'd had no problems from them. In fact, the last two years had been fairly peaceful.

Maybe it wasn't Rockslide, maybe it was Avalanche. Even after taking over the Temple, Cutter had been continuing to push his boundaries farther north. His ambition was to unite all the tribes under one rule—his. Had he attempted to go after Sandstorm while I was gone? Was that why? Because I was gone? Was this all my fault?

No. Not even Cutter was that stupid or desperate. A thousand different scenarios played through my head as I raced through the streets of Aramoor. I didn't care who saw me. I didn't even bother taking my more indirect routes through the back alleys and side streets. I kept to the most direct route, which unfortunately slowed me in other ways.

The larger roadways were packed with people leaving work and heading home, forcing me to slow in areas, as I had to navigate around the crowded sidewalks as well as the carriages and carts. The sun behind

me was dropping below the horizon, and the sky was beginning to fill with color. All that mattered was reaching the gates of Sandstorm and finding they were still there.

I sped up as I turned down our road and, coming over the hill, spotted the gates of Sandstorm ahead at the end of the lane. Several of the watchers spotted me and started shouting. A lone swordsman all in black was sure to attract attention.

"Protector!" I heard Toots shout at the top of his lungs. "It's the Protector! He's back!"

The gates started to part just as I reached them, and I was greeted by several of the Guard, who hopped out of the way when they saw I wasn't stopping. Why were they standing watch at the gate? A row of beaters stood behind them, all armed and ready for battle. Were we under attack?

One of the watchers was already running up the drive ahead of me. I chased after her, not stopping even long enough to speak with Toots, who was trying his best to welcome me back while at the same time asking a dozen questions about where I'd been.

I ignored them all and kept running.

In front of me, the girl was pouring everything she had into reaching the house as quickly as possible. She probably thought I was chasing her, because one glance over her shoulder had her running all the faster, but she wasn't fast enough.

I flew by her as I headed up the drive and straight for the house. To my delight, it was still there and seemingly intact. No fire damage or broken windows; not even the grass in front of the courtyard looked to have been disturbed, other than the normal trampling it got with a house full of rowdy street kids playing on it every day.

There were kids meandering around the courtyard, some playing in the trees on the side. Most I recognized, some I did not. I wondered if they'd had an influx of new kids from one of the other tribes. Several from Rockslide had migrated over after the battle two years ago.

Over on the right lawn, I could see Collen leading a group of beaters in drills. As soon as he spotted me, he left what he was doing and came running.

In the courtyard, Muriel looked up from where she was grooming Redwing. "Protector?" The hawk shrieked at me as I passed.

So far, nothing seemed to be out of place. No one seemed to be concerned. No bloodstains on the stone pavers, no chinks in the brick from arrows, swords, or spears. Had Overcaptain Tolin been misinformed?

I ran through the front door and straight into the backside of Tubby, who turned when he saw me.

"Protector!" Mouse's head popped up over top of Tubby's, as he was presently riding on the giant boy's shoulders. Squeaks and Petal were there as well, each peering around Tubby's thick legs. I wasn't sure what game had them so occupied, but it came to a quick end when they spotted me. In fact, everyone inside the long gallery stopped what they were doing.

"Ayrion, you're back." Bull, with his short-cropped hair, stepped out of the dining room on the right and started for me. He, too, was fully armed, mimicking me by wearing one sword on his waist and one on his back. I didn't stop to talk. Instead, I headed for the west wing and the stairs that would take me up to the chief's study. I passed the library on the right, spotting Gustory inside with a large gathering of kids sitting around him as he was no doubt using his magic to regale them with some wistful tale of adventure and intrigue. The traveling bard had become quite the asset to the tribe. I was certainly glad he had stayed around.

I turned the corner and ran straight into someone I hadn't seen since the last Guild meeting. In fact, seeing Toothless's face standing there

startled me enough that I drew my sword. His eyes bulged, and he fumbled back against the wall. Why was the Wildfire guard here? Was Red here? Were they in conference?

"He's with us," Bull called out.

I didn't have time to question it. The answers I was looking for were up two flights of stairs, so I took off running with Bull right behind me, trying to get me to slow down. At this point, I didn't care about anything except seeing that Reevie and Sapphire were still alive.

I reached the third floor and burst into the chief's room, sending Reevie nearly toppling out of his chair with a loud squeal. His legs caught under the desk and kept him from tipping all the way over.

"What in the bleeding—" He righted his chair and then got one look at me and his eyes narrowed. "You!"

I started to open my mouth, but Sapphire beat me to the punch.

"Ayrion? You're alive?" She leaped up from the long sofa on the left in front of the windows and ran over.

I leaned in for our usual kiss, but instead received only a firm hug before she promptly stepped back and pinched her nose.

"Oh, you stink."

"I see you're not dead after all," Reevie stated, still trying to pull himself together.

"And I see you aren't either."

"What?" Reevie didn't look his normal, cheerful self. Usually, when I made it back from a mission, he was the first to greet me, excited to see me home. Of course, I'd only ever been gone a week or two, not months at a time, and never without warning like what had happened on this occasion.

"Where've you been all this time, huh?" he said, his face hardening as he stood from his seat. "We haven't heard from you in nearly two months. No 'hey, Reevie, I'm going to be gone, leaving Aramoor, I'll see you when I get back!'" He grabbed a book from off the desk and threw it at me.

I caught it in midair.

Behind me, Bull shut the door to keep those filling the hall outside from seeing their chiefs arguing. Not that they wouldn't be able hear most of it through the door, and by the expression on Reevie's face, they were sure to get an earful.

"We had no idea what happened to you," he said, hardly taking a breath." We thought you were dead. No one would tell us anything. Sapphire even went to the garrison to try finding out where you were."

"You did?"

She nodded, but before she could say anything, Reevie continued.

"No surprise they didn't know anything. About what you'd expect from a group of soldiers. Dumb as stumps." He crossed his arms. "How are we supposed to run a tribe when one-third of the chiefs isn't around enough to even know what's going on?" He finally took a moment to catch his breath, his face flushed. "We could all be dead right now for all you'd know or care!"

Reevie plopped back down in his chair, apparently too angry to stand. I honestly couldn't blame him. I had been forced to leave in the dead of night without saying a word.

"I'm sorry," I said, first to Reevie, then Sapphire, and even to Bull, who had moved into the room a little further to feel like he was a part of the conversation.

"Sorry isn't good enough," Reevie shot back.

Sapphire looked at Reevie and sighed. I noticed, though, that she didn't correct him. She then turned to me. "Surely you see it was a difficult thing you put us through."

"It wasn't my decision," I said in my defense. "The king sent me and my roommates on a secret mission that no one was to know about, not

even the other lancers. I wasn't allowed to let you know that I was going or even where. The king didn't want to take a chance of any word getting out about what we were doing."

Reevie's face hardened even more, if that was possible. "And you thought we would blabber your secret across the city?"

"No. I'm just telling you what I was ordered to do."

"And what was it you were doing, if I might be so bold as to ask? What was of such great importance that you had to up and leave us all stranded, without the smallest word that you were even still alive?"

"I had to save the Elondrian ambassador and his wife from being murdered by the overlord of Cylmar."

The room went quiet.

Reevie sat there, his scowl still holding, though perhaps a bit softer around the edges. My heroic deed didn't seem to sway him much.

"You could have still found a way to let us know. I don't care what the king thinks. We're your family. We come first."

"I wish I had been able to, but I didn't know about the mission until we were being ordered out of our beds in the middle of the night and told to pack for a trip. They said someone would be waiting for us aboard the ship to explain the details of our mission. I had no idea what it was, or where, or how long it was going to take. You have to understand, I have sworn an oath to the Lancers. I have a duty there as well."

"Sounds like you need to make a choice, then," Reevie said before he had a chance to think better of it, or Sapphire to stop him. "Either you're a lancer or you're a chief of Sandstorm. You can't be both."

"Reevie." Sapphire turned, pulling her braid as she gave him a hard look. "I think we all need to take some time to think about this before we go making any rash—"

"Reevie's right," I said.

"What?" Reevie looked taken aback.

"What?" Sapphire looked even more so.

Bull just stood there.

"You heard me. Clearly my duty as a lancer is affecting my ability to do my job here, which I know is a burden to the two of you. You need someone who can commit. Unfortunately, I don't have that luxury. If I try to quit the Lancers, I'll end up in the stocks as a deserter, or worse. When the high king of the Five Kingdoms demands I do something, it's not like I can tell him no."

Reevie hmphed. "You could try," he mumbled under his breath.

"Would you?"

Reevie frowned but didn't respond.

"As a chief of Sandstorm, at least for the time being . . ." I looked at both of them. "I am still a chief here, correct?"

Reevie looked at Sapphire.

"Of course," she said.

Reevie then nodded.

"Good, then as my final act, I nominate Bull to take my place as the third member of the chieftains."

The others looked at me in shock. I felt strange even saying it. I'm not sure why I had. It had been building for some time, I guess. I knew it was the right thing to do, but finally admitting it was easier than I would have thought. This should have been a harder decision. My life since arriving in Aramoor had been centered around the tribes, and now I was stepping down.

The others stood there in silence, forcing me to be the first to speak. "Having three members allows there to be a final decision made at all times, and since Bull has been picking up the slack for me while I'm gone, and is familiar with the responsibilities, I believe he is the most logical choice."

"No," Bull said. "I'm not you. You're . . . you're the Protector. I

could never be that. No one can fill your shoes."

"And I'll always be the Protector as I'm needed, but as far as my role here in Sandstorm, I will relinquish that to you. I hope I will still be allowed membership or at least a place to lay my head when I'm not on lancer duty?"

Sapphire and Bull looked at each other, both almost too bewildered to speak.

"Of course," Sapphire said. "Wait, is this really happening? Are you really stepping down as chief? You were the one who got us these titles in the first place."

"Twice," Bull added.

She nodded. "Are you sure this is what you want?"

At that point, I wasn't sure about anything, but now that I was being presented with the option, something inside me felt it was the right choice. The guilt I had felt throughout this entire mission, with having to leave Reevie and Sapphire so unexpectedly, and the off chance that something might have befallen me while I was gone, was not something I wanted to repeat. I couldn't continue going on missions like this and be forced to worry about how that was going to affect the tribe.

I was being pulled in two directions, had been for a while, but for some reason, only one of those directions seemed to fill a longing in me I didn't even know I had. Maybe it had something to do with my Upakan heritage, that natural pull to be a warrior, to live up to my father's ring, or maybe it had something to do with me growing older, knowing I couldn't remain a street rat forever. Either way, the call of being a lancer was driving me in a new direction. I could either embrace it or run.

I looked at all three of them in turn, stopping on Reevie, who still hadn't said a word. I think he was more in shock that this whole situation had occurred than anything. His face was a mixture of anger, hurt, fear, and concern.

I smiled as best I could. "Yes. I think it's something we've all known was coming for some time. It just sort of sneaked up on us, is all." I turned to Bull. "You don't have to be *the* Protector to be *a* protector. You will do a fine job. I wouldn't have nominated you otherwise. I have no doubt in my mind that you are the right choice."

I looked at Sapphire and Reevie. "It's better this decision came from me than from the two of you."

Bull nodded.

Reevie still looked like someone had killed his favorite pigeon.

"If that's what you want," Sapphire said softly, not looking all that happy by the situation either.

"Good," I said, doing my best to change the subject before I changed my mind or started crying, or threw one of my swords into a wall. "Now that that is settled, will someone kindly tell me what's going on around here? Why am I hearing reports about a street battle between tribes large enough for word to spread all the way to the garrison? And why is Toothless standing down in the lobby?" I looked around the room, having forgotten all about the Wildfire guard until now. "Is Red here? Did someone try attacking Sandstorm? I didn't notice any damage on the way in."

The three looked at each other. Clearly something was needing to be said, but not one of them wanted to be the one to say it. It was Reevie who finally spoke.

"Wildfire was the tribe that was attacked."

"It was an ambush," Bull interjected.

Sapphire nodded. "They didn't stand a chance. Both Rockslide and Avalanche went after Red at the same time. Before the patrollers could be called, half the tribe was down or running for their lives. Toothless brought as many as he could here. He didn't have anywhere else to turn."

"And Red?" I asked, almost afraid to.

Sapphire looked at Reevie and nodded. "They took her and the skinny dark-haired one—"

"You mean Po?" I asked.

She nodded again. "They sold them to the Warrens Underground." Sapphire clicked her tongue as she gave her long blonde braid another firm tug. "No telling what terrible things are being done to them in there."

"Especially someone that looks like her," Bull said.

Sapphire gave him a hard look.

"What? It's the truth."

I leaned against the back of one of the chairs in front of Reevie's desk. "I can't believe they waited until now to try something like this."

"That's no doubt why they did," Bull said.

Reevie rested his elbows on the desk. "When you didn't show up for the last two Guild meetings, they probably figured this was their chance."

So, this *was* partly my fault. The guilt suddenly caught me by the throat.

"But that's not all," Reevie said and looked at Bull. "Tell him the rest."

Bull turned. "After they took down Wildfire and took Red and Po south to the Warrens, Cutter turned on Kore."

I almost laughed. "Fool. I told him not to underestimate Cutter. Cutter might play nice, but underneath is someone who's determined to have it all. What happened? Did he send Kore running, or did Kore beat him so bad that Cutter will think twice about stepping foot past King's Way East again?"

"Kore's dead," Sapphire said.

Now it was my turn to be stunned. "He's what? They killed Kore?"

"Wiped out nearly half his tribe," Reevie said. "The rest scattered to the wind, most likely picked up by patrollers. As soon as he did, Cutter swept out the Rockslide barracks and set up a station there, leaving a large part of his tribe there to keep the place running."

"We are flanked on both sides now," Sapphire said, her hand resting on the hilt of her sword.

"There were quite a number from Rockslide who decided to remain with Avalanche after Kore's fall," Bull added.

I wiped one hand back through my hair. "I can't believe Kore's dead. Wait, why didn't Cutter take over Wildfire's compound? It's a lot nicer than Rockslide's."

Sapphire smirked. "I don't think he likes the idea of living that close to the patrollers. Also, Rockslide is much more defensible."

"That's true." Rockslide was made up from the remains of an old lancer garrison that had been decommissioned decades ago. "And where's Cutter now?"

Bull rubbed the top of his nearly shaved head. "From what we've heard, he's staying right where he is inside the Temple."

I ground my teeth. "This might not have happened if I had been here."

Sapphire crossed her arms. "You don't know that. You can't put this on yourself. Kore and Cutter have been after Red since the day we first joined as chiefs, even before. They've always let their feelings be known about a girl running as chief."

"A lot of good it did Kore," Reevie said. "Got what he deserved, if you ask me."

I couldn't argue there. There had been plenty of times I wanted to put an end to Rockslide's former chief myself, and I almost did on at least two occasions. It was hard to believe he was really dead, though.

"There's only two tribes left," I said. "I guess we can assume that the

Tribal Guild has been abolished. Doubt there's any reason to show back up to a meeting. Probably the only thing you'd find is Cutter and half his Guard waiting to kill you." I glanced at the other three. "I guess I got out just in time."

"Oh, very funny," Reevie said.

"Sorry. Bad timing." I wanted to chuckle but couldn't. It was either that or cry. This was not the kind of news I was hoping to come home to. And still it was better than what Red and Po had to be going through. The thought of what might be happening to the two of them turned my stomach. I didn't know much about the Warrens, but from my limited time inside on lancer patrol, I knew it wasn't a place I wanted to be. Whether Sapphire wanted to admit it or not, in a way this was my fault, and I wasn't about to leave Red and Po at the mercy of those cutthroats.

"I'm going after them."

All three chiefs turned.

"Going after who?" Sapphire asked, as though hoping she didn't already know the answer.

"I'm going after Red and Po."

"Bleeding Hernia!" Reevie barked. "Have you lost your mind?"

"Probably, but I can't just leave them down there, not when I'm partly to blame."

"I hope you're not doing this because . . ." Sapphire shook her head. "Never mind."

I had a feeling I knew what she was going to say. "I'm doing this because Red and Po need help, and I'm probably the only one capable of giving it to them."

"I'll go with you," Bull said, tapping the hilt of his sword. He couldn't hide the tremor in his voice when he offered. Bull was my watchdog. Loyal as the day was long, and these summer days were certainly that.

"Not this time, I'm afraid. This time, I go alone."

# WILDFIRE

## Chapter 27

I T WAS A GOOD THING Commander Goring had given me the rest of the week off. I had no idea how I would have been able to sneak out of the garrison, cross the entire city, infiltrate the Warrens, find Red and Po, and somehow rescue them in time to sneak back into the garrison before anyone was the wiser. Just thinking about it made my head hurt.

I stood in my comfortable room at Sandstorm Manor, staring at the long mirror in the corner, admiring my new coat and pants. Unfortunately, they wouldn't prove all that useful in the Warrens. From what I remembered of the clans, they didn't dress like this. I sighed. Even in a den of cutthroats, a man wearing all black might stand out a little too much.

From what I had seen, most wore regular garb, along with at least one item of color: a purple sash or a green vest or a blue shirt. It wasn't quite so different from the street tribes, and since most of the Warrens

was made up of former street kids, I wouldn't be surprised to find that those practices had been passed down from the tribes to the clans.

Of course, I had no idea what the colors stood for, which clans they represented. In fact, I knew next to nothing about the place other than they'd as soon stick a knife in your gut as look at you. Yep, I was going to have to leave my leathers behind on this trip. I needed every advantage I could get, which meant blending in as best I could. That also meant leaving both my swords behind. That thought left me feeling worse than the loss of my clothes, but the weapons were too nice and once again would draw unwanted attention.

After a very delicious and quite extravagant supper—I'd almost forgotten how good the meals at Sandstorm were—I spent a good portion of the evening rounding up enough garments in my size to pull together a workable outfit. I decided to go with a red shirt instead of blue. It seemed appropriate, since it was Wildfire's members I was looking to recover.

I also found a decent enough sword from the armory. It wasn't anything fancy, but it balanced well in my hand and was newly whetted. After strapping it to my waist, I found a dagger for the back of my belt and a knife for my boot. Knowing where I was going, I was half-tempted to stick one in my other boot, one up my shirt, and perhaps another down my pants, but I restrained myself and settled on just the three.

Leaving the armory, I walked down to the library, where I found the majority of the kids listening to Gustory conjure another one of his famous bedtime stories. For my benefit, he told one of the lone Protector, who wanders the city at night, keeping the children safe from the big scary trolls that liked to eat them.

One of the younger kids pointed at Tubby near the back and shouted, "Troll!"

Everyone laughed, even Tubby, who stood and waved his arms in the air and began to growl, sending kids running out the door as he gave chase. The rest soon followed as they made their way up to bed, leaving me alone with the bard.

I smiled. "I liked the story tonight."

"I thought you would." He sat quietly on his stool and watched me. "Sounds like a very dangerous thing you are attempting to do, young man."

It seemed news of my mission had already spread throughout the tribe. "Can't argue with you there."

"You know, you don't owe them anything."

"Who?"

"Wildfire. Is it really worth risking your own life for two people who I doubt very highly would do the same for you? I know that sounds cynical, but common sense would say no." He stared at me a moment, then smiled. "But I guess they don't call you Protector for nothing." He packed up his pamphlet of loose papers, each holding some new story he'd written or discovered, a collection of fables at his disposal for whenever the need should arise. Once the last page was gathered, the bard headed toward the west wing of the manor, and no doubt the kitchen, to pick up his nightly glass of warm milk and honey.

"I can sneak in with you," a voice spoke behind me.

I turned and looked down. Mouse stood there staring up at me with as serious a face as I'd seen him with since our harrowing experience breaking into the Rockslide compound two years ago. He had grown some but was still small enough to scramble in and out of places he shouldn't be. His dirty brown hair was always disheveled, and he still carried his pigsticker on his side.

"Not this time," I said with a smile.

Mouse hung his head, but I could see relief in his eyes. I wondered what he would have done if I had said yes.

"We made a good team sneaking into Rockslide," he said. "Kore didn't even know we was there. Scared them all. Remember?"

I chuckled. "How could I forget? We scared them good, didn't we?"

Mouse grinned and whipped out his little belt sticker and jabbed at the air with it a few times. "We had them all thinking we was ghosts."

"I'm afraid this is one time I'll need to go alone. I appreciate you asking, but there are too many people here who depend on their head picker to risk having you get hurt."

"But what about you?" he asked. "You're even more important."

"I'm the Protector. This is what I do."

Mouse sighed and then did something he hadn't done in a long time—he gave me a hug. He then turned and chased after Squeaks and Petal, who were waiting for him at the end of the gallery. They waved at me and said good night.

I waved back.

Reevie, Sapphire, and Bull met me at the front doors.

"You sure about this?" Sapphire asked.

"Not really," I admitted.

"But you're going anyway," she added.

Reevie hmphed. "Of course he is. Palsy! He's Ayrion. Thick in the head as he is in the chest."

"I really can go if you want me to," Bull offered once more, and I shook my head.

"Best I go alone. Easier if I just have me to worry about."

He nodded, relief and disappointment on his face.

"If you don't hear from me by Eighthday, you might want to send word to the garrison. Find Overcaptain Tolin and let him know what happened to me."

"I hope it doesn't come to that," Reevie said.

Sapphire nodded. "I'll make sure he gets the message."

I looked at the three of them and smiled before walking out the door. I headed across the courtyard pavers and down the lane to the front gate, where Toots and Pike and even Collen were waiting.

"Thought you was gonna sneak by us without saying anything, huh?" Toots said, the side of his face glowing from the light of the torches at the gate.

"We heard you're going to the Warrens to try finding Red," Collen said, his darker skin blending well with his cape and hood, making him the perfect watchman. He was now the head of the beaters and was doing a fine job at keeping them trained. "Want me to come along?" He patted his sword at his waist. "I can if you need me."

I smiled. "I'll tell you the same as I told Bull: It's better if I go alone. Easier to get in and out of the place if I only have to worry about me."

Collen nodded.

"Watch out for everyone here," I said, then turned to Toots and Pike. "Keep a sharp eye out. I don't trust Cutter any farther than I can throw him."

"He won't be gettin' past us, Protector," Toots stated, elbowing Pike in the arm. "I can promise you that."

"Excellent," I said, giving them a salute.

All three, and a couple of the watchers and beaters standing nearby, raised their fist to their chest in response. With that, I turned and walked through the gate, which they had opened far enough for me to get through. I could feel their eyes on my back. I stopped just before cresting the rise and took one final look back at Sandstorm. I hoped this wasn't the last time I'd get to see it. With a heavy sigh, I turned and jogged down the street. I had one more stop to make.

It didn't take me long to reach Bailey Street, and I was halfway down the road when I heard horse hooves coming up behind me. I crossed over to the side of the road to let the rider pass, but the horse began to

slow, and I turned.

"What are you doing here?" I asked.

Sapphire hopped down from our tribe's one horse we now kept stabled at Sandstorm Manor and walked over. "I came to give you a ride across town. No sense in you running the entire way and being completely winded by the time you got there."

"How did you know I'd—"

"What, stop by the orphanage first?" She smiled. "Just a hunch."

She walked with me down the street, handing me the horse's reins to carry, since Pudding—named after . . . well, pudding, in particular the chocolate pudding Chef would make at Sandstorm—wasn't the most cordial of horses. She had a mind of her own and sometimes required a firm hand.

"I figured I best let Master Fentin and Mistress Orilla know that I'm back, just in case."

"Don't talk like that. Nothing is going to happen. You're going to do that thing you always do: get in, rescue them that need rescuing, and be back for morning eggs and grits."

I chuckled. "That thing I do, huh?"

"Yeah." She smiled and bumped me on the shoulder. I missed that closeness we used to share.

We headed up the road and into the narrow lane beside the orphanage, following it all the way to the back, where we tied Pudding off beside the kitchen door for her to nibble on some of Mistress Orilla's cabbages. I hoped she didn't do too much damage.

I peeked in the window, but no one was in the kitchen. I tried the door and was surprised to find it unlocked, so I opened it, and we went in.

"Mistress Orilla? Master Fentin?" I didn't call out too loudly, in case some of the kids had already gone to bed. We'd barely made it to the kitchen when Master Fentin walked in with a candlestick. He was wearing his long night shirt, clearly getting ready to go to bed himself.

"Who's there?" He raised the candle up to get a better look. "Ayrion, is that you?"

I smiled. "The one and only. Just returned from my adventures in Cylmar."

"Cylmar, you say?" The old man adjusted his spectacles higher on the bridge of his nose. He barely got them into place before the sound of boards creaking in the hall had him turning. "Look who's here, Orilla. It's Ayrion."

"So it is," she said with a scowl. "And where have you been all this time? I must say, we were worried out of our minds." She glanced past me and smiled. "You look lovely this evening, Sapphire, as always. Have you two eaten? I can whip you up a sandwich."

"As much as I would love one of your sandwiches, I just came by to let you know I had returned, before . . ."

"Before what?" Orilla asked, her face growing concerned.

"Before he goes and does something stupid," Sapphire said. "You heard about the tribal battle and what happened to the chief of Wildfire? Well, Ayrion's got it in his thick skull that he needs to go rescue her and her tagalong from the Warrens."

"The Warrens?" Mistress Orilla shook her head. "You remember what happened the last time you went in there?"

"Oh, I remember all too well," I said. "But I'm partly to blame for what happened to Red and Po. If I can do something, I need to try."

"But . . ."

Master Fentin laid his hand on his wife's arm. "A man needs to do what he thinks is right. Best we let him be." He turned to me. "When do you plan on going? Not tonight, surely."

I grinned.

He shook his head and started to open his mouth but stopped. "Best you be on your way, then. We're glad you are alive, my boy. Make sure you stay that way."

"I'll try my best."

Mistress Orilla reached into a bucket on the counter and tossed both me and Sapphire an apple. "Something to eat on the way."

I gave them each a hug, something I rarely did, then headed out the door, quickly pulling Pudding away from the vegetables before Mistress Orilla saw her. I helped Sapphire up into the saddle, then swung up behind her and turned the horse around, waving at the old couple, who were watching us from the window.

"I'm surprised you didn't take her up on her offer of a sandwich," Sapphire said.

"Are you kidding? After the supper we had tonight? I hope I don't have to do any fighting. I'm too full to move."

"Then maybe I should have just let you run across town after all."

I smiled. "I'm glad you didn't."

We rode up Bailey until it crossed Circle Drive, then took that south toward King's Way East, where we crossed over and continued into what was now Avalanche's territory. Not wanting to get spotted by any of Cutter's watchers, I directed us off the main road. Circle Drive would have eventually taken us down and around past the Temple, which was one place I didn't need to be.

"You know, you can leave me here, and I can go the rest of the way on foot."

Sapphire ignored me, and we continued on.

The horse's hooves echoed off the tightly packed ramshackle buildings that lined either side of the narrow streets. The residents in this part of Aramoor held a standard of living far lower than their northern counterparts. For some reason, the homes seemed even more run-down than what I remembered. Even though I'd lived in and around the Maze my first couple of years in Aramoor, it seemed my time spent in the north had changed my perceptions of how things should look.

I bet if I rode past the old Granary that I would hardly recognize it, or even believe that I had spent nearly half a year living under the floor of that dilapidated building and thought it quite nice. Well, maybe not nice, but at least adequate. Was I turning into a snob? I didn't want to think of myself like that, but I guess under the right circumstances, anyone could change, and not always for the better.

"I can't see where we're going," Sapphire whispered back over her shoulder, and I took the reins.

"I think I can," I said, still doing my best to keep many of my abilities as an Upakan—especially my magic—secret. The moon was nearly full, but a storm seemed to be moving in from off the Rhunarin, leaving the moon completely blanketed in heavy clouds. Using my enhanced sight, I guided Pudding as best I could around most of the potholes that covered the streets, and in Cheapside there were potholes aplenty.

The trek through the winding streets at the edge of the Maze eventually led us past the Pit, where I had first come across Tubby, or as he was more notably called at that time: Flesh Eater. The Pit rested on the corner end of Mora, a street which ran the length of the old city.

I pulled the horse to a stop alongside the brick wall that surrounded the Pit and slid off the back of Pudding. Taking a moment to stretch and check my weapons, I glanced around to see if I spotted any signs of patrol at the first Warrens entrance, which was just in view at the next bend.

There were several breaks in the old city wall that led into the Warrens, all of which were no doubt guarded. Several coincided with roads on the other side of Mora, leading into the lower parts of the Maze. I hoped the rain the clouds promised held off, but I could almost feel it

in the air. Smell it too. There was a shift to the wind, but not strong enough to clear out the low-lying fog that was already beginning to fill the streets. I could only imagine how much thicker the fog would be behind the covering of the old city's wall.

I looked up at Sapphire. "I guess this is it."

"I guess so."

I was surprised by the lack of emotional response. "Have I done something to upset you?" As soon as I said it, I realized how stupid it sounded. "I mean, apart from the whole leaving-and-not-telling-you-I-was-going thing. Are you still mad at me?"

She climbed down off Pudding, keeping a firm grip on the reins.

"You haven't . . . you know, kissed me once since I've been back. I've barely gotten two words out of you. What's wrong?"

"You want to do this now?" she asked. "We're standing in one of the most dangerous places in Aramoor, and you want to talk about our relationship now?"

"I might die tonight," I said, trying to layer on the guilt. It was a devious move, even for me, but I was willing to do whatever it took at that point to get her to open up. "You may never see me again, then how would you feel?"

She stepped forward and punched me in the chest, nearly knocking the wind out of me. "I told you to quit talking like that." She gritted her teeth. "Fine. It's difficult."

"What's difficult?"

"You think it's easy for me to stand here, this close to you, and not want to kiss you, to hold you in my arms?"

I scratched the top of my head. "I'm confused. So, you do still care about me?"

She hit me again. "Of course I care about you, ninny. That's the problem."

I shook my head again, more confused than ever. "What are you talking about? How could caring about me be a problem?"

She grabbed her braid and pulled with a huff. "Because I'd have to be blind to not see that your life is heading in a different direction than the rest of us. You know it, I know it; everyone but Reevie knows it, or at least will admit it to themselves. I don't want to be tied to someone who can only give me a small part of himself. And right now, it seems that's all you have to give."

I knew she was right. I just hadn't wanted to admit it. I was now a soldier who was also friends with the crown prince—his trainer, too. I was on speaking terms with the king and queen. I was being sent on secret missions for Elondria. My life was changing.

Apparently, that change was costing me Sapphire's affection.

"I'm sorry," I said, wanting nothing more in that moment than to put my arms around her, but knowing that was probably one of the worst things I could do right then. So, I fought the urge. "I think I've known it for some time but just didn't want to admit it. You and Reevie are my home. You two are what keep me grounded, but I see now that that's not fair to either of you. You have your own lives to live, and you don't need to be forcibly tied to mine."

She stepped forward and took my hand, holding it a moment as she stared at me in the darkness. I thought she was about to forget everything she had just said and embrace me. But she didn't. She finally released my hand and stepped back. "I'm glad you understand."

I took a deep breath. My heart felt like part of it had been ripped open, but there was also a small sense of relief there as well, which I was surprised to find. Everything was changing. I had a sinking feeling that the pain from this parting hadn't yet really taken hold. I hoped it didn't decide to grab me tonight.

I fought to push it all aside. Sapphire was right. I was an idiot for

bringing this up now. How was I going to focus on the task ahead when all I could think about was the way she smelled right then? The lilac perfume Noph had left her was intoxicating. I took a step back. It might not have been a large move, but it was a good start.

"I need to go before it gets too late."

"I know. Be careful, will you? Don't do anything stupid. If you end up dying for her, I'll kill you myself." Her brows lowered slightly as she realized how ridiculous that sounded, but she didn't correct it. She looked at me, face set. "The world needs you in it, Ayrion. Please come back alive."

"Well, I can't very well come back dead."

She started to punch me again but ended with a soft tap. Clutching Pudding's reins, she nodded for me to go.

I took a deep breath and took another step backward. This time it was easier, so I took a second, then a third, then finally turned and headed toward the first break in the old city's wall.

# WILDFIRE

## Chapter 28

THE SMELL OF LILAC FADED the farther I got from Sapphire, helping me to better concentrate on what lay ahead. Our conversation, though necessary, was poorly timed. Part of me was wishing I'd never brought it up, yet the other part was glad I did and that we had been able to make it through the uncomfortable ordeal and come out the other side, possibly the better for it. It was going to be hard seeing her around the manor house and not look at her in the same way.

I clenched my fists. I had to quit thinking about her.

Red and Po. They were the ones I was here to save. Saying their names helped. I wondered if they were still alive, and if so, what might have happened to them. As much as I didn't want to think about it, the very act of trying not to made it worse.

Without looking back, I headed into the Warrens, surprised to find no one standing guard. There was a torch mounted to a bracket just on

the other side of the wall, and even a stool underneath it, but no sign of whoever was supposed to be manning that post. Grateful for a bit of luck, I started up the street.

I'd barely made it halfway past the first building when someone called out behind me.

I could have kept walking and pretended I hadn't heard, but that would have been impossible to pull off unless I played deaf. For a brief moment, I thought about running, but that would have only started a chase that might have led to a hunt. With no other good options, I turned. The man was average height and build, with long brown hair that hung below the shoulders, half-covering the side of his face.

"Where were you?" I demanded, attempting to wrongfoot the guard. "Leaving your post in the middle of the night." I clicked my tongue and shook my head. "I was just on my way to report this to . . ." It just occurred to me that I didn't know who I would report something to. Did they have chiefs in the Warrens clans, or were they called something else? "Well, never mind. I guess since you showed back up, I won't have to. Next time, stay at your post."

I didn't give the worried-looking man a chance to say anything else and promptly turned and marched off like I knew exactly where I was going.

"Hold on! Stop!"

I balled my fists. Why couldn't he have just let it go? I spun back around. "What is it? You're making me late for a meeting."

"You didn't give me your name and why you was coming in so late. Where was you at?"

"Where I was at is none of your business."

The guard reached for his sword and started for me.

I didn't want to have a confrontation here. The point was to get in and out without being noticed. My hand slowly lowered for my own blade. If I had to, there were plenty of abandoned buildings for me to dispose of his body.

"There you are," a familiar voice called out near the entrance. "Why'd you leave so quickly? I told you to wait for me."

The guard turned, his hand releasing his sword as Sapphire came strolling into the Warrens, her shirt untucked and the top buttons undone quite provocatively.

"I, uh . . ." I didn't know what to say. "I told you I'd be back. There's no sense in you coming as well. I can handle my own business." What did she think she was doing?

The guard stood in the middle of the conversation, but his eyes were only on Sapphire, and the way he stared had me wanting to dispose of him right then and there.

Sapphire sauntered by, not paying the guard any mind, and walked over and kissed me. It was the kind of kiss I had been hoping for when I had first returned from Cylmar, but the kind of kiss I wasn't expecting to ever receive again. I lost my breath, even forgot where I was for a moment, and then she released me and slapped me in the face. "That's what you get for sneaking off like a common thief."

"I . . . I . . ." I better say something, or all of this was going to have been for nothing. "I'm sorry. I told you I had a meeting, and you looked so beautiful lying there that I didn't want to wake you."

She smiled and flicked the end of my nose. "That's very sweet. You're forgiven, then." She turned and started farther into the Warrens, grabbing my hand and dragging me with her. "Well, do you want to be late for your meeting? Come on."

The guard was so taken aback by the situation that he just stood there watching as we walked up the street and took the first crossroads to the left. We found a dark narrow passage between two buildings and quickly slipped inside, leaning against one of the old brick walls to catch

our breath.

"Well, that was exciting," she said with a nudge to my side.

"Exciting isn't the word I would use." My heart was still pounding. I wasn't sure if it was from the fear of getting caught, the anticipation of a fight, or that kiss. Who was I kidding? I knew exactly what it was. "Foolish is what I would call it." I turned and looked at her. "I could have handled a single guard. You shouldn't be here."

She turned as well, her eyes looking just to the left of mine, since it was too dark for her to see where I was. "It occurred to me that having two of us would make for a better cover. Someone walking through the Warrens alone is more likely to be noticed than a couple."

She had a point. A single man walking around in the dark was going to look more suspicious than a couple out for a stroll on a warm summer night. "Fine, but if anything happens, I want you to run for the wall and not look back."

"Of course."

I wasn't convinced. "I mean it. If anything happens, you leave me behind and run. You have an entire tribe who needs you." I wanted to say *I* needed her, but it would have only confused the situation further. Taking a deep breath, I reached down and took her hand and walked back out into the street. She didn't pull away.

"Just don't get any ideas about another kiss," she said as we headed deeper in. "That was the last one."

I smiled. "Too bad."

I caught a small upturn in her mouth as we picked up our pace.

I honestly didn't know where we were going. I had heard there were places in the Warrens that led underground. I could only imagine that was where the clans had set up their home. I know it would have been my first choice, but I was Upakan.

"Do you know where you're going?" Sapphire finally asked, after we'd been wandering through the empty streets for half an hour or so, seemingly without getting anywhere.

"Not really. I was hoping to run across—" We started around the next corner, and I jerked her back behind one of the buildings. I peeked around the side of the building and saw a group of four heading east toward the white wall of Aramoor, which bordered the outer perimeter of the old city. We were still a long way away from the white wall, but it was hard to miss, rising as high as a mountain in the distance. "This is what I was hoping to find," I whispered.

Sapphire glanced around the corner. "What? A group of cutthroats?"

"A way into the underground. We need someone to show us where it is."

"What are you going to do, walk up and ask them to point the way?"

"No. We're going to follow them."

"And what if they aren't going to wherever it is we are wanting to go?"

"We'll just have to take that chance. Besides, this late at night, I can't imagine where else they'd be going but to their beds."

"I can think of some places," Sapphire mumbled, but I ignored it.

"Come on," I said and started down the street, keeping close to the sides of the taller structures, where the shadows were the darkest. The sky lit and blinded me for a moment, just before the ground shook with a booming crash of thunder that had me grabbing my ears.

The men in front of us picked up their pace, and we matched them, nearly coming to a full run as the rain began to drop. Another flash of lightning showed the four disappearing to the right, and we raced to catch up. The rain was coming down harder now as we reached the edge of the lane and peeked around the corner.

The small street ended just ahead at what looked like a large stone latrine. The four opened the door and walked inside, one at a time, then

the door shut behind them. I glanced over my shoulder at Sapphire.

"Well, what are you waiting for?" she asked over the rising gusts of wind.

I took her hand, and we ran down the street, stopping in front of the stone edifice. If this was some sort of latrine, we were about to walk into a very embarrassing situation. The outside looked a little like one of those mausoleums they would bury important people in. I grabbed the handle and the door opened, far easier than I was expecting, so much so that I nearly hit Sapphire with it.

Another blinding flash lit the sky, and Sapphire tore past me and into whatever awaited us inside. I hopped in behind her and shut the door just as a deafening crash of thunder shook the stone around us. Just as soon the door was shut, I could hear the torrential downpour outside beating against the walls.

"Talk about good timing," she said.

There was a torch on the right, lighting a narrow stairwell that wound downward to what I could only imagine was the Warren Underground.

"Hurry," I said. "We need to catch up with the others."

"Why? We've already found the way in."

"Because from what I've heard in the barracks from Warrens prisoners we've captured, they have some kind of secret pass phrase for getting in."

"So didn't they tell you what it was?"

"No." I took off down the stairs, two at a time, listening intently for signs of the four who had gone in before us. I could hear something below, something like grating metal. We reached the bottom, which opened into a small antechamber, and on the other side was an enormous circular metal door. The outside of it had been engraved with what looked like a map, possibly the tunnels below the city, by the number of snaking lines. I'd heard they were quite extensive, though none of those prisoners we'd captured were willing—or perhaps able—to tell us much.

The four men in front of us were waiting as two muscle-bound guards pulled the door open. As big as they were, it looked like they were having a difficult time. I glanced over my shoulder at Sapphire, who was trying to peek around me. "That is why I wanted to hurry. Come on. We need to look like we're with them."

We pulled up our hoods and stepped out of the stairwell chamber and over behind the other men. I shook my arms to the side, flinging water across one of the men's legs. "Sorry. Looks like we made it just in time, aye?"

The man grunted.

"Feel sorry for those on watch tonight," I added, hoping to strike up a conversation.

"Just got off," one of the men in the middle said, taking a moment to try peering into our hoods, especially Sapphire's. His eyes lingered on her damp outfit, which was beginning to cling somewhat tightly.

"It's been a long day," I said with a fake yawn that turned out to be real by the end. "I think I might hit the bunk." I leaned over and put my arm around Sapphire's waist, and the man quit looking so hard.

"Yes, I can see why." He nodded at Sapphire with a wry grin.

"I'll thank you to keep your eyes to yourself," Sapphire growled, "or I'll cut them out and feed them to you."

The other men laughed.

"Quite the spitfire," the man in the middle said, smiling all the more, until Sapphire whipped a knife out of her shirtsleeve and spun it around her fingers. The man's eyes bulged. "My apologies. No harm intended. Just having a little fun." He turned back around and watched as the guards finished swinging the door far enough back for us to walk through.

"Your mouth is going to be the death of you one of these days," one of the men on the far side said to the other as they all walked through.

We followed them in, thankfully not being stopped by the guards. If the men had given some sort of pass phrase, it must have been enough that we were seen talking with them to not ask us as well.

Even better, Sapphire had kept her calm and didn't challenge the lech to a duel. She kept her knife in hand as we headed into what appeared to be some sort of meeting hall. On the right was a platform with several seats arranged with two on the first level, two on the second, and one prominent throne-like chair at the top. Several passageways led off the stone room, each with a colorful banner hanging overtop, which I guessed represented the different factions, though I had no idea what they were.

"Now what?" Sapphire whispered as we slowly moved to the back, trying not to appear to be staring too hard and doing our best to look like we fit in.

"I don't know," I said, "but I hope your outfit doesn't give us away." I just realized Sapphire wasn't wearing the same colors as me. I had a red shirt under my vest, but she was wearing purple, since most of her clothing was purchased to match that of Sandstorm.

"What do you mean?" Sapphire looked down at her outfit.

"If you haven't noticed, we're wearing two different colors. Look around the room. What do you see?"

Most of those in the meeting hall were divided into groups. Each group wore similar colors, matching that of the banners hanging over each of the tunnel entrances.

I sighed. "I just hope we don't draw too much attention being seen together like this. If people start to look, we might need to split up." It was going to be hard enough watching out for myself, but if I had to worry about Sapphire as well, things were about to get quite a bit more difficult.

"Wait here," she said, and before I could stop her or ask what she was doing, Sapphire left me standing against the back wall and headed over to a small group of people hanging around the tunnel with the red banner.

What was she doing?

Suddenly, she whipped out her dagger on one of the men, and I reached for my sword. What was she thinking? I started forward but stopped when I noticed no one else was rushing over. In fact, most of those in the room didn't even seem to notice or care. I waited and watched as the man slowly pulled off his shirt, which happened to be red, and handed it to Sapphire. From what I could hear, it sounded like she thanked him, then slowly backed away far enough to be out of weapon's reach before turning and walking back to where I was standing with my mouth agape.

"What in the Pits do you think you're doing?" I asked.

She smiled, then moved around to the other side of where I was standing so she could face the wall, and without warning, pulled off her top. I nearly swallowed my tongue. The group near the red tunnel watched, as did a few from two other groups nearby. She even managed to garner a few whistles.

She handed me her purple shirt and slipped on the red one she had just confiscated. She turned back around and smiled. "There, now we match."

I didn't know what to say. Those standing around watching finally turned back to their conversations. "Have you lost all reason? You just pulled a knife on a group of Warrens cutthroats and stole one of their shirts. Have you ever heard of the term inconspicuous? We are supposed to be blending in, not standing out. What are you going to do next, offer to bathe their chief?"

"You wanted us to be wearing the same colors . . . now we are."

"What did you say to him when you stuck your knife to his throat?"

"I said I had been forced to wear purple all day as a form of punishment, and I couldn't stand it any longer."

"And that's it?"

She shrugged. "Should I have said more?"

I threw my hands up, fighting to hold back the tongue-lashing I wanted to unleash on her, but as infuriating as it was, she had managed to get us into the same colors and with very little impact to us. Strangely enough, it might have opened up some opportunities.

"What now?" she asked.

"Now we try finding out where they are keeping Red and Po."

"And how do we do that?"

"The same way you just found a new shirt."

"By threatening to open their throats?"

"No . . . by walking over and asking. Come on."

It was Sapphire's turn to look surprised as she hesitantly followed me over to the same group of reds she'd just threatened a moment ago. The man who'd given up his shirt acted like it was no big thing and didn't even bother running to change into another. In fact, he seemed almost proud of his hairy chest and more than happy to show it off. It rivaled that of even Barthol.

I took off my vest and handed it to him as we approached. "Thanks for the shirt. I've had to listen to her complain about that purple one all day. She even tried telling me the color made her skin itch."

Some of those gathered laughed.

"Purple's not a very flattering color," one of the women said to Sapphire sympathetically, "which is why Shilvin wears it." She looked at the two of us. "Don't believe I've seen you in the meetings."

"We were newly inducted," I said. "Lost our tribe during the recent battle."

Some of those gathered nodded.

"Heard about that," the man with the bare chest said as he pulled on my vest. He was bigger than I was, so the front didn't close. "Sounded like a bad one."

"Good for us," another added. "Not so good for those up top. No offense, but recruits have been few and far between for the last couple of years. Those new chiefs of Sandstorm have been managing to keep the peace in such a way that there've been hardly a scuffle to recruit from."

"You keep track of what the tribes are doing?" Sapphire asked.

I, too, was surprised to know that the Warrens knew who we were.

One of the men wiped his nose on the sleeve of his arm. "Of course! How else do you think we fill our ranks? We bring 'em down and let them fight to see who we keep." He smiled, showing that he was missing several teeth, and those he had were black around the gums. "Good fun to watch, especially the criers. They tend to die first."

I gulped. "Die?"

Several standing around looked at me funny. "Yeah, something you should know if you was placed already. Who did you fight? Don't re-member seeing you."

My mouth dried up like an old prune, and I passed a quick glance over at Sapphire, but she looked as unsure about what to say as I did. My mind raced. "No, you wouldn't have seen us fight. We did enough fighting during the battle to garner someone's attention, because the blood had barely been wiped from our blades when we were offered a spot."

The others looked at each other a moment and then shrugged. The man with the vest finally spoke. "Fewer and fewer from the tribes have been making their way down, which is why the Underground isn't as full as it used to be. I even heard this new Sandstorm lot have set up

apprenticeships for its members." The man shook his head. "What's the world coming to when street rats start looking to better themselves? I tell you, it ain't gonna come to any good for us."

One of the women nodded in agreement as she picked at her teeth with a small belt knife. "It was rumored the king was in talks with one of the tribes in hopes of changing things. I guess it worked."

"The king?" I asked, taken aback. "The king wants the tribes broken up?" That was the first I'd heard about it. That didn't sound like the king at all. "Why would Rhydan want a tribal battle?"

"Rhydan?" The man with the vest laughed. "Not the high king, dimwit. We're talking about Crellin."

"Crellin?"

One of the women shook her head. "You really are new. Crellin is the king of the Warrens. Or at least, that's what he likes to be called."

"Oh." I smiled. "I guess that makes more sense than the high king trying to start a tribal war."

The man with the vest spat to the side. "I wouldn't put it past him. Don't trust none of those royals to do anything but what's right for themselves."

I wanted to tell him that the king wasn't like that. In fact, I'd found him rather pleasant and understanding, but it hardly felt the right time to bring it up.

Sapphire sneered. "I couldn't agree more."

I passed her a brief sideways glance, hoping she was just playing her part, but I had a feeling that the tone in her voice meant there was a least a small amount of truth behind her feelings. I wondered if that was how she saw it. Did she blame the king for pulling me away from the tribes?

I turned to the others. "We heard they brought Red in."

"Who?" the man with the vest asked.

"The chief of Wildfire. We heard she was captured."

"Ah, yes, they brought her and one other down a day or two ago, I think. The boy definitely looks like a crier. Can't wait to see him in the circle."

I sneered. "Serves her right for attacking us the way she did."

"I hope they torture her slowly," Sapphire added, once again sounding a little too convincing.

"No idea what they're doing with them," the man with the vest said, still doing his best not to look at Sapphire the wrong way.

"Got them in the cells, I reckon," another added.

"Any chance you think they'd let us in to have a poke at her? Wouldn't mind seeing her high and mightiness humbled in a dank cell. I lost one of my mates to her guards, and I wouldn't mind some payback."

"Cells are down there," the woman who'd been picking her teeth said. She pointed to one of the six tunnels that didn't have a banner hanging down over it. "They keep them next to the barrel."

"The barrel?" Sapphire asked.

The woman sighed. "I keep forgetting you're new. Best to save that conversation for later. It's one of those better-seen-than-heard situations."

Raised voices on the other side of the room had us turning. A fight had broken out between two men in opposing colors. Both had daggers. They circled and then leaped at each other at the same time. Both went down in a spray of blood as they each landed clean stabs at the same time, but the one on top managed to get his free before the other and plunged his blade over and over again into the man underneath until the man below stopped jerking.

I grabbed Sapphire's arm and pulled her toward the entrance to the tunnel while everyone's attention was on the fight. We made it inside and slowed, stopping once we were out of sight of the main hall.

"Did you see that?" she asked, her eyes bulging.

"Couldn't help but."

"I don't like it here," she said, then turned and stared down the tunnel we were in. "Any idea what they meant by the barrel?"

I shook my head. "Got a feeling we don't want to find out."

The tunnel was lit with sconces, fastened to the sides of the stone walls. Not all of the candles had been lit, but there were enough to see where we were going. We slowly made our way past one door after another. I had no idea where they led, and we had no time to stop to find out. I kept my eye open for some sort of barrel. If she was next to it, I suspected it would be noticeable.

Unfortunately, there were no barrels in sight—small, large, or otherwise.

I was beginning to wonder if they had sent us in the wrong direction for a good laugh when I heard shouts coming from a door ahead on the right.

"I'd know that harpy's voice anywhere," Sapphire said, and we headed for the door.

A couple of clan members stepped out of a room on the left, and I reached for my sword, but seeing the two of us, they headed back in and shut the door.

There was another shout and a loud crash, and the door we were heading for jerked open, and a large man with a thick beard and gold earrings in both ears stumbled out. He was wearing nothing but his long underpants, and even those seemed to be barely hanging on. He ducked, and a bucket flew over his head.

"Try that again and you'll lose more than your pride!" Red shouted from inside.

The man wiped blood from what looked like a bite wound on his arm. "Crellin owed me a favor, but you ain't worth the hassle! I'll make sure you go to the barrel for sure!" He stormed past, knocking Sapphire to the side as he did.

She raised her dagger and started to turn, but I grabbed her arm. "Let him go."

We rushed in through the opened door and quickly shut it behind us before anyone else came to see what all the commotion was.

I turned, and my breath caught in my throat.

"What?" Red asked. "You act like you've never seen a naked woman before."

WILDFIRE

## Chapter 29

RED WAS SPRAWLED across a large four-poster bed with one arm tied to the back post.

Sapphire and I pulled back our hoods. Red squealed, her attitude of complete unconcern vanishing, and she yanked the bedsheet over herself. "What do the two of you think you're doing?" She looked at me. "And where have you been? Where was Sandstorm when my tribe was being exterminated?"

"We didn't know it was going to happen any more than you did," Sapphire said, her hand tightening on her dagger.

"How did you get down here?" Red demanded.

"We walked," I said. "How did you?"

"What do you mean you walked? You just walked in here and no one stopped you?"

I looked around the room. "Where's Po?"

"They've got him in a cell a few doors down. Haven't seen him since the day before last."

"So, he might not still be there?"

"I don't know," Red said, still squirming uncomfortably under her sheets. "Why are *you* here?"

Sapphire walked across the room toward the bed. "We're here to rescue you, you trollop." She used her dagger to cut Red free.

Red rubbed the rope burn on her wrist, then looked up at Sapphire and smiled. "So, you came all the way down here just for me? I'm touched."

"It wasn't my choice," Sapphire was quick to point out.

Red frowned. "I'm sure it wasn't." She turned and pointed to a pile of clothes over by the fireplace. "How about doing a lady a favor."

"You, a lady," Sapphire scoffed. "Hah!"

I grabbed Red's clothes and tossed them on the bed, then turned around. Sapphire joined me, turning as well. I could hear the rustle of material as Red got dressed. While waiting, I walked over to the door and put my ear to it.

"We need to hurry," I said. "Whoever that was that came out of here earlier didn't look happy. He also didn't look like the kind of person to let something be."

"You can turn back around," Red said.

I turned cautiously and found her sitting on the edge of the bed, slipping on her boots. She pulled on her jacket, and we started for the door.

"You might want to leave that," I said, pointing at her red leather jacket, the same one she had purchased after I had first worn mine. "You'll stick out like blood on snow around this place."

"I'm not leaving here without my jacket."

"Fine. Then wear this." I handed her my cloak, since it had a hood. Of the two of us, Red needed to hide more than I did. I would just have

to keep my eyes lowered. "Now, where are the cells?"

Red pushed past the two of us and opened the door and peeked out. "This way."

We followed her, shutting the door behind us, and made our way farther down the tunnel. It wasn't long before we were stopping outside a door on our left. I knew it was the right one because I could already feel my magic beginning to wane. I'd forgotten about Po's ability. This was going to make our escape more difficult, since I wouldn't have my magic to fall back on.

"I hope he's still alive," Red mumbled behind me.

"He is," I said, without thinking.

She looked at me funny but didn't say anything.

This particular door had a small peephole about face level, but the covering had been shut. I knocked, and a piece of metal slid out of the way to reveal a set of eyes and part of a nose.

"What do you want?"

"Here to see the prisoner," I said.

"Not at this hour of the night." The piece of metal began to slide shut.

"Wait," I said. "We also have one to bring back." I grabbed Red and pulled her in front of the door so the man inside could see out, then yanked back her hood. She tried elbowing me in the gut, but I blocked it with my hand. "They've had their fun with her tonight and told me to bring her back."

"Give me a moment." The sliding peephole shut, and I could hear a lock from inside being snapped open.

Soon enough, the door parted, and the jailer stepped back to let us in. As soon as he did, Red snatched my belt knife and leaped on top of him, burying it in his chest. They both went to the ground.

I was speechless, but the muffled sound of voices coming down the hall had me grabbing the dead jailer's feet and dragging him the rest of the way in.

Sapphire quickly shut the door just as three clansmen walked by, then she turned on Red. "What in the name of Aldor do you think you're doing, you stupid tramp? Are you trying to get us all killed?"

Red stood and kicked the jailer's corpse for good measure. "Let's just say I owed him that."

"Red? Red, are you out there?" a whimpering voice called out from behind a door at the back of the antechamber where the jailer had set up his station.

"Po, I'm coming." Red grabbed the set of keys off the dead man's waist, and after trying several, managed to unlock the door. Behind it was a darkened corridor lined with locked cells. Before I had a chance to try hiding the jailer back behind his desk, Red and Po came traipsing back through the open door. Po looked the worse for wear, with two black eyes, a swollen lip, and a jaw that looked dislocated. We didn't have time to tend to his wounds, however. The longer we waited, the more likely we were to get caught.

I opened the door leading back to the main hall and peeked out. No one was coming. "Sapphire, give him your cloak. Anyone who looks like that won't be walking around here freely."

Sapphire took her cloak off and threw it over Po. He raised the hood to cover his face, and Red pulled hers up as well.

"We need to hurry, Ayrion," Sapphire said.

"I know." I took one more look out the door and slipped into the hall, motioning for the others to follow. I shut the door behind us and grabbed the jailer's keys from Red before she tossed them back inside. It was doubtful they would do us much good, but one could never be too careful.

I led them back down the hall, keeping just ahead to see if anyone

was coming before we turned another corner. "Come on," I said, and started into the next bend in the tunnel. We passed a few people in the hall, but they kept going without so much as looking our way.

I turned to see if the others were keeping up, and a door on my direct right opened just as I passed. I nearly punched the man in the doorway just on reflex.

"Hey, what you doing out so late?" he asked, his words slurred from an overabundance of ale, and by the sour smell of it, not the good kind.

"None of your business," I said, taking a cue from Sapphire and whipping out a knife. The man stumbled back into the room and shut the door. I glanced over my shoulder. "Hurry."

Rounding the next bend, I could see the end of the tunnel ahead, and I picked up the pace, stopping just inside the entrance where the shadows were thickest. There were a surprising number of people still gathered in pockets around the large meeting room. Not enough that we couldn't make it across without running into anyone, but enough that if something were to go wrong, we would be badly outnumbered.

Some were playing dice, others lounging about. There was a circle on the far side in front of the platform where another brawl was taking place, and those watching were cheering on the two fighters. I couldn't tell who was winning. They were both covered in enough blood that I wasn't sure how they were still standing.

I peered around the corner and spotted the metal door on the right. We just had to cross the entire meeting hall with no one noticing. Easy enough. I groaned inside.

"I don't want to go out there," Po said, quivering in Red's arms behind me.

I turned. "You go out there or get left behind. Your choice." I was a little surprised by my tone, but we were past the point of coddling. One wrong move could see us all killed. "Now stick together, and we'll get through this. Just act like you belong. Chat quietly, don't look anyone in the eyes, and you'll be fine. We'll take it slow. There's an opening between us and the door. That's our goal." I looked at each in turn. "You ready?"

They all nodded, even Po.

"Fine. Here we go." I took a step out, and the others followed right behind me, quietly chatting amongst themselves. A few of those gathered in one group on the right wall turned to look our way, but quickly enough went back to their own conversations. Those watching the fight on the left side didn't seem to notice us at all, and who would with the bloody battle in front of them?

I kept the pace slow, but not slow enough to appear to be dawdling. There was another group on our right near the wall, but I didn't turn to look, especially with me no longer having a hood to cover my eyes. From what I could see out of my peripheral, the group seemed to be made up of mostly women, many of whom were giggling rather loudly. I wasn't sure what had them so enamored, and I didn't really care. The door was just ahead.

We reached the halfway mark, and some provocative shouting behind us had me risking a quick look behind. A group of five men shot out of a tunnel on the right and headed straight for the passageway we'd just exited. My heart sank when I realized the man doing all the shouting was the same man Red had chased out of her room earlier. He was wearing a bandage on his arm, but at least this time he had his pants on.

"I demand justice be done! Look what she did to my arm!" His angry voice could be heard even after they entered the tunnel on the left.

I whispered over my shoulder. "Move. We need to get out of here."

Picking up the pace, our group made a straight line for the exit. We had to get those doors open before they realized Red was gone and found the dead jailer. We reached the other side of the room without drawing

attention, and I motioned at the two guards standing to either side of the door. "We're on watch tonight."

The two muscle-bound men looked at each other, then us. "Watch already went up an hour ago," the man on the right said.

"Yes, and if Edith back here"—I nodded toward Red—"had kept her mouth shut, we'd all be asleep in our bunks, but now we're all being sent up for punishment."

The two guards looked at each other, but they finally turned and released a lever that started a chain reaction of locks being snapped opened around the door. I gritted my teeth. The locking mechanism seemed to go on forever. What kind of ridiculous door was this? Finally, after what felt like an hour of waiting, the last lock released, sending a faint echo across the large chamber. When it did, the two guards put their shoulders to the metal and pushed.

*Come on, come on.* I was counting my heartbeats as I watched the door slowly begin to part. I could feel sweat running down my back. Even my palms were moist, one resting on my belt and the other on the hilt of my sword. *What is taking so long?* I wanted to leap forward and help them push. Surely it wasn't that hard to open.

The guards managed to get the enormous piece of metal opened just far enough for us to slip through, and I glanced over my shoulder. "Let's go."

I didn't get two steps before a booming voice behind us called out, "Sapphire?"

We all stopped at the same time, nearly tripping over each other. Behind us, leaning against the side wall, was one of the biggest men I'd ever seen. Not as big as Tubby, of course, but every bit as big as Barthol, possibly bigger. He was surrounded by a group of scantily clad women, the same women who'd been giggling and laughing earlier. I had purposely not looked in their direction, so I hadn't noticed the behemoth in the middle of them. He pushed the women aside and started toward us. On his back was a large battle-axe, its handle as thick as my arm.

"Well, well, well. If it isn't little Sapphire, all grown up. Almost didn't recognize you with all that hair. Didn't know you was old enough to be down here."

"I'm old enough to cut that tongue from your mouth," she said, a fierce look in her eyes. Her hand tightened on her dagger, and her other slid toward her sword.

Red and Po both backed toward me, leaving Sapphire to stand by herself. Whoever this man was, they all seemed to know him. Why didn't I?

"It's Kerson," Red whispered in my ear as she and Po moved past me, keeping their heads down as they inched their way toward the door.

*Kerson?* Why did that name sound familiar?

The big man smiled viciously at Sapphire but stopped just out of sword length. "I'd like to see you try."

Her hand wrapped around the hilt of her blade, but she didn't pull.

"What is someone like you doing down here?" he asked, not paying any of the rest of us any mind. "I heard you sold out Hurricane and took up with the likes of Sandstorm." He spat to the side.

I kept my hand on my blade as well and slowly inched my way forward to where she was standing. We didn't have time for this. They were sure to have found Red's empty chamber by now. The alarms were going to be sounding at any time.

"I didn't sell anyone out! Noph left and turned his tribe over to us."

"Yes, I heard my old tribe had taken on three chiefs." His smile vanished as he slowly reached over his shoulder and unhooked his battle-axe and pointed it at Sapphire. "And none of them is Spats. So. Where's. My. Little. Brother?"

The recognition hit me like a kick to the gut. Kerson was the former

chief of Hurricane. More importantly, he was the older brother of Spats, who I had kidnapped and shipped off to the other side of the Five Kingdoms. I tried swallowing, but my mouth had suddenly gone dry.

Kerson took a step forward, and I drew my sword and did the same, moving up alongside Sapphire, who had drawn her weapon as well. Behind us, Red and Po were nearly to the opening in the door, which had temporarily stopped as the guards were busy watching the confrontation with Kerson.

"Where is Spats?" Kerson bellowed. "Rumor has it that he disappeared in the middle of the night, and no one has seen him since. Did you have something to do with that?"

Sapphire shook her head. "No. But if I'd had the chance to do it myself, I can't say that I wouldn't have. He was a right stupid git who nearly got our entire tribe killed on more than one occasion. I don't know what happened to him, but I can say that I had nothing to do with it. I was the one, however, who had to step in and pick up the pieces after he left. Last thing I heard was someone spotted him boarding one of the schooners for the Blue Isles in the middle of the night."

Kerson frowned. "He was stupid, I grant you. But he was family . . . and no one messes with family." His eyes narrowed. "Seems you managed to profit rather well for yourself. Why is it that all the chiefs around you have a tendency to disappear in the middle of the night, conveniently leaving you to step in and take over?"

I looked beyond Kerson to the tunnel opening on the left, expecting armed clansmen to come charging through at any moment.

"Are you accusing me of something?" Sapphire sneered, her back bowing.

"We need to be going," I whispered to her.

"You haven't answered my question," Kerson said, taking a step forward, prompting me to pull Sapphire back. "Why are you down here?"

Kerson looked at me, possibly for the first time, as I was now standing between him and Sapphire.

I kept my head lowered, enough that he couldn't directly see my eyes. "She was here to see me," I said, forcing my way into the conversation, knowing Sapphire wasn't going to like it. "But it's time to go." I pushed Sapphire toward the door, stepping slowly backward myself but keeping myself poised in case Kerson tried anything.

"And who are you?" he asked, pointing at me with his giant axe as he matched steps with us.

"I'm no one." I turned and shoved Sapphire at the door, but before she managed to get through, the two guards moved in front.

"Are you too afraid to look at me, boy? I said look at me!"

We were out of time.

I slowly lifted my head, and Kerson's smiled dropped.

"You! I know you. The Upakan who runs the tribes. What is it they call you? Death's Shadow?"

I stared the enormous man down, running through scenarios of how I was going to get us out of here. None of them looked good. The longer we waited, the more attention Kerson was drawing. Even those over near the platform watching the fight were beginning to look our way.

"So, you're the one the tribes all seem to fear." He laughed. "They used to fear me. Tell me, are you the one responsible for my brother's disappearance?" Kerson grabbed his battle-axe with both hands as if ready to swing.

Suddenly, a bell rang from the tunnel we had exited earlier, and men came charging out.

"The prisoners are escaping!" one of them shouted.

"So much for the easy way," I said, glancing at Sapphire. "Go!"

Before I could turn back around, Sapphire had disarmed the first guard and kicked the second so hard between his legs he dropped to the

ground.

The hairs on the back of my neck stood up, and I spun just in time to catch a flash of steel before Kerson's axe split me in two. I was so used to having my visions that not having them was making me careless. I dove to the side and rolled, cutting down two men who had been standing against the wall near the door.

Spinning, I ducked, and Kerson's axe swung over my head and buried itself in the chest of a third attacker. He was the most surprised dead man I'd ever seen. Without even looking, I dove once more and kicked Kerson's legs out from under him. He went down hard.

I was on my feet and racing for the door by the time he managed to retrieve his axe from the dead man's chest. I tore through the opening and found two more dead guards on the other side, Red removing one of her daggers from the second one's chest.

"Run!" I shouted, and we all raced for the stairs.

Po was the first up, then Red. I followed behind Sapphire. I was in the well and up before anyone had made it out of the central hall. The stairs up seemed longer than they should have been.

Rain was still falling as we broke from the top and back out onto the old city streets. "Grab that bar!" I shouted, pointing at what appeared to be a loose rod in the metal gate next to the entrance. We all grabbed hold and pulled. It snapped off, and I quickly shoved it through the handle of the door, hopefully sealing off those inside. "That won't hold for long."

The night sky lit with another flash of lightning, and I took off running down the street. "Come on!"

The streets were dark, which made a hasty escape rather difficult, not to mention dangerous if we stepped in one of the many potholes making up this stretch of long abandoned roadway. Red had managed to grab the torch at the top of the stairs, which helped, but not much with the rainfall. Hopefully, it would also slow our pursuers, as they would need to find lighting of their own.

There was a crash behind us, and this time it wasn't thunder.

"I guess they're through," Sapphire said as we did our best to keep up a steady pace. Running was impossible; even a light jog was precarious. The best we could manage was a very fast walk as we moved from one street to the next, not really having any idea of where we were or how to get to the exit, other than to catch a glimpse of the city's white wall behind us with each new flash of lightning. As long as I kept the monolithic perimeter wall at our rear, I knew we were heading in the right direction, which would eventually lead to the old city wall on Mora Street and our way out of the Warrens.

Shouts rose all around us as we continued pushing forward. We were like mice in a trap. Those from the Warrens knew these streets, knew every nook and cranny. We knew practically nothing. There was no chance of recognizing anything in the middle of a thunderstorm.

A couple of quick glances over my shoulder, and I could see we had to stop. Po was beginning to fall behind, forcing Red to slow to wait for him. She didn't seem willing to leave him behind, a sentiment I doubted she would have felt for either me or Sapphire.

I found a narrow alley and pulled everyone under a set of stairs between two of the buildings to let them catch their breath. "We have to be getting close." I looked at Po. "Can you make it?" I had to shout over the now-deafening fall of rain.

Po nodded, but it was a weak nod, or maybe it was just him shivering. It wasn't exactly cold, but there were plenty of reasons around here to shiver besides the weather.

"Fine, let's go." We pushed our way through the narrow alley and back out onto the next street down.

Unfortunately, we weren't the only ones who had thought to take

that particular road, and we ran headlong into six armed clansmen—four men and two women.

They were just as surprised to see us as we were them, giving us a slight advantage. We knew that anyone we came across was an enemy, while they had to take the time to see if they recognized us before attacking. By the time they realized who we were, I had already dropped the first man, stuck my sword through the leg of the second, and was on to the third. Sapphire and Red rushed the two women.

Red wielded two long daggers, getting in close as she slashed and fought from up front, while Sapphire preferred her short sword, using her speed and agility to keep her attacker at arm's length before cutting the woman down.

Grabbing a second blade from one of the fallen, I faced down the remaining two clansmen. I spun through the street, water kicking up with each sweep of my feet, droplets flinging with each swipe of my blades. My moves were quick and precise, and before Red and Sapphire had a chance to clean their blades, both my assailants were writhing on the ground, one with a slash across his gut, the other with a calf that had been opened to the bone. The wounds weren't fatal if they were able to find someone who could attend to them, but they were enough to make sure they didn't follow us.

Red walked over to one of the men I'd dropped and leaned over with her bloodstained dagger before I pulled her back. "We don't have time for that."

Red jerked her arm away. "If you knew what they did to me down there, you wouldn't be saying that!"

"Oh, I've got a pretty good idea. Now come on!" I dragged her with me, and the four of us started moving once again. The torch, which had lasted surprisingly well through the rain, had been dropped during the scuffle and gone out, so we now depended solely on my Upakan eyes.

Each person grabbed hold of the one in front of them, with Red bringing up the rear. As fast as I dared, I led them down the street, keeping as close to the buildings as possible. Up ahead, another group emerged from a crossing street, and I quickly shoved everyone inside the nearest building, and we all ducked down beneath the glassless windows until they passed. I was beginning to get a strong sense of having done this all before as I thought about my last encounter with the Warrens Underground. It had gone just about as badly.

As soon as they passed, we were back on our feet. The fact that we'd run into two patrols in such a short time had to mean we were getting close to the old city's wall. We wiped the water from our eyes and the hair from our faces and headed back out into the rain once more.

We reached the side street that the last group had come from, and I glanced around the corner. There were torches ahead, scattered in front of a wide opening in the old wall, but we still had several buildings and at least one more street to pass before we reached them. I smiled inwardly. We'd made it across the Warrens. Now we just had to make it out.

"Any bright ideas?" Red asked, practically having to stick her lips to my ear to be heard.

"Yeah, don't get killed."

She grimaced, but I didn't exactly have anything better to tell her. It wasn't like I had some elaborately drawn-up plan on how to break out of the place. I'd been hoping to get in and out without anyone noticing. That certainly hadn't worked out.

"Just act like you're in one of the search parties and hopefully none of them will recognize us until it's too late." I thought a moment. "Even if we make it past the wall and into the Maze, we'll be stepping right into Cutter's territory."

Red raised both her blades. "Just let him show his face. I'll cut it off

and mount it on my bedchamber wall."

Scary thing was, she probably wasn't joking.

I led them around the corner, and we started down the side of the brick building, two away from the next street up, which was two more buildings away from the exit and those surrounding it. The lights were getting brighter the closer we got. So far, they hadn't noticed us, or at least no one acted as if they had, as they seemed to be milling back and forth in front of the opening.

We reached the final street and, not seeing anyone coming, rushed across. Even if there had been someone coming, it would have been impossible to tell in the middle of this torrential downpour.

Cautiously, we started down the side of the first of two remaining buildings. So far, no one was shouting or drawing swords. Of course, it looked like their swords were already in their hands. The closer we got, the closer to me the others pressed. If something did happen, it was going to be difficult for me to keep from hitting one of them with my sword.

We made it to the end of the first building. Only one more to go, and we would be surrounded by at least a dozen guards. The entire Warrens was now on alert. It was clear we weren't going to be able to talk our way through, which meant the element of surprise was going to be our best option.

I stopped just in front of the final building. We weren't close enough to see faces, but we were close enough that I was sure they could see us, and hopefully believe we were just another one of the many search parties moving through the city. Of course, the fact that we didn't have a torch or lantern might be a problem.

"We are going to have to fight our way through," I said. "There's no way they're letting anyone outside those gates tonight. We need to be fast and precise."

"You don't need to tell me how to fight," Red said with a smirk. "You just watch out for your own backside. As pretty as it is, we don't want anything to happen to it."

I grabbed her and pulled her to me. "You stick with me, or we all die. To fight through this, we need to fight together as one. We need to punch through their barrier. We can't do it if everyone scatters. Do you understand?"

Red gritted her teeth but finally nodded.

"Alright," I said, catching my breath. "All together. We'll try to hit them at the weakest point. The left side of the opening has the fewest people. Wait for my signal." I looked at Red. "You jump in front of me, and I'll cut you down myself."

Red smiled but moved back in line beside Po. She leaned in and whispered something in his ear. I didn't have time to worry about what it might have been as I started us forward, slow at first, shifting toward the left-hand side. There was about five people gathered under the left archway. This was it. Our one chance to break through. I hoped Po was up to—

"There!" someone shouted.

Behind us, a group emerged from the front of the building we had just left. How they knew it was us, I didn't know, other than the possible fact that we were the only group wandering about the city without any light.

"There they are!" I shouted back as we headed straight for the exit and the armsmen standing in front of it. I pointed to the group behind us. "It's them. They're trying to make a run for it!" It sounded absolutely preposterous and probably looked even more ridiculous, but the more confusion I could muster, the better our chance of getting through. "Watch out! Here they come!" I pointed my weapon behind me at the

coming group. We were now close enough to see the faces of those gathered. They certainly looked confused.

I raised my sword once more and yelled at them. "Attack! What are you waiting for, Crellin to come up here and give you his permission?" A couple of the men started toward the oncoming group, but most seemed frozen in place, as two sets of searchers were shouting to attack each other.

I didn't stop, pushing us forward, continuing toward that left side. How much closer could we get? We had about fifteen feet to go. Ten. We weren't going to get any closer without giving ourselves away. "Now!" I rushed the four at the corner wall, dancing between their blades. They barely had time to raise them, and I dropped the first two almost before they knew what had happened. Red and Sapphire took the remaining two, and we broke through the lines only to find another, larger search party waiting on the other side. Where had they come from? They were blocking our route into the Maze, leaving us only one option: run down Mora. We couldn't have had worse luck.

I grabbed Sapphire, who was busy cutting down another clansman, and pulled her back. Red and Po were already running up Mora, having come to the same conclusion I did. Except, no doubt realizing just as I did that there was no way to outrun the entire Warrens. We still had to pass by at least three more openings before we reached the old shipping yards, and alarms bells were already beginning to ring, letting the others know that we'd been found.

We weren't going to make it. I shoved Sapphire toward Red and Po. "Run!"

As soon as she did, I turned to face the onslaught. There was no way we could have outrun them. But if I was able to hold them back long enough, it just might give the others a chance. I reached for my magic, but it wasn't there. I borrowed a curse from Reevie—"Bloody Bile!"—

then cut down two men as I fought to keep the rain out of my eyes.

My swords never stopped, spinning from one side to the other, deflecting, blocking, parrying half a dozen blades at once. I reached for my magic once more, feinting, ducking, weaving my way through the steel, fighting to stay just ahead of the deadly blades.

And there it was. I could feel my magic beginning to swell. Po must finally be far enough away. *Come on!* I reached for it again, and this time it boiled up within me, burning through my body as it filled me with its familiar heat. I swiped at the nearest attackers and then retreated, letting my visions take over as I turned to face the coming horde.

I was panting as I watched them come. The first wave was nearly on top of me when I raised my blades. *I am Death's Shadow.*

The first wave hit, and my arms and legs took over, moving almost on their own. I danced and spun and slipped between their weapons like nothing even I had seen before. It was like I had become a wraith; nothing could touch me. I cut and sliced and stabbed and carved my way through the attackers with a force that scared even me, dropping bodies as fast as falling petals from a pulled daisy.

But no matter how much magic I expended; I wasn't invincible. I took a cut to my left arm, dodging a thrust to my back. I took another to my right leg in exchange for missing an axe to my neck. Each wound burned, but I kept on fighting. I couldn't stop. If I stopped, I was dead.

I stumbled backward as the last of the first wave dropped at my feet, splashing in puddles of blood and water. Unfortunately, in the time it took me to cut them down, three more groups had shown up. I hoped the others had gotten out—Sapphire especially. Sandstorm needed her.

My breath was ragged. I had tried to control it, to focus my strikes and movements to conserve as much energy as I could, but I knew this was it. The only solace I had was that I wasn't going down alone, and that I had been able to save my friends in the process. If this was my end,

it was going to be one they never forgot.

Kerson shoved his way through to the front, his enormous battle-axe over his shoulder. He looked at the pile of bodies at my feet and then at me. "So, for once the rumors are actually true."

I wondered what rumors he was referring to. There were so many.

Another flash of lightning lit the street, and I blinked under its brightness. The thunder rolled and the ground began to shake, but even after the thunder had passed, the ground was still shaking.

Kerson raised his axe. "I'm going to enjoy this." He roared and led the charge, his axe over his head.

The stone under my feet trembled as I raised my sword. There weren't that many of them, were there? No. I recognized that sound. Even over the storm, I heard the familiar pounding of horse hooves.

Ten feet away, Kerson began to slow, the others right behind him. Then they stopped altogether. What were they doing? I turned and nearly yelped when an entire regiment of horsemen came billowing out of the storm behind me. Overcaptain Tolin yanked back on his reins to keep from trampling me underfoot.

Room Eleven was right behind him, already half-dismounted and rushing to my side. To my undying amazement, even Dakaran was there, sword in hand and looking ready for action.

"Heard you might need some help," Barthol said with a grin as he stared out at the Warrens gathering. "This is starting to become a regular thing."

Gellar laughed. "Told them it was the Warrens that needed the help."

"Draw swords!" Tolin shouted, and the sound of ringing steel overpowered that of the rain.

Kerson and the rest of the Warrens stared at the lancers, then slowly began to back away. He pointed at me with his axe. "This ain't over!

One of these days, boy, mark my words, you and I are going to meet face-to-face!"

The clans melted back inside their walls on the right and disappeared into the night. Stumpy walked out from a small side street on the opposite side of Mora from the Warrens, three waterlogged individuals beside him. Sapphire ran over and hugged my neck.

"We didn't get too far before they showed up," she said, motioning to the lancers.

I smiled. "Come," I said to all three of them. "I'll introduce you."

Red and Po stayed to the side, not wanting to get any closer to the lancers than they had to. Sapphire, on the other hand, walked over and let me introduce her to each of my roommates. She had met several of them after my first trip into the Warrens, but it had been a couple of years. She had even locked swords with Stumpy.

"I remember you," Dakaran said. "Would never forget a face as beautiful as yours." He lifted her hand and kissed it.

"Alright, alright," I said, grabbing her hand back. "She doesn't need royalty slobbering all over her."

Sapphire, however, didn't seem to mind, and even managed a formal curtsy.

"How did you know I'd be here?" I asked them.

"Where else would you be," Waylen said, "but getting into trouble?"

"And no better place to find it than here at the Warrens," Fipple added, pulling his hood back over his topknot, now that the battle was over.

Stumpy smiled. "It was your little friend. The healer. He said you might be needing some help."

"Reevie stepped foot in a lancer garrison?" Sapphire asked, almost as amazed as I was.

Tolin walked over, wiping the water from his face. "I suggest we save

this conversation for when we are safely away from here." He put his hand on my shoulder. "It's good to see you alive, again. I would have hated to have to explain to the king how you managed to rescue his ambassador and then went and got yourself killed in a foolish attempt to single-handedly purge the Warrens."

"It's my fault," Red said, walking over with Po in tow. "Don't blame him. He came to rescue me from the Underground."

"You actually went down there?" Gellar asked.

"We did," I said, nodding toward Sapphire, "foolish as it was."

"And I'm sure it will be an interesting story once it's told back at the garrison, but for now . . ." Tolin turned. "Lancers, mount up!"

Dakaran smiled at Sapphire and Red, then back at me. "You'll have to tell me all about it when you get back." He chuckled and mounted with the rest of the regiment.

Stumpy produced two extra horses. "Thought you might need these."

I looked up and was shocked to see that one of the horses was Pudding. "Where did you find him?"

"Found him hiding under a porch's overhang a couple streets down."

I looked at Sapphire, and she shrugged. "I forgot to tie him."

I took the horses and watched as Stumpy and the rest of Room Eleven mounted and then turned and rode back up the street.

We quickly mounted as well, me and Sapphire on one horse, Red and Po on the other. Not wanting to find ourselves in another confrontation with Avalanche, we decided to take the very long way home, by means of heading north until we crossed the Tansian and then following the water up and around the north side of the island. From there, we headed east until we reached Circle Drive.

Red started to turn her horse north.

"Where do you think you're going?" I asked.

"Home."

"That's not home anymore, not unless you want to share a room with some members of Avalanche."

She gritted her teeth.

"Well?" Sapphire asked. "Are you coming or not?"

"What, with you?"

"Why not?" I asked. "I've accepted your hospitality before. Time you accepted ours."

Red looked up the empty street and sighed, but with nowhere else to go, she guided her horse back in line with ours. "I guess I could suffer your hospitality for one night."

Sapphire shook her head and groaned.

Hurricane    Avalanche    Rockslide    Wildfire    Sandstorm

Believe it or not, things actually settled down at Sandstorm Manor, even with the arrival of our new houseguests. Sapphire remained civil as long as Red kept out of her way, and the two managed to get along enough to keep from sticking a blade in the other.

My meeting with the king and queen went even better than I had hoped. It was rather exciting to stand in the throne room with my roommates and be publicly recognized at court. We were each awarded medals of commendation by the king's own hand and had our triumphs sung, quite literally, by a bard who the ambassador and his wife had hired to express their gratitude for their rescue. Nothing like having your exploits proclaimed in front of the aristocracy to the tune of "The Blushing Milkmaid."

The whole experience had my roommates in a bit of a whirl. It was

all they talked about for the rest of the week, at least until our formal meeting with the ambassador and his wife. Along with treating us to a lovely meal at their estate, they sent us each away with enough gold to match two years' worth of our lancer pay.

My roommates were impossible to be around after that.

But it was more than the gold and the singing bard that had made it all worth it. The gift of seeing my father and brother once again was more than I could have ever hoped for, not to mention the change in status that me and my roommates had earned within the lancer community. As word spread of what we had done, the stigma of being Room Eleven quickly vanished once and for all. Others nodded to us when we passed. Exaggerated rumors spread through the ranks of our conquests, and we were glad to let them continue, even indulging in embellishing them here and there when we got the chance.

We were actually getting requests to join what some lancers were calling the Black Guild, which I could only assume had something to do with my new coat. Tolin, in an unexpected turn of events, granted me special permission to wear my black leathers instead of my usual lancer uniform. He said that it seemed to give the men confidence when I was around.

Over the next several months, our little group of seven turned into seventeen, and then twenty-seven. In fact, I had to eventually put a limit on the number of entrants, because I was finding that I couldn't keep up with the training schedule.

With Dakaran's help and his father's ear, the king granted us permission to continue our training at the palace, which unfortunately was garnering quite the audience of nobles. The aristocracy found it all rather exhilarating, until I finally had the rooms barred during training due to my men being unable to concentrate, as the noblewomen would gawk and wave.

My two lives were still trying to find balance. My duties at Sandstorm had been greatly diminished as Bull took over my empty seat as co-chief. He was a natural leader, and the tribe flourished. Thankfully, I was allowed to keep my room on the third floor and granted full access to chief meetings, if and when I was around to do so, which seemed to be growing few and far between, as my duties at the garrison and the palace only increased.

Reevie continued his studies, spending three days a week practicing with Physicker Saban. Reevie was already beginning to garner quite the reputation throughout the city as the most accomplished young healer around. It was almost humorous to watch as he, too, found his time at Sandstorm beginning to wane with the added responsibilities of a growing practice. Being the good-natured young man that I was, I never teased him about it.

Fine, maybe I did a few times.

Red remained at Sandstorm, at least for the time being. Even after taking up residence, she never seemed to really fit in, somehow remaining an outsider. I think more by choice than anything. Having been the head of her own tribe for so long made it difficult to be relegated to just another member of someone else's. To Sapphire's credit, she was good at listening to Red's opinions, of which there were many, and using what she thought would work for Sandstorm, but the two never became close.

Days turned into weeks and weeks to months as time seemed to fly by. I never believed Master Fentin before when he said the older he got, the shorter the days became. I now knew what he meant.

I sat in my little reading cubby in the corner of my room and stared out the long windows at the trees below and the kids climbing in them, quietly sipping on my spiced apple cider. My life was changing, and there was a sadness I felt at what I was losing in the process. The greatest pain was the loss of the closeness I used to have with Reevie. I missed

my times spent under the Granary, when it was just the two of us fending for ourselves with no other pressure than to figure out where our next meal would be coming from. I smiled. Those were the days.

I couldn't help but wonder at how far we'd both come since Reevie had found me lying in a puddle of my own blood and brought me home to nurse back to health. I wondered if, knowing what all that would have involved and the direction it would eventually take him, he would have still done it.

In my heart, I knew the answer.

Our meetings now were friendly nods as we passed in the corridor on our way to our separate lives. Perhaps it was always meant to be. We were there for each other when we needed it most, and even though we didn't still share that same closeness, I knew Reevie would be there for me if I ever needed it, and I for him.

Sapphire was the other half I was missing. My heart still ached at times, especially in the quiet of the evenings, knowing that what we had was gone. But it wasn't like I didn't understand. She needed someone who would be around, someone she could depend on. Unfortunately, I wasn't that person, at least not right now. I wasn't sure I'd ever be.

That was the funny thing about life here in Aramoor. One moment you're on top of the mountain, and the next you're being crushed under it. But it's what we choose to do in those difficult times that defines who we are, something I had to learn the hard way. Part Upakan, part street rat, part lancer . . .

One thing was for certain. My life was anything but boring.

# The End of WILDFIRE

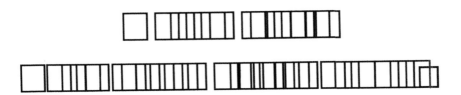

## Dear Reader,

**I** HOPE YOU enjoyed this fifth book in the Street Rats of Aramoor series. If you found the story entertaining and would like to see more, then please consider helping me reach that goal by leaving a quick review on Amazon.

Reviews are very important. They help encourage other readers to try the book while at the same time showing Amazon that the book is worth promoting.

~ Thank you in advance!

Want to be notified when the next book comes out? If so, go to this address: *www.michaelwisehart.com/join-the-wielder-council*

**<< Keep reading for a FREE offer >>**

## Author Note

**L**OVE FANTASY MUSIC? Stop by the shop, *Aramoor Market*, and take a listen. Over 30 minutes of original fantasy score, inspired by The Aldoran Chronicles. You can also grab the digital hi-resolution images for each of the maps, as well as the character art.

« *www.michaelwisehart.com/aramoormarket* »

### For the Latest News
« *www.michaelwisehart.com* »
« *facebook.com/MichaelWisehart.author* »

## << Keep reading for a FREE offer >>

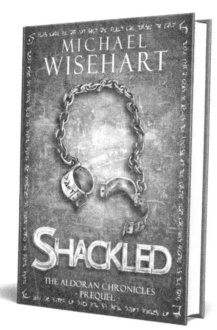

**I**F YOU WOULD LIKE to get a FREE copy of the prequel to the Aldoran Chronicles series, go to the address below. The prequel is vital to the ongoing story.

« *www.michaelwisehart.com/aramoormarket* »

*Born in a world where magic is not only feared, but outlawed, Ferrin's choice to use his abilities brings the Black Watch to his doorstep. Caged alongside a helpless band of half-starved wielders, he formulates a strategy to escape. Armed with nothing more than his sarcastic wit and a determination to never give in, Ferrin attempts the impossible.*

# Acknowledgements

**T**HANK GOD for the doors and windows He's allowed to open in order for me to reach this point.

I want to thank my parents *Mickey and Julie Wisehart* for their unending loyalty, encouragement, and support over the years. None of this would be possible without you—love you both.

I want to thank my Author Team, whose endless talent, time, and dedication have made this project possible:

## AUTHOR TEAM

I want to thank my cover illustrator, who took a written description, along with some reference photos, and brought the kingdom of Cylmar to life in a very dark way—*Dongjun Lu "Russell"*

I want to thank my interior illustrator for her creativity in designing our first look at the Warrens—*Elwira Pawlikowska*

I want to thank my cartographer, who managed to take a maze of jumbled ideas and turn them into the capital city of Aramoor—*RenflowerGrapx*

I want to thank my content editor, whose red pen never seems to run out of ink—*Nathan Hall*

I want to thank my line editor, who always finds the most appropriate word choice—*Danae Smith*

I want to thank my copy editor, who keeps my scripts clean and my readers happy—*Crystal Watanabe*

## About the Author

ICHAEL WISEHART graduated with a bachelor's degree in business before going back to school for film and starting his own production company. As much as he enjoyed film work, the call of writing a novel got the better of him, and on April 14, 2014, he started typing the first words of what would become two epic fantasy series: The Aldoran Chronicles and the Street Rats of Aramoor.

He currently lives and writes in North Georgia.

# Glossary of Terms

## Street Tribes of Aramoor

**Avalanche** [*a-vuh-lanch*] Tribe color is white. Chief is Cutter.

**Hurricane** [*her-ĭ-cane*] Tribe color is blue. Chief is Spats.

**Rockslide** [*rock*-slide] Tribe color is green. Chief is Kore.

**Sandstorm** [*sand-storm*] Tribe color is purple. Chief is Noph.

**Wildfire** [*wild-fire*] Tribe color is red. Chief is Red/Kira.

## *Months of the Year*

**Aèl** [*ay*-el] First month of the year.

**Sòl** [*soul*] Second month of the year.

**Nùwen** [*noo-win*] Third month of the year.

**Manù** [*mah-noo*] Fourth month of the year.

**Toff** [*toff*] Fifth month of the year.

**Kwàn** [*quon*] Sixth month of the year.

**Nor** [*nor*] Seventh month of the year.

**Èldwin** [*el-dwin*] Eighth month of the year.

**Kùma** [*koo-muh*] Ninth month of the year.

**Akòsi** [*uh-kah-see*] Tenth month of the year.

**Èshan** [*ee-shon*] Eleventh month of the year.

**Zùl** [*zool*] Twelfth month of the year.

# New Character Glossary

*(Introductory characters not mentioned in prior books)*

**Bosko** [*Boss-ko*] Stableman at the Ram's Head Inn in Ecrin. Tells travelers he can get them anything they may need: women, weapons, drink.

**Brishad** [*Brĭ-shod*] Leader of a clan of Sil'Rhivanni who travel through Cylmar. Older man with a long white beard and colorful cape.

**Crellin** [*Krell-in*] Head of the Warren Clans. Prefers the title of king over chief.

**Dovan** [*Do-vun*] Head of the Fisher Guild in Ecrin. A thug.

**Dreese** [*Dreese*] Chandler at Dorwall. Found hanging from his own store sign.

**Egert** [*Ee-gert*] A tower guard in Overlord Saryn's castle.

**Forang** [*For-ang*] Ecrin street tribal chief whose territory surrounds the overlord's keep.

**Gorman** [*Gor-man*] Elondrian ambassador kidnapped by Overlord Saryn. Husband of Neina.

**Jasna** [*Joz-nuh*] A younger server with a hooked nose working at the Ram's Head Inn in Ecrin. She has a pretty sister who the soldiers like to stare at.

**Jkovis** [*Juh-ko-vis*] Owns a shop in Ecrin that sells maps, among other things.

**Kelsi** [*Kel-see*] Sister of Jasna. Works at the Ram's Head Inn.

**Lorn** [*Lorn*] Husband of Ayrion's sister, Rianna.

**Matty** [*Matt-ee*] Drunk woman at the Spotted Pike Inn tavern. Only person brave, or drunk, enough to give Ayrion a straight answer about the killings. Older with grey streaks in her hair and bright green eyes.

**Mirna** [*Mir-nuh*] A middle-aged woman working at the Ram's Head Inn in Ecrin.

**Moric** [*Mor-ick*] Jailer on duty in Overlord Saryn's castle.

**Neina** [*Nee-in-uh*] Wife of Ambassador Gorman. Kidnapped by Overlord Saryn.

**Neven** [*Nev-en*] A little picker inside of Ecrin who conned Ayrion and his roommates out of their money. He later helps them garner a map of the interior of the overlord's keep.

**Nezrit** [*Nez-rit*] New magistrate of Dorwall. Killings began the day he arrived.

**Petrija** [*Peh-tree-juh*] Sil'Rhivanni healer.

**Pradjic** [*Pray-jic*] A fisherman in Ecrin. Used to be Jasna's father's right-hand man before Jasna's father's boats were stolen from him by Dovan.

**Pudding** [*Puud-ing*] The horse at Sandstorm Manor, which Sapphire enjoys feeding.

**Ratko** [*Rat-ko*] The head of a small troop of Cylmaran soldiers who frequented the Ram's Head Inn.

**Stanis** [*Stan-iss*] Ecrin blacksmith who works in Fishtown.

**Thorin** [*Thor-in*] Blind man who begs near Aramoor's East Gate. Walks with a staff.

**Tobar** [*Toe-bar*] Innkeeper for the Spotted Pike in Dorwall. He was average height and skinny with brown hair and brown eyes and three-day stubble. No distinguishable features. A very forgettable person.

**Vulkina** [*Vul-kee-nuh*] Ecrin street tribal chief whose territory runs from the east of Rodon Hill south to the fish market.

**Zivota** [*Zĭ-vo-tuh*] Noted merchant in Ecrin who was looking to hire protection for a shipment he was sending to Rhowynn.

**Zlatin** [*Zlay-tin*] Former boat captain and father of Jasna and Kelsi. His title and boats were taken from him by Dovan.

### Stop by and visit:
www.michaelwisehart.com

Printed in Great Britain
by Amazon